The Ghost Comes Out

THE SISTERS SPURLOCK

ISBN 978-1-0980-2582-3 (paperback)
ISBN 978-1-0980-2583-0 (digital)

Copyright © 2020 by The Sisters Spurlock

All rights reserved. No part of this publication may be reproduced, distributed, or transmitted in any form or by any means, including photocopying, recording, or other electronic or mechanical methods without the prior written permission of the publisher. For permission requests, solicit the publisher via the address below.

Christian Faith Publishing, Inc.
832 Park Avenue
Meadville, PA 16335
www.christianfaithpublishing.com

Printed in the United States of America

To our mother, who never let
us give up on our dreams
—DSW and SSR

To my husband, who read every word
of this book and gave wonderful advice.
I love you more than you know
—SSR

CHAPTER 1

1964

It was the summer in the small rural town of Grayton, Tennessee, and what took place there is still talked about today. Some say what happened that summer could've occurred in any community in the south. Citizens in Grayton didn't happen to share that thought. They were just the unfortunate ones to live through it all.

Just over the state line in Mississippi, things were heating up with the civil rights movement. What was going on was a movement called Freedom Summer, a crusade to increase the black vote. Along with this cause came the murder of three of its organizers. Those who lived in Grayton had no idea what was taking place just over the Tennessee line nor did they care. They had problems of their own, and that summer, secrets that were hidden behind closed doors were secrets no more.

Grayton was the seat of Dakota County, located about thirty miles south of the town of Savannah. The population was 762, but by the end of that summer, there were six less citizens and a town turned upside down by suspicions, innuendos, and a place no longer safe to leave doors unlocked.

CHAPTER 2

THE FIRST DAY OF SUMMER BREAK

Rosalee and Tatiana Scholl woke up early that first day of June. It was the first day of summer break for Rosalee. Tatiana, or Tati (pronounced Tat-ee) to her sister, wasn't old enough for school, but was a quick learner. Every day, Rosie, as Tati called her, would come home from school and teach her what she'd learned. It didn't matter that it was the first day of Rosie's summer break. Rosie was a born instructor, and teaching and learning didn't take a vacation.

"If ya don't practice, Tati, ya neva gonna learn. Ya don't wanna be one of those slow learnas, do ya?" asked Rosie.

"No, I don't, Wosie," Tati said.

"Tati, I'm gonna have to put ya in speech class. Ya gotta practice yua *R*s. 'Member those slow learnas?" It just so happened that Rosie was the speech teacher too.

Tati didn't know what a slow learner was, but by Rosie's tone, she knew it wasn't good. Rosie always talked about this boy in her class named Jimmy Smothermon. Jimmy was what Rosie called a slow learner. "It took him all year in the first grade t'learn the alphabet an' write his name. Yep, he's a slow learna all right."

Rosie had just completed the second grade, and she knew everything there was to know, or at least she thought she did. She knew how to read on the fourth-grade level, write on big lined paper, could

THE GHOST COMES OUT

add and subtract up to twenty and count to one hundred. So, what else did she need to know? And to Tati, she was the smartest person she knew.

Both Rosie and Tati lived with their mother, Victoria. She was not only beautiful on the outside, but even more so on the inside. She was short in stature. In fact she stood only at 5'1¾", but she was very proud of that ¾ and would let everyone know it. She had light-brown straight hair, which she wished was curly, with skin as smooth as silk. Despite being poor, anyone who knew their mom thought they were the luckiest kids in Grayton.

Victoria worked at the Grayton Board of Education. She was the secretary to the superintendent, and the town agreed their mom was the best thing that ever happened to Superintendent Marcus Peters.

Rosie and Tati were brushing their teeth when their grandmother, Ree, called.

"Rosalee an' Tatiana, breakfast's ready. Make sure y'alls hands ah warshed!" shouted Ree.

Their grandmother, Ree, took care of them when their mom was at work. Ree was their father's mother. She was only fifty-six that summer, but her hair was already completely gray. She looked and acted much older than her years and not the typical grandmother. She was short, chubby, and not the warm grandmotherly type. She wasn't much taller than Rosie, and her eyes were as blue as the sea. When she got mad, her eyes became darker and more vibrant. The sisters didn't think she liked them. She wasn't the cheerful type, and they thought they were more of a burden than a pleasure to her.

They all lived together in a 1900-era Victorian home. It was badly in need of repair. The exterior of the house required a lot of cosmetic work. One might say it needed a face-lift, perhaps two. The gutters were riddled with holes, and weeds had made a home in them. The paint on the house was chipped off, and one could see the original paint color underneath, which was yellow. The holes in the roof were many, and the Scholl family prayed for dry days with no rain because the water would pour into the girls' bedroom upstairs. The inside was no better. There was no centralized heating. They used little floor heaters, and Victoria and her two girls would snuggle together on cold winter nights for warmth. The paint on the walls was coming off in big chunks. On a cold day, the girls would take paint pieces off the walls and compare who had the biggest piece. That is until Ree found out what they were doing and had them select their own branches off of the buckeye tree to use to whip them.

Rosie and Tati came down the front staircase, and waiting for them at the bottom of the staircase with his tail wagging was their basset hound, Midas. Midas went everywhere the girls went, and today he was ready to eat. Each of the girls loved on Midas for a minute, and then he followed them into the hall. The hall led into a big kitchen. Ree had her back to them when they came into the kitchen.

Without looking, she said, "Rosalee, please make sure Tatiana's hands ah clean, t'day. Ya know her nails ah always dirty, an' Lawd only knows where they been!"

"Yes, 'em, I washed 'em myself, Ree. They look pretty clean, an' Tati ain't eatin' her boogers, no mo," said Rosie.

Rosie was always taking up for Tati because Ree never addressed Tati. Perhaps she thought Tati was too young to understand, or maybe she thought Tati was one of those slow learners. Tati was very small. She had just turned three in April, and her blond hair seemed to fall in her face. She had a sweet almost angelic look on her face, and anything Rosie told her was gospel.

"That dawg is useless. Rosalee tell ya sista t'put ' im outside!" commanded Ree.

Rosie just looked at Tati. Tati picked up Midas's leash and led him under the table. She told him to be quiet. It was as though Midas understood he needed to be silent.

Breakfast was their favorite meal, because that meant after they ate, they had the entire day to play. The one good thing about Ree's breakfast was the cereal. She would buy the twelve cereals in a snack pack. The girls loved them until they got down to the last of the cereals. Neither Rosie nor Tati particularly liked cornflakes. They saved them to the last hoping someone else would eat them or perhaps they would just disappear. No such luck. Today, there was a snack pack of cornflakes cereal at each of their plates. The girls had assigned seats

THE GHOST COMES OUT

at the kitchen table. Rosie sat next to Ree, and Tati sat on the other side of Rosie. Tati believed Ree arranged the seating like that because she didn't like the sight of her. It was a good thing she sat on the other side of Rosie because Tati hated bacon. Ree cooked it until it was black and tasted like burnt paper, but every morning, there were three pieces at their seats. Tati would pick a piece of bacon up off her plate. She dropped her hand under the table, and Midas would eat her bacon. She did this three times. Midas watched over both Rosie and Tati, and in turn, he was fed…well. Rosie would eat her bacon and sometimes ask for more. It was hard to believe she could eat like that because she was skinny and very active. Rosie looked like their father. She had his beautiful dark-auburn wavy hair and blue eyes. She also had his disposition and seemed to handle any situation that came up. Ree favored Rosie and would give her ten cents for every auburn hair on her head. Rosie made sure she would split it with Tati.

"Ya jest as pretty, Tati. Ya git whateva I git, okay?" Rosie said to Tati handing her five cents.

"Wosie, ya my bess fwend. I love ya, Wosie," Tati responded.

Their father, Jeb Scholl, worked at the Grayton Plastics. It was a factory on the west side of town. Jeb stood about 6'1" and was very strong. He had to be. He was the supervisor of over twenty-three employees and was well respected and loved. During this time, the Vietnam War was well at hand, and Jeb's number for the draft was low. He was to have been deployed in August of '64, but fate stepped in.

On January 4, 1964, Jeb had driven to Stockton, the neighboring big town, for tools and supplies. It was snowing lightly on his trip down. On his return trip to Grayton, the snow had picked up. For those who live in the south, an inch of snow is enough to call a state of emergency, and most southerners aren't used to the white stuff and, well, just can't drive in it. Jeb was taking his time on Highway 69 as he headed back to Grayton. All of a sudden, a red Studebaker station wagon appeared over the hill. The wagon was swerving over the entire road and coming straight for Jeb. He slammed on the horn, pumped the brakes, and swerved to miss it but hit a telephone pole instead. The pole came crashing down on the car, killing Jeb instantly. Even though 1964 brought with it front seat lap belts in cars, his car was an old 1955 Chevy Bel Air, which were not equipped with the safety devices.

The station wagon neither slowed down nor stopped. It was as though it had no idea of the accident it caused.

Ree interrupted the quiet and stressed in a sharp tone, "Rosalee, make sure ya sista eats all her breakfast. We can't 'ford t'waste no food, an' I ain't gonna pay fo waste, ya understand? We ain't the Montagues, ya know? I know y'all not used t'good cookin', so 'preciate it when ya git it, ya hear?"

Ree was referring to their mother, Victoria. She wasn't the best cook in the world. In fact, she wasn't much of a cook at all. She would laugh about how she could burn water. One time, she did just that. Victoria loved to read, and when she got caught up in a good book, she seemed to forget everything else. Shortly after they married, Victoria was reading James Baldwin's *The Fire Next Time*. She left water on the stove to boil. She lost track of time, and the water evaporated and burned the bottom of the pot. The pot caught on fire and burned the stove. Luckily, no one was hurt. When Jeb came home, he was relieved Victoria was okay and remarked, "I hope that book was worth it, Vicki. You know I didn't marry you for your *culinary talents*," he said with a laugh. And he took her out for dinner at the Grayton Burger and Shake joint. That became their Friday night date place.

*****

Ree was drinking her first cup of Folgers instant coffee. This would be the first of many that day. She had a habit of watching her stories and drinking java. Rosie and Tati never bothered Ree during her story time. This was "Ree's time," and she didn't let you forget it.

After breakfast, Rosie took the initiative and asked Ree if they could go play.

"Ree, can Tati an' I go outside an' play? We won't go pass the stop sign on our bikes, an' we won't play with Valerie an' her little sista. We know they white trash," said Rosie.

THE GHOST COMES OUT

"First of all, her name is Tatiana. Why must y'all give each other nicknames? Secondly, ya beds mus be made, rooms straightened, an' put ya playclothes on. What ya have on now are school clothes, plain an' simple. Make sure Tatiana brushes her heya. Also, please put ya sister's heya back from her face. We may be po, but she ain't gotta look it. If she were mine, I'd put a bowl on her head an' cut round the bowl. If her mother ain't gonna do somethin' with her heya, I will!" Ree said in a huff as she marched out of the kitchen.

"Will Wee cut my head off, Wosie? I kinda like it," Tati said just before tears came spilling down her cheeks. Rosie reached over and gave her a hug.

"Don't worry, Tati, Momma ain't gonna let her touch ya head or hair. Me an' Momma'll take care of ya. Asides, Ree's all talk! I heard that phrase on Mister Ed the other night," Rosie said with a laugh.

"Now, let's git t'owwah chores, then we can have some fun," Rosie said.

From the hallway, Rosie and Tati heard Ree say, "Rosalee, y'all need t'warsh y'alls plates an' dry 'em afore ya leave the kitchen, ya hear?"

"Yes 'em," said Rosie as she and Tati ran a little water over the plates and put them in the strainer. A little food was left on them, but they didn't care. They would be eating from them again at lunchtime.

Summer days in Tennessee were hot, and especially on the Tennessee River. It was like desert hot. You know, you're barely outside, and you're already drenched in sweat. That day, Rosie, Tati, and Midas had just gotten outside in the hot sun when they saw Monty Hutchins, their neighbor next door. Monty was their best friend. They both seemed to share him. Monty was a year younger than Rosie. He looked up to Rosie just like Tati. Rosie was a whole grade above Monty, and that's serious business when you're in elementary school. Monty was almost as tall as Rosie with dark-brown hair. He had a couple of teeth missing up front and was always sticking his tongue through the spaces.

"Hey, Monty, whatcha doing? Ya wanna go ovah t'school an' maybe play fo square?" asked Rosie. "We could go an' git Valerie an' her little sista, DaisyBelle, an' see if they wanna go too."

"Wosie, I thought ya said they was white twash," noted Tati.

"Now, Tati, ya know Ree calls anybody who's po…white trash," explained Rosie.

"Ain't we po, Wosie?" Tati asked.

Rosie looked down at Tati and replied, "We sure ah, Tati. We sure ah."

"So, Monty, wanna come?" invited Rosie.

"Sure, why not," Monty answered. You could tell he'd do just about anything to be around Rosie. He had a major crush on her.

They all headed down to the creek. To get to Valerie's house, they needed to cross the creek, and since it hadn't rained for weeks, the stream was dry. They ran down and then up the bank. When they got on the other side of the creek, they could see Valerie's mom and dad, Mr. and Mrs. Shelby. They were both outside by their 1954 red Studebaker station wagon. Mr. Shelby was a car mechanic, and he had it running pretty good.

"I told ya yua drinkin' has gotten outta control, an' now ya so drunk ya can't even work!" yelled Rita Shelby.

Carl Shelby pushed his wife against their car.

"Don't ya talk t'me like that, woman! I'll drink anytime I wan. I bring home da bacon, don't I?" Carl said as he slurred his words. He raised his hand to hit her when Valerie came running out of the house.

"Please, Papa, don't hit Momma," pleaded Valerie. Valerie had just completed the fifth grade. She was a tall girl, much taller than the boys in her class, and had blond frizzy hair. She kept it in a ponytail most days, but today it was down on her shoulders.

Rosie, Tati, Midas, and Monty stopped in their tracks. They were frozen. None of them had ever seen a mother and father fight, and Valerie was in the middle of it. Even Midas understood he shouldn't make a noise.

"All right, ya take huh. Imma gonna go fin' someone who's mo lovin' an' kinda t'me!" he said. Carl Shelby pushed his wife into Valerie, which caused them both to fall to the ground.

Carl got into his car laughing as he sped off. The station wagon swerved all the way down the hill and out of sight.

THE GHOST COMES OUT

Rita and Valerie were both crying and consoling one another.

"I hate him!" Valerie said. "Imma sick an' taared of him usin' ya like a punchin' bag, Momma."

DaisyBelle came out of the house, and the screened-in door slammed behind her as she ran down the steps. "Momma, ya okay? Val?" she asked.

DaisyBelle had gotten her name from her mother and sister. Rita had decided on naming her Daisy, but Valerie insisted she be named Belle because her fifth-grade teacher, Mrs. Tullock, had told her *belle* means "beautiful" in French.

"Momma, please name huh Belle. It's the most beautifulest name in the world," said Valerie.

"Okay, honey, why don't we combine the names an' call huh DaisyBelle?" suggested Rita. "She gonna love huh name."

Even Carl had no problem with the name they picked. He could've cared less. He wasn't even at the hospital when DaisyBelle came into this world. Carl was with Erleen, his girlfriend, in Stockton. It was only after Rita and his new daughter came home that he saw DaisyBelle for the first time.

DaisyBelle was small for her age. She was seven years old and had been held back in first grade, so she was going to repeat it. She wasn't one of those slow learners Rosie talked about; she just had too much going on at home to do well in school.

The three Shelbys hugged one another tightly. "I promise, this'll end. We ain't gonna stay in this house with him much longa. I tried once t'end this, that didn't work. I promise this'll end soon!" said a reassuring Rita.

Rita led her daughters into the house and closed the door.

CHAPTER 3

SUNDAYS

Sundays in the south meant just one thing—church. Everyone in Grayton went to morning services. Now, not all attended the same one, but everyone would go. There were plenty of Christian churches to choose from to find a spiritual home. Each church stood next to one another. It was called Christian Row. It started with the Methodists, followed by the Baptists. Next came the Presbyterians and the Church of Christ, and last on the row was the Pentecostal Church.

The Church of the Southern Baptist of Grayton was located on the other side of town. This was the only black church in Grayton. It was also the most spiritual of all the churches in town.

There was only one Catholic family in Grayton, the Amatos. They had to drive to Stockton to attend mass.

Grayton did not have any synagogues. The closest synagogue was in Memphis, which was a two-hour drive from Grayton. Didn't really matter because there weren't any Jewish families around town anyhow.

Grayton Pentecostal Church

No one ever knew how many people attended Grayton Pentecostal Church because there were no windows in that concrete building. The structure was actually built to be a storm shelter, but it kept getting bigger and bigger, and before you knew it, the parishioners at the Pentecostal Church claimed it as their home.

Rumor had it, there were rattlesnakes on-site for the parishioners to handle during the worship service. The snakes were kept in a container. Rosie came home one day from school saying Mikey Steele's father, Jimmy Bob, was bitten by a snake while at church. He did not seek medical attention and died later that same afternoon.

"Ya not gonna b'lieve this, Tati, but his arm swelled up the size of fo baseball bats! If Imma lyin', Imma dyin'," said Rosie. That was only said if it was the gospel truth.

"Did it hut, Wosie?" queried Tati.

"Did it hurt? Ya bet it did, Tati! 'Member when ya got stung by that wasp last summa an' ya cried?" wondered Rosie.

"Oh, yes, Wosie. It hut so much," Tati stated.

"Well, what ifin there'd been a million wasps that stung ya? That's what it felt like, Tati," explained Rosie.

Rosie swore it was the truth, and from that day forward, Tati was scared to death of snakes.

Grayton Baptist Church

Rosie, Tati, Victoria, and Ree attended Grayton Baptist Church. In fact, they had their own pew. Now, if you're a regular at church, everyone knows who sits in what pews. There's an unwritten rule by churchgoers you don't sit in someone's pew. That's just how things were.

One Sunday, the Scholl family was tardy for morning service. Ree had gotten up later than usual. This was not normal. Ree was a stickler for routine and punctuality.

"Imma gonna ask Jesus t'forgive me fo sleepin' in. Ya know He don't like slackers, heathens, or people who are late t'hear the Lord's word," stressed Ree.

"Which one is yua, Wee?" Tati wondered.

Before Ree could take a step toward Tati, Victoria stepped in and put her arm around Tati.

"Either ya do somethin' 'bout that child of yuas or I will!" cried Ree.

The look on Ree's face was enough to sober the town drunk, Lucian, and that was one of the only times either Tati or Rosie could recall that Ree looked directly at Tati. But before Ree had time to collect her thoughts, Victoria spoke up.

"I believe Jesus will forgive us for being a little late this morning, Ree. I'm sure he's just glad we're in his house to worship." Victoria had the sweetest disposition, and since Jeb's death, she felt even more protective of her daughters.

Victoria knew her mother-in-law was less than happy when Jeb had asked her to marry him. Ree and her best friend, Emma Jean, had always imagined their kids would grow up and marry each other. Emma Jean had a daughter, Velma Lee, and she seemed to push Velma Lee onto Jeb every opportunity she got. So, it was a shock when Jeb brought Victoria home to meet Ree. Victoria was a city girl, and Ree thought Jeb needed a country wife like Velma Lee.

Victoria knew Ree had not gotten over Jeb's accident. Well, she hadn't either. It had only been five months. Every night when Victoria was in the shower, she cried. She wept for lonliness, and she wept for her girls losing their father. She turned on the water to drown out the noise. She didn't want the girls to hear her. They needed to think she was getting on, and her strength was their strength. The hardest thing was living with Ree. Ree's mood had gotten worse since Jeb's death. Jeb knew how to handle his mother, but it was different for Victoria. She told herself someday she could afford to move out on her own with her two girls, but until then, she was going to make the best of this situation.

Ree was still fuming from Tati's question when the Scholls arrived at the church door. They proceeded down the main aisle to their pew, the second row from the front. When they got to their pew, there were two strangers sitting there, a man and a boy. They looked up at the Scholls. Ree glared down at them.

"Who ah you?" asked Ree. "Unless Jesus Christ Himself gave ya permission t'sit there, ya better git up an' out of owwah pew!" shouted Ree Scholl.

"Which ah them, Wee, slackas or hevens?" asked Tati. Luckily, Ree didn't hear that question. She was too focused on the interlopers.

The man got up and motioned for the boy to rise too. They never darkened the door of the Baptist Church again. Additionally, no one ever sat in the Scholls' pew again except the Scholls.

Grayton United Methodist Church

The man and boy who had been kicked out of Ree's pew at the Baptist Church found a home at Grayton United Methodist Church.

Harry Miller had asked around at the Methodist Church to ensure the second pew was not taken. When he was assured it was not, then he and the boy, Dean McCauley, made it their pew, and they had found their spiritual home there.

While their attendance in church was regular, neither Harry nor Dean ever joined a Sunday school class.

The minister, Pastor Allan Boyd, wanted to get the child more involved in church. During Holy Week, Pastor Boyd asked if Dean could attend the traditional Easter egg hunt sponsored by all the local churches. The excitement on Dean's face was undeniable as he looked up at Harry.

Immediately, Harry responded, "No, we have plans," and that was the end of that. Dean dropped his head and stared at the ground. There were tears falling down his cheeks.

Why won't he allow the child to participate? There's something odd about the two of them. I believe the Lord is calling me to pay them a home visit and invite both of them to Sunday school and Wednesday night service. I just need to try harder, thought Pastor Boyd.

Harry was very protective of Dean. He always had his arm around the boy in church, much like a father or grandfather might do, but he was neither. Harry was approximately in his early fifties, and Dean looked to be about nine years old. The relationship between those two would be explained that summer of '64.

Grayton Presbyterian Church

Monty Hutchins and his family attended Grayton Presbyterian Church. They considered their church the fun-loving congregation that accepted anyone who needed a church family and home. Monty's little brother, Alvin, was just two the summer of '64. Monty's uncle, Bradley Bacon Haas (pronounced Hays), attended this church too, and he was in charge of ringing the bell for the morning service. Every Sunday, Bradley, or "Bake" as he liked to be called, would take his nephews, Monty and Alvin, up to the belfry in the church and let them ring the bell. Bake loved sharing this activity with his only nephews.

*****

Bake Haas worked for the newspaper the *Grayton Gazette*. He was the chief reporter. Quite often he was called out to cover the town's headline news like when the Meyer's two cows got out and were found at the playground of Grayton Elementary School. The kids were having a great time playing with the cows. There was one picture where the fourth-grade girls were trying to get the animals to jump over the rope. The caption read: EVEN COWS CAN GET A WORKOUT AT SCHOOL. Bake also covered the story of Clara Magnus, who delivered her baby in the public library. It turns out that Clara's water had broken earlier that morning, and on her way to the hospital, her husband, Tommy Joe, dropped her off at the library to pick up the book *Dr. Spock's Baby and Child Care* to read in the hospital while in labor. This was their first baby, so neither Clara nor Tommy Joe realized there would be no time for reading. Nor did they know just how quickly their baby was going to make his appearance into the world. Clara hadn't read that far in the book when her baby's head began to crown. The librarian, Ethel Craighead, a spinster, had never seen a live birth. When Clara dropped to the floor, Ethel yelled, "No, you cannot have your baby here. It's not allowed! The carpets have just been cleaned, and there are sanitary issues." Neither Clara nor her baby paid the slightest attention to Ethel. The baby was born there on the library floor. Ethel resigned the next day.

Another member of Grayton Presbyterian Church was Daphne Montague. Daphne was the daughter of Franklin and Louise Montague and their only child. They were the first family of Grayton. Franklin's ancestors founded and settled the town in 1789.

Daphne lived in the mansion that overlooked the town. She was in her midthirties and was a beautiful woman. Miss Daphne, as the townfolk called her, married once when she was younger. When she graduated high school at the young age of sixteen, she married her tutor, Johnson Davis. They had eloped to the big city of Stockton. When her father, Franklin, found out about it, he had the marriage annulled, and Johnson Davis left town and was never heard of again.

Louise Montague died six months later of a broken heart, and Franklin died six months after that in a hunting accident.

What went on inside that mansion, only the Montagues knew, but the summer of '64, everything came out at last. What once was hidden behind the marbled columns was now for the citizens of Grayton to know and comment on, and of course they did.

Grayton Church of Christ

The Grayton Church of Christ had worship down to the ticktock of the clock. Members were preparing the weekly Lord's service exactly at the time the Presbyterians were ringing the church bell to leave. Since there was only one restaurant in Grayton that was a buffet-style family place, the Come an' Gettit Café, it was nice when the patrons were staggered and didn't come at once.

The Shelbys attended this church. During service, Carl Shelby was the epitome of a devout Christian parishioner. He had Rita and the girls walking in front of him. He spoke to everyone he saw and walked out of his way to address the elders.

"Hey there, Elder Rodgers, is that '63 Chevy truck of yuas still giving ya trouble? I thank I can fix'er at a low cost," said Carl.

"Really? I'm kinda tempted t'take it back to the dealership. It's only a year old," said Eric Rodgers. Carl knew he could fix the truck with just a turn of the wrench. When Elder Eric Rodgers brought the truck into Agnes's Garage and Repair earlier that week, Carl had seen a loose bolt. He had chosen to keep that from Elder Rodgers when he came to pick the truck up. He quoted a price of $11 for repairs.

"I tell ya what, I know I gave ya an' estimate of $11, but if I can't fix'er fo less than $10, I will take it t'the dealership myself," said Carl.

"Well then, we have a deal," said Rodgers as they shook hands.

Carl would simply tighten the bolt and charge Elder Rodgers $9. That would be enough money to travel to Stockton, have a few drinks, and meet up with his girlfriend, Erleen. He didn't think his wife, Rita, knew about Erleen. Oh, how wrong he was.

Rita hated what she saw Carl doing, but loved going to church. This was the only time she actually felt like a family, and she loved to parade her two girls, Valerie and DaisyBelle. She loved her daughters and cherished time with them. She prayed daily for God to show her a way out with her girls. She felt the time was near. Watching Carl make his rounds, she felt physically ill by what she was witnessing. *I know it'll be soon*, she thought to herself. *God, let it be soon.*

As soon as the service was over, Carl would go back to drinking again. No one at the church had any idea Carl had an alcohol problem. He was a closet drinker, but unfortunately for his family, he had given them a key to the closet. They tried desperately to hide it from outsiders, but the summer of '64, everyone in town knew what he was hiding.

The Church of the Southern Baptist of Grayton

On June 5, 1964, Martin Luther King Jr.'s book, *Why We Can't Wait*, was published. A beautifully written account about racial segregation in America. The book suggests that 1963 was the beginning of the Negro Revolution and uses King's "Letter from a Birmingham Jail" as the main focus.

The residents of Grayton had no idea that Martin Luther King Jr. was making strides in America toward integration for people of color. In Grayton, no one knew or seemed to care what happened beyond the city limits. The churches were segregated, and while there

THE GHOST COMES OUT

were numerous white churches in the town, there was only one black congregation, the Church of the Southern Baptist of Grayton.

All the people of color of Grayton attended this church. If the other congregations' members had ever visited a Sunday service at this church, they never would've gone back to their own. Not only was the music inspirational but so was the message. Reverend Andrew Anglin Greer was the pastor of this church. He had not only heard Martin Luther King speak but knew him personally.

The staff of Daphne Montague attended this church.

Silvia Smith worked for Miss Daphne, and she did not like her one bit. She was Miss Daphne's personal maid and didn't particularly like working for white people. Silvia was married to Jackson, and they had two children, Johnny and Billy.

When Silvia and Jackson had been married four years, Jackson had taken himself a girlfriend who happened to be Silvia's cousin, Bernice. Silvia was devastated Jackson would take up with anyone, much less her cousin.

"Fool's Hill… Fool's Hill… He goin' ovah Fool's Hill," Silvia's mother would say. "Don take it personly, they all do it. He comin' back, doncha worry. He be back."

Sure enough, after five months of listening to Bernice nag about this and that, Jackson came back. "I learn my lesson, Silvie, won't be goin' ovah Fool's Hill no mo'." And that was that.

Jackson was Miss Daphne's chauffeur. Miss Daphne's father, Franklin Montague, did not think it proper for young ladies to drive themselves, but after the death of Mr. Montague, Daphne tried driving. She couldn't seem to get the hang of it and totaled two brand-new 1960 convertible Porsche 356 cars. She never drove again.

Clayton Smith, brother of Jackson, was Miss Daphne's gardener. There were no grounds in Grayton more beautiful than Miss Daphne's. The citizens of Grayton thought Clayton to be a miracle worker. He only needed to lay his hands on dying flowers, and they came back to life. Even though he was black, he did attend the Garden Club regularly. He was the only man invited or welcome, but when it came time for refreshments to be offered at the close of the meeting, he was expected to serve the ladies. Clayton didn't seem to mind this, though.

"How can you stan servin' those high an' mighty white folk, Clayton?" Silvia asked in disgust.

"I don't mind helping out one bit, Silvia," Clayton replied. "I like teaching anybody about flowers. If you'd put your mind to it, you might learn something too," he told his sister-in-law with a smile. His smile melted most women's hearts—black and white.

"Ya gots it all wrong, Clayton. They's jest tryin' t'put ya in yua place," argued Silvia.

"God put me here to help people. I will help anyone who needs it," Clayton stated firmly.

Clayton prided himself on what God had given him. Not only was Clayton gifted with great looks but he had a knack for speaking. He worked at enunciation and articulation. He had watched Sidney Poitier films over and over and had practiced speaking in the mirror. And like Demosthenes, he even put pebbles in his mouth in an effort to speak more clearly. He valued education and wanted someday to go to college, but until then, he was thankful for working for the Montagues.

With Clayton's good looks, many of the women at the Garden Club would've liked to have gotten to know Clayton a lot better, despite his color. Several women slipped him their numbers, but Clayton never acted on any of their passes.

On November 19, 1963, Martha Duncan, the president of the Garden Club, was hosting the group in her home. She excused herself when the refreshments were being prepared. She knew Clayton was in the kitchen, alone. She all but assaulted him while he was preparing the food. She wrapped her arms around him while he held a tray of lemonade and cookies in his hands.

"I can't stand it any longer, Clayton. I want ya so badly. Take me now! Take me into the bedroom and rip my clothes off!" Martha said with urgency. She put one hand on his head to bring him closer to kiss him and the other went to rub the joystick between his legs.

Clayton was so shocked and scared, he dropped the tray with the lemonade and cookies. The glasses broke, and the cookies scat-

THE GHOST COMES OUT

tered everywhere. The door to the kitchen came flying open with the ladies of the Garden Club coming in to see what the commotion was.

Looking at Clayton, Martha yelled, "You dum niggah! You will pay for this!" She looked at Daphne Montague and said, "He will work for me for three weeks to pay this off!"

Miss Daphne simply reached into her purse and took out a hundred-dollar bill. She laid it on the kitchen table and turned to Clayton and said, "I believe it's time for us to go. I was getting tired of this club anyway."

Neither Daphne Montague nor Clayton ever attended another Garden Club meeting.

CHAPTER 4

ROSIE'S SUMMER SCHOOL

Rosie and Tati woke up early the next day. They wanted to see their mother before she went to work. Even though it was summer break, their mother still had to make a living. She was Superintendent Marcus Peters's secretary and his girl Friday. Talk was he couldn't do anything without Victoria Scholl. She kept him focused and knew his schedule inside and out. When Victoria's husband, Jeb, died suddenly in the car wreck, Victoria took a week off to plan the funeral, settle the estate, and take care of Rosie and Tati. Marcus ended up calling her after three days begging her to come back to work. He tried to be strong for Victoria, but he was literally lost without her. She knew more about running his job than he did.

Marcus Peters was vain—extremely vain. Never was there a mirror made that he didn't like. His hair was his vanity. Before he went anywhere, he would "fix" his hair. Before he got out of a car, he would "fix" his hair. No mirror was ever passed without him first "fixing" his hair. When the weatherman called for rain, Marcus would have his trusty umbrella by his side and his hat. No rainwater was going to touch his hair. The townfolk made fun of him, behind his back of course, and would often mimic him, but what he didn't know…

He was twice divorced and just simply couldn't please his wives in the bedroom. He wasn't interested in sex. In fact, his first wife, Lydia, told others they only had sex once on their honeymoon.

THE GHOST COMES OUT

"He told me on our wedding night that we didn't need to have sex every night," Lydia revealed. "Sad thing is we didn't have sex much at all after that."

He would much rather have a platonic marriage as opposed to a real one, and both his ex-wives had found comfort in others. He got married only to please his parents. They were eager for him to have children, but that was the last thing he wanted. He disliked kids.

Oddly, he was superintendent of Dakota County Schools. He had gotten this job only because his father, Wyndell Peters, knew every member on the Dakota school board. They all were indebted to him for various reasons, and so he decided to call in all favors at once; and thus, Marcus Peters became superintendent.

The one area Marcus was good at was running. He would run five miles every day after work no matter the weather. The men who sat downtown in the square outside of Bender's Five and Dime would wait for Marcus to do his daily run. Folks said you could set a clock by him and he never skipped. All day long he sat behind a desk and dreamed of running in the afternoons. Marcus was such a dedicated runner that the summer of '64, he hosted the Dakota County 5 Mile Race. The proceeds were supposed to go to funding a new playground for Grayton Elementary School, but he had other plans for that money, and it wasn't to finance a playground.

*****

"Momma, we just wanna give ya a hug b'fore ya lef fo work," said Rosie. Both she and Tati gave their mom a hug and kiss.

"Momma, I love ya, tis much," stated Tati as she held out her arms wide.

"I love you girls more than you'll ever know," Victoria asserted. "Now, you be good for Ree, okay? I'll see you tonight."

The girls walked her to the porch and waved goodbye as she got into her car, a used 1962 Ford Fairlane. The 1955 Chevy Bel Air had been totaled in the crash, and this was the replacement she got from the insurance money. When the car salesman heard how much she had to spend, the cost of the car coincidentally was that exact amount—$2,216…hmmm.

They came back inside and took their places at the kitchen table. Midas knew to crawl under the table next to Tati. This was his favorite meal too.

Rosie spoke up first as she stuffed a piece of bacon into her mouth. Tati was busy giving her three pieces of burnt bacon away to Midas.

"Ree, can me an' Tati start owwah own summa school? We could use that ole barn in back that no one uses. I b'lieve it's impotant t'keep the mind sharp. I could hep Tati with her *R*s. Ya know she jest simply can't git 'em right," explained Rosie.

"Well, y'all need t'clean it up first. Make sure it looks good. Schools should be clean 'cause God likes cleanliness, ya know?" emphasized Ree.

"So, if we clean it up, can we use it?" asked Rosie.

"I guess so. I don't see no reason why not," Ree replied.

They cleaned their dishes off and made up their beds and headed out of the house.

So, Rosie, Tati, and Midas ran to the old barn in back of their house. "Wosie, its dudty," said Tati as they looked inside.

"I know it's dirty, but we can clean it up, ya know? We can git Monty t'hep us. He needs t'come t'owwah school too. I noticed him readin' the otha day, an' he had t'ask me fo times what a word was. Now, I'm not sayin' he's a slow learna, but he needs hep," said Rosie.

Midas and the girls ran next door to the Hutchinses' house. They were just about to knock on the door when Bradley Bacon "Bake" Haas came out of the house in a hurry.

"Why, hello, girls! What do you have planned to do today?" he asked as he patted Midas.

Rosie stepped forward and said, "We gonna start a school in owwah barn. We want Monty t'hep us. He could use some hep in his readin', ya know?"

"I think that's a brilliant idea!" said Bake. "What are you going to do, Tati?" he asked as he bent down to give her a hug.

THE GHOST COMES OUT

"Wosie says I need hep with my *ah*s. She's a speech teacha too," added Tati.

"Tati means her *R*s. She really needs my hep, ya know," Rosie said firmly.

"Well, I believe you girls have it all figured out. Have a great day. I'd like to come see your school when it's finished. Maybe I can take pictures to put in the paper," said Bake.

"Thanks, Mista Bake. We'd like that," stated Rosie.

As Bake got in his old beat-up 1959 Ford Ranchero, Monty must've heard them talking and came running outside.

"Howdy, Rosie an' Tati, how y'all doing?" asked Monty.

"Me an' Tati are here t'see if ya want t'hep us fix up our ole barn as a school. Imma gonna be the teacha 'cause Imma goin' in the third grade," Rosie explained.

"Sounds good t'me," noted Monty. "Mom says I have t'take Alvin t'day. She's gotta git her hair done. Tati, you can play with Alvin, can't ya?"

"I can take cawa Alvin 'cause Imma olda than him," Tati proudly stated.

"Tati, we gotta start with ya speech class t'day, okay?" Rosie stated.

"Okay, Wosie. I will wuk hod," said Tati with earnest.

Rosie said with a grin, "I know ya will, Tati, yua my sista."

Monty and Rosie went to work at the barn behind the Scholls' house. Tati took care of Alvin, and Midas managed to chase a couple of field mice away. They cleaned and threw away a lot of old boxes. They swept and asked Ree if they could use some fold-out chairs for the school.

"Well, I guess seein' it be fo educational purposes, but don't ya break 'em. I only have eight of 'em, ya know," explained Ree.

"Thanks, Ree. Me an' Tati will take care of 'em," said Rosie.

By the afternoon, they had two more students wanting to enroll in Rosie's summer school. Valerie and DaisyBelle Shelby asked if they could join. Rosie was especially happy because not only could Valerie help teach, she could give some needed one-on-one for DaisyBelle, who was repeating first grade.

"How did y'all know 'bout owwah school?" Rosie asked.

"Well, we stopped by Grayton Burger an' Shake t'git a soda, an' we saw Mista Bake, an' he tole us 'bout it. He seemed 'cited 'bout yua school, Rosie," Valerie noted.

"Yeah, my Uncle Bake's the best," said Monty with pride.

"Momma said we could come if ya say is okay," said DaisyBelle.

"I say everybody's welcome. We can have at least eight students 'cause we got eight chairs," explained Rosie.

*****

Harry Miller and Dean McCauley were out walking their German shepherd, Lucy. They happened by the Scholls' house, and Midas perked up and went running toward Lucy. The kids went running after Midas. Lucy was a well-disciplined dog and did not growl or attack Midas. The canines seemed to have an understanding of sorts and just smelled each other.

Rosie stepped forward and said, "Imma Rosalee Scholl, but everybody calls me Rosie. We live here. Who'r you?"

Harry was about to speak for Dean, but he didn't have to.

"I'm Dean McCauley. Do you all live in this house?" he asked.

"Nope," Rosie said. "Me an' Tati live here an' owwah dog, Midas, too."

Rosie introduced the kids to Dean.

"Ya not from 'round here. Where ya from?" Valerie asked.

Before he could answer, Rosie spoke up.

"Yua his dad?" Rosie asked Harry.

Harry declined to answer and said, "We need to get going now, Dean."

"Ya can leave 'im with us, if ya want. We have room fo three mo students," insisted Rosie.

She explained they were starting their own summer school and he was welcome to attend. Dean and Harry looked at one another. Dean's eyes were pleading with Harry to let him stay.

"Okay, but I'll be back in an hour. Dean, Lucy must stay with you," said Harry.

THE GHOST COMES OUT

Harry left reluctantly. He kept debating in his head if leaving Dean was a good idea. He felt better that Lucy was there with Dean. This would give Harry time to do things he couldn't otherwise do with the boy around. He could make the calls he needed and check in to make sure things were going accordingly, and having Lucy there with Dean actually made him feel better.

"So, what grade ya in?" Valerie asked Dean.

"Uh, I don't go to regular school. I get taught at home," Dean said.

"Why do ya do that? Yua daddy not like school? Ya how old?" asked Valerie.

Dean said almost in a whisper, "I'm nine years old, and it's just how we do it."

Rosie took over from here. "Ya read, Dean?" she asked.

"Oh, yes, I'm a good reader. I just finished reading *Charlie and the Chocolate Factory* by Roald Dahl," Dean said.

"Okay, we can use ya t'hep the little ones read," said Rosie. Rosie didn't want to let on she hadn't read that book yet. At her school, they weren't supposed to read that book until the fourth grade, and she was just going into the third. *I jest might read it anyway*, she thought. She would be the teacher, but Valerie and Dean could be her helpers.

"Rosie, I wanna be called Val 'cause Momma an' DaisyBelle call me that," Valerie proclaimed.

"I don't thank we gotta problem with that. From now on, we gonna call Valerie… Val," Rosie instructed.

"Imma gonna call ya Val too," Tati stated softly.

As they were cleaning and getting ready for school to start, Midas and Lucy started barking. Their incessant growls wouldn't stop. The children ran out to see what they were barking at, and there underneath some hay behind the barn was a snake. It was a big western cottonmouth. Although any snake at all seemed big to the kids. Monty picked up Alvin and ran. The other children took off running toward the house, except for Tati. She didn't or couldn't move. She was literally frozen in place. She remembered the story Rosie told her about Mikey Steele's dad being bitten by a snake at church, only to die later that same day. The kids were yelling as they reached the house.

Ree came out of the house and said, "What in tarnation is this ruckus? Rosalee, whas going on?"

Rosie shook her head and yelled, "There's a snake undaneath some hay b'hind the barn!"

Ree looked around. "A snake?" she asked and then looked around. "Where's ya sista? Where's Tatiana?" yelled Ree.

Rosie looked around and realized she wasn't with them. Without hesitation, she ran back to the barn, all the while Ree was yelling at her to stop. Rosie saw Tati just standing looking at the snake while Midas and Lucy were shielding Tati from the reptile. The snake looked like he would strike at any minute as the dogs kept barking at him. Rosie came up behind Tati, picked her up, and carried her away just as Ree came toward them carrying a 12-gauge shotgun. She took one look at the cottonmouth, took aim, and blasted that snake to smithereens. Then she looked around to see if the snake had a nest. It did. She took care of the unhatched eggs too.

As she came up on the porch, she said, "Yua school is safe now." And she walked into the house.

*****

Later that evening, Victoria came home to hear about the girls' day. She hugged her two precious daughters tightly and whispered, "Thank you," to Ree over their heads.

"I am so very thankful you were there, Ree, to take care of the situation," said Victoria.

Ree simply shrugged and excused herself. She said she wasn't feeling well and set off to her bedroom.

"Wosie, Midas an' Wee saved me, Momma. I was scawed."

Midas perked up when he heard his name. Rosie and Tati rubbed and hugged him.

Victoria's eyes filled with tears. "I know you were scared, angel. I'm just so thankful you have the best big sister who loves you so."

"I love Wosie so much," said Tati, and she hugged her so tightly.

THE GHOST COMES OUT

Later, when Rosie and Tati had fallen asleep and Victoria was in her room, she had time to reflect on the day's events. She couldn't help but feel as though she was the luckiest mother in the world. The Lord may have welcomed her Jeb into his kingdom earlier than she wanted, but he left two precious angels for her to watch over and love. Victoria always felt Jeb around her, especially during her prayers. She was just finishing her prayers when…

"AAAHHH!" someone yelled, and then *THUD!*

CHAPTER 5

Not Ready to Go

Victoria heard the scream and raced into the direction from which it came—Ree's bedroom. She opened the door, and there lying on the floor was Ree. She rushed over to her as blood was coming out of a wound at the top of her head. Victoria quickly gathered a washrag from the closet and put it on the wound. Her mother-in-law was not conscious nor was she moving around. In 1964, there was no 9-1-1. The only number to call in case of an emergency was zero. Victoria ran to the hall phone and dialed 0 to get the operator.

"This is the operator, what is your emergency?"

"This is Victoria Scholl at 202 West Pillow Street in Grayton. My mother-in-law has fallen and hit her head. She is unconscious, and we're in need of an ambulance. Please hurry!" Victoria said urgently.

"Yes, ma'am, I will connect you to the Stockton Medical Center," replied the operator.

Having heard the commotion, Rosie and Tati came into Ree's bedroom. They immediately went over to their grandmother. "Is huh dead?" asked Tati. Tears had already formed in her eyes and were spilling onto her face.

"She ain't dead, Tati. Is her, Momma?" asked Rosie.

Victoria didn't answer Rosie's question. She just said, "Go get more washrags and wet them first. Put them on her wound," said Victoria calmly.

Then Victoria heard someone on the other end of the line and began.

"Hep me, Tati!" said Rosie.

Rosie looked down at her little sister and gave her a hug.

"Everythang's gonna be okay, Tati. Ya jest need t'hep me, okay?" Rosie stated.

"I won't cwy no mo," said Tati drying her eyes.

Victoria got off the phone and went over to Ree.

"Girls, I need for you to be brave, okay? Ree's going to be fine. We just need to be strong for her. You know how Ree frowns on tears," emphasized Victoria with a smile.

It seemed like an eternity, but they began to hear a siren in the distance. Ree was beginning to come around, but was very confused. Her pulse seemed to be racing, and her color was pale, but at least she was semiconscious.

The ambulance pulled up, and two men got out. They brought a stretcher with them to the front door.

Victoria ran to the door to let them in. "She's in the back, follow me," she directed.

When they got back to Ree's room, they looked at the woman and felt her pulse.

One of the attendees smiled briefly at Rosie and Tati and said, "Okay, girls, looks like you've done a good job. Now let us take over, okay?"

"I thank she's gonna be okay. We put wet cloths on her," explained Rosie.

"Uh, we put cloths on huh," echoed Tati.

"Thanks, girls. You did a fine job," said the attendant with a smile.

They asked Ree several questions, but she just mumbled answers. Nothing coherent.

The second attendee asked Victoria what Ree's name was and her age. He raised an eyebrow when Victoria told him Ree's age. With her hair completely white and worried wrinkles, the paleness of her face made her look so much older than her fifty-six years.

"Her pulse is 150. Her blood pressure is 190/120. We need to get her to the medical center STAT," stated the driver.

They loaded Ree up and were in the ambulance before Victoria and the girls could get ready to follow the emergency vehicle in their car.

When they arrived at Stockton Medical Center, Ree was being examined by the emergency doctors. Because of the girls' ages, they were not allowed to go back, but one of the young nurses named Sammie Jo assured Victoria that she would watch them so Victoria could go back into the room where Ree was. Just as she rounded the corner, she heard someone yell, "CODE BLUE! CODE BLUE!" All of the doctors and nurses on the floor came rushing into Ree's room.

Rosie and Tati followed the nurse, who was looking after them, racing to Ree's room. They saw their mom and rushed to her. They were told to go and wait in the waiting room.

Victoria, Rosie, and Tati stayed in the waiting room for hours. Rosie and Tati both fell asleep on either side of their mother. Victoria had an arm around both of her girls. They needed comfort and reassurance, and so did she. Victoria would nod off but would wake up at the faintest of noises. At 4:12 a.m., the emergency room doctor came into the waiting room and walked over to Victoria.

He said, "Your mother-in-law went into a cardiopulmonary arrest. She had a heart attack, but amazingly she is resting comfortably and is talking now. She's asking to see you, Mrs. Scholl. I will send a nurse in to watch your daughters."

The same nurse, Sammie Jo, came into the waiting room with Rosie and Tati, while Victoria was led back to Ree's room.

"Hello, Ree," Victoria said when she came into the room. She bent over the bed and held Ree's left hand. It seemed so cold, and Victoria tried to warm it in hers. Ree had a little more color in her face, but she looked as if she'd aged twenty years. Ree smiled ever so faintly. She was weak, but determined to say something to Victoria despite the tubes in her arms and the mask on her face.

"Toria," Ree said ever so softly and labored. "I...not...red...t...go."

That was all she said as she closed her eyes and went to sleep.

CHAPTER 6

MIDAS SEIZES THE DAY

Victoria stayed with Ree for another forty-five minutes until a nurse came in and told her to go home. "We'll look after her, Mrs. Scholl. You need to get some sleep, and your girls are asking for you too," she added with kindness.

Victoria took her daughters home just as the sun was coming up. By then, Rosie and Tati had had enough sleep and were hungry for breakfast, but not before knowing how Ree was.

"Do ya thank she'll be okay, Momma?" Rosie asked.

"I love huh," Tati stated.

Victoria couldn't help but smile lovingly at her daughters. She was so lucky to have such caring and loving girls.

"Yes, I think she's going to be okay, but we'll need to be very careful around her. She'll need plenty of rest, and we'll need to wait on *her* for a change," Victoria added.

"Let me cook you some breakfast," offered their mother. "I know my cooking isn't as good as Ree's, but I'll try," she added laughing.

"Me no like bacon, Momma, but Midas do," said Tati with a big smile.

"How about if we give Midas some dog food today, and I'll make you some scrambled eggs with your cereal. Does that sound good?" Victoria inquired.

"That'd be great, Momma. Can we open a new snack pack? Me an' Tati don't like cornflakes," said Rosie as she made a face.

"Sure, my precious angels. Go ahead and open a new snack pack. How about if you save the cornflakes for me? I love them," said their mom. She really wasn't crazy about cereal, but cornflakes were as good as any of the other brands.

"Yea! Ya hear that, Tati? No mo cornflakes fo us!" Rosie shouted.

"Yea! No mo conflakes fo us!" echoed Tati.

As they were eating their breakfast, someone rang the doorbell. After the night they had last evening, everybody froze. Victoria walked out of the kitchen and down the hall toward the front door. She was followed by her three shadows—Rosie, Tati, and Midas.

Victoria opened the door, and there on her doorstep were Rita, Val, and DaisyBelle Shelby holding a beautiful bouquet of flowers. They had to be picked from the Montagues' garden because no one else in town had a garden like the Montagues, and they wouldn't miss a few.

"We are sorry t'botha ya, but we noticed the ambalance at yua house last night an' thought we'd come ovah an' see if we could hep ya in any way," said Rita as she presented the flowers to Victoria.

"Oh, how thoughtful of you. Thank you so much for the bouquet, do come in," said Victoria.

"Girls, take Valerie and DaisyBelle into the kitchen and put these flowers in a vase. Would you girls like some scrambled eggs and cereal?" asked Victoria.

Val and DaisyBelle said in unison, "Yes! Thank you!"

So the girls went into the kitchen to eat, and Victoria showed Rita into the den. They both sat down on the couch.

"I'm sure you're wondering about the ambulance. My mother-in-law, Ree, took a fall last night hitting her head. She got to the hospital and then went into cardiac arrest. We were with her all night. The girls and I just got home about an hour ago. We will need to go back to the hospital in a little while," explained Victoria.

"Then, please lemme hep. Ya don't need t'take them girls back t'the hospital. I know they're too young t'go back an' see their grandmother in her room, an' I can stay here, if ya don't mind. I can watch the kids so they can still have their summa school. My girls love comin' heeyah so much, an' I would love t'hep ya out, if I could," offered Rita.

Victoria had no idea the secret Rita was keeping. Rita wondered if Victoria knew would she be as accepting of her and her girls. She badly wanted to tell her, but not today. Her secret would have to wait.

"How kind of you, Mrs. Shelby. I will accept on one condition," Victoria said.

"Whas that?" asked Rita.

"If you let me take you all out to eat tonight," Victoria insisted.

"Ya don't need t'do that, Mrs. Scholl. What're neighbors fo?" prompted Rita.

"That's my one condition, and my name is Victoria," she added with a smile.

Rita was hoping Carl would not be home when they went out to eat. She did not want him to cause a scene nor did she want anyone to know he had a drinking problem. Too late. The entire neighborhood was aware of Carl's problem, and the fact he liked to put his hands on Rita was no secret either. No neighborhood mother would allow their children to go play at the Shelbys' house.

Rita replied, "It's a deal. It'll jest be me an' the girls. An' call me Rita."

"Great. We can make a girls' night out. How does that sound?" asked Victoria.

Rita couldn't help but think Victoria was as lovely a person as she'd ever met.

"Yes, that sounds great!" agreed Rita smiling.

While Victoria was at the hospital sitting with Ree, the four girls, Monty, and Dean were busy learning in the old barn turned into their school.

"Do ya thank yua dad'll let ya stay a little longa t'day, Dean?" wondered Monty. He and Dean had hit it off, and he wanted to get to know him better.

"Nah, Harry's a real stickler for time. But that's okay. I get to be with you guys for as long as he'll allow it," said Dean with a smile.

"Why ya call yua daddy, Harry?" Val wanted to know.

"Uh, well, he just likes it that way," Dean responded, and nothing else was said.

Dean was so excited that Harry would let him be a part of this group. Harry had never let him out of his sight. Lucy, the German shepherd, was with Dean again that day.

While Dean was at school, Harry went back to their house and made several calls to Chicago. He had to check in to let his boss know how things were going. He had just hung up the phone when there was a knock on the door. No one ever came to their house, and before he answered the door, he put his trusty Smith and Wesson .38 in the back of his pants, just in case.

"Who is it?" Harry demanded.

"It's Pastor Allan and Frances Boyd from Grayton United Methodist Church," said the pastor.

Damn, if I wanted company, I would have asked you to come over. Don't just show up at my doorstop, thought Harry.

"Just a minute," Harry said, and he opened the door just a little. He really didn't want company and thought that would be a hint to the pastor and his wife to make this unannounced calling short and sweet.

"Hi, Mr. Miller, we thought we'd come over and let you know about the exciting events taking place at our church this summer. We noticed you and Dean are there every Sunday for church, but there are so many other things we would love to share with you and we're sure you'd want to be involved in," said the pastor.

Now Pastor Boyd had been at this church for ten years. Frances, his wife, was already getting itchy about moving to a bigger town. She had her sight set on Memphis. She wanted to be the wife of the pastor of Greater Memphis United Methodist Church. This was the biggest Methodist Church in the south. The pastor was quite happy where he was, but his wife was not. She'd been in this small town far too long for her liking. She couldn't understand why her Allan was not as popular as Reverend Andrew Anglin Greer of the Church of the Southern Baptist of Grayton. *He thanks he's all that 'cause he know Martin Luther King Jr. Well, somethin's gotta change*, she thought.

THE GHOST COMES OUT

"I...er...we need t'move to a different area. Imma thankin' we've done all the 'good' we can do in this town. What 'bout movin' to a bigga area...say... Memphis? Spreadin' the good word in a bigga town is mo of a challenge, don't ya thank? Oh, an' by the way, Allan, I was in yua office at church, yesterdee, an' I did some spring...er... summa cleanin'. I burnt all of yua sermons. It's time ya started t'write some new refreshin' sermons. Don't ya thank? Nobody wants t'hear a sermon they've heard b'fore, don't ya thank? An' Imma gittin' taared of them nosy women's club askin' me 'bout finances. Them's nosy, don't ya thank? Do somethin' 'bout it Allan," Frances insisted.

Frances had a habit of ending a question with "don't ya thank." The ladies of the Conference of Methodist Churches would use that phrase every time they saw Frances, hoping to break her of that habit, but Frances was oblivious. She had no idea that was her catchphrase.

For most men, the thought of having a wife like Frances would be enough to arrange a homicide, but not Allan. He was as fine a man as there ever was. He loved Frances's flaws and believed in their marriage. He also believed that if God wanted them to move, he would make it happen.

"I really appreciate the call, Pastor and Mrs. Boyd, but Dean and I are quite happy with the lovely message you deliver every Sunday," said Harry. He was sure that would let them know he just wasn't interested, but he was wrong.

It always amused Frances Boyd when someone would open their door just a crack. The harder a parishioner tried to keep her out of their house, the harder she tried to get in. Frances was not going to allow this man to keep her out of his house. Her curiosity was already piqued by the relationship of Harry and Dean, and she was determined to find out exactly what it was.

"Oh, my goodness, Mr. Miller, Imma feelin'...weak," said Frances, and sure enough if she didn't drop to the ground where she was. Both Allan and Harry carried her into Harry's house. They laid her on the couch. Harry ran to get a rag and water and dab her head with a cold cloth.

Mission accomplished, thought Frances. When Frances was determined, nothing was going to stop her. She had always wanted to go into theater, so faking an illness was nothing she hadn't practiced before.

The living room had only a couch, chair, small end table with telephone, and TV, and because Harry hadn't expected company, he hadn't shut his bedroom door. She could see there was a small bed and a big bed in the master. *Hmmm,* she thought. *They share a room? How strange when there are two other bedrooms.* She glanced at the telephone table. There were various numbers written on a pad. All the numbers had an area code of 3-1-2. *Now, who would he be callin' in Chicago?* thought Frances. Quickly, she committed one of the numbers to memory before Harry picked up the pad and turned it over.

Frances would eventually find out who was on the other end of that phone number. If only she'd minded her own business, but that was impossible—and one more event that unfolded the summer of '64.

*****

Rita was up at the Scholls' house when she heard a banging on the front door. It startled her, and Midas too. The dog had not gone with the girls today to school. He too had had a long night waiting for the Scholls to come home, but the noise at the door woke him up. Rita walked to the front door and peered out. Midas followed behind. She saw her husband, Carl, at the door. She could tell he was already drunk. Rita opened the door slowly. Carl pushed his way inside the house.

"Well, well, well, I wondered wha this place look like on the insi," slurred Carl. "Coul use a man's hep. P'haps the widow might be lonely." Carl smiled.

"Carl, please don't cause a scene. Imma watchin' Victoria's girls while she sittin' with her mother-in-law at the hospital," said Rita.

"Aren ya a good neighbor hepin' the little widow an' her girls?" Carl remarked.

Just then Carl saw Midas looking at him. The animal began to growl. He was the best-tempered dog until he sensed danger, and he now detected something wrong. It looked like Carl was going to pat Midas as he reached down, but he kicked the dog instead. Midas was sent flying half-way across the room. He stayed on the floor for a minute and then limped away down the hall and into the kitchen.

"Carl! Why'd ya do that? He did nothin' wrong. Midas is a sweet dawg. Why ya hurt 'em like that?" Rita yelled.

"He shouldn growl at me! Now, ya be a good little wifey an' fix me somethin' t'eat," demanded Carl.

Rita knew if she didn't, there would be hell to pay, so she went into the kitchen to cook something for Carl. Just like her kitchen, the Scholls didn't have a lot of food in the cupboard or fridge, but at least they had cornflakes and bacon. That was more than she had in her pantry. So, cornflakes and bacon was what she fixed him.

Rita had just finished making the bacon and was putting it on the table. Carl pushed her toward the table to hurry her up, and in the process, the plate in her hand went flying. The bacon and the plate hit the floor. Midas grabbed the bacon and took off through the hole in the screened-in door to the outside.

Carl couldn't believe the dog had taken his food, and for a brief moment, he was stunned. It could've been the alcohol that caused him to pause, but shortly thereafter, he recovered. He looked at Rita and said, "Well, ya did it, didn ya? Ya let that mongrel git my food." Then, he slapped Rita right in the face for being so careless. He left a big red mark on her face as he left the house in total disgust and headed to Stockton and Erleen.

Even though Rita's face hurt from the slap, she thought it was worth it. *To see the look on Carl's face afta Midas grabbed the bacon off the flow an' headed out the door was well worth the pain an' the red mark on my face*, Rita thought with a laugh.

"Midas, me an' you gonna be great friends," Rita said to herself.

CHAPTER 7

Summer School Is Integrated

A baby doesn't come into this world with preconceived prejudices. A baby will smile at anyone who is loving. Babies do not know color, sexual preference, religious choice, or nationality. This is how it should be for everyone, and this is how it was for these children in Grayton.

"Rosie, Tati, come on and grab some cereal, eggs, and bacon before your school starts," shouted their mother, Victoria, from the bottom of the stairs.

Rosie and Tati came running down the stairs followed closely by Midas. Now, Midas wasn't supposed to be an inside pet, but after he helped save Tati from the snake, no one minded him being inside, not even Ree. And no complaints were heard from Midas either.

Today was one of Victoria's days off. She was at the table when the girls and Midas came down to the kitchen.

"Momma!" cried both girls with delight.

"We f'got ya had off t'day!" shouted a happy Rosie.

"I thought I might check out your school. I also have a surprise for you too," added Victoria. She walked around to the other side of the table and pulled out eight little chalkboards and eight boxes of chalk from a brown paper sack.

"This like Kissmas, Momma!" said an excited Tati.

THE GHOST COMES OUT

"Momma, where'd ya git these? These are jest what we need t'make owwah summa school great!" shouted Rosie.

"I told Mr. Peters about your school, and he donated these to your school. I told him he could give them to you himself, but he had so much on his schedule, so he gave them to me to present to you. So, you know what that means, don't you?" asked Victoria.

"Yes 'em, we need t'write a thank-ya note t'Mista Peters," replied Rosie.

Looking at Tati, Rosie said, "I'll hep ya write yuas t'Mista Peters, okay, Tati?"

"Thank ya, Wosie. I dunno how t'wite yet," explained Tati.

"That's 'nother thang I gotta hep ya with, Tati," said Rosie shaking her head. "Momma, I got my hans full, don't I?"

Victoria said with a laugh, "A good teacher's job just doesn't end at 3:00 p.m., and you're a good teacher, Rosie."

The girls finished their breakfast and headed out to the barn for school. Monty was already there waiting.

"What took y'all so long?" asked Monty.

"Ya early, Monty. We're always on time too. God don't like no slackas, ya know?" asserted Rosie.

Val and DaisyBelle were just walking up to the barn, and DaisyBelle was carrying a Marian doll. Tati's eyes were so big when she saw the doll. This was the only thing she had wanted for her birthday, but Victoria couldn't afford it. After Jeb's death, money was very tight. Victoria had promised Tati she would get her a Marian doll just as soon as the life insurance check came in, but the new car took every penny of that check. They were just barely getting by, and since Ree was in the hospital, spare change went for gas to and from the hospital. Victoria was still determined to get Tati the doll as soon as she could.

The Marian doll had first made an appearance in 1960. It was the hottest doll on the market, and every little girl wanted one. One could buy the Marian doll as either a blonde, redhead, or brunette. In 1963, Mippie, Marian's little sister, was introduced. The market wanted to cash in on both sexes, so Hall and Hodge were introduced for boys. Marian's Fantasy House and her magic car were out then too. The doll was so popular the stores could not keep them in stock. To think DaisyBelle had her own Marian doll. Tati thought she was the luckiest girl in the world. She dared not ask if she could touch it, but DaisyBelle asked her if she would like to hold her, and it didn't take a second invite for Tati to reach out to take Marian.

Even though DaisyBelle's parents were poor, if not poorer than the Scholls, Carl got the doll for his youngest daughter by winning it in a poker game. There were periods of normalcy where Carl could actually be civil, but they were too few and far between. DaisyBelle was the only one in the family he seemed to care about. DaisyBelle loved her sister, Val, and she shared the doll with her, but Val didn't care about the doll the way DaisyBelle did.

"You can hold her an' comb her hair if ya wanna," DaisyBelle said to Tati. With each doll came a comb and brush, an extra change of clothes, as well as a swimsuit and stand. Tati was so excited she almost dropped Marian on the ground. She could not believe she was holding Marian in her own hands, and was getting to brush her hair too. Rosie realized she was not going to get a lot of work out of Tati today. So, she thought today would be a good day to give DaisyBelle some one-on-one attention with her reading.

Dean McCauley showed up a little late that day. Lucy wasn't with them when Harry dropped him off.

"Where's Lucy?" Val inquired.

"She wasn't feeling well. She has an upset tummy," said Dean. He didn't want to tell them the real story. Lucy was his best and only friend, and he couldn't talk about her without tears forming in his eyes.

"Dean, I'll let you stay for two hours. I'll be back precisely in two hours," Harry said, and off he went. He had to make his usual calls to Chicago and had just enough time to get home to do it. He also thought he'd go to the Grayton Grocery Mart for supplies. He didn't like taking Dean with him if he could avoid it.

"Boy, yua dad has a tight leash on ya, don't he?" asked Monty.

Dean did not answer. Instead he asked Monty if they could play ball during their recess time. Monty quickly answered with a resounding yes. Dean had been taught to never answer questions about himself or Harry. Dean was happy in this town, and now he'd made some friends. He didn't want to have to move again.

During free writing time, the children could write any story on their new boards or, as in Tati's case, practice writing letters. Val wrote a letter to her mother, Rita. She loved her mother, and her dislike for her father seemed to be growing daily. Val knew when he had been drinking because he would slur his words and grab at her. He smelled like a stale wine or beer bottle and dried urine. Val tried hard to protect her mother and sister. But it wasn't her job, and Rita knew it. She would do anything for her girls, but lately she had something on her mind. Something that just kept eating at her. She had a secret, and it was a big one—and no one to confide in. She badly wanted to talk to Victoria, but feared what might happen. She knew the Scholl girls were nice and came from a good family, so she was happy her girls could play with them. Perhaps after a time, she might talk to Victoria. Getting it off of her chest would be good, but for now, she'd just have to keep it to herself.

The next activity was recess. All the kids would play ball or four square or just chase each other. Tati and DaisyBelle were playing with Marian and styling the doll's hair in a long ponytail that hung down her back. They were so immersed in their task that Tati did not see her mother come to visit. Rosie ran to her mom with arms opened wide, and Tati even left Marian to hug her mother. Val, DaisyBelle, and Monty hugged her too. Rosie introduced her mom to Dean, who felt immediately drawn to Victoria. She was so much like his own mother, and oh how he missed his mom. He missed her so much that he physically ached. If only he could see her.

Victoria joined in and played with the kids when they heard a wonderful sound. Yes, it's the sound we all love to hear when we're little. The sound of bells. The sound of music. The sound of the ice cream truck! Victoria surprised them when she told them they could each get one ice cream of their choice. They ran to the street to stop the truck.

That summer, the ice cream man was Joe Puckett, but the kids called him Mr. Joe. Mr. Joe was a scam artist, flimflam man, and quite frankly a racist. He also was very particular about who he waited on. That is until he met Victoria Scholl.

"Tati, ya know not t'talk. Mr. Joe don't like that," warned Rosie.

"I know, Wosie. I won't say nothin'," Tati responded.

The kids were in a line and waiting for Mr. Joe to wait on them.

"Today, I wanna tell y'all about a contest Ice Cream World is havin'. Fo every ten cents ya spend, Imma gonna give ya a ticket. On July 4, Imma gonna pull out a ticket, an' if ya have the same numba on yuas, then ya win a pony," Mr. Joe explained.

"A PONY!" The kids screamed.

"Thas right, a pony. Now, how many ice cream treats y'all wantin' t'day?" Mr. Joe demanded.

"Oh, Momma, ya know I always wanted a pony. I wish fo a pony every time I blow out my birthday candles," Rosie said to her mother. Rosie thought if she had a pony, she would let every kid in the neighborhood ride it whenever they wanted. She and Tati would brush and feed it daily. She'd even picked out a name for the pony, Lucky. She chose that name because she would be the luckiest third grader in Grayton if she won it.

All the kids got an ice cream and a ticket for a chance to win the pony. As they were eating their treats, two young boys came up to the truck. They had their money in their hands ready to buy an ice cream.

"I wanna chocolate bah, an' my brotha wanna a vanilla," explained the bigger boy.

Mr. Joe shook his head and said, "Nah, I don't sell t'no niggahs. Now, get outta heah!"

Victoria heard the transaction. She couldn't believe her ears. She turned toward Mr. Joe and said, "You will serve these two boys, or I will report you first to the NAACP! Secondly, I will call the *Grayton Gazette*. I'm sure they would love to write a story about the ice cream man refusing to serve business to two boys of color. You may not be aware, but yesterday, June 19, the Civil Rights Act passed 73–27. Your business would be gone like that!" she said as she snapped her fingers. She looked down at the two boys with nothing but love in her eyes. "Put your money away, boys, your ice cream is on me."

Mr. Joe served them but threw their ice cream in their direction so they had to catch them before they hit the ground.

"I believe you're forgetting something, Mr. Joe," Victoria demanded.

"Whattcha want now?" yelled Mr. Joe.

"I believe these boys get a ticket a piece so that they too might have a chance to win the pony," responded Victoria sweetly.

Mr. Joe threw two tickets on the ground and then sped away in his truck. He was so mad he forgot to turn on the bells and music, and without the warning, children did not come out to meet him. He lost quite a few sales that day.

The two boys thanked Victoria for her kindness.

"Thank ya, ma'am. Me an' Billy had money t'pay," said the bigger boy with a smile.

"You just keep that until the next time," Victoria said.

"Yes 'em. Thank ya, ma'am," both the boys said in unison.

Rosie came forward bringing Tati by her hand.

"Imma Rosalee, but everybody calls me Rosie. Imma goin' into third grade. Y'all wanna come t'owwah summa school? We got two chairs lef, an' we have lots of fun. This here is my sister, Tati. She jest turned three. How old are y'all?" Rosie inquired.

"Imma Johnny, an' Imma eight, an this here is Billy. He be seven," replied Johnny.

The other kids crowded around and welcomed Johnny and Billy. Rosie's summer school was now full, and for the first time in the history of Grayton, Tennessee, a school was integrated. It only took a few minutes to show the Grayton adults how easily children of different races could get along. Oh, if only the adults had paid closer attention, but that was not to be that summer of '64.

CHAPTER 8

REE COMES HOME

"Today is a very special because Ree's coming home," Victoria explained to her girls. "Are there clean sheets on her bed?"

"Yes, 'em. Me an' Tati put new ones on this mornin'," stated Rosie.

"Yes, me an Wosie put towels in huh bathwoom too, Momma," added Tati with a smile.

"Great, thanks, girls. I just want everything looking as nice as possible for her. What do you think about getting some fresh flowers to brighten up her room?" asked Victoria.

"Oh yes! Yes!" agreed both girls.

"Ya always thank of everthin', Momma," said Rosie.

"It's 'cause ya the best, Momma," echoed Tati.

Victoria wrapped her arms around her daughters and squeezed them closely. They gave her such strength, and she prayed continually thanking God for her girls.

"Okay, let's go get some flowers and put them in her bedroom, then we can go to the hospital and bring our Ree home. How does that sound, girls?" asked Victoria.

"That sounds great!" cried Rosie.

"That sounds gwait!" echoed Tati.

They went downtown to the Grayton Florist and bought the prettiest colored daisies that Mr. Wooldridge had in his shop. They rushed home to put them on Ree's bedside table so they would be there when she came home.

"I thank they are beautiful! Ree's gonna love 'em, Momma. An' she's gonna love us fo gittin' 'em, won't she, Momma?" asked Rosie.

"I hope so," said Victoria.

"Okay, everybody, ready?" asked Victoria. Midas was sensing the excitement, and his tail was wagging. Victoria looked down at him and said, "Sorry, Midas, you're going to have to stay here."

Midas seemed to understand, so he went to the kitchen and lay down under the kitchen table.

They arrived at the Stockton Medical Center just in time for breakfast to be served to the patients. Rosie and Tati stayed in the waiting room. There were several little play cars on a table that were there for children to enjoy, so the girls were entertained while Victoria went back to see Ree.

When Victoria entered Ree's room, she heard her mother-in-law arguing with the same nurse, Sammie Jo, who Victoria had seen before.

"I told ya, I don't like runny eggs. I thank I need t'teach yua cook how t'cook. She don't know how," argued Ree.

"I'm sorry, Miss Ree, I'll be sure to let the chef know," she insisted. Sammie Jo turned to look at Victoria with a huge smile on her face.

"I'm so sorry,' said Victoria.

"Don't be," Sammie Jo said with a laugh, "she's going home with *you* today." And she left the room.

Even though Ree professed not to like the eggs, she ate them anyway. In fact, she ate all her apple sauce, cereal, and toast, and complained during the entire meal.

Victoria helped Ree get dressed after breakfast. Nurse Sammie Jo came back in to give Victoria Ree's medicines and to go over her discharge papers. Sammie Jo was almost giddy when she wheeled Ree, in the wheelchair, down to the front of the medical center to Victoria's car. The girls were so excited to see Ree. They ran over and gave her numerous hugs. Despite her manner, Victoria could tell she was happy to see the girls.

"Now, git in the car, Rosalee an' Tatiana. We don't have time fo this," said Ree.

They drove home, and the girls couldn't stop talking and catching Ree up on everything that had happened while she was away. They told her about the new boys they had added to their school.

"So, now ya got eight kids, do ya?" Ree wondered.

"Yes, 'em, we do," responded Rosie.

"Well, take care of my chairs, ya hear? I only have eight of 'em," Ree reminded the girls.

When they got home, they helped Ree into the house and back to her bedroom. The girls were so excited to show Ree her room and the flowers.

"Look, Wee, we got ya flowuhs," said Tati shyly.

Ree looked at the flowers. "Now why ya do that? They gonna die. Ya want me t'die, girl?" Ree demanded of Tati.

"I sorry, Wee," said Tati.

Tati was just about to cry when Ree added, "Plastic flowers don't die. Why d'ya thank I only have plastic flowers in my room? Ya need t'thank fore ya act."

Tati didn't want Ree to see her cry, so she turned her head and looked at Rosie. Rosie took Tati's hand, and the two girls walked out of the room.

Victoria helped Ree get in bed and made sure she was comfortable. Then, she picked up the vase full of flowers, took them out of the room, and closed the door to Ree's bedroom. Not a word was spoken.

CHAPTER 9

AND THE FUN BEGINS

The Scholls' house

"Hey, Tati, we gotta git up. We be late fo school, an' ya know Jesus don't like no slackas," said Rosie in a hurry.

"I comin', Wosie. Don't wanna be no slacka," said Tati. Neither Rosie nor Tati really knew what a slacker was, but both had heard their grandmother, Ree, say it so many times they understood it wasn't good.

"Midas, ya betta huwe, ya don't wanna be no slacka," Tati said to Midas.

He looked up at her and followed right behind her as though he understood what she had said. They raced down the stairs to see Ree at the bottom of them. She had an angry look on her face, and her piercing blue eyes were even brighter blue than usual. In fact, the look she gave the girls was of pure hatred. The girls stopped short when they got to the bottom. Tati was already beginning to tear up in fear of what Ree was going to say.

"Who ah ya, an' whattcha doin' in my house, little girls?" demanded Ree.

THE SISTERS SPURLOCK

On the other side of town, Silvia Smith's house

Silvia was in the kitchen making breakfast for her kids. She was cooking ham, biscuits, grits, and eggs. She always made a big deal about breakfast. "Is mos impotant meal fo kids," she told her sons, Johnny and Billy.

"I don't know if I want ya playin' school wid them people," said Silvia to her sons, Johnny and Billy.

"Oh, Momma, please? They was so nice t'us," said Johnny.

"Yeah, an Miss Scholl bought owwah ice cream fo us," added Billy.

"Now, why she buy two lil black boys ice cream? I jest don't trust someone whose han I can't see," said Silvia.

Clayton had just entered the house to hear the discussion.

"Why don't you let me take the boys to the summer school, Silvia? I can check things out, and and if it doesn't look reputable, they won't stay," said Clayton. "Besides, what better thing for the kids than to be in school, right?"

"This ain't a real school. This is put on by white folks. I don't like it. Don't like it one bit," Silvia argued.

"I'm not going to take no for an answer, Silvia. These boys want to go, and I'm going to take them," Clayton insisted.

Silvia didn't argue. She accepted that Clayton was going to take his nephews to the school. She didn't like it, but she didn't argue.

Silvia had a beautiful house to live in, rent free. This was furnished by her employer, Miss Daphne Montague. She had more groceries in her cupboard than anyone in the white community. It was given to her and her husband, Jackson, by Miss Daphne. She wanted her employees to be happy and well taken care of. At Christmas, her employees were given bonuses. This was unheard-of in Grayton, but Daphne Montague took care of her employees, and they each loved her…except for Silvia. No matter how hard she tried, Silvia was not going to like her. That is until the secret on Montague Hill came out.

"Are you ready, boys? I believe summer school is calling," stated Clayton with his beautiful smile.

THE GHOST COMES OUT

"Yessir! Thanks, Uncle Clayton," said the boys.

*****

Harry Miller's house

Dean was at the kitchen table and eating a brown sugar cinnamon pastry. These were his favorite toaster pastries, and Harry made sure the pantry was invariably stocked with plenty of them.

"Harry, I was wondering if I could invite one of my new friends, Monty, over to spend the night," said Dean. "He's very nice, and he's taught me a lot of different games, and well, he's my best friend."

He dared not say "since Lucy's no longer here." He knew Harry felt badly over what had happened, but it just wasn't fair. Harry had taken Lucy to get her bathed and her nails clipped while Dean was at school. When he went to pick her up, she wasn't there. The groomer said she'd somehow gotten out, and she'd looked and looked for her but to no avail. This did not make sense to Harry. Lucy was not only trained but she would not leave. She was a rare kind of German shepherd. She was entirely white, and Harry knew she was worth quite a bit of money. When Harry told Dean about it, he went into his room and cried himself to sleep.

Harry looked down at Dean with concerned eyes. "You know we can't have anyone over. If I could, you know I would allow it, but right now, things just aren't good," said Harry. "I'm bending my own rules to allow you to attend the school as it is. I'm sorry, but the answer is no, Dean."

Dean knew it was a stretch, but he wanted to be like any other kid. He wanted to have sleepovers, he wanted to be on a baseball team, he wanted to go on vacations, but his was a different circumstance, and he knew what was at stake.

Tears started to fall down his face. They hit the pastry that was still uneaten on his plate. Harry had to turn away from the table. He couldn't stand to watch Dean getting upset. It was such a shame that this sweet boy couldn't play intramural sports and be like other boys, but Harry knew the fewer people who knew them, the better. He didn't want to have to move again. This was the first town they had been to where both Harry and Dean felt at home. He just couldn't risk it.

"Dean, you need to hurry and finish because summer school starts in fifteen minutes," said Harry.

*****

The Shelbys' house

"Whatcha thank yua doin'?" Carl demanded of this wife, Rita.

Carl was still on an all-night drunkathon, and Rita had spent the entire night trying to calm him down. For some reason, he was madder than ususal. Rita suspected it had something to do with his girlfriend, Erleen, in Stockton. She couldn't know how right she was. Carl had arrived at Erleen's house the night before, only to find she already had a gentleman caller. Tuesday nights were Carl's time to go to Stockton. That Tuesday, he had gotten a bouquet of flowers to give her as a surprise. Unfortunately for him, it was he who got the surprise. The gentleman caller turned out to be David Harness, a mechanic who worked with Carl. Turns out David and Erleen had been seeing each other for quite a while, and Erleen was not going to stop seeing him either. She told Carl to hit the road, and that's exactly what he did, but before he left, he flattened every one of David Harness's car tires. He thought about keying the car, and then thought of something better—he smashed the front window with a tire iron, then departed.

When he eventually got home, he was in one foul mood. Rita shut the door to the girls' room. She wanted to muff as much of the sound as she could.

"I asked ya a question. Whatcha thank yua doin'?" Carl repeated.

"Please, Carl, the girls are gettin' dressed. Let's discuss this afta they leave fo school," said Rita.

"Wha the hell ya talkin' 'bout, woman? School's out fo summa!" yelled Carl.

"I know, Carl, 'member they go t'the Scholls' house, an' they have summa school. Don't ya 'member comin' ovah there the otha day? I fixed ya eggs," said Rita.

"Oh yeah, that damn dawg ate my bacon!" screamed Carl. His face seemed to grow darker as he recalled the scene.

Val came running out of her bedroom and rushed to her mother's side. "Don't cha hurt Momma again, ya hear me? I won't let ya!" shouted Val.

"Oh ya won't, will ya? Well, well, looks like ya have a replacement, Rita."

And before Val could move, Carl stepped forward and, with a closed fist, hit his eldest child in the jaw. Val fell to the floor. He had knocked her unconscious. Rita knew it was just a matter of time before he transferred his aggressions onto his children. She screamed and ran to Val. DaisyBelle raced out of her bedroom carrying Marian, and when she saw Val lying on the floor, she dropped her doll.

"She asked fo it, didn' she?" Carl laughed.

And just like a mother cub protecting its young, Rita, with fury in her eyes, grabbed the closest thing available…a chair…and in one smooth move that would've made even a heavyweight champion take notice, she broke the chair over her husband's head. In the boxing world, it would've been classified as a TKO.

*****

The Hutchinses' house

Monty Hutchins had overslept. He had stayed up late the previous night watching the last airing of *The Twilight Zone*. He was mesmerized by that show and was quite upset that it would be the last time on air. His hero was the host, and he wanted to grow up and be a storyteller of science fiction too. He lay in his bed thinking about the episode when he heard talking downstairs. He thought he heard Uncle Bake talking. He adored his uncle, and if he couldn't be a science fiction writer, then he wanted to be a reporter like Bake. He dressed quickly then ran downstairs to the kitchen, and sure enough, his mom, Bake, and little brother, Alvin, were all eating at the kitchen table.

"Well, little buddy, I was beginning to wonder if you had been taken into the twilight zone," he said to Monty with a laugh.

"Did ya see it, Uncle Bake? Wasn't it the greatest episode? And t'thank it's the last one," Monty said with disappointment.

"I know, Monty. I'm just as disappointed as you, little buddy. I too was glued to my television last night," Bake stated as he thought about the last episode of the Twilight Zone.

"It's always a shame when parents don't know just how special their kids are. Which brings me to why I am here. I thought I'd go to your summer school with you today, Monty. I'd like to take some pictures for the paper and do an article. What do you think?" Bake wondered.

"Really, Uncle Bake? That's the best news eva! I know Rosie's gonna be excited. Ya know, it was her idear, right?" asked Monty.

"I want to hear all about it, but let's wait until we get there and the word is idea. There's no *r* in idea, little buddy. Now, I don't want to lose the excitement, so go and brush your teeth. I've got an errand I must do, so I will meet you over at the Scholls' house," Bake explained.

CHAPTER 10

THE BUCKEYE TREE

At precisely 8:00 a.m., Monty showed up at the barn made into the school in back of the Scholls' house. No one was there.

Huh, that's weird. They ain't here yet, thought Monty. That thought had just popped in his head when Dean, Harry, Clayton, Johnny, and Billy came ambling up.

"Hey, guys, where's Rosie and Tati?" asked Dean. No one seemed to know, so the four boys amused themselves by chasing each other around the barn.

Rosie, Tati, Midas, and DaisyBelle were the last to arrive. They came together. DaisyBelle was once again carrying her Marian and holding her tightly as though someone might take her away. Tati was holding Marian's brush and comb in her left hand and Rosie's hand in her right. Midas ran to Dean with his tail wagging. He was looking for Lucy. Dean bent down to pat Midas. *Lucy's gone, and I don't know if she's ever coming back. I'm sorry, Midas,* Dean thought as he looked into Midas's eyes. Midas seemed to understand and went to sit beside Tati on the ground.

"DaisyBelle, where's Val?" Monty asked.

"Uh, she's sick," said DaisyBelle, clutching Marian ever so tightly in her arms. Even though Tati was three years younger, she felt a kindred spirit in DaisyBelle. She put her arm around DaisyBelle.

"Okay, let's git started. There's so much teachin' t'do an' not 'nuff time," said Rosie. Harry and Clayton laughed.

The kids had been working for some time when Bake Haas came up. Clayton and Harry had stayed around to observe the kids reading and writing.

Bake Haas introduced himself to the boys as well as Harry and Clayton.

"Nice to meet you, Mr. Haas," said Clayton. "Aren't you a reporter with the *Grayton Gazette*?"

"Yes, I am, but please call me Bake. Everyone does. I actually came to do a story on the summer school. I didn't realize it was integrated," he said, looking at Johnny and Billy, "but leave it to the children to show us adults the way, right?" asked Bake. "Mr. Clayton, I believe you're the gardener for Miss Daphne Montague, right? No one knows flowers like you. Your garden is the most beautiful in our lovely town," Bake remarked.

"Why, thank you, Mr. Bake, I love what I do, and it is my honor to work for Miss Daphne," said Clayton with a huge smile. One could tell he adored his job and his employer.

He's a strikingly handsome Negro, Bake thought. *I'll bet he's got black women coming and going.* Having exhausted everything he could out of that conversation, Bake turned his attention to Harry. "So, it's Mr. Miller, right? Where do you come from? I believe I know everyone in this small community, and your face is not familiar," asked Bake.

"We moved here a year ago," Harry said, and that's all he said, and he glared at Bake, as if to say, "Don't ask me anything else because that's all you're getting."

Bake held Harry's glare. *There's something about this guy I do not like. I don't trust him. I'll do some checking on him when I get back to the office. Now what was Harry's last name? Note to self: Miller*, thought Bake.

"Well, I guess we have a school mascot, don't we?" Bake said with a laugh.

"Hi, girls, and who is this?" Bake asked pointing to the doll. DaisyBelle said nothing.

Tati spoke up, "She's huh best fwend. Huh name's Mawian, an' we love huh." Bake smiled a big grin and kneeled down to get a better look at the doll.

THE GHOST COMES OUT

"I can see why, Tati, she's a princess," added Bake.

Harry turned to Dean and quietly whispered, "I'll be back as soon as school's over. Don't go anywhere until I return, okay?"

"I won't, Harry," said Dean in a whisper, and then Harry left.

Interesting, thought Bake. *Dean just called his dad by his first name. Why? What kid would call his father by his first name? I must find out more about these two.*

Bake was a very good reporter. He also had an unusual talent for being able to hold two conversations at once. He could be in one discussion but able to listen to another in an adjoining room. His hearing skills were incredible. His boss told him that's what made him such a good journalist. Bake learned he had this ability at an early age. He would be talking to his friends but able to hear what his parents were saying in the next room. He never missed a thing, which could also be a curse. When Bake was six years old, he was watching television in the living room with his sister while his parents were in the kitchen smoking a cigarette. After dinner in their household was a time for adults to talk and children to watch TV. It was Bake's favorite time of the day, but he simply couldn't turn off his ability to listen in on his parents. Much to his detriment, he heard his father say to his mother, "Ya know I love you an' the children, Gail, but bein' what I am, I simply can't live this way no more. Ya know it's jest a matta of time 'fore I'm found out. It ain't fair to ya, Gail. You're still young. You can fin' someone who'll treat ya right an' love ya. I ain't that person. I'll be sendin' ya money every month fo you an the kids, but I ain't gonna be a part of their lives. It jest ain't fair."

And with that, Bake's father left them. Never to see them again.

Gail never remarried. She never gave up the hope that one day her husband would come home. She died waiting.

Bake was busy taking pictures of the kids writing and reading. He told them this story would probably be on the front page. Rosie was thrilled to hear it, but was still reeling from what had happened that morning. She was a very resilient third grader. When Ree had stopped both sisters at the bottom of the stairs and demanded knowing who they were and what they were doing in her house, Rosie knew something was not right with her grandmother. She knew she needed to take charge of the situation and felt Tati tense up next to her.

"Ree, yua funny," said Rosie. "Ya know me an' Tati are yua granddaughtas. Lemme an' Tati hep ya back into bed. Ya know ya shouldn't be outta bed."

So, the girls led Ree back to her bed, and Tati went to get a glass of water for Ree and placed it on her bedside table.

"Whas wong with Wee?" Tati asked Rosie as they walked out of Ree's room.

"Shhhh! Wait til we git outside," said Rosie with some urgency.

"Don't know whas wrong with Ree, Tati. We gotta tell Momma when she gits home t'night. Now, we don't wanna dispoint owwah friends. We're runnin' late fo school," Rosie reminded Tati.

When they walked out of their house, they saw Rita talking very seriously to DaisyBelle. Rita had a concerned look on her face. She hugged and kissed DaisyBelle and then turned and walked away. Tati ran to DaisyBelle, who was holding Marian in her arms. DaisyBelle gave Marian's brush and comb to Tati to hold. She loved being able to play with Rosie and Tati but was so worried about Val.

Immediately after Carl knocked Val to the floor, Rita and DaisyBelle had gone to her aid. Rita picked Val up off the floor and carried her to her room. She was resting on her bed in the room she shared with DaisyBelle. Val had an ice pack on her face.

"I wan ya t'go t'the Scholls t'day, DaisyBelle. I'll take care of Val. She wouldn't wan ya t' worry 'bout her. Everythang's gonna be okay. Ya jest go an' have fun with Tati. Don't forgit Marian," Rita reminded DaisyBelle.

"Momma, is Papa gonna be okay too?" DaisyBelle inquired.

Rita said reassuringly, "I'll be takin' care of yua fatha, I promise."

DaisyBelle gave Val a hug.

Rita turned to Val and said smugly, "I'm gonna walk ya sista t'the Scholls, but I'll be right back, okay, honey? Don't worry 'bout Papa, I'll be takin' good care of him when I git back. Ya understand me, honey?" Val simply nodded and smiled slightly. She knew her mother would do anything to protect her and DaisyBelle. *I kinda feel*

THE GHOST COMES OUT

sorry fo Papa. Nah, he gonna git whas a comin' t'him, she thought, and suddenly her head didn't hurt nearly as bad.

The afternoon passed in a flash. Bake had already enough photos to go with his story, so he went back to the *Grayton Gazette*. Clayton was walking around the property and noticed a tree on the Scholls' land. He called the kids over.

"Do you know what kind of a tree you have here?" asked Clayton.

"Uh, yesssir, my Ree calls it a buckeye, but me an' Tati git branches off so Ree can use um as switches t'spank us if we bein' bad," Rosie explained.

Clayton answered in his smooth-spoken way, "You're so right, Teacher Rosie. It's called a buckeye tree, and those nuts on the tree are called buckeye nuts. Look here." He pulled one out of his front pocket.

"Whas so great 'bout the tree, Uncle Clayton?" inquired Johnny.

"Why, this buckeye has gotten me out of a lot of trouble. It brings me good luck," Clayton informed them. "You all need to carry one in your pocket. I wouldn't go anywhere without mine."

The children got down on the ground and began picking them up. "Don't take all of them, friends, leave some for others," Clayton stated.

Before each child put a buckeye in their pocket, the children made a wish on them. DaisyBelle's wish was for her sister and father. *I hope Val's gonna be okay and that Momma's gonna take care of Papa*, she thought.

Dean turned his buckeye over and over again in his hand. *I wish Lucy would come back and that someday I could see my momma again*, he thought.

Monty didn't really believe it, but what did he have to lose? *I wish Rod Serling would do 'nother TV show.*

Rosie grasped hers tightly in her hand and wished, *I wish Momma an' me an' Tati could win some money so we could git a pony.*

Tati wished, *I wish Wee like me, an' if Imma doin' somethang t'huh, Imma sorry.*

Johnny looked at his buckeye and thought, *I wish me an' Billy could go to real school with our new friends.*

Billy put his buckeye in his pocket and thought, *I wish fo ice cream man t'come back 'cause Imma hungry fo ice cream.*

As the buckeyes were being put into the children's pockets, the first of wishes came true. The children heard the familiar noise at the same time and began jumping up and down. It was the ice cream man. That's right, Mr. Joe was back.

"My wish came true, Uncle Clayton!" cried Billy. "I jest wish fo the ice cream man t'come. This here buckeye works!"

The boys and girls ran to the street to meet him. He stopped his truck. He was afraid not to for fear Victoria would report him to the NAACP if he didn't.

Rosie whispered to her sister so only she could hear, "Me an' you don't have no money, so we ain't gittin' nothin' t'day, okay?"

"Is okay, Wosie. We jest happy fo owwah fwends," Tati replied.

DaisyBelle stayed back with Rosie and Tati. She didn't have money either. Clayton watched as the girls stood back from the line. He surmised that they had no money to pay for the ice cream, and he recalled what his nephews had told him about Mr. Joe's first visit.

"Don't forget these precious girls. They need some ice cream too," said Clayton politely. Mr. Joe pushed three ice cream bars toward Clayton.

"I believe we need seven tickets for the pony you're giving away," said Clayton. Mr. Joe threw the tickets in his direction. Clayton took the ice cream bars and handed them to the girls and gave each child a ticket for the chance to win the pony.

"Uh, Mista Clayton, we don't need no ice cream 'cause me an' Tati are full, but since ya got 'em fo us I guess we'll eat 'em. Thank you, Mista Clayton," Rosie said with a smile.

Clayton looked down at the girls with a million-dollar smile. He stuck his hand in his pocket and withdrew two dollars. He proceeded to spit on the two-dollar bills, and then he handed them to Mr. Joe, who recoiled in disgust.

"I refuse t'take these wet dollas spit on by some niggah man. So gimme my money, boy!" demanded Mr. Joe.

THE GHOST COMES OUT

"I'm afraid, Mr. Joe, that's all I have, sir. So, I guess you can either take it or not," said Clayton with his classic smile.

Mr. Joe got into his truck and nearly ran them over as he turned his vehicle around. His left front wheel hit the sharp curb, and when it did, the tire went flat in seconds. Clayton went over to retrieve his money, which had fallen off the truck as it spun around.

"Ya ain't heard the last of me, boy!" said Mr. Joe as the truck went up and down due to the flattened tire.

"Maybe not, but today, I have," said Clayton in a whisper as he put his lucky buckeye back into his pocket.

CHAPTER 11

THE SECRET HOUSE

He had inherited the property years ago, but only now knew what he wanted do with it. Every weekend for the past year, he came out to the property and, little by little, had built a small storage house that looked like a cottage. It was the size of a one-car garage, but plenty of room to store his collectibles. He painted the outside of the house a khaki color so it would blend in to match the wooded environment. It was hard to find, and if you didn't know it was there, you wouldn't see it.

He hadn't planned the exact day or time but felt secure that there would be a sign to let him know when the time was right. He started collecting his current craze in 1961. As he looked around the room, he smiled at the thought of what pleasure his collectibles would bring. He put on the shelf his newest purchase. "Perfect," he said to himself. He had a couple of more items to buy before his collection would be complete. He was so excited he had to fight himself from acting too quickly. Everything needed to be perfect, and he mustn't act before the timing was right.

As he closed the door to his new getaway, he whispered, "Not long now, not long now."

CHAPTER 12

THE MANSION ON THE HILL

Daphne Montague was perhaps the least understood woman in town. She hated being on display as she called it. She just wanted to be like everyone else, but she wasn't. She was a Montague and had an image to uphold.

"You're not like other children, Daphne. You're a Montague. Be proud and honored that you come from the family who founded Grayton," declared her father, Franklin.

"Yes, dear, you should hold your head high everywhere you go because your blood is special. You are like royalty in this town. Franklin, I believe when we pass, the townfolk should bow. What law needs to be passed to get that to happen, Franklin? We are Grayton royalty," professed Louise.

Louise Montague was a child of privilege. She didn't know what it was like to be around children whose parents were not millionaires. She was born of wealth and would marry money. When she first laid eyes on Franklin, she knew he was the one for her. Franklin, however, was smitten with Louise's little sister, Stella. He would send Stella flowers and candies hoping to win a date with her. Louise intercepted every delivery and told Franklin her sister just wasn't interested. She made sure he knew she could be the shoulder he needed to lean on, and soon Franklin and Louise were a couple. Stella was never the wiser to any of it.

"I just want to be like other kids. I want to go to Grayton High School. I don't want to be homeschooled and tutored anymore. Please let me get to know the other kids in town. The only time you let me out of this mausoleum is to go to church, and then we have to leave early because you don't want anyone asking you to join any church clubs," Daphne noted sadly.

She had just turned fifteen and was already three years ahead of her peers at Grayton High School. Nevertheless, she wanted to be a regular teenager. Her only friend was her tutor, Johnson Davis. He was ten years her senior and had watched Daphne grow into a beautiful young woman. He'd oftened dreamed about kissing her, but she was still a minor, and her parents were always around and watching. So, he would wait until she was eighteen and of age to make up her own mind, and then he'd make his move.

Louise said in a serious tone, "That's silly talk, Daphne. You're not like other kids, and you never will be. You will be graduating early from high school next year when you're sixteen, focus on which sister school you would like to attend. As you know, I'm a Vassar graduate, and you would be a legacy. I would love to write to my fellow alum and tell them my daughter will be a Brewer, but being a Blue at Wellesley is nothing to sneeze at either. You see, Daphne, we're giving you the freedom to choose." And with that, the discussion was closed.

Daphne began taking books out into the garden to watch nature and read. She also would turn her home radio up so she could hear Perry Como singing "Till the End of Time." She would often get lost in her own thoughts. It was a beautiful spring day when the new gardener came in to weed the flowers. He stopped working when he saw Daphne.

"Uh, sorry, Miss Daphne, I didn't know you were out here. I won't bother you. I'll come back later," said the gardener with a beautiful smile. He was just about to leave when…

"Oh no, don't stop. I'm just reading boring Shakespeare. I have to write a paper, and I'm just not in the mood. So, what's your name?" Daphne inquired. *He's got the most beautiful smile…and those muscles. I wonder what it feels like to be in his arms*, she thought.

THE GHOST COMES OUT

"My name's Clayton. I'm Jackson's younger brother," explained Clayton. Jackson Smith was Franklin's chauffeur. He had been with Franklin for five years and was a devoted employee. When Clayton turned eighteen, Franklin asked his boss if he could use a good gardener.

Franklin's response, "Because he's your brother, Jackson, I will give him a try, but understand my wife is very picky about her gardens."

"Yessir, I promise he won't lettcha down. Clayton don't jest have a green thumb, he gots green hans, sir. You see," said Jackson.

That was six months ago, and Clayton had settled into life at the mansion very easily. He did indeed have green hands and had turned the Montague gardens into a mini Versailles.

"Hi, Clayton, I'm Daphne. I love how you have made the gardens come to life. Daddy talks about you all the time, and Mother believes her gardens will make *Better Homes and Gardens* before the year's out. You're a real hit around here. How old are you anyway, Clayton?" queried Daphne as she twirled her hair around her finger. She was not only intrigued but could not keep her eyes or her mind off of his broad chest.

"I'm eighteen," Clayton responded. He then added, "I'll let you get back to your reading. I think you'll appreciate Mr. Shakespeare when you allow yourself to be drawn into his plays, Miss Daphne. I'll finish up later," Clayton said as he turned around to go.

Daphne stood up and came closer to Clayton. He stood about 6'1", and she came up to about his chest. She couldn't deny that Clayton was gorgeous, and the fact he was a man of color only fascinated her more. She had never gotten this close to a Negro, and she had the urge to touch him, but she thought better of it because just around the corner came her tutor. *Oh great,* Daphne thought. *I wish he'd give me a little space, always hovering over me—what a suckup and pest.*

"There you are, Daphne. What are you doing out here? You might catch something out here in this air," Johnson Davis said while sizing up what was going on between Daphne and the gardener. "You need to finish your paper on why Hamlet pretended to act mad."

"Don't care why he pretended to be mad, but I'll tell you why I am if you'd like to hear it!" Daphne said in a huff and ran past him into the house.

Johnson turned to Clayton and eyed him up and down. "Don't you come near Miss Daphne again, you hear? I would hate for the Montagues to have to excuse you from their employment for patronizing with their daughter. Understand, boy?" Johnson said in a harsh tone.

Clayton looked very pleased as he smiled, waved, and said, "Yessir, wouldn't want to step on grass you've already claimed as yours." And he gathered his tools and walked off whistling "Till the End of Time."

CHAPTER 13

THE DAKOTA COUNTY 5 MILE RACE

Victoria came home from work to find Rosie, Tati, and Midas upstairs in their bedroom. Rosie and Tati were huddled together with Midas. The door was closed, and they were quiet. In fact, Rosie and Tati were playing the quiet game. Victoria opened the door to their bedroom, and both girls jumped.

"What's wrong, girls?" asked a concerned Victoria. She walked over to both girls and sat on their bed hugging them tightly. "Are you okay?"

"Uh, Momma, me an' Tati are so glad yua home. We had a 'currence with Ree," Rosie told her mother.

"You mean an occurrence?" suggested Victoria.

"Yeah, when we got ready fo school, we came downstairs, an' Ree was there. She didn't even know who we were, Momma. She wanted t'know why we was in her house. Me an' Tati took her back to her bed, but she wasn't actin' like Ree," Rosie explained.

"Yeah, huh wuhdn't actin' like Wee, Momma," echoed Tati.

"Tell you what, girls, I'll go down and see about Ree. You girls stay here, and what would you say to us all going to Grayton Burger and Shake tonight for dinner?" offered their mom. Victoria was very concerned over what the girls had told her, but she couldn't let on to the girls she was worried.

"Can we, Momma? Do we have 'nuff money t'go?" asked a concerned Rosie.

"Yeah, can we, Momma?" repeated Tati.

"You bet we can, girls. We deserve it," stated Victoria. "Now go ahead and put your shoes on, and I'll call you when we're ready."

The girls were so excited and were jumping up and down. This was indeed a treat. Since their father died in January, they had only been out to eat once. They simply couldn't afford it. They had to watch every penny, and going out to eat simply wasn't in the budget, but Victoria was determined to do something remarkable for her girls, and this was indeed special.

Victoria made her way down the stairs to see Ree. She half expected her not to know who she was either, but she was surprised.

"Hi, Victoria," Ree said. "I didn't hear ya come home. The girls with ya?"

Victoria had to hide her shock. Ree was fine and was even asking about Rosie and Tati.

"They're getting ready because I'm taking us out to eat tonight at Grayton Burger and Shake," said Victoria.

"Ya rob a bank, Victoria? We ain't the Rockefellas, ya know," Ree said shaking her head.

Victoria laughed. "No, I didn't rob a bank, but I think we need a family night out, and I'm paying, so let's go!" She called upstairs for the girls to come down, and they came running down the stairs followed by Midas. "Sorry, Midas, this is just for people." The dog went to the window to watch as the four of them got into the car.

When they got to Grayton Burger and Shake, Victoria's boss, Marcus Peters, was there. He was getting a burger to take home and putting up notices for the first Dakota County 5 Mile Race. When he saw Victoria, he smiled, but then his eyes fell to the girls. *Oh no,* he thought. *Kids, great. I cannot let them touch me. Otherwise, I will have to shower, again. And my hair, if they touch my hair, I don't know what I'll do. It was looking especially good after my run today.*

"Hello, Victoria, and how are all the Scholls?" Marcus wondered as he looked at the girls and Ree Scholl.

"Hello, Mista Peters. Whatcha doin'?" inquired Rosie.

THE GHOST COMES OUT

"I'm putting up notices for the first Dakota County 5 Mile Race. You girls are going to enter, aren't you? A portion of the proceeds will go to buy a new playground for Grayton Elementary School," said Marcus. He tried to sound as though he was really interested in what the child was saying. *Now, what was her name again? Rosemary, Rosemarie, oh, what is it? Oh yeah, Rosie's her name. Now, what's the youngest kid's name? I have no idea. Nor do I care. I know things are tight with Victoria and her family, but hey, Victoria can afford $1 a piece to enter. She makes good money. I pay her $0.75 an hour. Six hours on the clock, and she could pay for the four of them to enter the race and have $0.50 leftover. Even the old woman could walk in it. They wouldn't have released her from the hospital if she weren't better, right?*

His thoughts were interrupted when he heard Victoria say, "Okay, girls, we've bothered Mr. Peters enough. Let's find a booth before they're all taken. I'll see you tomorrow. Have a nice night." And she smiled at him as they left to take the far booth in the corner.

Marcus's order was ready, and he paid quickly and left before anybody else stopped to talk to him. He got into his 1963 Buick Riviera and sped off. That car was his baby. It was as close to a child as he would ever have. He drove to an old dirt road and pulled off. His house was located approximately a mile off of Highway 69. No one knew where he lived, and he liked it that way. There was a trail in back of his house that hikers would use, but that was very seldom. The trail was approximately a five-mile stretch, but it was rare when anyone used it, and it was starting to get overgrown. After his last marriage ended, he moved away from town and its people. His mail was delivered to a post office box in town right down the street from the Dakota County Board of Education.

The Dakota 5 Mile Race was scheduled for Saturday, June 21, and Marcus was excited about it. He wanted all of Grayton's citizens to participate. Marcus thought he was a shoe in to win the race. *Who else in this godforsaken place trains daily other than me? And the more who enter the race, the more money I'll be putting in Bank Marcus Peters. Perhaps I can take a most needed vacation to an island where no one knows me. Yes, that sounds like a wonderful idea. Oh my,* he thought as he caught his reflection in the mirror. *I must try to find someone else to cut my hair. I don't think Stephanie knows what she's doing.* Before he even sat down at his kitchen table, he had to fix his hair. He was actually going bald, and Stephanie was doing the best she could with the head of hair she had to work with. She had told him many times that the comb-over was not the most complimentary of hairdos. He just wouldn't listen. *That's better,* he thought as he fixed his hair to his liking.

Unaware to Marcus Peters, someone else had a piece of property close by. It was approximately one hundred yards away from his house and right off the trail. Oh, if he had only known what would take place in that small khaki-colored cottage, perhaps he would've stopped it or at least called Sheriff Charles Hall, but that was not to be.

As the week wore on, the kids and community were getting excited about the 5 Mile Race. Half of the proceeds would go for the playground at the elementary school, and the other half would go to the winner of the race.

"Me an Billy are gonna run, an' we plannin' on winnin'," Johnny declared with a big smile.

"Yeah, we gonna run like the wind, ain't we, Johnny?" Billy asked his big brother with an equally beautiful smile minus a few baby teeth.

"Me an' Tati have saved $0.50 a piece. Momma said she would let us earn the rest b'fore Saturday," explained Rosie. She looked at Tati and smiled.

"We gonna uhn some money, wite, Wosie?" Tati asked her big sister. Anything Rosie said was pure golden to Tati.

Tati had been playing with DaisyBelle's doll, Marian. Whenever she got the opportunity to brush and style her hair, she took advantage of it.

"Uh-huh, we are, Tati," said Rosie.

"Hey, Dean, ya gonna run?" Johnny inquired.

Dean just shrugged. *Maybe Harry will let me enter too,* Dean thought. *If only Lucy were here. Maybe we could run together. Oh, Lucy, where did you go? Please come home.* He reached in his pocket and squeezed his buckeye.

THE GHOST COMES OUT

"Monty, ya gonna enta the race?" Billy wanted to know.

"Ya betta b'lieve it!" Monty said with excitement. "Me an' Uncle Bake gonna run t'gether."

"DaisyBelle, ya thank y'all will enter?" asked Rosie.

"I dunno. I hope so," said DaisyBelle. Things were different in DaisyBelle's house since the morning her papa had hit Val. She couldn't put her finger on it, but things just seemed different in the house. It had been a week since the incident, and she had not seen her dad. No one brought his name up either. The bruise on Valerie's face was pretty much faded, but she had not returned to school. *Maybe Momma'll let me an' Val run in the race. I wish I could be with the other kids*, DaisyBelle thought.

Unbeknownst to Dean, but ever since Lucy had gone missing, Harry was hot on her trail. That dog meant far too much to Dean for Harry not to find out what happened to her. While Dean was at summer school, Harry was out looking for Lucy.

Harry had gone back to the groomer, Mary Louise, who had bathed and clipped Lucy's nails. He drove his car and parked it one hundred yards from the groomer's house and walked the rest of the way. He didn't want Mary Louise to know she had company. In her driveway sat a 1964 Volkswagen Beetle. *How in the world could a groomer afford a car like that?* Harry thought. As he approached her front steps, he heard voices coming from within the house.

"I tole ya, Mary Louise, ya betta git rid of that dawg, or that dawg's owna is gonna come back. Is too risky keepin' that dawg in the basement," said a woman's voice.

"Ya know my sista, Erleen, in Stockton? She say she got somebody who might wanna dog like this, an they pay top dollah. I make nothin' runnin' this groomin' business, an' ya thank that car in my driveway cost nothin'? I had to sleep with the mechanic five time 'fore he give me that stolen car, an' trus me, he ain't a good lay eitha," Mary Louise said with a laugh but added, "The moment I see that white German shepherd comin' through my door, I say 'thank ya, Jesus. Imma gonna make some money.'"

Harry knew the groomer had done something with Lucy, but now he had the information confirmed, and he was going to take back what was his. As he made his way around the back of the house, he pulled a handkerchief from his coat pocket. The backyard looked like a dumping ground. It contained discarded wrecked cars, and debris was everywhere. He located many empty soda bottles in the backyard. *I only need one*, he thought. *I'm so glad these people live like pigs. It makes my job so much easier.* He recovered a garden hose that had been discarded. Harry cut out the section of the hose that was not damaged with holes. He quickly made his way to the basement door. *I'm so glad no one in this town ever locks their doors. You never know who might be coming in*, Harry thought with amusement. As he made his way in the basement, he heard a noise. It sounded like a whimper. He walked toward the sound and opened a door. When the door opened, the figure lying on the floor looked up and started wagging her tail. He had found Lucy. Lucy tried to get to Harry, but she was tied up. Harry reached into his pocket and pulled out his trusty Buck knife. He never went anywhere without it, and he freed Lucy from her ropes.

"Okay, girl, we're going home, but first we have a debt that must be paid. You need to be very quiet," Harry said to Lucy after he had rubbed her. Lucy knew not to whimper or make a peep.

Both Harry and Lucy made their way back through the basement and out the door to the backyard. When they crept toward the front yard, Harry told Lucy to stay where she was while he went toward Mary Louise's new VW beetle. He used the hose he had to siphon some gas out of the tank, and it went into the bottle he had taken from the backyard. Lastly, he shoved his handkerchief into the bottle. He motioned for Lucy to come to him. She obediently came and sat by his side. He had just made his own Molotov cocktail. He pulled out his Zippo lighter and lit the handkerchief and threw it at the VW beetle. It exploded as it hit the car. The car went up in flames, and Mary Louise came running out of her house. She looked at her vehicle in dismay and then saw Harry and Lucy standing in the street watching.

"Don't ever mess with a boy and his dog!" Harry yelled, and he and Lucy turned and walked away from her house.

*****

THE GHOST COMES OUT

The entire town turned out the day of the race. Some came to watch, but most came to run or walk the five miles. Everyone agreed it was for a great cause, and the kids badly needed a new playground. Daphne Montague did not enter the race but pledged $100 for the playground. Everyone cheered when she arrived to watch the race.

Well, everyone but her own employee, Silvia Smith, who could be heard shaking her head and whispering, "She ain't so good. All huh money's from huh rich dead daddy. She ain't done nuttin' fo this town."

Marcus Peters had been up since dawn. He was so excited anticipating he would get half the proceeds because he was a cinch to win. On his kitchen table were brochures of different cruises he thought he might take with the winnings. He'd never been out of the country and had heard so much about the Cayman Islands. *Yes, I believe I will go to the Cayman Islands and snorkel. Perhaps I will love it so much I won't come back. Maybe they could use a superintendent. They must have schools down there for the little illiterate village kids*, he thought with a laugh.

The judge of the race was none other than the sheriff of Dakota County, Charles Hall. Sheriff Hall was the best thing that had ever happened to Grayton. He was a local boy who had been born and raised in Grayton and knew everyone in town. He had gone to college at Southwestern University in Memphis and had studied criminal justice. He went on to law school at Memphis State thinking he would practice law in either Memphis or Nashville. He was offered a position at the prestigious firm of Dicken, Wade, Hamm and Gouge and was about to accept it when he came home for Christmas. His father, John Kevin, or JK, had fallen while putting lights on the Christmas tree and broken his hip. If that wasn't bad enough, their dear friend Sheriff Braxton Hughes had suffered a massive heart attack and died in the courthouse. Grayton was a buzz over the holidays with who would replace him. There was only one person the people of Grayton wanted, and that was Charles Hall. There was a quick election, and Charles took over after the holidays. JK was there to watch in a wheelchair. His hip was mending, but he wasn't ambulatory yet.

THE SISTERS SPURLOCK

The starting line for the race was between BANK and the sheriffs' office. Grayton Elementary School's first-grade teacher, Miss Sadie Hargis, had drawn a yellow line across the road to designate the start, but she didn't stop there. She wanted all the participants to feel special, so along the five-mile route, she had drawn flowers, and in each flower was the name of one of the participants. Sadie would go the extra mile for all her students. One might say she was married to her job because she believed she was tied to her craft. Free time was spent in her garden. Sadie was one of those teachers everyone loved and no one forgot. During the summer of '64, both Sheriff Hall and Sadie Hargis were two of the townfolk whose names were mentioned not only in town but also in both Nashville and Memphis.

The anticipation for the race to begin was almost as exciting as the race itself. Monty and Bake were pinning their numbers on their shirts when the Scholl family showed up. They were followed by Billy, Johnny, and their Uncle Clayton, who seemed to be in their own zone.

"I'm gonna be takin' the lead right away," bragged Johnny with a big grin.

"Is that so?" questioned his uncle. The three of them huddled together and said a prayer. Those around could clearly hear Clayton Smith say, "Lord, we know You're in charge, so we're not asking for special favors. We want anyone who enters to do their best but remember it's all in fun. We ask that You be with the children because they are our future."

The three said, "Amen," together.

Rita, Val, and DaisyBelle approached the group. Val and DaisyBelle were wearing their numbered shirts. DaisyBelle was holding Marian in her arms. She too had a number on the front of her shirt.

"Ya wunnin, DaisyBelle?" asked a smiling Tati.

"Yep, I'm 'cited. Somebody paid fo us t'enta. Ain't people nice, Tati?" asked DaisyBelle. Someone wanted to make sure the Shelby girls ran in the race, so their fee had been paid. No one knew who had paid their entry fee.

THE GHOST COMES OUT

"Yeah, they ah, DaisyBelle. Mawian looks puwetty," said Tati pointing to Marian. "Is she wunnin too?"

"Nah, I'm gonna let Miss Hargis hold huh. She gonna take good care of huh," DaisyBelle said and gave Marian a big hug.

Harry, Dean, and Lucy joined the others. Even Lucy had a number on her collar. She was ready to run.

"Lucy's back!" Monty exclaimed. "I know ya so 'cited, Deano. Can Lucy run too?"

"I thank they gonna let anyone or thang run that has $1." Johnny laughed.

Dean turned and spoke to Harry quietly so that only he heard.

"Thank you, Harry, for letting me run in the 5 Mile Race. I wanted to be with my friends and run with them," he said.

"I know how badly you wanted to run, Dean. Now, understand Lucy must be with you at all times. You cannot let her get ahead of you. You must run the race with her by your side," instructed Harry.

"I know. I promise we'll run it together. I'm not going to let Lucy out of my sight," noted Dean.

He bent down to give Lucy a big hug as her blue eyes never left his face. He was her best friend, and her tail wouldn't stop wagging. If dogs could talk, she would've said she was glad to be home.

Bake Haas moved closer to Harry and Dean to listen to their conversation. *There's something not right about those two. Why does Dean call Harry by his first name? Where are they from? Why is Harry so concerned about Dean's safety? I will find out the story behind them. I think I'll talk to Sheriff Hall. He must know something, and I can get a good story because that's what a good reporter does,* thought Bake.

Everyone was warming up when the runners heard a familiar sound. It was the sound of music and bells, and yes, Mr. Joe Puckett, the ice cream man, had just pulled up. A woman and child jumped out of the truck with Mr. Joe. It turned out the woman was his wife and the child was his daughter, Dorothy. Now, Dorothy was eight years old and a year behind Rosie in school. Even though she'd been held back in first grade, that child had an attitude. She was a big girl like her mother and father and was never late to the dinner table. Talk was if the table had been made of food, she would have eaten it too.

THE SISTERS SPURLOCK

When she stepped out of the truck, she had a big triple-decker ice cream cone in her hand. She saw Rosie and edged her way through the crowd to talk to her.

"Ya runnin' in this thang, Rose?" Dorothy asked sarcastically while eating the last of her treat. "I bettcha don't win. Ya ain't that fast, ya know."

Tati had asked Rosie why Dorothy would call her Rose and not Rosie. Rosie responded, "She do it t'aggravate me. I don't let it git t'me 'cause I'm smarta," Rosie would say with a big smile.

"Yep, me an' Tati are runnin' t'gether," replied Rosie. "Why ya not runnin', Dorothy?"

She responded, "I gotta hep Papa sell ice cream. We gonna make lots of money t'day."

"Seems t'me ya eatin' most of yua daddy's ice cream. I guess ya gonna have t'pay him a lot, huh? Why, I b'lieve ya must be his best customer, right, Dorthy?" asked Rosie before turning to Tati and straightening her number. She didn't see Dorothy leave, but those around heard her as she pushed her way back through the crowd.

About this time, Pastor Allan Boyd and his wife, Frances, were making their rounds through the crowd when Frances spied Harry and Dean. They were her special targets. Ever since they'd made an uninvited visit to Harry's house, Frances was all up in their business. She had her little helpers at church find out any information about them. The only piece of information she had garnered was that they bought a lot of pastries at the store. In fact, the local grocery, Grayton's Grocery Mart, had to order more than usual because Harry had bought their entire supply. *Great*, thought Frances. *I'm no closer t'knowin' what's goin' on with those two than I knew b'fore. I do believe God wants me t'know their business, an' I will not disappoint him, so Imma jest gonna have t'do my own diggin'.*

"Why, hello, Harry an' Dean, are y'all both runnin' in the 5 Mile Race?" Frances inquired while pushing her way into Harry's personal space.

"No," Harry said curtly, hoping his one-word answer would shut Frances up. He was not in luck. This only made Frances more determined than ever.

"Why, I don't know yua dawg, Dean. What's his name?" Frances asked. She actually knew more than she was letting on. She had asked some of the church parishioners, and they had told her the dog's name was Lucy.

"It's a she, and her name is Lucy. She's my best friend too," added Dean as he patted and loved on the animal.

"Why, I b'lieve she's a German shepherd, yes? She must've cost ya a pretty penny, Harry. I don't b'lieve that breed comes cheap, do they, an' she's completely white. Why, I bet that makes her more sought-afta, huh? Perhaps ya need t'put a collar on her saying, 'I'm expensive,' don't ya thank?" Frances advised laughing.

"Sorry to interrupt, dear, we need to go sign in ourselves," urged Pastor Boyd. "Good luck, and we'll see you at the finish line."

Pastor Boyd interrupted his wife because he knew she was stepping over the line with Harry. *Obviously this man does not want us to know what's going on between him and his son*, he thought. Pastor Boyd was still not convinced they weren't father and son. He thought it odd that Dean addressed Harry by his first name, but perhaps that was just their relationship.

Frances wasn't the only one watching Harry and Dean. There was another person there at the 5 Mile Race. They never took their eyes off of Dean. Wherever he went, observant eyes were on him and took pictures of Dean and his dog, Lucy.

Ten minutes later. "If I may have your attention please," said Sheriff Hall on the loudspeaker. "I would like to thank everyone for coming out today to our first, and hopefully, annual Dakota County 5 Mile Race!"

The crowd broke out in applause and cheers. This race was as exciting as the county fair, which was coming up next month. There were several runners from Stockton who had heard about the run and wanted to enter. Every citizen of Grayton seemed to be in attendance, even one whose deepest secrets would be revealed before the summer was out and would change the town of Grayton forever.

"I would like to call up a very special person who conceived, organized, and spearheaded this great event. Please give our own Superintendent Marcus Peters a welcoming applause!" acknowledged

Sheriff Hall cheerfully. Marcus Peters slowly made his way up to the front. He loved the applause and adulation from the people. Just as long as no one touched him or his precious hair.

Because Marcus was the first one to sign up for the 5K, his number was 01. He also thought it might be indicative of the order in which he would place in the race.

"Hello, fellow Graytons! I am proud to announce that we have raised $1,200 for the Grayton Elementary School playground. I would also like to thank Daphne Montague for her generous donation of $100 for our playground," praised Marcus.

The Garden Club heard Daphne's pledge and contributed $101.

"I can guarantee the children of Grayton will love their new playground equipment. We will have the fanciest school playground in all of Tennessee!" shouted Marcus.

The crowd went crazy. The boys and girls were jumping up and down in anticipation of getting the new equipment.

Sherriff Hall came back up to speak, "Now, I need for all runners to take their places. If you are walking the five miles, would you kindly step to the back. I know we have several runners here today from Stockton, and I believe Mildred Schweizer told me we have a few from as far as Memphis. We welcome each of you to our 5 Mile Race. If you are running or walking with pets, Mildred is coming to hand out paper bags in case your pet has to go during the race. You know we want our streets free of debris and waste." Charles laughed, and the audience joined in.

He allowed Mildred a few minutes to hand out the bags.

The runners were set at the starting place, which was at BANK. Clayton, his nephews, Marcus Peters, and Dean and Lucy were up front. There were several runners who were not from Grayton who took their places up front too. They looked like they had been training for this event. The walkers had assumed their positions at the back of the pack. Rosie, Tati, Val, and DaisyBelle were in the middle along with Monty and Bake.

"Okay, on your mark, get set, GO!" and the starting gun went off.

THE GHOST COMES OUT

Marcus Peters took off like a shot followed by several runners no one knew. They all seemed to stay in a tight little group. Clayton Smith and his nephews, Johnny and Billy, weren't far behind, and Monty and Bake were following at a close distance. Dean and Lucy were a surprise to the townfolk. They were running in tandem and were a crowd favorite. The sweetest, cutest, and most adored runners of the 5 Mile Race were Tati, Rosie, Val, and DaisyBelle. They ran the race together. While they did not have a chance of winning, they didn't enter the race to win. They entered it to be together.

As the faster runners passed the first mile, Marcus was still in the lead, but just barely. He had two runners close on his heels. He didn't turn around for fear they'd pass him. He couldn't believe anyone could be as fast as him. *How dare someone from another county come in and win this over me,* he thought. *I have to win this race. I've already put a down payment on a cruise to the Bahamas and the Cayman Islands. I can't lose!* The others coming up behind the front-runners were Clayton, Dean, and Lucy. Clayton was surprised to see how fast Dean could run, but kept encouraging him along the way.

"Next hill at marker 1½ is a killer, so pace yourself, Dean," said Clayton. "We can run this together if you like." Dean was getting winded, so he just nodded.

At the two-mile marker, Marcus was about ten seconds over the next two runners, and following closely behind were Clayton, Dean, and Lucy. Monty and Bake had fallen farther behind, and runners were passing them on both sides. Johnny and Billy had started too fast and were farther behind as the four girls were actually gaining on them. Many people who had started out running the 5 Mile Race had gotten so winded they walked the remainder.

As the 3¾ mile appeared ahead, Marcus was feeling a little giddy. The two runners who were on his heels had fallen farther behind. What he didn't know or see was there were two individuals and a dog who were gaining on him. Marcus knew this course like the back of his hand and knew he had two hills to go before the finish line. Clayton, Dean, and Lucy were on Marcus's heels. This was going to be a neck and neck race. Marcus was getting scared because Clayton knew the route too. What none of the runners knew was that Mr. Joe was at the top of hill 2. He was waiting for Clayton and his nephews. He didn't like that they were in the race anyway, and then he saw how fast Clayton was. *Over my dead body a niggah's gonna win a white man's race. It ain't gonna happen*, he said to himself. The second hill was in sight for the three runners and Lucy. As they approached the second hill, Mr. Joe stepped out and threw a watermelon at Clayton's head.

"Here ya go, boy. Enjoy the melon," Joe shouted with a laugh. The melon missed Clayton and hit Marcus instead. Marcus went down. Clayton stopped to see about Marcus.

"Go on, Dean, you and Lucy go and win this race," shouted Clayton.

Marcus was dazed but okay. He would have a big hematoma on his head and a black eye the next day, but he got up, and Clayton placed his arm around him and carried him the remainder of the way. Marcus and Clayton heard the crowd going crazy as Dean and Lucy crossed the finish line first, but as they got closer, the spectators got even louder as they saw a man of color carrying a white man toward the finish line. That was one of the greatest stories Bake would ever write.

As Rosie, Tati, Val, and DaisyBelle crossed the finish line holding hands, there wasn't a dry eye in town. The town agreed that was the sweetest act of friendship, and Victoria and Rita were there to hug their girls tightly.

Dean received $100 for winning the race. Harry was so proud of Dean he couldn't stop smiling. Dean gave his money to the Grayton Elementary School playground except for $1. He bought Lucy a bone.

"I couldn't have done it without you, Lucy," he acknowledged as he hugged her tightly.

The pictures that were taken of the winners and runners that day are still viewed at the Grayton Library. Dean and Lucy's picture was taken over and over again, but one photographer took more than thirty pictures of them. Dean never knew or saw the person who took his photograph thirty times. He would later find out who was there to watch him run.

THE GHOST COMES OUT

Marcus Peters recovered from his physical injury. It took him longer to bounce back from the loss of the down payment he had put on his cruise; it was nonrefundable. He pressed charges against Mr. Joe, who received one day in the county jail for assault and two months' probation for his crime. Mr. Joe lost money from his business that day. While he was out attempting to do Clayton harm, Dorothy ate two boxes of ice cream bars. He had a loss of profit and a criminal record. Not a good day for Joe.

And the one who was there just watching was not disappointed. The time to act was getting closer and closer. If only he could reach out and take what he wanted, but no, he had to remind himself, "Slow and steady wins the race."

CHAPTER 14

RITA GETS THE NEWS

It was two days after the Grayton 5 Mile Race, and everyone was still abuzz. The citizens of Grayton just loved talking about it again and again. They marveled at how fast Dean and his dog, Lucy, ran the race. They talked about how Clayton gave up winning in order to help Marcus Peters cross the finish line. If they only knew what the run cost Marcus Peters, they would've had a good laugh, but he kept that to himself.

Two elderly ladies, Elizabeth and her sister, Barbara, were in town shopping at Grayton's Grocery Mart and were heard discussing the race.

"Those precious little girls who ran the race holding hands at the finish line were the sweetest things I ever saw. Don't ya thank so, Lizabeth?" questioned Barbara.

"Ya know I can't see. Why ya keep bringin' that up?" Elizabeth retorted. "I heard all the shoutin' an commotion. It must've been a spectacle."

"Ya know I can't hear, what ya say?" asked Barbara.

And that went on and on for quite a while until they had finished shopping and left. Elizabeth's son, John, was outside in the car waiting to take them home.

If they had only stayed a few more minutes at the grocery store, Elizabeth would have heard some shocking news, and Barbara would have seen the excitement going on, and perhaps between the two of them, they could've figured it out, but it was just as well. They would find out soon enough anyway.

*****

It was approximately ten in the morning when Sheriff Hall received a disturbing call. It was from Buckley Flohr, a farmer about five miles out in the county. Buckley had a 456-acre farm and a pond that was located at the front of the property. He had just done his morning milking when he saw something disturbing close to the pond. There was a portion of his fence that was down close to the road and tire tracks that led from the fence to the water. He went over to investigate and saw a car in the pond. *Now I wonda how long that been there?* he thought. He immediately called the sheriff.

"Charles, this here's Buckley Flohr. I just 'scovered a car in my pond," said Buckley. "Is mostly submerged, ya know. Ya thank someone might be in it? It looks like a red car. Ya want me t'try an pull 'er out with my tractor?" asked Buckley.

"No, stay right where you are, Buckley. I'm on my way," Sheriff Hall said as he hung up the phone and raced to his car. Because nothing ever happened in Grayton, it was a shock to the residents when the police siren went off. In fact, those who heard it in town all came running out of their establishments to see what was going on.

It took Charles six short minutes to get to Buckley's farm. When he arrived, he saw Buckley out by the pond. Charles ran up to him and looked at the car in the water. He turned to Buckley. "Get your tractor, we need to pull this out immediately."

Buckley had his tractor close by and drove it over to the pond. He got out his chain and hooked it to the back of the car and slowly pulled the vehicle out of the water. When it came out of the pond, there was water pouring out from the car doors. It was a red Studebaker station wagon, and there was an occupant inside. Charles ran over to the vehicle, and what he saw started the summer of secrets in Grayton. Carl Shelby was lying on the front seat—very wet and very dead.

THE SISTERS SPURLOCK

On the way over to Rita's house, Charles practiced what he would say. To Sheriff Hall, it was a known fact Carl Shelby was a drunkard and womanizer. In fact, he thought the whole town knew except maybe his church family. They refused to believe he was anything but a good, genuine, and holy family man. After all, he was always at church on Sundays. As a mechanic, Carl tried to give his spiritual family financial breaks on car deals, or at least that's what he told them he was doing. Those who knew him best would never have used the adjectives *good, genuine*, and definitely not *holy* to describe Carl.

So what am I going to say to Rita? I'll offer my condolences and then tell her it appears to be an accident. Most likely, Carl fell asleep at the wheel and crashed into Buckley's fence and landed in the pond. The coroner will have to make the final decision, but I'm sure it was an accident. Yes, that's what I'll say, Charles thought. As he would later learn, looks are deceiving.

Charles arrived at Rita's house and noticed how run-down the house looked. The grass needed mowing, and the screened-in porch had a big hole. It looked as though someone had come and thrown something through it. The hole was approximately the size of a grapefruit. As he approached the front door, he could hear voices inside. As he got closer, he heard singing. It was quite nice to hear such joy this early in the morning. *Too bad he was going to change the mood in that house*, he thought.

He knocked on the door and announced who he was.

"This is Sheriff Hall," he said loudly. Immediately, the singing stopped. The door opened, and there standing with Rita were her two daughters, Val and DaisyBelle. He had just seen the two daughters run the 5 Mile Race with the Scholl girls. He couldn't help but think how precious Val and DaisyBelle were.

Rita opened the door slowly. "Sheriff, ya wanna come in? Whas this 'bout?" she asked somberly.

Charles started through the door. He smiled down at the girls and said, "Rita, could we talk in private?"

"Ya scaring me, Sheriff. Whas goin' on? My girls can hear. Them's my rocks, ya know?" explained Rita.

THE GHOST COMES OUT

"Okay, then. Rita, girls, I'm afraid I have some bad news. I'm so sorry to have to tell you, but we found Carl...and he's dead," Charles said very gently. He went on to explain, "We found Carl in his station wagon in Buckley Flohr's pond."

Rita didn't say anything. She didn't move, but when DaisyBelle began to cry, she immediately went to comfort her. Val just stared at Charles. There was no reaction or emotion on her face. *That's odd*, Charles thought. *I just informed her that her father is dead, and she doesn't react. It's as though she knew, I'm sure she's just shocked. Who wouldn't be?*

Charles went on, "He must've fallen asleep at the wheel and crashed into Buckley's fence and drove into his pond. I'm sure it's an accident, but the coroner will have the last word. Rita, we know Carl had an...er...problem." He didn't want to say more because of the girls.

DaisyBelle ran into her room to get her doll. This was the last gift she had received from her father, and she hugged it tightly hoping if she did that, he would come back. *The innocence of children*, thought Charles. *How beautiful and how sad. I've literally broken this child's heart, and I can't do anything to stop it.*

"I will be in touch, Rita, but if there's anything I can do to ease your pain. Please let me know. Is there anyone I can call to come over?" wondered Charles.

"Uh, yes, there is. Would ya...please call Victoria Scholl? I thank if she an' her girls come ovah, that would be a big hep to both me an' my girls," she suggested.

Rita was trying her best to comfort her daughters. She would do anything to protect them, and seeing her little girl so upset made her think. *Could I have tried harda to be a betta wife? What could Ida done to stop this?* she thought.

Charles interrupted her thoughts and said, "I will run up to Victoria's house now."

Charles's heart beat faster when Rita mentioned Victoria's name. From the moment Jeb Scholl introduced him to Victoria, he couldn't help but think Jeb was the luckiest man. Victoria was not only beautiful and smart, she was also so nice; and when Jeb had unexpectantly died, he wanted to run to her and comfort her, but he didn't know her well, and it just wasn't right to console a friend's grieving widow. Now, he had an excuse to pay her a call. He thought about how sad that these two young neighbor women were now both widows.

What he didn't know was how it seemed to be related. He would find that out later.

When he reached Victoria's door, the door opened up before he even knocked. Hurrying out was Rosie and her little sister Tati followed by their dog. They would've run into Charles had he not reached out and caught them.

"Hello, little ladies," he said happily. "What's the hurry?"

"Hello, Mista Sheriff, owwah summa school is late t'day 'cause we gonna have a water party," Rosie replied with a smile. "Ya here on 'fficial business?"

Charles kinda chuckled and said, "I was hoping to see your mother. Is she here?"

"No, she jest lef fo work," said Rosie.

"Yeah, she jest lef fo wuk," echoed Tati.

Charles was disappointed when he heard Victoria wasn't there. His heart actually sank a little.

"Ree's here, ya wan me t'git her?" Rosie prompted. Midas was busy smelling Charles's shoes. The dog seemed to approve because he lay down at Charles's feet.

"Wee's heuh," said Tati.

"Could you tell her I need to speak with her a second?" requested Charles.

The girls went running back into the house yelling for Ree. Midas looked up at Charles, who bent down to pet him. "You are a sweet fella, aren't you?" Charles noted.

The girls came back, and Ree appeared in the hallway walking slowly. Charles couldn't help but notice she was having trouble getting around after her heart attack. His father, JK, was older than Ree by eight years, but one would never know it. Charles had noticed at the 5 Mile Race how old she looked. She had aged so much since Jeb's death. *Wasn't that just five months ago?* he thought. He remembered when he was younger how he and others would come and play

THE GHOST COMES OUT

at Jeb's house after school. *Wow, that seemed like a lifetime ago*, he thought.

"Why, hello, Sheriff. How ya doin'? Whatcha doin' here?" Ree demanded.

"Hello, Miss Ree. I need to talk to you about a police matter," he said. He looked down at Rosie and Tati. He didn't think they needed to hear what he was going to tell Ree.

Ree understood and said, "Go on, girls. Git ya selves ready fo ya water party an' make sure everybody gits a turn sprayin' with the hose. Ya need t'be good hostesses. An', Rosalee, look out fo ya little sista."

"Yes 'em, I will. Tati be okay, she's with me. Bye, Mista Sheriff," responded Rosie.

"Bye, Mista Shawiff," repeated Tati.

"Tati, ya jest not gettin' the hang of those *R*s. Whas a teacher to do?" Rosie asked laughingly as she and Tati went down the porch stairs. Midas happily followed.

Now the summers in west Tennessee are extremely hot, and when you're poor, you have to make fun things out of anything you can. This was the case in Grayton. No one in Grayton had a swimming pool but Daphne Montague. But the kids didn't care. They didn't need a pool to have fun. They had a spigot on the house, and they would hook the hose up to it and spray each other. Running around getting filled up like a car gets gasoline, but of course it was water. This was one of the fun times that summer of '64 in Grayton, Tennessee.

Meanwhile…

"So, whas up, Sheriff?" asked Ree. Ree had always liked Charles. She had known him as a boy, but was not happy when he became sheriff. She just couldn't get over the fact that he and her Jeb had grown up, and now Charles was the elected officer in the county and her Jeb was gone. In her mind, Charles would always be a boy. She could still see her Jeb playing with Charles and his friends in the backyard.

THE SISTERS SPURLOCK

"I've just come from the Shelby house. We found Carl Shelby in his car dead in Buckley Flohr's pond. Miss Rita wanted to know if Victoria and the girls would come down and be with them. I think she finds great comfort with your family," explained Charles.

"So, he drunk hisself t'death, did he? I never like that Carl. He was not a good man," said Ree, and she added, "He was not like my Jeb. He was po white trash."

"Nobody was like Jeb, Miss Ree. He was a good and honest man. He shouldn't have died so young," replied Charles.

"No, he shouldn't!" Ree said suddenly. "I never know why God took 'im. I guess he needed an honest man t'help St. Peter at the golden gates, ya thank?" asked Ree.

"I'm sure you're right, Miss Ree," Charles replied.

What came next, Charles wasn't prepared for.

Ree looked at Charles with loving eyes and said, "Jeb, now you go an' git the girls, okay? They need t'hep the Shelbys."

"Yes 'em I will," said Charles. And Ree reached out to hug him.

She let go of him and stood back looking Charles squarely in the eyes. "I've missed ya, Jeb. Glad ya came home."

CHAPTER 15

THE CORONER SPEAKS

Grayton's coroner was Tyler Bush, known commonly as Ty. He was elected as coroner and had been one for two terms. When Carl's body was delivered to his office, he thought this would be an open-and-shut case. He had spoken with Sheriff Hall and had gotten the details from him. As he began to examine the body, he couldn't help but notice a lump on the front of Carl's head and an open head injury at the back. *If Carl had been asleep when he crashed into Buckley Flohr's fence and ended up in his pond, how did he get a head injury at the back of his head? And how long had Carl been in the pond?* These were the questions that needed answers. Although Ty was no MD, he thought his friend Marshall Cross, the pathologist in Stockton, needed to have a look at this. He also didn't think this would be an easy case.

*****

The phone was ringing in Marshall Cross's office. He slowly walked to pick it up. *Figures,* he thought, *the one time I actually get to sit down and eat my lunch, the phone rings.*

"Stockton Pathology Department," Marshall said as he answered the phone.

"Hey, Marshall, this is Ty Bush. How you doing, my friend?" asked Ty.

"Oh, hello, Ty. What's up? Had I known it was you, I'd have eaten my lunch first." Marshall kidded.

"I'm sure you would've," Ty quipped. "Actually, I'm calling about a body I have here in my office. There's something strange here. I don't believe it was an accident, and I could use your help on this one. Can you make it over here this afternoon?"

"Of course, I'll come," said Marshall. "You're puzzled, aren't you?"

"Yes, I'm afraid I am," said Ty. "Come round back when you get here, and I'll let you in."

Later that afternoon

Ty heard a noise on the door in back of his office. He opened it to find his good friend Marshall Cross. He extended his hand out, and Ty eagerly shook it. Marshall was in a jovial mood, but he could tell Ty was ready to get to the business at hand.

"So, what have we here?" Marshall asked as he made his way to the body on the gurney. He pulled back the sheet and saw Carl's dead naked body on the table.

"Where's your washroom, Ty?" Marshall asked.

"First door on the left, but don't you be looking in my drawers, you hear?" Ty teased. Ty and Marshall had girlie magazines they kept in their work bathrooms. Neither one would dare take them home for their wives to see.

The procedure for the autopsy took three and a half hours to complete, but when Marshall took one look at Carl's head before performing the autopsy, he said, "I can tell you right now that this was not an accident."

After Marshall had completed the procedure, he explained to Ty, "This was just as I expected. The large bulge on the front of his head did not cause his death. He may have suffered a major headache from it, but it would've gone down in a day or two, and aspirin would've helped alleviate the pain. The protrusion at the back of his head was such an injury that blood seeped outside of his brain. In other words, he had a subdural hematoma, and that's what ultimately killed him. Something hit his head with a great force. I'd say he was in that pond for at least seven days. There was also no water in his lungs. He was dead before his body and car were pushed into the pond. You've got yourself a homicide, Ty."

*****

Rita, Val, and DaisyBelle were getting ready for the day. The girls were just finishing up breakfast and were going to go to the Scholls' house for summer school when a knock startled them from what they were doing.

Val was closest to the door, so she went to see who it was. Rita and DaisyBelle were right behind her. Standing at the door was Sheriff Hall, and Val opened the door to let him in.

"Hello, Rita…girls," Charles said as he tipped his hat. "Rita, I need to speak with you, please."

"'Course, Sheriff," Rita said. "Girls, why doncha go 'head an' go on up t'the Scholls."

"Momma, I don't wanna leave," insisted Val. "I wanna stay with you."

"Please, Momma," added DaisyBelle and squeezed Marian, who was in her arms.

Rita looked down at her girls and held out her arms to hug them. She said quietly, "Val, ya need t'take care of DaisyBelle. An', DaisyBelle, yua can take care of Marian."

Both girls were on the verge of tears. Rita gave them a reassuring hug. She told them when she picked them up maybe they would have a picnic lunch. She told them they could ask Rosie and Tati, if they wanted to. This seemed to make them feel a little better, but both girls hung on to their mother before she let go of them and ushered them to the door.

She turned to the sheriff and said, "I'm gonna walk my babies up the street. Be back in a minute," said Rita. She wasn't gone long. Charles appreciated the fact that she put her daughters' welfare above all. *Perhaps that's what happened with Carl,* he thought.

"Okay, Sheriff, this 'bout Carl?" Rita inquired as she came through the door.

"When was the last time you saw Carl, Rita?" wondered Charles.

Rita was totally unprepared for his question. She sat down on the couch and thought about it. "Last time I saw Carl was a week ago. Yep, that's right, it was seven days ago," said Rita.

"Was Carl here at the house?" questioned Charles. Rita couldn't help but notice Charles was writing everything down.

"Uh, yeah, he was here, an' he was in a foul mood," Rita added. *Why is he writin' all this down?* wondered Rita.

"Rita," Charles said softly, "I know Carl has been rumored to lay his hands on you. Did you guys get into a fight that day?"

Rita looked up with tears in her eyes. "Yeah, we did, but he didn' lay his hands on me. He hit my Val instead." And the floodgates opened wide.

Rita put her face into her hands and sobbed as Charles watched her. He gently reached over and patted her back. Charles thought he'd figured out what happened. *Carl hit Val, and Rita must've picked something up and whacked Carl on the back of the head. Did she put him in the car and drive him to Buckley's farm and run the vehicle into the water?*

Before Charles could ask Rita any more questions, she volunteered the next bit of information.

"I pick up nearest thang I could, a char, an' smashed Carl with it," cried Rita. "He d'served it. It was only matta a time 'fore he started on my babies. I couldn let Carl hurt 'em, ya know? They's all I have." And she collapsed onto the couch.

She may have wanted him dead before he hurt their daughters, Charles thought. Charles still had questions for Rita. *How did Carl get out to Buckley's farm? Could Rita have driven out there and pushed the car into the pond while he was knocked out? But how did she get him into the car? Could the daughters have helped?* Charles wondered. He waited until Rita's sobs slowed down to ask additional questions.

"Rita, what happened after you hit Carl with a chair?" he asked gently.

Rita thought about it for a minute before she replied.

THE GHOST COMES OUT

"DaisyBelle an me got Val off the floor. I made her an ice pack t'put on her face. She was layin' on her bed with the ice pack on her face when I lef," said Rita in between sobs. "I tole her I was gonna walk DaisyBelle up t'the Scholls fo summa school. Carl was layin' on the foor when I lef. Didn' wan nobody t'know what had happened. I may not be an educated woman, but I gots my pride, ya know? And mor n anythang else, I love my girls!"

"When you got back from the Scholls' house, what happened then?" asked Charles.

"Huh, funny how I jest 'membered. Carl was gone when I got back," said Rita. "I was glad. Didn' wanna see him…now, he's dead." And sure enough if she didn't start crying again.

"Did you not wonder where he went? Or why he had not come home later?" asked Charles.

"Nah, I thought he gone t'see that harlot ovah in Stockton," Rita looked up as she said it.

"Who are you talking about?" asked Charles. He had heard Carl had a mistress in Stockton but didn't think Rita was aware of it, and he didn't know the woman's name.

"Don't know an' don't care!" Rita exclaimed. "Now, Sheriff, I wanna go lie down." If Charles thought he was going to get any more information from Rita, he was wrong.

"I'll just show myself out, Rita," said Charles, and he left.

*****

Summer school was going along as usual. Rosie was trying hard to get everyone to concentrate. They just wanted to play. Lucy and Midas were playing tug-of-war with a rope. They were not only the school mascots, but they were their protectors too.

"We don't have many more days lef of summa school," said Rosie. She wasn't expecting all the grunts and groans when she said that.

"Whatcha mean not much days lef, Rosie?" asked Monty.

"The county fair's comin' up, an' Momma wants us t'hep out. Me an' Tati are gonna enter the pie-eatin' contest, ain't we, Tati?" asked Rosie. "So we gotta practice eatin' some pies, right, Tati?"

Tati was thrilled when she heard her name. She and DaisyBelle had just changed Marian's clothes from swimsuit to her evening gown.

"Yep, we gonna git t'eat a pie," Tati responded with a smile.

"We also hep each year with the animals. We git t'hep put ribbons on the winners," said Rosie. "If ya wanna hep, Val, you an' DaisyBelle can work with us at the fair."

"We'll ask Momma. She doesn't like fo us t'leave her fo long," Val replied sadly.

Rosie gave her a big hug and said, "Me an' Tati know whatcha feelin', Val. We jest been there." The four girls hugged each other, and then Rosie said, "Tag, you're it, Val." They all ran off together laughing.

"What y'all gonna do at the fair, Billy an' Johnny?" Monty wondered.

"Momma an' Daddy are gonna hep Miss Montague make pies, an' Uncle Clayton tole me an' Billy we can hep him park cars," stated Johnny.

Monty asked with excitement, "He gonna letcha drive?"

"Nah, we wish. Me an' Billy jest stand an' show people where t'park," explained Johnny.

"You gonna do anythang, Deano?" Monty inquired.

"I dunno. I'll ask Harry tonight," said Dean. He didn't think he would get to participate. He had been lucky to have been able to run in the 5 Mile Race. He didn't want to push his luck.

"If ya wanna hep Uncle Bake an' me, we could use ya. Me an' Uncle Bake are gonna take pictures of people. Uncle Bake's always tellin' me there's a story b'hind every picture. Ya thank Harry'll letcha hep us?" Monty appealed.

"I'll ask him," said Dean. He added, "Thanks for thinking about me, Monty."

"Of course. Ya my best friend, Deano," said Monty. A feeling came over Dean that he hadn't felt in so long. He had a best friend who really liked him. He felt so warm, and no one but his mother had ever called him Deano. He was beaming from ear to ear when Harry came to pick Dean up, but Harry was curt. He didn't address any of the children. He just said, "Dean, Lucy, let's go."

When they got back to the house, Harry told Dean some news he didn't need or want to hear.

"Dean, I'm afraid we're going to have to move again. Go and pack your stuff. We're leaving first thing tomorrow morning," Harry asserted.

*****

Charles needed to get to the bottom of where Carl had been. *Had Carl been to see his mistress? What was her name?* Charles needed answers, and he needed them now. So he picked up the phone and made a call.

"Agnes's Garage and Repair, this is Wally speaking," answered Wallace Hull.

Wallace, or Wally as everyone called him, was one of the finest people in town. He loved his job, and he adored his garage. His first marriage to Agnes Tucker had ended in divorce. She said he loved his garage too much even though he had named the garage after her. He was never home, and when he was, he was tinkering with an old luxury car from the 1940s, the Delahaye. He found someone two years later who appreciated Wally's love for cars. Her name was Josephine Marlene Mokes. She worked in the shop with him, and never were two people made for one another more than those two.

"Hey, Wally, this is Sheriff Hall. How you doing?" Charles asked.

"Oh, hey, Sheriff. We're doin' okay, but it's hard, ya know? We lost one of our own. Jest don't git it," Wally said sadly.

"Yes, that's why I'm calling. I need to ask you some questions. Is now a good time to come over?" Charles inquired.

"Yep, that'd be fine. We're here jest talkin' 'bout Carl," Wally replied.

Sheriff Hall got over to Agnes's garage in less than five minutes. He walked through the glassed door, and the mechanics and Wally's wife, Marlene, were there. They were drinking coffee and smoking. Charles did not smoke, but you'd never have known it by the way his clothes smelled. He washed them every night to get the stinch out, but to no avail.

"Hello, everybody," Charles started, "I'm sorry to be here during a time like this. I know you're upset about the death of one of your own."

"Well, I'm not!" David Harness asserted. "Carl was one mean son of a bitch. And ya know what, Sheriff? He weren't that hot of a mechanic eitha!"

"Now, David, ya know he was a pretty good mechanic. We know why ya didn't like 'im," Wally replied, and the others just nodded.

Charles was surprised to hear someone who worked with Carl talk about him like that.

"David, could we go outside and talk?" invited Charles. He held the door open for David, and the two walked outside to talk. David took a drag of his cigarette. He was angry and wanted to punch something. A lot was weighing on his mind.

"So, David, why did you not like Carl?" Charles wanted to know.

David looked directly at Charles and said, "He didn't understand that he had overstayed his welcome. He was a lyin', cheatin' dirtbag. His wife d'served betta...an so did Erleen!"

This was the first time Charles had heard the name *Erleen*. *Could this be the woman he heard about over in Stockton?* "Who's Erleen, David?" asked Charles.

David didn't realize he had said her name out loud. "Uh...she's jest a woman I know," David said softly.

"What's she got to do with Carl? She the woman over in Stockton? She got a last name?" Charles prompted David.

"Uh, yeah...last name's *Yoder*. Howja know, Sheriff?" David asked.

"Grayton's a small town. People talk. Mechanics talk. So, might as well tell me what happened 'cause I'm gonna find out. Both of you seeing Erleen Yoder?" Charles surmised.

THE GHOST COMES OUT

"Yes, I mean no. I mean...well, this is what happened. Carl used t'come in here an brag 'bout how he got Rita at home an' this woman in Stockton too. One day he comes in an' tells me he's gonna see her afta work. So I want t'see if he was tellin' the truth. I follow him t'Stockton. Sure 'nough, he has this woman there named Erleen. She was so purty. I thought why he gits two women when I don't have one? Ya know what I'm sayin', Sheriff? Anyway, Carl goes an' sees Erleen on Tuesdays and Thursdays. So, I jest happen t'go over one day, an' me an' Erleen hit it off. I love her, Sheriff," David explained.

"Okay, so when did Carl find out you were seeing Erleen too?" asked Charles.

"Yeah, well, I was taared of Carl seein' my woman, so I was there on one of his regular days t'see her. Ya oughta seen him when he seen me with her. I thought his eyes would pop out of their sockets. Ya know, she chose me over Carl? She tole me she never really liked him. She got tarred of him bein' drunk all the time. Anyway, b'fore that son-of-a-bitch left, he flattened all my B.F. Goodrich taars an smashed my window with a taar iron. Can you b'lieve that? I thank he got what he d'served!" declared David.

"What was that, David?" asked Charles.

"Ya know, he's dead," said David shrugging.

"Last question, David, did you see Carl again after that? I'm sure you were mad enough to do something, right?" *I've got him right where I want him. He definitely had something to do with Carl's death*, Charles thought. But what came next out of David's mouth was something Charles wasn't prepared for.

"Yeah, I was mad as hell. He was jest a sore loser, an' it cos me three week's salary t'git my car fixed. The one I feel sorry fo is his wife an' kids, but with his $10,000 life insurance, Rita oughta be a happy widow," said David.

CHAPTER

16

DEAN'S LUCK

Dean had just gotten used to being a part of the Grayton community. He had established himself with his friends at Rosie's summer school and was getting used to being singled out by Pastor Boyd's wife, Frances, at the Methodist Church. Every Sunday when Dean and Harry would arrive for Sunday services, Frances Boyd made a special trip over to see both of them. It seemed to Dean as though she was pumping them for information. In all truth, she was. She was fascinated by them. *Where are they from? Why did they come here of all places? Who'd they know in Chicago?* she wondered. She didn't want to tip her hand, so she didn't come right out and ask them about Chicago.

"We're jest so happy y'all are here. Where was it y'all said you was from?" she asked Harry one Sunday. "We need t'know in case ya want t'transfer yua membership t'our little Methodist Church here in Grayton."

"We haven't decided yet," said Harry, and that was all he was going to offer.

Haven't decided what? If ya goin' t'transfer yua membership? Or if ya gonna stay in Grayton? Which is it? This man is insufferable. If he thanks Imma givin' up findin' out what's goin' on with the two of 'em, then he's sadly mistaken. The harder ya push Frances Boyd away, the more I wanna stay, she thought with a big smile. *Looks like Imma jest gonna have t'make a call t'the phone numba I memorized when I was at yua house. Somebody in Chicago's gonna get a call from little ole me.* Frances couldn't hide her excitement as she said, "Well, y'all have a wonderful an' blessed day."

"Harry, why do we have to leave? I was just beginning to feel home here. I've got real friends, and today Monty told me I was his best friend. Please, Harry. You know what else? Monty called me Deano. You know the only other person who's called me that was Mom," said Dean pleading.

Harry bent down and looked Dean in the eyes. "You know I don't want to leave, but today I got a call from my boss. Apparently someone from around here has made a phone call to Chicago. You know what that means, right?"

"Who? Who knows about us, Harry?" Dean wanted to know.

"You didn't tell anyone of your friends, did you, Dean?" Harry questioned. *I'm sure Dean accidentally mentioned it to one of his new friends. He must be more careful at the next place we go*, Harry thought.

"You know I didn't. I don't talk about us ever," argued Dean. He thought to himself, *I know I didn't say anything about where we are from or why we chose Grayton or anything. I've been so careful.*

"Harry, I'm begging you. Please call and ask if we can stay. I've never felt more at home than this place," cried Dean.

Harry went over to hug Dean. He felt so badly for this child. *I suppose I could call again,* he thought. Just as he was about to tell Dean he would make one last attempt, there was a knock on the door. Both Harry and Dean jumped. They weren't expecting anyone and were afraid they had been found. After tucking his gun in the back of his pants, Harry crept over to the door slowly. Someone knocked at the door again. Harry opened the door slowly and saw that nosy Frances Boyd from the Methodist Church. *Oh great*, he thought. *She's just what I need.*

"Uh, hello, Mrs. Boyd. This is really not a good time," Harry said with exasperation. This time he was not going to allow this woman in his house even if she did faint.

"Nonsense, Mr. Miller. Any time's a good time fo a spiritual chat," said Frances as she pushed her way into the house.

Allan had refused to go with her this time. "I don't think Harry likes us just showing up at his house. There are a few patients at the hospital who could use some cheering up. Won't you go with me and help raise their spirits? You're so good at that, and our church members just love it when you come," Allan suggested.

"Allan, ya know I wanna be there, but I feel as though God's leadin' me t'make a visit on Harry an' Dean. I know ya understand bein' the godly man ya are an' all," she added sweetly.

The last place I wanna go is the hospital. Talk 'bout a downer. Oh, I'm so tired of holdin' the hand of the sickly. They gonna t'die anyway, why should we go outta owwah way? We might even catch what they got. No, I wanna go visit our new friends. Now that I know they have a connection t'Chi-town, I need t'know these two. Oh my, what if they had connections to a big Methodist Church in Chicago? I really like that windy city, an' I know they gonna love me, Frances thought.

She brought with her a vase full of flowers she'd picked at Daphne Montague's house. She was always taught to bring something with you when you go a visiting, and she knew Daphne wouldn't be missing any of her flowers.

When she got into the room, she noticed there were suitcases out. "Are y'all goin' somewhere?" she asked. "Not back t'Chicago already?" She let it slip before she knew it. *Oh no,* she thought. Just looking at Harry, she knew she'd overstepped. Harry's face grew dark, then almost as quickly, it faded. He pretended not to hear.

"Thank you for the flowers, Mrs. Boyd. Please sit down, won't you?" asked Harry. He now knew the person who had called Chicago. He wanted to find out as much as he could about what she knew.

"So tell me, Mrs. Boyd, are you originally from Grayton?" Harry asked. He was taking note of everything she said and did. He was also memorizing every facet of her face. Eye color, blue; hair color, brown; hair parted on the left side; approximately forty-three to forty-five years old; has a mole on her left cheek; a slight overbite; bites fingernails; snorts when she laughs. *Yeah, that oughta be enough to describe Frances Boyd to my boss,* Harry thought.

"Why, I shouldn't talk 'bout me, but since you asked. Well, me an' Allan met when he was in college. I always wanted t'go, but my family jest didn' have the money. I was a workin' at a restaurant near the college campus when Allan walked in. It was like love at first sight, ya know? Imma 'riginally from Hattiesburg, Mississippi. Can't ya tell with my accent?" She laughed, and then she snorted. "I love Grayton, but Imma thankin' Allan's talents are wasted in this small town. I thank he needs t'go to a bigga town or city like…"

"Chicago?" Harry offered. He finished Frances's sentence for her.

"Uh, well, yes, that would be lovely. Y'all know Allan, an' don'tcha thank he'd be betta suited fo someplace like that?" Frances suggested. She was fishing for a compliment or anything to make her think Harry might help her in her endeavors.

"You know, I think he just might. Why don't we keep this conversation between the two of us? I'll make some calls and see what I can do. Would that be okay with you?" asked Harry.

"Yes, yes, notta word t'no one! Tick a lock as they say. I would love t'surprise my Allan with a new parsonage in a bigga city. That way he could minista more t'the needy, don'tcha thank?" asked Frances. She didn't even wait for an answer. Frances was on cloud nine. She even looked at Dean when she said her goodbyes. *Could my dream be comin' true? Windy city, here I come!* she thought.

After she left, Harry looked at Dean and said with a smile, "No worries, Dean. We're staying. You can go and unpack."

Dean went into his room and pulled out the buckeye he kept in his secret drawer. *First, getting Lucy back, and now I get to stay. This really does work*, he thought and slid it into his pocket.

CHAPTER 17

VAL TALKS

Sheriff Hall went to visit the one person who might be able to shed more light on what happened to Carl: his own daughter Val. According to what he had been told, Val had not gone to the summer school at the Scholls' house that day. She had stayed at home due to the incident with her father. Rita said she had an ice pack on her face when she left Val to walk DaisyBelle to summer school.

Charles was legally allowed to question Val without parental permission, but he thought with everything she had been through, it would be better to ask Rita first. So, Charles went back to the Shelbys' house. When he drove up the driveway, he saw Victoria and her daughters playing in the front yard with Rita and her girls. His heart skipped a beat when he saw Victoria.

"Sheriff, what can I do fo ya t'day?" Rita wondered.

She wasn't very warm, but then maybe she had something to hide, and I'm sure she was getting tired of me making my unexpected visits to her house, Charles thought.

"Hello, Rita, Victoria," he said as he touched his hat out of respect. "Rita, I need to talk to Val."

Rita was visibly upset. "Why ya need t'talk t'Val? She's jest a kid," Rita said indignantly.

Victoria looked at Rita and Charles. "Perhaps the girls and I need to go," she suggested. But one look on Rita's face told her she needed to stay. Rita needed Victoria there for comfort. So, Victoria stayed but went and played with the girls to give the two of them some privacy.

"Rita, you told me Val was at the house with Carl the day he hurt her, and when you got back from taking DaisyBelle to summer school, he was gone, right?" asked Sheriff Hall.

"That's right," said Rita as she thought for a moment. "Okay, I'll let ya, but I wan Victoria there when ya question her." *I hope Victoria would be fine with that,* she thought. Rita went to talk to Val and reassure her. She told her just to tell the truth.

"That's fine," said Charles.

Rita went and talked to Victoria and asked her if she would stay and be there while Sheriff Hall questioned Val. Victoria readily agreed. She would do anything to help Rita and her girls. So, Rita, DaisyBelle, Marian, Rosie, and Tati went up to the Scholls' house to play.

Victoria, Val, and Sheriff Hall went into the Shelbys' house. Victoria and Val sat on the couch while Charles took a chair in front of them. He took out a little notebook.

"Val, this is not something you need to be scared about. I would just like for you to tell me what happened on the last day you saw your father," Charles explained very softly. He knew she was fragile, had just lost her father, and was only eleven years old.

She looked up at Charles and said, "Ya know he hit me, don'tcha?" asked Val. Victoria had no idea what this child had gone through, and listening to what Val said, Victoria moved closer to her and put her arm around her.

"Tell me about it, Val," encouraged Charles.

"Papa was bein' mean t'Momma, again. I heard him yellin' at her. I came outta mine and DaisyBelle's room an' tole him not t'hurt her. So, he looked at me an' hit me instead. It hurt. I fell on the floor. I don't 'member what happened next 'cause I was knocked out, but Momma says she picked up a chair an' hit Papa ovah the head. He fell too. It knocked him out. He d'served it, ya know? Ya don hurt kids," cried Val, and she fell into Victoria's arms.

Victoria rocked her softly. Charles had never liked Carl, but now he loathed him. *To hurt a child is a line no one should cross*, he thought.

"Val, what happened then?" asked Charles.

"Uh, I kinda was dizzy, but Momma an' DaisyBelle heped me up. They heped me git in bed. Momma made me a ice pack. Momma was cryin'. She kept sayin' how sorry she was. Momma's wonderful. She loves me an' DaisyBelle," Val asserted. "After that, Momma tole me she was gonna walk DaisyBelle up to yua house, Miss Victoria," she said as she looked at Victoria. "She didn' wan DaisyBelle t'miss summa school, an she didn' wan nobody t'know 'bout what Papa did. She tole me she'd be back in few minutes."

"Did your dad get up after your mother left?" Charles asked.

"Nah. Afta Momma an' DaisyBelle lef, I heard the door open. I thought, 'How could Momma have walked DaisyBelle to ya house,' Miss Victoria, 'an' b'back so fast?' But it weren't Momma," Val explained.

"How do you know?" Charles questioned. He was writing everything she said down in his notebook.

"I heard Papa say, 'Why ya here? Whatcha doin' in my house?' The voice I heard was not Momma's. It was a low voice," Val added.

"What did the voice say? Could you tell if it was a male or female voice?" Charles curiously questioned Val.

"I thank the voice said, 'You'll find out,' but I really dunno. I thank it was a man, but I don't know who it was. I jest 'member it was low. Afta that, the door slammed, an' I heard Papa's car leave. I was so glad. I didn' wan t'see him. I know he was my papa an' I loved him, but I didn' like 'em. Don't thank he eva liked me eitha. He did love DaisyBelle," Val said with a half smile. "Everybody love DaisyBelle," she continued.

After that, Victoria kissed her forehead. "And everybody loves you too, Val," she said as she rocked her slowly.

"Val, I have just one more question. When did your mother come back?" inquired Charles.

"I dunno, a few minutes lata," said Valerie between sobs.

THE GHOST COMES OUT

Victoria kept rocking her and telling her over and over again it was going to be okay. Charles wanted to reach over and hold the two of them.

Instead, he got up and turned to Victoria. "May I go and ask your daughter Rosie a couple of questions?" *I need to establish a timeline,* he wondered.

"Of course, Charles, you do what you need to do. I'll stay here with Val," said Victoria in a whisper over Valerie's head.

Charles left Rita's house and drove up to the Scholls. He found Rosie, DaisyBelle, Tati, and even Midas playing tag in the front yard. *Oh, to be a kid again. What a wonderful time in our lives, and we don't realize it until we're older and looking back,* Charles thought. When they caught sight of him, they stopped playing. Rita and DaisyBelle went to the porch and sat on the porch swing when Charles came up.

Rosie, who was the boldest, came forward and asked, "So, did ya git the information ya needed, Mista Sheriff?"

Charles said with a laugh, "Yeah, kind of, but I was hoping you might be able to answer a question for me, Rosie."

"Sure can, Mista Sheriff," Rosie stated. Tati and Midas had walked up beside Rosie. Tati carried Marian in her arms. "Sure can, Mista Shawiff," repeated Tati.

"Do you remember when DaisyBelle came to summer school without Val?" asked Charles.

Rosie looked over at Rita and DaisyBelle.

"Yessir, I do. Me an' Tati were wonderin' where Val was, but DaisyBelle told us she was sick. Probly got the stomach bug. Ree's always gittin' it, ya know. Anyway, her an' DaisyBelle talked fo a minute fo DaisyBelle came ovah to us. They was serious talkin', ya know? Momma always does that when she don't want me an' Tati t'know whas goin' on." Rosie motioned for Charles to come down so she could whisper in his ear, "Tati's jest too young t'hear some thangs, ya know?"

Charles laughed and nodded his head. He touched Rosie and Tati on the head and thanked them both for helping him. *All of these girls are blessings from God, and sadly all are now without a father,* he thought.

"Rita, Rosie, Tati, and DaisyBelle, y'all have a wonderful day. I believe I've gotten all the information I need," he said. He got back into his car and checked the Shelbys off his list for now. He had confirmation of a timeline for Rita. He knew she hadn't pushed Carl's car into Buckley's pond, but he had to find out who did. *Who was the voice that Val heard? Was it a male, or could it have been a female? Next on the list was Erleen Yoder and David Harness. They had good reason and probable cause*, he thought.

Before Charles could put his car in gear, his walkie-talkie went off, "Sheriff, this is Shelia, come in please, over."

"Shelia, this is Charles, over."

"We have a 189, sir, over."

"Ten-four, Shelia, be right there."

Charles didn't bother turning on the siren. He didn't want to scare anyone because a 189 in Grayton meant that a noisy reporter was poking around the office. *I knew it would just be a matter of time*, he thought. *Oh, Bake's got his antenna up.*

When he got to the office, his secretary, Shelia, was trying to ward off Bake's questions. By the look on her face, he was making her mad, and no one wanted to be around Shelia when she got mad.

"Hey, Sheriff Hall!" Bake said happily. "I need some answers about the death of Carl Shelby. What do you make of it? Accident? Suicide? What are your thoughts, Sheriff?"

Bake could not contain his joy. This was the biggest thing that had happened in Grayton since he became the top news reporter of *Grayton Gazette*. *If I do a good job reporting on this, perhaps I should submit it to the* Tennesseean *or the* Commercial Appeal. *This could seal my future. Take it slow, Bake*, he said to himself.

"Bake, I've just come from the Shelbys' house. Please don't harass them, yet. Give them a day to grieve and make arrangements," said Charles.

"So, the body's been released to the funeral home?" asked Bake, who was busily taking notes in his notebook. "Do you think it will be an open or closed casket?"

THE GHOST COMES OUT

Oh good, Charles thought. *He doesn't know.* "Uh, just hang on, Bake. I'll let you know when I know something, okay?" Charles asserted.

"My sources tell me, Sheriff, it's not an accident or suicide…but a murder. Now will you answer my questions?" asked Bake.

Too late, Charles thought. *He already knows.*

CHAPTER 18

JOE'S AUDITION

The Ku Klux Klan had not invaded the sweet town of Grayton, but there was a small group forming in Stockton. Truth be known, there was one citizen of Grayton who badly wanted to join the KKK, and he had just gotten out of county jail. Most people knew him as Joe Puckett, but the kids all knew him as Mr. Joe, the ice cream man.

Story had it that Joe's wife, Raveleen, made him his own white robe. She cut out the eyes and mouth and hemmed them back just right so only the eyes and mouth showed. She made a cone out of cardboard and glued that inside the hood of the robe. Then hemmed the other sheet so that it hung down to his feet but not long enough to trip over. He would need to make a hasty retreat in case he was out burning crosses or beating up Negroes. He needed the flexibility to run fast. Raveleen even put Joe's initials on the robe in case there happened to be a mix-up. She wanted Joe to have the one she made for him. Neither Raveleen nor Joe really understood the purpose of the white robe was to be anonymous.

Raveleen made this for Joe's forty-fifth birthday. When he unwrapped the package, witnesses say they actually saw tears in his eyes. This was a proud moment for Joe, but not one that would last. Joe had heard there was to be a meeting over in Stockton behind Jim Fisher's Bar and Grill at 7:00 p.m. on that Thursday. Joe was determined to be there and couldn't wait to put on his new robe. He left Grayton at approximately 6:20 p.m. He wanted to arrive in Stockton

THE GHOST COMES OUT

a little early. He drove over to the town in his robe and headgear. He was proud, and he thought the stares he received as he drove over were just those who were envious of him. *Perhaps them are KKK wannabees,* he thought with a smile.

When he got to Jim Fisher's, his heart was beating fast. It was as though he had just been through a workout. That idea tickled Joe because he was a very large man and had never worked out a day in his life. Joe parked in back and knocked on the rear door of the establishment. The door slowly opened, and the man who was standing there was someone who was about Joe's age. He swung the door open wide to reveal four other men inside. All were smoking cigarettes and drinking beer. When they saw Joe standing at the door, one laughed so hard he spit his beer in another's face, which caused them to laugh harder.

"Who the hell ya think ya are?" asked one.

Another said, "Why, he's the gran dragon, I guess." And they laughed again.

Joe merely stood there. His face got hotter and hotter as they made fun of him. He could feel the heat coming off of his face. He was glad to have the hood over his face so they couldn't see it.

"Don'tcha know ya have t'be voted in? An then there's a 'nitiation, ya know?" said another guy.

"Hey, guys, did ya see this? This fellow has his monogram on his robe, ain't that sweet?" And then the entire room broke out in an enormous round of laughter. They didn't stop.

"Tell ya what, fella, give us yua phone numba, an' if we want ya, we'll call ya," said the guy holding the door.

Joe wrote his name and number on the back of a ticket order.

"If we wantcha, we'll call ya," they shouted as he left. Joe got back into his car and took off his hood. He drove back to Grayton in silence, but convinced himself he'd get a call. After all, their objective was all the same. Right? Joe waited by the phone for an entire week just hoping and praying for a call. It never came. Poor Joe, even the rejects didn't want him.

This rejection only seemed to spur him on even more. *They gonna see. They all gonna see. As long as I have breath in me, I'll show 'em what Imma made of,* he thought. It wasn't much longer that he had to wait. The timing was coming when Joe Puckett did show them what he was made of. Oh, if only he'd had sense to stay out of it, but he didn't. The time was nearing for Mr. Joe to act.

CHAPTER 19

TIMIN'S EVERYTHING

He took the shortcut out to his private building. No one ever used the trail that connected the town to the county. The trail had been built for hikers, bikers, runners, or walkers during the Let's Get Grayton Healthy phase. Because of the lack of interest in getting Grayton in shape, the trail had overgrown. Weeds, dandelions, crabgrass, and any other type of unwanted vegetation was present on the path. In fact, the trail was so overgrown that one could not decipher the tracks from anything else. He felt confident in walking the trail because the only other types of civilization he saw leading to his house was of the nontalkative kind. Many deer and rabbits would scurry as he made his way through, but nothing with just two legs did he ever meet.

When he arrived at the cottage, he marveled at his own handiwork. Because of the color he painted the building, it was hard to see among the bushes, trees, and grass. He had been careful not to disturb the surroundings. As he made his way inside, he paused and looked around. *This truly is a dream*, he thought. He placed the last of his collectibles on a shelf. "There," he said, "perfect." He stood back to survey the exhibit. Nodding in satisfaction, he sat down and drew out his blueprint. *The first thing on the agenda is how to get rid of our good Sheriff Hall. He may be from Grayton, but underestimating him would be a mistake.* He laughed to himself as he scurried to finish the last of his plans.

"I've got it!" he said out loud. "When the clock strikes twelve, the fun will begin!"

CHAPTER 20

IS IT FOR REAL?

"Wake up, Tati!" shouted Rosie, but Tati didn't much more than move. Rosie went over to get her up when she realized something was wrong with her sister. She hadn't been herself the night before when she went to bed with a low-grade fever and refused Ree's delicious spaghetti. Victoria had given her some baby aspirin hoping that would take care of the fever. Now, something was visibly wrong with her. She was broken out in small red blisters over her entire body. She even had them on her face. Midas was by Tati's side. He had sensed something was not right with her and had stayed by her side all night.

Rosie ran from the room shouting, "Momma, Momma, come quick! Somethin's wrong with Tati!"

Victoria ran upstairs as fast as she could. She knew her baby had not felt well, but now she was really worried. She met Rosie at the top of the stairs.

"What's wrong, Rosie?" Victoria asked urgently.

"Momma, she's got these bumps all ovah, an' she's rayed," answered Rosie. She was so concerned about her little sister.

Victoria knew instantly what was wrong with Tati before she got into their bedroom. It had to be chicken pox.

Now in '64, there was no vaccine for chicken pox. It was just one of those childhood diseases that you really wanted your child to be exposed to at an early age because the sooner they had it, the sooner they were immune. Rosie had gotten chicken pox at the age of two. In fact, she only had two little pox on her stomach. She had a fever, but thankfully, she had missed a bad outbreak.

When Victoria saw Tati lying in bed with those nasty blisters over her face and body, her heart just sank. *My poor baby*, she thought. She reached down to feel Tati's head, and sure enough, she was hot. Everyone in the Scholl household had gotten chicken pox earlier, so they were immune, and now little Tati had them.

"Hey, my little angel. How are you feeling?" Victoria asked lovingly.

"I no feel good, Momma, an' I itch," Tati informed her mother while scratching her blisters.

"I know it itches, honey, but you must try not to scratch. You don't want them getting infected," Victoria explained.

"I twhy, Momma," Tati replied in a small voice.

"I know you'll try, my angel," Victoria repeated.

Victoria bent down and picked Tati up in her arms. She was going to put her into the tub.

"Rosie, go down to the kitchen and ask Ree to give you all the oatmeal she has left. I know we're almost out. Let's put that on our grocery list, okay?" advised Victoria.

Rosie ran down the stairs as though the house was on fire. She loved her little sister, and if she could help in any way, she was determined to do so.

"Ree! Ree!" Rosie called as she ran into the kitchen. "Momma needs all the oatmeal ya have. Tati's sick."

"Why in tarnation do y'all need the oatmeal? Is that child gonna eat it all? We need t'save some fo othahs, ya know?" answered Ree.

"I dunno, but she needs all of it," commanded Rosie.

Ree walked over to the cupboard and was complaining as she went. "Make no sense," she kept muttering.

She reached into the cupboard and brought down the last of the oatmeal and gave it to Rosie.

"We're gonna have t'git more, ya know? We ain't made of money." Before she finished her little tirade, Rosie had already taken off with the oatmeal and had run back upstairs. Victoria helped Tati undress and was in the bathroom sitting on the stool with Tati in her

THE GHOST COMES OUT

lap and a towel wrapped around her. She was rocking her little girl in her arms as the tub filled up with water.

"Here, Momma! I brought all we had," Rosie said excitedly. "Whatcha gonna do, Momma?"

"I'm going to give Tati an oatmeal bath. This will help her from scratching at the blisters. She has the chicken pox. I'm going to let you pour all the oatmeal into the tub, can you do that for me, honey?" requested Victoria.

"Ya bet I can, Momma," said Rosie. She turned to Tati and said, "This is gonna hep with yua scratchin', Tati?"

In a very sad voice, Tati said, "Tank ya, Wosie."

Tati got into the tub and just enjoyed the way the oatmeal made her feel. Victoria told her to lean back, and she held her while Tati soaked in the tub. The oatmeal helped Tati to refrain from scratching her blisters. Tati stayed in the tub until she grew tired.

"Are you wanting to get out now, angel?" Victoria asked her daughter.

"Yes, Momma. I tiuhed," said Tati. Victoria and Rosie helped her out of the tub and into her pajamas. Then, Victoria carried Tati to bed. She looked down at Rosie and said, "You're going to need to cancel summer school today. I don't want anyone else coming down with the chicken pox, okay?"

"Okay, Momma. Ya know everyone's gonna wanna come an' see Tati," explained Rosie. "I guess I can't let 'em, huh?"

"No, honey, they'll just have to wait until she's better and not contagious," explained Victoria.

"DaisyBelle's gonna be upset. Tati's her best friend. Well, other than Marian," noted Rosie. "I'll go an make a sign so everybody'll know, okay, Momma?"

"That's a great idea, honey. I'll stay with Tati," said Victoria.

Rosie left the room and went and got her little chalkboard that Marcus Peters had given them. She wrote in her best handwriting, "No school t'day. Tati's got them chiknpoks," and she left it at the barn door.

It wasn't long until the doorbell started ringing. Just as Rosie had predicted, everyone wanted to come and see Tati.

"Whas all the fuss?" Ree asked in exasperation. "Would ya please tell yua little friens t'stop ringin' that bell?"

Rosie just pretended Ree hadn't said anything and went about answering the door and any questions that their friends had. When Rosie opened the door, there standing in the doorway was Rita, Val, and DaisyBelle with her doll, Marian.

DaisyBelle offered Marian to make Tati feel better.

"Stay right here. Imma gonna take it to her," Rosie stated.

Rosie went upstairs to share with Tati.

"Look, Tati, DaisyBelle wanted Marian t'be with ya durin' yua illness. Ain't that sweet?" asked Rosie.

"I don't wan huh t'git sick too," remarked Tati.

Rosie went back downstairs to give Marian back to DaisyBelle. She explained why she was returning the doll. But what DaisyBelle, Val, and Rita did next was one of the sweetest acts of kindess anyone in town had ever heard of. They took Marian home and got out DaisyBelle's red Doh kit. They tore the Doh into little bits and rolled them into little circles. They placed these all over Marian's body and took the doll back up to the Scholls' house.

They rang the door, and Rosie came running down the stairs.

"Now, wha? I was jest gittin' in t'my stories!" yelled Ree.

When Rosie opened the door, there was no one there. She looked down, and there on the stoop was Marian covered in red Doh dots. She looked like she too had chicken pox. She ran upstairs yelling the whole way, "Tati! Tati! Look who's got chiknpoks!"

Victoria met Rosie at Tati's door. "Shhh, honey, I think she's finally gotten to sleep," informed Victoria.

"Look, Momma! Look!" cried Rosie with excitement. Victoria looked down at what Rosie had in her hand. A big smile came over Victoria. "Oh my," she said. "I guess we'll just have to put her with Tati. We've now got a hospital room of chicken pox patients, don't we, Rosie?"

"Yes 'em, we do. Can I put her with Tati? Jest thank, Momma, when Tati wakes up, she can have her friend too," Rosie said with a smile.

THE GHOST COMES OUT

Victoria and Rosie stared down at Tati and Marian both covered in red dots. Victoria motioned for Rosie to come with her. Midas, who had been standing guard over Tati, got up and walked toward the door. They left the bedroom and closed the door.

"This would be a good time to go to the store and get more oatmeal and some food you and Tati would like. You can get anything you like, okay, honey?" Victoria insisted.

"But I not sick, Momma, Tati is," said Rosie.

"And who's doing an outstanding job of taking care of their little sister?" Victoria asked with a smile.

"Me, Momma. Imma takin' care of her, right?" appealed Rosie with a huge smile.

"Yes, you are, and you need to stay strong to help her, don't you?" Victoria questioned.

"Yes 'em. I gotta stay strong, right, Momma?" Rosie nodded her head.

"Okay, let's go tell Ree where we're going and exactly what's going on. I know she feels like she's left out. I need to call Mr. Peters and tell him why I did not show up for work. Knowing Mr. Peters, he will probably quarantine the office," Victoria said with a laugh.

"Rosie, you go and get our grocery list off of the fridge, okay?"

"Uh, Momma, can we git some grape juice? I know how much Tati loves it, an' well, I do too," Rosie requested with a grin.

"You bet we can, honey," Victoria responded.

Victoria went to Ree's bedroom and knocked on her door.

"Come in!" yelled Ree. "Whatcha want?"

"Hi, Ree," Victoria said sweetly. "I wanted you to know Tati's got the chicken pox. She's got a fever. She's upstairs in her room asleep. I've given her an oatmeal bath, and now she's sound asleep in her bed. If she wakes up, would you get her something to drink? There's orange juice in the fridge."

"Orange juice ain't cheap. Why we got that? Ya spollin' those kids, ya know," retorted Ree.

Victoria ignored her and asked, "Will you look after her if she should get up?"

"I'll do my bes. I ain't a nurse, ya know," Ree exclaimed as she turned her attention back to her stories.

Rosie was in the foyer waiting for her mother when Victoria came down the hall. "Let me give Mr. Peters a call, and we'll be on our way."

Victoria called Marcus Peters and told him what was going on. And just like Victoria predicted, he insisted she stay away until the contamination period was over. He never had chicken pox. Somehow he had escaped them when he was a child, and now to come down with them at his age would be horrible. After he hung up the phone from Victoria, he proceeded to clean everything in both of their offices. *Great, when was the last time I saw those kids? Oh yeah, the 5 Mile Race. What a fiasco that was. Was she carrying the disease then? How do I know I won't come down with them? I remember she came within five feet of me. I think I might have a fever. Should I call the doctor just in case? Should I leave town? But where can I escape these horrible diseases? Oh, if only I could've escaped to the Cayman Islands,* he wondered.

Victoria and Rosie drove to the Grayton Grocery Mart. They greeted Mabel, who was the only cashier in the store. She also happened to be married to Stuart, who owned the market.

"Hi, Victoria and Rosie. How y'all doin' t'day?" Mabel asked as she greeted them.

"We are good, Miss Mabel, but Tati ain't. She got them poks. Ya know the kine ya git from chickens," explained Nurse Rosie.

"Oh, I'm so sorry to hear. Ya know oatmeal heps with the itchin'," said Mabel, "but we are out of it. Jonas Neal took the last of it this mornin'. Ya know April? She's got 'em too."

"Oh, no," said Victoria. "It looks like we're gonna have to go to Stockton. I hate leaving Tati that long, but with the baby aspirin I gave her and her bath, she ought to sleep for a while. Let's go to Stockton." She and Rosie got in their '62 Ford Fairlane, and off they drove to Stockton.

Tati woke up from her nap and found Marian right beside her. She smiled. She got out of bed, picked up Marian, and went in search of her mother and Rosie. She walked down the stairs carrying Marian as she went. At the foot of the stairs was Midas. He perked up when

THE GHOST COMES OUT

he saw her, and she bent down to rub him. She walked toward the kitchen hoping to find her mother or Rosie in there, but no luck. Ree must've heard a noise in the hallway because she came out of her bedroom and saw Tati.

"Who are ya?" yelled Ree. "Whatcha doin' in my house?" Before Tati could respond, Ree again yelled at Tati.

"I say, who are ya? Whatcha want? Ya need t'git outta my house! Take that mongrel wit ya!" shouted Ree.

Tati tried to speak, but nothing would come out. She stared at Ree and couldn't move. Tati was on the verge of tears, and that combined with the fever made for a bad combination.

Ree walked closer to Tati and said, "I tole ya t'git out! Now git!"

And she led Tati and Midas to the door. Tati hung tight to Marian. The doll gave her strength. When she reached the front door, Ree shoved her out and slammed the door on her. Her small figure stood on the front porch looking for Rosie or her mom. Midas looked up at Tati and wagged his tail. He wasn't going to leave her, and at least she had him by her side.

Tati thought she would go and look for her mother and Rosie. She thought maybe they were at the barn, so she walked toward the shed. She thought maybe Rosie or one of her other friends might be there for summer school. No luck. Nobody was there. So, she started out walking toward the road but got turned around. She walked toward town but saw a little trail. She walked on the path for what seemed like an hour until the tracks began to get overgrown with weeds, crabgrass, and dandelions. Some of the weeds were as tall as Tati. By now she knew she was lost. Tati and Midas walked on and on, and then they came upon a small cottage painted in a khaki color. She thought someone might live there, so she went to knock at the door. No one answered it. She looked down at Midas, who was right by her side. Tati tried the knob of the door, which was actually unlocked. She twisted the knob and opened the door.

"Hellwo," Tati said. She and Midas walked in. What came next could only be Tati's imagination and the fever, or was it? The room was dark, but when the light from the door came in, she saw the most beautiful sight of all…a room full of dolls… Marian dolls.

CHAPTER 21

REE'S FAULT

Sheriff Hall was in Stockton interviewing Erleen Yoder.

"So, you're saying you did not see Carl Shelby again after he caught you and David Harness together?" asked Charles.

"Now jest why would I? Did ya know he smashed David's window an' flattened his tires? I told ya I was done with him. Sorry he's dead, but I thank it's karme," explained Erleen.

"You mean karma?" Charles corrected her.

"I dunno, but I know if ya hurt someone or their propty, it'll come back an' bite ya, an' that's jest what it did to Carl," explained Erleen. *It also came back t'bite my sista, Mary Louise. I tole her not t'take that German shepherd dawg. She jest wouldn't listen. She got what was comin' t'her too. Shame, I gots all the brains in our family*, Erleen thought.

"What about David? Do you know if he saw Carl after that day?" questioned Charles.

This just doesn't make sense, Charles thought. *I don't believe Erleen or David or Rita saw Carl again. Who else would want Carl dead? It just doesn't make any sense.*

"I tole ya already, no! But did I tell ya that me an' David are gittin' married? Did I tell ya that? Yep, he asked me right in that char you're sittin' in now. That mus be a good luck char or somethin'," added Erleen.

THE GHOST COMES OUT

"Well, thank you, Miss Yoder, for your time. I may have additional questions for you," explained Charles.

As he was making his way toward his police car, he heard Shelia's voice on the radio.

"Sheriff Hall, come in please, over." No response. "Sheriff Hall, come in please, over," Shelia repeated.

"Shelia, this is the sheriff, over," Charles replied.

"Sheriff, we have a 10-57, over," reported Shelia. A 10-57 was the code for a missing person.

"Shelia, copy that, who are we looking for? Over," questioned Charles.

"A child, three years old, Tatiana Scholl, over," replied Shelia.

Charles almost dropped the receiver. "Did you say Tati Scholl, over?" Charles queried.

"Affirmative, Sheriff. Over," said Shelia.

Before Shelia had answered back, Charles put the siren on and was speeding as fast as he could toward Grayton. Nothing was more important than finding a missing child, and because it was Victoria's daughter, he would do anything to help her. On the way over, he kept thinking she couldn't have gone far. *She is only three years old. How far can a three-year-old go? Where could she have gone?*

When he arrived at the Scholl house, he found Victoria racing all over the yard calling Tati's name. When she caught sight of him, she raced toward him and fell into his arms.

"Charles, you've got to find her. She's sick. She's feverish with chicken pox. It's all my fault. I left her to go to Stockton to get more oatmeal for her chicken pox. I left her. I left her asleep with Ree. Why did I do that? What was I thinking? I left my baby when she needed me most," cried Victoria.

"Victoria," Charles asked lovingly, "why would Tati have taken off? I'm sure she's around here somewhere."

"That's just it. She woke up, and Ree didn't recognize her with the spots on her face and ordered her out of her house. The good thing is she does have Midas with her. He wouldn't leave her side. I just know he wouldn't," Victoria noted, reassuring herself.

"Where's Ree?" inquired Charles. "I'd like to talk to her."

"Uh, she's in her bedroom, I think. I know she feels just awful about this, but I told her. I told her to watch my baby." And then Victoria broke into a sob.

While this was going on, Rosie had called her summer school friends to help find Tati. They came at once. Dean, Harry, and Lucy came; Johnny and Billy brought Clayton; Val and DaisyBelle were there with Rita; and Monty came over from next door with his uncle, Bake.

"Rosie, we'll go look downtown. She may have wandered down there," said Bake. "Monty and I will go there."

"Me an' my girls'll go look in the barn an' back of yua house," stated Rita.

"Johnny, Billy, and I will go down near the river," said Clayton. He didn't want to think that Tati would go there, but she might have been fascinated by something she saw.

Charles went into the house to find Ree. She wasn't in her bedroom. She wasn't anywhere. *Oh no*, he thought. *She's gone to look for Tati herself.* He didn't want to alarm Victoria. He knew she had enough on her plate, so he thought he'd keep that bit of information to himself.

Charles approached Rosie and said, "I'm going to give you the biggest job of all."

"Okay, Mista Sheriff, whas that?" Rosie wondered.

"You are going to stay and take care of your mother. She needs you more than you know. Can you do that for me, Rosie?" Charles requested.

"Ya bet I can, Mista Sheriff. Momma needs me t'hep her, an' thas what Imma gonna do. I need t'be here when Tati gits back too," explained Rosie.

If only everybody was as wise as you, Charles thought. Before he could get into his car, the sky reacted to the situation by bringing down rain—hard rain. *If Tati and Ree both missing wasn't bad enough*, he thought.

Victoria yelled at Charles as he got into his car, "Please find my baby! She's going to be wet and cold, and her momma's not there to protect her."

THE GHOST COMES OUT

"I won't be back until I have Tati with me, I promise, Victoria," Charles shouted back, and he pulled out with the siren blaring.

Meanwhile…

"Useless…my fault…all my fault. Ya jest useless, Ree. Ya such a useless person, Ree. Ya good fo nothin'. Is my fault. Is all my fault. I didn' know. I didn' know," Ree said to herself. She kept mumbling over and over again what she had done. *I'm gonna find that baby if it's the las thang I do*, she thought.

She had started out toward town but had gotten lost, and then came the rain. It was falling in sheets, and Ree could barely see in front of her. She needed to find shelter but wouldn't stop until Tatiana was in her arms. She started out on what looked like a trail, but the weeds, crabgrass, dandelions, plantain, and purple loosestrife were everywhere; and the more she walked, the more disoriented she became. Had Tatiana come this way? She doubted it, but she called her name just the same.

"Tatiana! Tatiana!" cried Ree. With all the rain falling, her voice seemed to just echo back to her.

"Tatiana! Tatiana!" she cried louder, but to no avail.

She walked slowly using her hands to shield the water off of her eyes in order to see. Ree walked for a good twenty minutes in the pouring rain. She was shaking, but she didn't know it. Her body temperature was dropping, but she didn't feel it. Night was coming, and the thermometer was falling, and still the rain continued. All at once Ree heard a noise. She shielded her eyes and… *What is that standing in the rain? It looks like a statue…frozen*, she thought.

CHAPTER

22

DAPHNE HELPS OUT

Daphne went looking for Clayton on the grounds of her mansion. She couldn't find him anywhere. *Where is he?* she wondered. *I need to discuss something very important with him. He told me he'd be in the greenhouse. Maybe he's with Jackson.* So Daphne headed into the garage. She stopped walking when she overheard Silvia and Jackson talking in the kitchen.

"I tell ya she ain't lost. She probly hidin' or somethin'," Silvia stated to Jackson.

"I don't thank so, Silvie. Clayton an' the boys went t'hep fine her. She got the pox, ya know?" Jackson insisted. "I thank we need t'pray she okay," he added.

"Nonsense. Is waste of a good prayer," Silvia argued.

Daphne couldn't help herself but interrupt them. "I'm sorry, Silvia, but I couldn't help but overhear you. Where did Clayton go?" Daphne asked.

It was Jackson who answered, "Miss Daphne, little Tatiana Scholl is missin'. She has the pox, ya know. Clayton, Johnny, an' Billy went t'hep out. They's been gone fo an hour. If ya don't mine, I'd like t'hep too."

"Of course, you need to go! I will go as well. It's our duty to help out," Daphne remarked.

"It raining, Miss Daphne, lemme bring the caw round front so yous don't git wet," Jackson explained.

THE GHOST COMES OUT

"I'll get umbrellas. We may need several for other volunteers who might not have one. Silvia, would you make some homemade chocolate chip cookies? When that precious child is found, she might want something sweet. Also, make a big pot of chili and cornbread. We can take that to the house so they won't have to worry about dinner, and no one makes chili like you, Silvia," Daphne acknowleged with a smile.

Daphne was as good a person as there was in Grayton. She wanted to fit in, but because she lived in the mansion on the hill, everyone thought she was untouchable and unapproachable. After the Garden Club fiasco, she chose to stay close to the house. She had heard Silvia's boys talking about how they loved the summer school at the Scholls' house and how they were such good friends. When Clayton, Johnny, and Billy ran in the 5 Mile Race, she had watched closely. Daphne's heart melted when she saw how the girls ran across the finish line together holding hands. When Clayton had sacrificed the race to help Marcus Peters finish the race was the highlight of her year, until *her* news that is.

When Jackson and Daphne left for the Scholls' house, the rain was beating so hard that it took them ten minutes to drive 1½ miles. After they left, Silvia said to herself, "She need t'mine huh own business. Make me nervous she spyin' on us. Can't have private conversation without huh listenin' in. Ain't right. It ain't right. I fix cookies an' chili 'cause I wanna do it, not 'cause she tole me to. Nobody make chili like Silvie," she repeated with a smile.

When they got to the Scholls' house, out on the front lawn was a woman and a child of about six or seven huddled under an umbrella. *That couldn't be the missing child*, Daphne thought. *That must be her sister. The one who started the summer school.*

Before Jackson could get out of the car to help Daphne out, she was out of the vehicle with umbrellas in hand and running up the sidewalk to Victoria and Rosie. Before she reached them, she already had one out and handed it to Victoria.

"Hello, Mrs. Scholl. I'm so sorry to meet you under these circumstances, but I'm here to help you in any way I can. Oh, please forgive my manners. I'm Daphne Montague."

Everyone in town knew who Daphne Montague was, but at that moment, Victoria's whole thought process was on her baby, Tati. Rosie's the one who spoke up, "Hi, Miss Montague. Imma Rosie. We're waitin' fo Tati t'come home."

Daphne smiled at Rosie and said, "Let's get your mother under the shelter of the porch."

"Yes, 'em. Momma, we need t'git unda covah, 'kay?" Rosie asserted.

Victoria allowed Daphne and Rosie to help her on the porch out of the rain. Daphne turned to Rosie and said, "Let's go inside out of this rain. You need to keep your strength for when Tati comes back."

When she said that, Victoria looked at her for the first time and asked, "You do think she'll come home, right? Charles said he won't come back without her. She's my baby, and she's sick. She's got the chicken pox, and I'm not there to help her."

And she started to cry. Daphne reached over to comfort her. She reassured her saying that everything would be okay. She would be coming home, soon.

Jackson came through the door and volunteered to go look for Tati.

"Can I take the caw an' look fo little Tati, Miss Daphne?" Jackson asked.

"Of course, Jackson. Please use the car. I'll stay here with Mrs. Scholl," insisted Daphne.

"Momma, I gonna go with Johnny an' Billy's daddy. He needs my hep," said Rosie.

Rosie reached over and kissed her mom. Victoria turned around and gave her a big bear hug.

"You be careful, honey." And she looked at Jackson and said, "Drive safely and come back with both of my babies, okay?"

"Yes 'em. We do what we can," Jackson assured her, and he and Rosie went out in the rain.

After they left, Daphne brought a blanket over for Victoria. "You're shivering," she remarked.

THE GHOST COMES OUT

"Oh, am I? I didn't notice," answered Victoria. "I can't stop blaming myself. My baby has the chicken pox, and I left her to go get more oatmeal from Stockton because our grocery was out. I left her with my mother-in-law, and I should've been here with her. She needed me, and I let her down. What kind of mother does that?" Victoria questioned.

Daphne looked at Victoria with tears in her eyes and said, "A good mother, that's who. You did exactly what any good mother would've done. You left her to go to Stockton so that she would feel better from the itching of the chicken pox. You were only thinking of your child. You are a good mother as I hope to be…one day."

"Oh, thank you for your kind words, Miss Montague," Victoria said. "I only pray my baby comes home safely. It's raining, you know, and she's only three. She was feverish when I left."

Daphne hugged Victoria tightly and said, "I believe with all my heart she's going to be found and will come home, soon, and please call me Daphne."

Daphne felt such a kindred soul to Victoria. She could only imagine what was going on in her mind and so badly wanted to help.

"Daphne, you don't have children, do you?" asked Victoria. *Of course, she doesn't*, Victoria thought. *She's not married.* Any other time, Victoria would've apologized for that question, but at that moment, her mind was on Tati. She didn't even hear Daphne's answer.

"No, not for another seven months," she said.

CHAPTER 23

REE'S RESCUE

As Ree guarded the rain out of her eyes, she saw a figure just standing in the pouring rain, not moving. Could this be real? She heard a dog barking and barking. As she slowly approached the frozen figure, she noticed she was standing in front of a little cottage. *And what's that in the cottage? Those dolls or what?* she wondered. She quickly forgot about what she thought she saw and focused on the figure. It was a little girl, and next to her was a dog. It was Tati and her dog, Midas. Midas barked louder when he saw Ree, but Tati was still.

"Tatiana!" she called. Tati didn't move.

"Tatiana!" she called louder. Still, Tati didn't move. *What is wrong with that girl? Why won't she come t'me? I know she ain't hard a hearing. Whas wrong?* thought Ree.

As Ree came closer to Tati, she realized why she wouldn't move. A snake was preventing Tati to come closer. Midas was standing guard. He wouldn't allow Tati any closer to the snake. Snakes love the rain because they can hunt for frogs during the wet weather, so they aren't afraid.

"Sssssss…NNNNN…AAAA…KKKKKK…EEEE!" shouted Tati. Tati was terrified of snakes after Rosie told her what happened to Mikey Steele's daddy, Jimmy Bob.

Ree rushed forward and grabbed Tati. She didn't wait for the snake to make its move. She was determined to rescue her grandchild. Even if the snake had bitten her, she wouldn't have felt it. Her adrenaline was racing, and she didn't have time to think about the consequences. It was time for action, and nothing was going to stop her.

"No snake's gonna keep Ree from huh granchile," Ree shouted as she picked up Tati and ran. Midas advanced toward the snake, but the reptile retreated, and Midas followed behind Ree and Tati.

The rain came down harder, now. It was beating against their skin, and every step made it more difficult to walk. Ree and Tati were both soaked to the bone, but neither one felt it. Midas was with them every step they took. He wasn't about to leave them. Tati hung on to Ree's neck for dear life. She wanted so badly to go home. "Momma?" she asked in a soft voice.

"Thas where Imma gonna take ya, Tati. Imma takin' ya home," said Ree in Tati's ear. That would be the first and last time Tati would hear her grandmother say her name.

Meanwhile…

It was now 8:30 p.m., and the rain hadn't let up one bit. Clayton, Johnny, and Billy returned to the Scholls' house.

"Miss Victoria, we haven't found her yet, but we're not stopping either," said Clayton. "We just came in to get a warm drink if that's possible. We went to the elementary school, but she wasn't there, either."

Then Clayton noticed that Daphne Montague was there. Everyone in the room saw his eyes light up when he saw her, but Victoria was too busy focusing on what Clayton had just told her.

"Thank you so much, Clayton, Johnny, and Billy. I know you're just as concerned, and I appreciate all you have done and are doing to bring my Tati home," said Victoria choking back tears.

"Victoria, you stay put. Clayton and I will go make hot chocolate for everyone," responded Daphne.

Just after they left for the kitchen, Jackson and Rosie returned with Silvia. Jackson had dropped Rosie at the front door, and he and Silvia drove around to the back of the house where the kitchen was located.

THE SISTERS SPURLOCK

In the kitchen

Daphne and Clayton hurried to the kitchen. Making the hot chocolate was of utmost importance, then they would talk. While Daphne got the cocoa powder from the cupboard, Clayton retrieved the milk from the fridge. Both of them noticed how sparse the cupboard and fridge were. As they put the pot on to boil, Daphne turned to Clayton. She looked at him deeply and said, "This may not be the time, Clayton, but you're going to be a daddy!"

Clayton couldn't help himself and pulled Daphne close to him. It was a long passionate kiss. So engrossed were they that neither one was aware that standing at the kitchen door was none other than Jackson and Silvia with chili, cornbread, and chocolate chip cookies.

In another part of town

"Rain's so hard I cain't see, young'un. I cain't go much furtha," Ree explained looking at the precious cargo she was carrying, Tati.

"I love ya, Wee," said Tati in a weak little voice.

She was now drenched, and the fever was causing her to see things that might not be there. She saw Marian dolls everywhere. Some had red dots on them and some didn't. Tati smiled when she thought about the room she had seen, or had she?

Ree and Tati took cover underneath a tree. It wasn't much cover, but it did give Ree a rest. Her arms were so tired, and her strength was depleting. She didn't think they could find their way back. She sat down and held Tati in her arms and rocked her singing a song she'd learned as a child.

> My arms were made for rockin'
> When Jesus comes a knockin'
> I will not let Him take my baby now.
> He knows I need my baby
> So He'll let me keep her maybe
> And together we'll enter His kingdom somehow.

Ree sang this over and over again until Tati closed her eyes. Ree leaned back against the tree and prayed.

Two Groups Form into One

"The rain's just getting harder, Dean. I think we're going to have to turn back. I'll bet she's been found and is back at the house safely, now," Harry insisted.

"Please, Harry, I think Lucy can pick up on Midas's scent. Let's give it a little longer. Tati's so sweet and well, she's kind of like a little sister. She and the other girls are the closest I have to sisters," Dean pleaded with Harry.

"Lucy, go! Find Midas!" shouted Dean. Lucy took them in a direction they had not gone before. She took them through weeds, overgrown grass, poison ivy. It was difficult for them to see, but they ventured on. Lucy seemed to be on to something. They saw a light coming from the direction they were going and followed it. It would fade in and out, but Lucy headed straight for the light. They were getting closer and closer to it, and all the while they were calling, "Tati! Tati!"

They saw a figure ahead, and when they shouted Tati's name again, it turned around. It was none other than Sheriff Hall. He had a flashlight and was using it to search for Tati. They were thrilled to see one another and together formed a lookout party for Tati. They hadn't gone far when they thought they heard a noise, and Lucy picked up the scent. She was almost running.

They yelled "Tati! Tati!" over and over until they heard a small little voice say, "Ovah here."

Lucy saw Midas, and the two started sniffing, and tails were wagging. They found Ree and Tati taking cover under a tree. Tati was safe in Ree's arms, but both were soaked to the bone, and Midas hadn't left their side.

When Ree saw Charles, she said, "I...found...ya...baby, Jeb. I...found...ya baby."

In one swoop, Charles picked up both Ree and Tati and ran with them. He ran all the way back to his car. He was a strong man, but adrenaline had kicked in, so he was able to run holding both of them. He pulled blankets out of the trunk and wrapped them around Ree and Tati. Both Ree and Tati were shivering, now. It's as though they waited until they were found before giving in to the cold. Harry, Dean, and the dogs piled into the back seat of the police car, and Charles put the siren on.

"Shelia, come in, over!" said Charles.

"This is Shelia, over."

"Call Dr. Elsworth Walker, tell him to stand by, over."

"Affirmative, Sheriff, over," said Shelia.

"This is an emergency, over," noted Charles.

"Ten-fifty-seven. Found. Repeat. Tati Scholl found. Over."

"Great news, Sheriff! Over," Shelia exclaimed.

Dr. Walker was at home with his wife, Florence. They were just sitting down to eat when the phone rang.

Florence looked at her husband smiling and stated, "You know it's for you. Who else would call us during dinner hour?"

Dr. Walker got up and answered it. He listened and then hung up the phone.

"So, what's the emergency?" Florence queried.

"It appears little Tati Scholl got lost in the rain and is in need of care," he replied.

The phone rang again, and this time it was Charles Hall.

"Dr. Walker, this is Sheriff Hall. Tati Scholl and her grandmother were both caught out in the storm and are cold to the bone. Tati's infected with the chicken pox and had a fever before getting wet. I know being out in the rain didn't help her fever one bit, and her grandmother is extremely wet and cold too. Would you please meet us at the Scholls' house as soon as you can?"

"Absolutely, Charles. I'm on my way, now," Dr. Walker responded.

Turning toward Florence, he said, "Dinner will have to wait. Can you keep it warm for me?"

"Of course, dear. I always do. It will be here when you get back," answered Florence with a smile. "Please give the Scholls a hug for me. They are so sweet and have gone through so much this year."

THE GHOST COMES OUT

Luckily for Dr. Walker, the rain had subsided when he got into his car and headed toward the Scholl residence.

Meanwhile...

"Oh, my precious baby!" Victoria cried out when she saw Tati.

She reached out her arms for her daughter. She didn't even look at Charles when he brought her in soaking wet. Her focus was on Tati and getting her into a warm bath.

She looked in her precious face and said, "I'll never leave you again, my little angel."

And she ran with her into the bathroom to put her into the tub. She had no idea Ree was waiting in Charles's car.

"Rosie, will you help me, honey?" she asked.

"Ya betcha, Momma. Hey, Tati, ya gave yua sista an' Momma a scare," Rosie said affectionately.

"I saw…wy, Wo…sie. I saw…wy," Tati responded shivering.

Victoria just held her and, through tears, exclaimed, "You have nothing to be sorry about, angel,"

"Wee…s…ave…me," Tati said through the shivering and shaking.

"What did you say, honey?" asked Victoria. *I thought she said something about Ree*, she thought.

"Tati, Rosie has some oatmeal she's going to put in your bath. This will help with the chicken pox and will make you warm all over," Victoria said lovingly.

Rosie poured the oatmeal into the bathtub while Victoria lowered Tati into the warm tub. Tati kept shivering, but when she got into the tub, the warmth soon enveloped her, and she wasn't shivering as much. Both Victoria and Rosie were attending to Tati when there was a knock on the bathroom door.

"Rosie, will you see who that is, honey?" asked Victoria.

Rosie went to the door and opened it, and standing there was Sheriff Hall.

While Victoria had been attending to Tati, the sheriff was attending to Ree. After he gave Tati to her mother, he went back to the car to retrieve Ree. She had her eyes closed. She was now shivering uncontrollably. The rain and cold had gotten to her. As Charles was helping her into the house, she suddenly had difficulty walking and was experiencing trouble seeing.

"I can't walk, J-J-J-Jeb. I ain't…seein' t-t-t-too…good, either…dizzy. It…okay…'cause… I b-b--brung…yua baby…h-h-h-home, Jeb. I…b-b-b-brung…huh…home," Ree said slowly.

She had gone into a sudden cardiac arrest. Charles tried catching her as she went down but was dead before she hit the ground. Dr. Walker arrived right after, but there was nothing he could do other than declare Ree's time of death.

CHAPTER 24

TATI'S HOME

"Hi, Mista Sheriff," Rosie said with a smile. "We givin' Tati a bath t'warm her up."

"Rosie, I really need to speak to your mother for a minute. Do you think you could take over giving Tati her bath so I may speak with her?" Charles requested.

"Sure," Rosie stated. "Tati, Imma gonna give ya yua bath, now, 'kay?"

Victoria got up and went out in the hall to see what Charles wanted. She left the door open just a crack so if Tati called for her, she could be there in a jiffy.

"Please forgive me, Charles. I didn't even thank you for bringing Tati home. You told me you'd bring her back, and you did. Thank you so much!" said Victoria. She laid her hand on his arm, and his heart skipped a beat.

"I didn't come up for that reason, Victoria. I'm afraid I've got something else to tell you. Uh, did you know that Ree went out to look for Tati?" Charles asked.

"What? No, she was in her bedroom," said Victoria.

What was it Tati had said? 'Ree saved me,' I believe those were the words she said. I just didn't listen to her, Victoria thought.

"She must've snuck out, but she got caught in the rain too. Victoria, it was actually Ree who found Tati. When we came upon them, they were under a tree soak and wet, and Ree was rocking Tati," Charles explained.

"Oh, I must go and thank her! I'm sure she's soaked to the bone like Tati." Victoria stuck her head in the bathroom. "Girls, I will be right back. Tati, I won't be two minutes. I must go and see about Ree," she stressed.

Charles reached out and grabbed Victoria by her arm. "No, uh, I'm afraid I've got some bad news for you, Victoria. If I could sugar-coat this in any way, I would, but Ree suffered a major heart attack... and died," Charles said gently. "The coroner's on his way over here, now," he added.

"No! No!" cried Victoria. "I can't believe it. Where is she? I must see her," exclaimed Victoria. Charles reached for Victoria and held her, and as he did, the tears began to fall.

Before she could go and see Ree, Dr. Walker was coming up the stairs to see Tati. He saw the tears in Victoria's eyes and knew she had been told about her mother-in-law.

"Victoria, allow me to offer my sincerest condolences. If there's anything Florence and I can do, please let us know." Dr. Walker looked at Victoria and held out his hands to her.

She took them and looked at him and asked, "It was sudden?"

"Yes, it was, my dear," he said. "I know you've gone through so much and are just learning of the new sadness. I'm so very sorry." There was an akward silence before he added, "I understand our little Tati has the chicken pox and a fever too?"

"Yes, she's just a little angel, and she's been through so much. Dr. Walker, this is going to shake her. Ree saved Tati, and now...she's dead. How do I tell Tati and Rosie?" cried Victoria through tears.

"You allow your heart to do the talking. I promise you God will put into your mind the words needed to say to your daughters when the time is right. He never lets us down, does he? Right now let me take a look at Tati," Dr. Walker said gently.

Victoria collected herself for a minute before going back into Tati.

Charles went downstairs to wait for the coroner while Victoria rinsed Tati off, and she and Rosie helped Tati into her pajamas. They

THE GHOST COMES OUT

took her into Victoria's bedroom because there was water all over the floor from the rain in the girls' bedroom. Waiting for them in Victoria's bedroom was Dr. Walker. He took one look at Tati, and his heart softened. She was such a small child, and she'd been through so much.

"Hi, Tati. I hear you've had an adventure," Dr. Walker said kindly.

"Uh...huh. I...was...in... Mawian's...house," said Tati.

"Well, I'm sure you have lots to tell when you're better," Dr. Walker said. "Now, let's take a look at you." He felt her forehead, and there was no doubt she had a fever, but he had to check it rectally. Tati knew what was coming, but she felt so bad she didn't care. She simply laid on her stomach while he took her temperature.

"Just as I thought...102.8," he said to himself. "Rosie, can you go get your sister some orange juice? How does that sound, little Tati?"

"Dr. Walka, can Tati have some grape juice? That's owwah... ur... I mean...her favorite," Rosie explained smiling.

"If that's what she wants, then by all means, grape juice it is," Dr. Walker replied with a smile.

"O...kay," said Tati slowly. "I weal tiuhed."

"I'm sure you are tired, honey. Let's get you some grape juice, and then maybe you can go to sleep. I'll stay right here with you, okay?" Victoria insisted.

Rosie ran down the stairs to the kitchen. Even at eight years old, she knew something was going on because they hushed up when she came into the room.

"I need t'git Tati some grape juice," said Rosie excitedly. "Imma gonna take care of her 'cause she needs me. I'll probly be on call all night!"

Clayton laughed and said, "Yes, ma'am. Your sister needs you, and nobody can take better care of her than Miss Rosie."

"Thanks, Mista Clayton," Rosie said with a smile. She then turned to Silvia and asked, "Ma'am, ain't ya Johnny's an' Billy's mom?"

Silvia looked down at her and declared, "I am."

"Do I smell cookies unda that nakin by any chance?" Rosie asked with a smile.

Silvia's whole demeanor changed. "Ya bettcha, little teacha. Ya wanna try the best chocolate chip cookies in Grayton?" she bragged.

"Yes 'em, I do!" exclaimed Rosie, and she reached to take one. She took a bite, and as she was chewing, she said, "These ain't the best cookies in Grayton, Miss Silvia...these the best cookies in the world!"

Right then Rosie had made a friend with Silvia. Something that Daphne had tried years to do, but the result was not the same.

"Ya thank I could take one up t'Tati? This might make her betta, ya know," explained Rosie. And Silvia gave her two to take up.

"Ya, might git hongry on the way up, little teacha!" Siliva replied with a big smile.

Rosie went to the fridge and poured the grape juice into a glass and took that and the cookies back upstairs to Tati. She came through the bedroom door just beaming.

"Tati, I brung ya the best chocolate chip cookies. Johnny an' Billy's mom made 'em. They good too!" Rosie said with excitement.

Tati lifted her head, but it hurt so much she just laid it back on the pillow.

"Ya thank... I could...eat 'em lata? I...vewy...tiuhed," Tati said as she closed her eyes.

Now Rosie was really concerned. She'd never known Tati not to eat chocolate chip cookies or drink her favorite juice.

With tears in her eyes, she asked Dr. Walker, "Is T-t-t...ati gon...na die?"

Victoria rushed over to hold Rosie. As Dr. Walker explained, "No, Tati's going to be just fine, but we need to bring that fever down, and juice and rest will really help. Do you think you can help your mother take care of Tati, Rosie?"

Rosie's tears dried up when she discovered she had an important job to do.

"Dr. Walka, I'm not only a teacha, Imma nurse too," Rosie said with a grin.

Rosie went in to sit by Tati's side just in case she needed her. Victoria listened as Dr. Walker gave her instructions on what to do to get Tati's fever down. Then, he said he would come back in the morning to check on Tati before he went into his office.

Charles came up the stairs after the doctor left. The coroner had taken Ree's body to the morgue. When he got to the top of the staircase, Victoria turned to Charles and said, "I cannot believe Ree risked her own health to go out and find Tati…and now she's dead. Charles…did she say anything about where she found Tati? Did Tati see her when she had the heart attack? Do you think her going to look for Tati caused her death?"

Victoria broke into a wail of tears, and Charles just held her. They stood like that for a few minutes before Charles answered her.

"I've no idea where she found Tati. I only know when we found them, they were taking cover under a tree, and Ree was rocking and singing to Tati."

Looking down at Victoria, he continued, "She loved Tati, and she wasn't about to let her go. To answer your next question, no, Tati was upstairs with you when Ree died. I was bringing her into the house, and the attack occurred."

Do I dare tell Victoria that Ree had confused me with Jeb? Charles wondered.

"I'm so sorry, Victoria. Miss Ree was a big part of my childhood. I'm a believer in destiny. I believe if Ree had been in her room lying down on her bed, the result would have been the same. I also believe she died doing exactly what she wanted to do, and that was rescuing Tati," added Charles.

Victoria looked at Charles and, for the first time, thought how nice and gentle he was. He had gone the extra mile for Tati, and for that, she would always be grateful, but it was more than that. She was beginning to have feelings she hadn't felt in some time. She allowed Charles to hold her while she cried, but something else was happening to Victoria, and it felt good. It was nice to be held by a man, again. She felt safe, secure, and wanted. No one would ever replace her Jeb, but this was nice, and for the first time since Jeb's death, she felt good.

What happened next, no one could have predicted.

*****

Because of the size of the small town, Grayton did not have an official fire station. It was made up of townfolk who called themselves the Grayton Volunteers. The Scholls' house was still reeling from Tati's disappearance and Ree's sudden death, but nothing could've prepared them or the town for what happened next. The volunteer fire alarm started sounding. It was actually a military surplus air-raid siren. It started low and then got louder and louder, impossible for the entire town of Grayton not to hear the noise.

There were twenty-five men who made up the Grayton Volunteers. It was their duty to work and assist during any fire. The last Grayton blaze was at the Robbinses' farm. There had been an oil lantern that had overturned, and it caught the house and barn on fire. Luckily, no one was injured, but the only thing that withstood the flames was Garnett Robbins's black cast-iron skillet found in the basement. His son, Kenneth Hall, never used another skillet to cook in after that.

There were two men who were responsible for sounding the alarm. They were the Dixon brothers, Jefferson and Chuck. They were confirmed bachelors and lived right next to the firehouse. They had just finished their dinner when they heard a loud boom. Both men raced to the window to see Marcus Peters running down the street yelling, "Fire! Fire!"

The brothers looked at one another, and without hesitation, both headed for the firehouse. It was actually Jefferson who got to the switch first. He was faster than his older brother and beat him soundly by fifteen feet.

Since there hadn't been a fire in Grayton in seven years, the men were a bit rusty on what to do. With the sounding of the alarm, it brought most every member of the town who were ambulatory. Men, women, and children came running toward the firehouse eager to lend a hand, but mostly out of blatant curiosity.

"The color'd church's on faar!" yelled Petie Smyth.

CHAPTER 25

THE BEST AND WORST OF GRAYTON

Petie Smyth was part of the volunteers, and because he was first to the firehouse, he drove the engine. There were at least sixty people at the Church of the Southern Baptist of Grayton helping with hoses and carrying buckets of water to extinguish the blaze when the Smiths arrived with Daphne Montague. An assembly line of people were passing buckets of water to help kill the fire. It was a blaze and smolderingly hot. Clayton, Jackson, Billy, and Johnny immediately sprang into action helping to carry one of the hoses. Harry Miller and Dean joined the bucket line while Lucy stayed right by Dean's side. Monty and his Uncle Bake were busy taking pictures for the *Grayton Gazette*. This was big news for Bake, and this coupled with the murder of Carl Shelby could put him on the map. He wasn't about to miss this opportunity to sensationalize these stories.

When Charles heard the alarm, he and Dr. Walker got into his police car and raced to the fire. They saw Marcus Peters on the way and gave him a lift to the church.

Damn! Isn't it enough that I alerted the town of the fire? Do I have to help put the damn thing out too? I was having such a good run too. What if a spark should touch my hair? It would go up in smoke with all the hairspray I have on it, thought Marcus.

Over in the distance just out of the view of the church, sat Mr. Joe and his wife Raveleen. They were under a tree eating fried chicken and singing Martha and the Vandellas' new release, "Dancing in the Street." When they heard the alarm, Mr. Joe and Raveleen raced to the scene. Dorothy joined them shortly afterward.

"Where ya been, Dorthy? Ya look a mess. Why don't cha git yuaself cleaned up once in a while," Joe remarked while he chewed on a drumstick.

"Will do, Pops. Momma, can ya pass ovah a thigh an' leg? I'm hongry!" Dorothy replied while wiping spilled gravy on her shirt.

They weren't about to help but thought they'd bring their dinner and enjoy the "show" while they ate.

Silvia was distraught. She never cared when something happened to the white folks. She thought they deserved whatever occurred, but this was her church.

"Tell me, Jesus, the revrend ain't in there?" shouted Silvia to the heavens. "He jest can't be. He know t'git out."

A hand reached over and touched her on the shoulder. It was the Reverend Andrew Anglin Greer himself. He was a sight for sore eyes as Silvia gave him a huge hug and thanked Jesus over and over that he'd been saved.

"Silvia, Jesus saved me. I was going t'work on Sunday's sermon at the church, but I got a stomach bug. Queenie Mae made me stay home," the reverend explained and then added as he looked at the fire, "Imma so glad she did."

With that, Silvia began to cry. The good reverend held her while the tears fell onto his shirt.

"What we gonna do? We gots no church. We gots no hymnals. We gots no place to call owwah home. We gots nothin'!" cried Silvia.

Reverend Greer looked down at her and said, "We don't needs a building, Silvia. We gots the Lord in our hearts. We don't needs books. We gots more music in us than any book can contain. Jesus is our heart, an' *he* is our home, so we always gots a place! We gots each otha, an' no fire's gonna take that away. Now, I want ya t'dig down deep, an' I want ya t'start singin' like ya ain't eva sung before, ya hear?

THE GHOST COMES OUT

Ya know ya gotta voice of an angel, an' this time I wants ya t'sing so that the angels in heaven will stop what they doin' an' join right in."

And with that, Silvia looked up to the heavens and began singing "Go Tell It on the Mountain." And the louder she sang, the quieter the fire seemed to be getting. Everybody there joined in singing with her. As the crowd grew, the louder the singing got. All the pastors from the other Grayton churches were there singing, rejoicing, and working to put out the fire.

Frances Boyd was organizing the bucket brigade. One wouldn't actually say she was working, but she was a hell of a good delegator, and with the soot she was covered in, one might think she'd been in the fire.

In the middle of it was Daphne Montague. She was working as hard as anyone to put out the fire. Her beautifully coifed blonde hair had fallen and was touching her shoulders. She had never looked as beautiful as she did at that moment. Daphne had turned momentarily to accept another bucket of water from the man behind her, Harry Miller. She had her back to the fire and, thus, never saw it coming. Another explosion occurred inside of the church, and it sent debris flying as Daphne turned toward the eruption. Some say it was a miracle no one was killed. Others say the angels protected them because only one was injured… Daphne. Part of a wooden pew hit her. She went down, and immediately blood began spewing from her face. The bucket brigade came to assist her. Someone yelled her name, and when Clayton heard who had been hit, he dropped the hose and ran to her side. He shoved everyone out of his way and picked her up in his arms and began praying.

"Ya let go of huh, niggah!" screamed Mr. Joe, who came running down the hill toward Clayton. "She ain't a darkie, an' ya need t'take yua hans off Miss Daphne. Ya germs gonna kill her."

Charles sprinted toward Joe afraid he was going to attack Clayton.

"Joe, you leave him alone! We need to get Miss Montague help. You need to just back away!" Charles yelled as he caught a hold of Joe.

Dr. Walker witnessed the accident and raced forward. He was doing his best to examine Daphne while Clayton was holding her. She wasn't responsive, and her vitals weren't good. She needed to be transported to a hospital immediately. "Clayton, she needs medical attention. We need to get her to the hospital STAT! Call for an ambulance!"

Silvia approached her brother-in-law. "Clayton, ya know we needs t'git Miss Daphne t'the hospital. Jesus is watchin' ovah her. Let Doc do what he do," said Silvia in a sweet sisterly tone.

It wasn't a question. It was a statement. Silvia knew her boss was badly injured, and whatever bitterness she had felt in her heart toward Daphne, it suddenly evaporated. She no longer felt hate in her heart but love. Miracles do happen, and Silvia's heart softened that night.

Clayton heard no words until he heard the sheriff ask, "Does anyone know who Miss Daphne's next of kin might be? Does anyone know?"

"Me…it's me… Sheriff. She…she…she's…my…wife," sobbed Clayton as he looked at Daphne.

The crowd assembled was so quiet the only audible sound was the water from the hoses and the fire itself. No one could believe what they had heard.

"And, Sheriff?" Clayton said as he held his wife in his arms.

"Yes?" Charles answered. He knew many secrets about the families in this town; after all, he was the only law enforcement personnel in Grayton, but he wasn't prepared for that one, and the hits just kept coming.

"Daphne… Daphne's…pregnant…two months…with my child," weeped Clayton.

CHAPTER 26

COLOR'D CHURCH GOES UP IN SMOKE

Bradley Bacon Haas, a.k.a. Bake, was on top of the world. He felt as though his luck was changing. He had yearned to have his byline on every article on the front page at the *Grayton Gazette*, and his wish came true. This was by far Bake's best work since the two Montague suicides. The headline simply read, "Why?" He asked that question over and over in the article. "Why did the Negro church burn? Did the thunderstorm start it? Was it arson? Was there something more sinister about this fire? Could the Ku Klux Klan have started the fire to send a message? These questions are on everyone's mind, and they must be answered," Bake wrote in his article. His pictures were so vivid and real they even captured the very moment Daphne Montague was hit by the flying debris.

"Daphne Montague, Grayton's own local celebrity, was hit by flying debris from the fire. She was taken to Stockton Medical Center. Her condition is unknown at this time," he wrote. What his article didn't say was that gossip was already flying in Grayton regarding Daphne and her gardener, Clayton Smith. The Grayton citizens were abuzz with the news that not only was Clayton her husband but they were expecting a baby together.

Years earlier when the citizens of Grayton thought Daphne Montague had run away and married her tutor, Johnson Davis, it had actually been Clayton Smith she had married. Franklin and Louise Montague had paid Johnson Davis $10,000 to spread the word he'd married Daphne, keep his mouth shut about Clayton, and leave town. He complied. Six months later, Louise Montague was so distraught she died of a broken heart. The truth was she died of a broken heart only because she shot herself with a .22 caliber revolver in the chest. Franklin did his best to cover it up, but sadly he died six months later the same way his wife had. It was ruled a hunting accident. Bake Haas had uncovered the sordid truth and had written about both suicides in length. He sensationalized the story considerably, and his readers were thirsty for more. The paper was such a hit that it sold out at the Grayton Grocery Mart, and one hundred more papers had to be printed to satisfy the readers' curiosity.

The Garden Club

"Can you believe Daphne was married to Clayton the entire time? Why, I do believe I smelled his sweat on her the last time she was here," said Loralee Cline with disgust.

"What about her poor parents. Bless their hearts I bet they just wanted to die when they found out," JoEllen Ford added.

"They did, JoEllen. They killed themselves, or did you miss that part in the story?" retorted Loralee.

"Daphne always thought she was better than the rest of us," said Martha Duncan, president of the Grayton Garden Club, at the next meeting.

"Yeah, to think all along she was married to that niggah." Marcy Creech laughed. The other Garden Club members readily agreed, but what none would admit was they would've traded places in a minute if they could've had one romp in the sack with Clayton.

Grayton Grocery Mart

The two elderly sisters, Elizabeth and Barbara, were shopping at Grayton's Grocery Mart in the square. They were talking about what Barbara had read in the newspaper that morning over breakfast.

THE GHOST COMES OUT

Barbara turned to her sister and asked, "Can you believe Miss Daphne is married?"

"I didn't even know she was being courted, did you, Barbara?" questioned Elizabeth.

"Did you say she went to court? I didn't read about that, sista," answered Barbara.

"No, I said I didn't know Miss Daphne was dating anyone," responded Elizabeth.

"You say you'd like some dates? I don't think Grocer Hunter sells any, but we could go to Stockton," said Barbara.

And their conversation went on and on like that until they eventually left the store.

At the summer school

When Johnny and Billy came to summer school, Rosie, Val, and DaisyBelle met them with big hugs while Midas and Lucy wagged their tails excitedly.

"We jest so sorry 'bout yua church. Momma's makin somethin' t'bring to ya. Tati wanted t'be here, but she still has the pox. We jest so sorry," Rosie proclaimed.

"We gonna be okay," said Johnny earnestly.

"Yeah, we already gots some place to hold our church. We gonna worship in the back of Grayton's Grocery Mart," added an excited Billy. He was thinking that during the sermon when he and Johnny got bored, they could sneak some candy from the store. He was thrilled they were going to be having worship inside the mart. *Maybe we can get some soda pop too*, he thought.

"If ya couldn't find a place, ya know ya could use owwah school. It's fo everyone," explained Rosie.

"Ya know ya can count on yua school family, right? We love ya too," Val reminded Billy and Johnny.

"Yes, we do," added DaisyBelle.

"Thanks, girls. We good though," Johnny replied.

Monty was busy thinking about what had been discovered with the fire. He just couldn't resist asking.

"Hey, how 'bout yua uncle an Miss Montague? Uncle Bake said he neva saw that comin'. What 'bout Miss Montague? She okay?"

"We jest 'cited 'bout the baby. We hopin' fo a boy. We be cousins," explained Billy happily. He didn't want to discuss anything else. He and Johnny had been sworned not to say anything about Daphne, and he wasn't about to tell.

"I'm just so glad you guys are okay and you've got a place to worship. Family is so important, and now you can add another baby to yours," said Dean. He was thinking about his mom. He missed her so much and prayed one day his family would be whole.

Stockton Medical Center

Clayton had not left Daphne's side the entire night. He thought if he were to leave, she might need him, and he couldn't bear to disappoint his wife. She had regained consciousness but was disoriented. Her first concern was for her child, and when she discovered the baby was fine, she was able to rest. Clayton's love for her seemed to grow with each passing minute.

The doctors at Stockton Medical Center knew they had an interesting case in front of them. The patient was a thirty-four-year-old female in good health. She had been involved in an accident caused by flying debris from a fire. She was also two months pregnant. The trash had actually hit her in the face and had caused major damage. The patient's head was covered in gauze and bandages, and she had received twenty-two stitches as a result. The plastic surgeon on call was Dr. John Buchannan, and he had done a remarkable job on her face that she would not require any additional surgery for the scars.

Dr. Jaycee Malcolm had been called in from Memphis. He was the best ophthalmologist in the south. He had done his preliminary exam on Daphne and called Clayton outside of the room to talk.

"What's the matter with my wife, Dr. Malcolm? Is she going to be okay?" Clayton pleaded.

"Mr. Smith, your wife has a corneal abrasion. Apparently when the rubble hit her face, it hit both of her eyes, specifically her corneas.

THE GHOST COMES OUT

Her right cornea is torn beyond repair. Her left one is very scratched but perhaps will heal itself in time," said Dr. Malcolm.

Clayton begged, "I don't understand, sir."

"Mr. Smith, right now, your wife is totally blind," he explained.

CHAPTER 27

THE FUNERALS

Grayton had only one funeral home, Embry's Funeral Parlor. It was owned and run by the Embrys. It had been in their family for three generations. The family had a secret weapon, Kimmie Embry. She was without a doubt the best mortician in the south. One would have to look high and low to find anyone better in the business than Kimmie. People were amazed at her talent. The bodies were made to look as natural as though they were merely taking a nap and would wake up at any moment.

Victoria had gone to the funeral parlor to pick out Ree's dress and casket. Not only did she have to purchase another casket, she had to put this one on credit too. The Embrys were nice, but they were also businesspeople, and they liked selling the very best coffins. Victoria chose a simple walnut wooden casket lined in satin with a satin pillow to match. Even though it was the least expensive, it set Victoria back $300. *It could be $3,000. I simply don't have that kind of money lying around. If I pick up another job, I could have both Jeb's and Ree's caskets paid off in two years,* thought Victoria.

Marie "Ree" Ramsey Scholl looked prettier and younger in death than she had in life. When Victoria first saw her in the casket, she couldn't believe how youthful she appeared. The dress she had chosen for Ree was one she only saw her in once. It was the dress she had worn to her and Jeb's wedding. It was the shade of blush, and it

THE GHOST COMES OUT

looked beautiful on her. Victoria was pleased with the choice she had made. *I think this dress makes her inner beauty shine forth*, she thought.

"Would you please make sure these matching shoes are on her feet?" Victoria asked Kimmie. "I wouldn't want her feet to get cold."

"Yes'em. We'll do our best," Kimmie replied. *I know this is hard on the family, but there's not a lot of room in the casket, and it's hard to fit everything into such a small space, but I'll do the best I can because Miss Ree was always good to me as a child. She made a special popcorn ball for me every Halloween, and she always made sure I was invited to all of Jeb's birthday parties. I can't believe it's been just a few months ago I was preparing Jeb for his forever home. How sad for this family*, she thought.

Deciding whether or not to keep the casket open or closed was a debate Victoria wrestled with in her mind. Having to tell the girls about Ree's death was hard. She knew it would be especially hard on Tati. Not only was she healing from the chicken pox but hearing Ree had passed away was not going to go well. Victoria decided to tell both of the girls at once. She thought they could lean on each other that way.

Victoria went into her room and sat on the side of the bed next to Tati. Rosie crawled up next to Tati. Rosie had taken her job as nurse seriously and would put her hand on Tati's forehead to see if her sister was warm. She would look at her mother and smile to let her know Tati had no fever.

"I've got some news I need to share with you," said Victoria sadly.

"Momma, are ya sad?" asked Rosie.

Tati tried to repeat what Rosie asked but just gave up and looked at her mother.

"You know that you two are my sunshine, moon, and my stars, right?" appealed Victoria. The two girls nodded with smiles as their mom spoke on.

"Do you know who else thought you were out of this world?" The girls just looked at their mother with a question on their faces.

"Ree did," Victoria replied.

Before Victoria could speak again, Rosie asked, "Where is Ree? I didn't see her downstairs. She still in bed? I'll bet she's still restin', right, Momma?"

"There's something I need to tell you both about Ree," Victoria paused. "She's gone to be with your daddy in heaven," Victoria added.

Tati looked at Rosie. Rosie just laid it out and asked her mother, "Ya mean Ree's dead?"

Tati looked again at Rosie and began to cry. Victoria reached over and put her arms around both Rosie and Tati. As they cried, Victoria rocked them back and forth until the sobbing stopped.

"Wee save me, Momma. Is my fault?" Tati wondered.

Victoria squeezed her even harder and said, "No, my little love. Ree's heart gave out. It is no one's fault."

They all stayed in that embrace for several minutes until they heard the doorbell ring.

At the door was the flower delivery man, Simon. He had a beautiful peace lily to deliver to the Scholl family. When Victoria saw it, she laughed to herself. "Ree wouldn't have liked that it was real."

That same day…

While Victoria was at the funeral home, she ran into Rita Shelby. Rita was there picking out a casket for Carl. Both of the funerals were to be held on the same day, just in different rooms. When the two women saw one another, they ran toward one another and hugged. Both women had gone through so much, and they appreciated the fact they didn't have to say a word. They just knew.

Rita was appreciative of Victoria's friendship and often wondered, if she knew the truth, would she still want to be her friend, but this was not the time nor the place to discuss her secret.

Like Victoria, Rita had to put the cost of Carl's casket on credit. She was unaware Carl had an insurance policy. She knew nothing about it or who the beneficiary was. One of the benefits at working at Agnes's Garage and Repair was a life insurance policy. Every employee had a $10,000 life insurance policy on them with their families as the beneficiaries. Carl had never bothered telling Rita about the policy.

THE GHOST COMES OUT

He didn't think it important, and he never thought he'd precede her in death, so what was the point?

Both services were set for June 30. Ree's service would go first at 11:00 a.m., and Carl's would follow at 3:00 p.m. This would give those who wanted to attend both services an opportunity to do so. Sheriff Hall was especially glad. He would be with Victoria and her daughters for Ree's service and then would watch the crowd at Carl's. Who knows? In law enforcement, he'd learned that the criminal often likes to attend the service just to see what everyone knows and to be close to the family.

Flowers began to pour into the funeral parlor for Ree. It looked and smelled like a florist shop. There was every flower imaginable in the room where Ree's body was residing.

Sadly, there was only one arrangement in Carl's, and that was given on behalf of the funeral home. Rita simply couldn't afford an arrangement. She was barely able to make ends meet and had purchased the casket on credit. Little did she know that shortly she would be receiving a nice insurance check in the mail.

When Victoria, Rosie, and Tati saw that Carl had only one arrangement, they quickly took the cards off of half of the arrangements that had been sent for Ree's funeral and took them into Carl's room before Rita or her daughters returned. When the Shelbys came back, they were shocked to see how many flowers Carl had received. They were pleased, especially DaisyBelle.

"See, I tole y'all Papa had many friends," remarked DaisyBelle with a huge smile on her face.

Rita and Val were surprised, but both were happy so many people had remembered Carl. *I can't b'lieve he had this many friends. Did I misjudge him? No, he was horrible t'me an the girls. It's best he dead,* thought Rita.

Ree's Funeral

The whole town seemed to come out for her funeral. Marie "Ree" Ramsey Scholl had been a fixture in Grayton. She had grown up and married in the town. She never wanted to live anywhere else.

This was the place she raised her son and where she called home. The house she grew up in was the same one in which she married and raised her son. No wonder it was falling in all around. She never believed in home improvement no matter how much it needed, so the house seemed to be imploding upon itself.

Ree knew about everyone in Grayton. When Jeb was growing up, Ree would often have ten boys sleeping at her house. She was the woman every kid wanted to have as a mother, but in her later years, she had developed dementia, and the youthful mother was replaced by a strict, rigid, and sad woman.

When Victoria, Rosie, and Tati came into the room, everyone stood as they made their way to the front. Tati still had some spots on her face but had scabbed over, and she was noncontagious. Her fever had been normal for two days, and she was holding Rosie's hand as the two entered.

The service was given by the minister of Grayton Baptist Church, Pastor Theodore Lester. He had known Ree all his life and talked about his youth spent at her house with Jeb. Theodore's remarks were so uplifting that after he left the pulpit to sit down, someone got up and asked Theodore to baptize him. What an emotional service that was.

After the service, they went to the cemetery on the hill for the burial service. Frances Boyd, wife of Pastor Allan Boyd of the Methodist Church, couldn't contain herself and sang "How Great Thou Art" a cappella. Those who attended wished she hadn't. Frances wasn't getting enough attention, and how could she remedy that? Well, breaking out in song was the answer. Victoria smiled and thanked her before she could sing another song.

"Don't ya thank the service needed a song, Mrs. Scholl? I jest knew ya wouldn't mind, I always say a church hymn can be sung anywhere, don'tcha thank?" explained Frances.

"Well, thank you for thinking of Ree," Victoria replied.

Sheriff Hall recognized the awkwardness of the situation and hurriedly took Victoria and the girls away in his squad car.

THE GHOST COMES OUT

Carl's Funeral

Sheriff Hall was the first to arrive at the funeral parlor. He wanted to make sure he saw everyone who came. Sadly, the only people who showed up were the summer school children and their parents. Not even Stockton's own Erleen Yoder made an appearance. Rita was glad she wasn't there. She didn't want to have to explain to her daughters who that woman was. Rita was disgusted that none of the mechanics at Agnes's Garage and Repair came, that is until the gravesite service. Wally himself came racing up to the cemetery. He was still in his work clothes, but he at least showed his face. He had with him an envelope. After the service was completed, he went over to talk to Rita.

"Miss Rita, I'm sorry 'bout yua loss. Ya know Carl was a good mechanic," Wally acknowledged.

"Thank you, Wally. Imma glad ya came. He'd a been happy yua heeyah," responded Rita.

"Uh, this here's an envelope an inside is a policy. Ya know Carl had a life 'surrance policy, right?" Wally queried.

"I don't know what yua talkin' 'bout, Wally," Rita replied.

"Well, when anyone works fo me, they git life 'surrance policies. This here one's fo $10,000," Wally explained.

"What's this gotta do with me?" Rita asked.

"'Cause yua the beneficiary," responded Wally.

Rita nearly fell to the ground. *What is he trying to tell me? Does he mean what I think he means? No, that jest couldn't be. Fortune don't follow no Shelbys*, thought Rita.

"Ya need t'fill out the form, an Grayton Life will send ya a check for $10,000," Wally explained.

Rita's eyes filled up with tears. She and the girls embraced in a group hug. They were beside themselves. *I can't believe that useless piece of manure left us this. Is the nicest thang yua eva did was t'be dead, Carl*, thought Rita.

Sheriff Hall watched the entire exchange. No, she did not know there was a policy. *There's no way she could have reacted the way she did if she had known. Where do I go from here? The only people in atten-*

dance were the girls' friends and their parents. How sad, and what bad fortune for this murder investigation, thought Charles.

Meanwhile…

DaisyBelle made her way over to Tati. They hugged.

"Ya lookin' betta, Tati. How ya feelin'?" DaisyBelle asked sympathetically.

"I okay," answered Tati. "Ya think yua momma will let ya come ovah?" Tati asked.

"Lemme ask her, okay? Oh, how's Marian? She still have the pox?" asked a concerned DaisyBelle.

"I dunno, I brung huh home," answered Tati.

CHAPTER 28

REE'S LETTER

After the funerals, both the Scholls and Shelbys were exhausted. They both had many things to deal with. The Shelbys were deciding what to do next. Do they stay in Grayton or leave to make a new life for themselves? With the help of the $10,000 insurance policy, they had many decisions to make.

Victoria, Rosie, and Tati were busy cleaning out Ree's bedroom. Victoria wanted to get the house ready in case they had to sell it. Neither she nor Ree had ever discussed what to do with the house if Ree should die. It just wasn't talked about, and after Jeb's sudden death, neither one wanted to venture in that direction.

Rosie had the task of cleaning out Ree's bedside drawers. She and Tati marveled at all the buttons and marbles Ree had collected. Why she wanted to keep them, only Ree knew, but it was fun to play with them.

Tati was playing marbles with Midas while Rosie kept cleaning out the drawers. Tati's strength wasn't up to par yet, but she was getting stronger every day, and Rosie was still on call while her sister was recuperating.

When the last drawer was almost empty, there was an envelope at the bottom. It had Victoria's name on the front and was sealed. Rosie brought it to her mother.

"Momma, I b'lieve this is fo you," she said handing her mother the envelope.

THE SISTERS SPURLOCK

Victoria looked it over and sat down on the edge of Ree's bed and opened the envelope. Her daughters huddled around her as she took out some papers, and as she opened the first page, she began to read,

Dear Victoria,

If you reeding this, then Im with Jesus. No need to worrie bout me, I ben calld home to be with my Lord.

I aint no good at showin emoshun. I spose I never felt good enuff for no one to love me. I thank ownlee reeson Jeb's dad marryed me caus all othr girls was takin but ya alwayz showd and told me you loved me. Lookin back now I spoz none of us Scholls dservd some one like you or your girls in owwah lif.

I aint no good with the girls. I didnt want them gettin to clos. I didnt under stand how to love them. Rosalee is so like my Jeb. I didnt want to get to clos for fear she mite die to. The litle one Tatiana lookd so like you Victoria. I just coodn't let her know I liked her but you no I did rite? I reely love her. Wood you tell her?

One day I see you agin. Till then I wate with my Jesus til yall come home. One last thing I have a bank acount at BANK, ownly bank in Grayton. I neva took money out, didnt blieve in it. The acount number is JKR051761. The boy at BANK is Ricky Phelps. He tack good cair of you. Show him this letr.

Maybe some day when you think of me you smil?

Your mother in law,
Ree

THE GHOST COMES OUT

P.S. The house now blongs to you and your girls. Do some rpairs. House needs it.

Victoria and her two girls began crying not because Ree had left them anything but because she had actually loved them. None of them had ever heard her speak a word of love, and to think she was now gone, and they only heard about it now.

"Okay, that does it. Promise me, girls, we will never go a day without telling each other we love one another, promise?" proclaimed Victoria.

"Ya got it, Momma!" exclaimed Rosie while blowing her nose.

"Me too, Momma!" shouted Tati, and they shared a group hug, and even Midas wanted in on the fun.

"Now, I believe we've done a good job this morning. Since summer school was called off for the week because of the funerals, I think I need to take my two special girls to Grayton Burger and Shake. What do you think?" Victoria inquired with a knowing look and smile.

The girls started jumping up and down. "Yes, Momma!" they both squealed in delight.

"Momma, can we go to BANK while we're out? Ya know me an' Tati never been in there? Do we need t'dress up?" Rosie asked excitedly.

The only bank in town was called BANK. It wasn't called the Bank of Grayton or Grayton National Bank. It was just called BANK, with all capital letters. No one ever knew the story behind it. Everyone just accepted it.

Victoria laughed. "No, you can wear your playclothes. Well, I guess we could go. Would you both like that?"

"Me an' Wosie wanna go, Momma," Tati said with confidence.

*****

When they got to the restaurant, they saw Marcus Peters.

"Hey, Momma, there's yua boss. Hi, Mista Peters!" shouted Rosie as she and Tati ran up to him.

Oh no, Marcus thought. *Shouldn't that child still be quarantined or something? Is she safe to be around people? Since I haven't had chicken pox, is she still carrying that disease? Oh no! What if I got chicken pox in my hair? Would it all fall out? Oh damn, I must call Dr. Walker and ask him when I get home.*

"Hello, Scholl family. How are you? I'm just getting a lunch order to take back to the office. Victoria, I know you've got your hands full, but I could really use you back at work as soon as possible," stressed Marcus.

"I need to find someone to take care of the girls while I'm at work. You wouldn't let me bring them to work with me, would you?" asked Victoria sweetly. She already knew the answer, but she was hoping he might change his mind.

"Uh, I would, Victoria, but you know the policy. Oh, how I wish I could change it," Marcus explained unconvincingly. *Hell no, you can't bring them to work. They're disease carriers, and who knows what they'll be coming down with next?* he thought.

"I know you would, Mr. Peters. Don't worry about it. I'll be back at work on Monday," responded Victoria. *I'll see if Rita might be able to watch the kids next week so that they can still have their summer school,* she thought.

"Great! Well, here's my order. It's always a pleasure to see all the Scholls at once. Toodles for now," he said hurrying out before either child laid their hands on him.

"Don't know 'bout yua, Momma, but yua boss is always in here an' always in a hurry," remarked Rosie watching him go.

Victoria laughed and said, "How right you are, honey. Now, let's find a table."

After lunch, the three Scholl girls ambled up to BANK. The girls entered BANK as though they were going into a library. Rosie turned to Tati and put her finger over her lips. So, Tati put a finger over her lips. Since they had never been in a bank at all, they didn't know how to act but were on their best behaviors.

Victoria went to the first teller (there were only two) and asked to speak to Ricky Phelps. It turned out that Ricky Phelps was the branch manager. He had his own office, and when the teller made

THE GHOST COMES OUT

him aware someone needed to speak to him, he rose from his chair and came to speak to Victoria.

"Good afternoon, ma'am. I'm Ricky Phelps. Ramona tells me you need to speak to me. What can I do for you today?" he asked smiling at Rosie and Tati.

"I'm Victoria Scholl. My mother-in-law—" Victoria got no further in her explanation before Ricky interrupted her.

"You do not need to explain further. I know why you're here. Please know how very sorry I am about your loss. Your mother-in-law is the reason I'm here in this job. After her husband, Charles Sr., passed away, Ree became the soul beneficiary of her husband's estate. Charles's dad made a fortune in the lumber business and left it all to his son. When Charles Sr. died, it was left to Ree. She never took out a penny from her account, not even for her husband's funeral arrangements because they had been paid for prior to his death. Ree got me this job. I had been the manager at the Grayton Grocery Mart, and she thought I should aim higher. When this job came open, she went to the board of directors and demanded they hire me, or she would take her money elsewhere, oh, but I'm sure you know how special she was. I won't go on anymore except to say it's a privilege to meet you, and I hope you'll plan on doing further business with us here at BANK," proclaimed Ricky as he showed them into his private office.

There were only two seats opposite Ricky, so Victoria held Tati in her lap.

"I'm afraid I'm at a loss, Mr. Phelps. My daughters and I were cleaning out Ree's room and found this envelope. Inside of it was this letter explaining Ree had an account with you. I did not know she had an account, much less that she had money in it. She stated in the letter that I was to present this to you," explained Victoria as she handed the letter over to Ricky. He read it.

Ricky got up from his seat with the letter in his hand and walked around where he was standing above Victoria, Rosie, and Tati. He pulled his chair over to them and sat down just inches away before he spoke.

"If you didn't know Ree had an account with us, then I'm afraid what I'm about to tell you will come as a shock," he paused before continuing. "Other than Daphne Montague, your mother-in-law has the largest account in our bank." He paused again. "And now that belongs to you."

CHAPTER 29

SUMMER SCHOOL ENDS

Monday

This was the final week of summer school. All the kids were excited but sad that their summer school was coming to an end. Rita watched the kids while Victoria was at work. With the windfall Victoria received, she could readily afford to pay Rita for the babysitting/chaperone job.

When Ricky Phelps wrote a number on a piece of paper at BANK and gave it to Victoria to read, she nearly fell out of her seat. The amount written on the paper was $264,081.22. The girls were watching to see her reaction. She merely smiled and said to Ricky, "I will be in touch very soon. Thank you so much for your time, Mr. Phelps."

After leaving BANK, Victoria knew she would never have to work another day in her life, but providing a good role model for her daughters was extremely important, and besides that, she loved her job. Being the superintendent's secretary was a sought-after position. When she married Jeb, she wanted to work to help support their family, and Marcus Peters had provided her the opportunity, and she wasn't going to let him down. So, just as she had promised Mr. Peters, she was back to work on Monday.

Summer school

"I thank we had the greatest summer school eva. Everybody agree?" Val shouted as the rest of the boys and girls cheered.

"You've done a terrific job, Rosie. I learned a lot and met my best friend, Monty, here," proclaimed Dean. Lucy looked at Dean and wagged her tail as though she knew what he had just said.

He put his arms around his German shepherd and whispered in her ear, "No one could ever replace you, Lucy."

"Yeah, me an' Deano are buddies!" exclaimed Monty.

"I'm jest glad y'all had fun an' learned somethin'. Tati, we still need some work on those *R*s, but we're gittin' there, ain't we?" Rosie asked.

"Yes, we ahh. Ya the best teacha, Wosie," Tati remarked affectionately to her sister.

DaisyBelle looked at Tati smiling and said quietly, "I thank ya doin' great, Tati."

Tati reached over and gave her a hug. Midas, who was watching, started wagging his tail in appreciation. Tati put her arms around him and gave him a big hug too.

"Me an' Billy are glad we come down," added Johnny. "Momma axed us if we gonna have a gradiation. Ya thank we could, Rosie?"

"I thank we can do whatever we want. Who wants a gradiation?" Rosie questioned. "I thank we need t'vote. All in fava of a gradiation, raise yua right hands."

First, Rosie and Val had to explain to Tati and DaisyBelle which was their right hands. All agreed for a summer school graduation, and it was passed.

"I thank we need t'ask owwah mommas what we do at a gradiation," noted Val.

"I'll ask my Uncle Bake, he'll know," said Monty excitedly.

"I'll ask Harry, he'll know too," added Dean. *I only hope Harry will let me be a part of this. He's been distracted and very quiet lately,* thought Dean.

"All I know is yua momma, Johnny, had betta make some of her chocolate chip cookies. They the best in the world," Rosie insisted.

THE GHOST COMES OUT

"They ahh good," responded Tati patting her tummy.

So all eight kids agreed they would discuss it with their parents that night to see what they needed to do to make this graduation a success.

Dean's house

Harry was getting accustomed to Dean going to summer school for a few hours while he worked at home on business. It also allowed him time to drive over to Stockton to grocery shop. Harry preferred going there because no one knew him and no one asked any questions. He had just pulled into his driveway and unloaded the groceries when there was a knock on his door.

Now who can that be? Dean's still in school. He had talked to his boss while in Stockton, so he knew everything was going as planned. *It would be nice to sit down in front of the television for a few minutes before I need to pick up Dean and Lucy. Well, I'll get rid of whoever this is,* he thought.

Harry went to door and opened it just enough to see who it was. *Oh no, not again,* he thought. *She just won't take no for an answer. Oh well, the boss told me what to do.* He opened the door wider to let her in.

"Hello there, Mrs. Boyd. How wonderful of you to come and pay me another visit. So, what can I do for you today?" Harry asked pleasantly.

"All right, if I come in, Mista Miller, it's awfully hot out heeyah, don't ya thank?" asked Frances Boyd while pushing her way into the house. She had barely gotten inside when she looked around. *Why, it's jest like the last time. He hasn't changed a thang. How odd. The door was open t'the master bedroom, an' jest like b'fore, a full bed an' a single. That is jest weird, an' there's only a little table in the otha bedroom. Why would both of 'em sleep in one room? This place really needs a woman's touch,* she thought.

"Guess yua wondrin' why I'm back. I always say helpin' neighbors is what we should do, an' bein' the Christian I am, I wanna hep ya. Don't ya thank that's the Christian way?" suggested Frances.

"You know, I do, Mrs. Boyd. I think you were called to do God's will," responded Harry.

"I was jest wondrin' if ya had time to thank of anyone ya could call in that Chicago City of yuas that could hep my wonderful husband, Allan? I would love t'surprise him. Don't ya thank that would be a great surprise?" Frances insisted.

"I do indeed, Mrs. Boyd. You know I was talking to my boss just the other day about you," replied Harry.

"Ya were? Really? I mean of course ya were. My Allan's the finest man, an' bein' in a bigga area like Chicago t'spread the word is jest what the Lord wants fo us—er, him. Don't ya thank?" Frances asked.

"I do, ma'am. I really do," Harry answered. "Now, you agree this should be a total surprise, right?"

"Yes, sir, I do. Uh, what did yua boss say? Uh, could ya tell me yua boss's name? I would love t'call 'im personally or thank him personally," Frances exclaimed. She was so excited. *I'm gonna get out of this godforsaken town an' move up into a real city—Chicago. I can't wait t'tell my family back home. They never thought Ida eva make it. I can't wait t'rub it in their faces that Imma—I mean we're movin' t'Chicago. Chicago, look out, heerah comes Frances—uh, Frannie Boyd!* she thought.

Frances was so caught up in her thoughts she missed out on what Harry was saying.

"Please forgive me, Mr. Miller. My mind was elsewhere. Would ya mind repeatin' what ya said?" Frances asked apologetically.

Yeah, I'll just bet your mind was elsewhere, Harry thought.

"I was saying that my boss is coming down on Friday. Perhaps we could all get together. How does that sound to you? We've got a lot of connections in Chicago, and I've talked about how talented and devout your husband is. My boss is anxious to meet you and insists it's only the three of us, but this must be a complete secret from everyone. Would that be a problem?" asked Harry.

"No, no, no, of course not, Harry. I can call ya Harry, right? I was jest thankin' if we're gonna be such good friends, I need t'call ya Harry, an' yua can call me Frances or Frannie, if ya prefer. My bess friends call me Frannie, an' I b'lieve we're gonna be friends, don't ya thank?" insisted Frances.

No one—not one single person ever called Frances *Frannie*. It could be because she enjoyed talking about herself so much she never had a best friend. But whatever the reason, she just thought since she was going to the big city that she would reinvent herself. *I know Chicago'll love me. Maybe Harry an' his boss'll git my Allan that big church in the center of town, the United Methodist Church of Chicago,* Frances thought.

"Oh my goodness, Harry. Do ya thank yua boss'll want my Allan t'come an' be head minista at the United Methodist Church of Chicago? This would be my dream—er... I mean *owwah* dream come true," answered Frances. She could barely contain herself.

"I guess you'll just have to wait and see, Frances... I mean, Frannie," Harry replied with a laugh. He added, "I just had an idea—no, it's no good. I'll see you on Friday, Frannie."

"What? What? Please don't stop. What was yua idea, Harry? Imma sure it's gotta be great. Please tell me!" insisted Frances.

"Okay, well, I was just thinking perhaps we could make this more of a windfall for Pastor Boyd if we pretended you were leaving him for another pastor in a bigger town. Then when he finds out that he's been chosen for a church in Chicago, and he goes to the windy city, and in front of the church is y-o-u! What a wonderful surprise!" explained Harry.

Frances kind of laughed. "Uh, do ya thank he'd go fo that? I mean...well, I'll be honest with ya, Harry, since we're such good friends an' all. Allan an' I have been havin' some marital problems, lately. I even told 'im I was gonna leave 'im fo someone else if he didn't git us out of this loser town. Ya know Imma woman with needs, an' this place jest ain't doin' it fo me. Do ya blame a woman like me, Harry? I'll betttcha ya ain't eva been with a pastor's wife b'fore, have ya?" Frances asked while she inched closer to Harry. She began unbuttoning her blouse with her right hand while her left hand was reaching out to caress Harry, and that's when he stopped her.

THE SISTERS SPURLOCK

"Frannie, don't tempt a man like me. I'm only human, and you are some woman," Harry said uncomfortably. *The very last woman on Earth I would go for is this broad*, he thought.

"Oh, I was only teasin' ya, Harry. Imma one-man woman, ya know. I like yua plan, Harry, what do I need t'do? I cannot wait t'see Allan in Chicago with me on the front steps of the church. He's gonna be so shocked!" exclaimed Frances.

"Great, this is what I was thinking," Harry explained as he laid out his plan for her.

Frannie said, "Okay then, I'll see ya on Friday at 8:00 p.m. at the old shack on Cardinal Dr. right b'yond the city limits. I need t'leave my letter fo Allan, right? Oh, I can't wait!"

After Harry saw the car pull away, he called his boss.

"The plan is in motion," he said and hung up.

CHAPTER 30

DAPHNE COMES HOME

Sheriff Charles Hall's office

Shelia arrived early to work. She had so much to do, and Sheriff Hall had told her he wouldn't be in until 9:00 a.m. She thought, *I'm so glad he's comin' latta. He works so hard an' neva stops. Someone is always asking fo hep, an' he simply can't say no, an' with the fair comin' up, I know, I'm gonna introduce him to Bertha. She would make a good wife, an' she can cut faar wood and*—Shelia didn't get to finish her thought when the phone rang.

"Grayton Sheriff's Department, may I hep ya?" Shelia answered.

"I need to speak with Sheriff Charles Hall," the voice said.

"I'm sorry, but Sheriff's not in yet. Can I take a message? This is Shelia."

"Well, Shelia, would you tell Sheriff Hall to contact Arnold Deal at ###-3-9-0-8? I'm Stockton's fire investigator," said the voice on the other end.

"I sure will. Ya have a nice day, okay?" replied Shelia, but the man had already hung up.

THE SISTERS SPURLOCK

The Scholls' house

"I think I could ask Mr. Peters if he would hand out a certificate to each of you," Victoria told the girls the night before. "Would you like that?" Victoria asked her daughters.

I'm sure Mr. Peters would do that. I mean, after all, it's helping educate children, and that's what it's all about. Yes, I think he will do it, she thought.

"Ya betcha, Momma!" Rosie answered. "This is gonna be the best gradiation in the world!"

"Best gadiation in the wuld!" echoed Tati. Even though she still needed assistance on her *R*s, she had learned all the letters of the alphabet, and that was quite an accomplishment for a three-year-old.

The Shelbys' house

"Ya know how proud I am of ya girls? This has been a rough summa, but it's gittin' betta, an' it's 'cause of ya girls. Do ya know how much I love ya?" Rita asked her girls with pride.

"We love ya, Momma!" cried both Val and DaisyBelle.

Rita went over to the little record player and put on Manfred Mann's new 45 single record, "Do Wah Diddy Diddy." Rita and her daughters loved that song the first time they heard it, and Rita had bought the 45 record as a surprise for the girls. They began dancing and singing. They were having such a good time together, and for the first time, they didn't need to worry about money. Rita felt liberated. She was not only free from Carl but had his life insurance policy and would be receiving a check soon in the mail. Oh, to be so liberated and free from worry, but if they only knew, they were being watched from a face staring at them through the bedroom window. They were simply oblivious. In that moment, they were alive and carefree, but it wouldn't last.

THE GHOST COMES OUT

The Hutchinses' house

"Momma, are ya 'cited 'bout our gradiation? Maybe I can git Uncle Bake t'come an' take pictures. Whattdoya thank?" asked Monty excitedly.

"Well, I suppose it won't hurt t'ask, but ya know Bake's very busy. I know y'all have had a good time with ya friends, Monty, but what 'bout Alvin? He's missed seein' his big brother. Perhaps ya might take him with ya t'summer school fo the 'mainder of the week? I thank it'd be good fo him, an' ya know those little girls Tati an' DaisyBelle jest love havin' him round," Mrs. Hutchins insisted.

"Okay," Monty said with a sigh. "I guess it'd be all right." *I know, Deano an' I can play chase with the others, an' the younger girls can take care of Alvin. Yeah, that'll work*, he thought.

While Monty was helping Alvin to get cleaned up for dinner, Bake came ambling through the kitchen door.

"How's my favorite big sister and two favorite nephews?" he asked sneaking a bite of Mrs. Hutchins's famous meatballs.

"Did I time it right again? Are you having your famous spaghetti and meatballs tonight?" Bake asked jokingly.

"Ya know we are, Uncle Bake. We have spaghetti an' meatballs every Monday night," said Monty laughing.

"Hey, Uncle Bake, ya thank ya could come t'owwah gradiation on Friday an' take pictures fo the paper?" Monty asked pleading.

"You mean your graduation? I'll ask my boss, but I think I can make it. What time, my little nephew?" Bake answered while giving Alvin a big hug.

"Don't know yet, we're talkin' 'bout that tomorrow. I'll let ya know, okay?" Monty said enthusiastically. Alvin, who was standing beside Bake, started jumping up and down.

The Smiths' house

Johnny and Billy couldn't wait to get home to discuss the graduation with their parents. Both Silvia and Jackson were in the kitchen when the boys came flying through the front door.

"Guess what? Guess what? We gonna have that gradiation, Momma!" shouted Johnny.

"An' Rosie wants t'know if ya can make some of yua cookies?" added Billy.

"Why, course I can! That Rosie's a little firecracka, ain't she, boys?" Silvia replied with amusement.

Jackson turned to his boys and said, "T'day is inpotant. Miss Daphne's comin' home, an' we needs t'do anythang we can t'hep her. Me an Momma are countin' on you boys t'hep out."

Billy spoke first, "Ya know we love Miss Daphne, Daddy. We gonna hep her in any way."

"Yep, we gonna hep Uncle Clayton too. He might need us, ya know," Johnny proclaimed.

Jackson and Silvia looked at each other. They were proud of their boys. Since the news had come out about their Uncle Clayton and Miss Daphne, the dynamics in the Smith family changed. No longer did they feel as though they were employees, they felt like they were family, and Silvia and Jackson had taken turns with Clayton to stay with Miss Daphne in the hospital. Silvia was also eager to have a baby in the family. She couldn't wait to be a nanny to the baby, but first they must make sure Miss Daphne was okay.

Around 3:00 p.m., Daphne's car drove into the circle of her driveway. Clayton was behind the wheel, and Daphne was sitting as close to him as she could get. Since the town now knew she was married, she was going to let them know just how happy she was despite her blindness.

Silvia saw the car first and called to Jackson and her boys that Miss Daphne had arrived. They came outside to meet her. Silvia came up to the side of the car and opened it for Miss Daphne.

"Miss Daphne, I here fo ya, an' so is Jackson an' owwah boys," Silvia said proudly.

Daphne turned toward Silvia's voice and smiled. She had bandages covering both eyes. Her blond hair was touching her shoulders, and her hands were feeling their way across the front seat toward the door.

Clayton spoke up, "I'm going to carry you in, honey."

THE GHOST COMES OUT

"Now, what did we just talk about in the car, Clayton? I must learn to get around, and I will before our baby's born. I am not going to be dependent on everyone, agreed?" Daphne requested sweetly.

I have totally misjudged her. Even though she blind, she not gonna let it ruin her life. I do believe God gave huh this baby b'cause he saw somebody special, thought Silvia.

Daphne got out of the car and breathed. "Tell me, Clayton, are your roses in bloom?"

"You know they are, honey, but they are our roses, and not one of them is as beautiful as you," Clayton said reaching for Daphne's hand. Daphne blushed a deep red.

"Johnny, Billy, how's summer school going?" Daphne inquired while reaching to take the boys' hands.

"Miss Daphne, we havin' a gradiation on Friday, ain't we, Billy?" Johnny asked eagerly.

"Yep. Miss Daphne, would ya like t'come?" Billy asked suddenly.

Before Daphne could respond, Silvia interrupted, "She probly need huh rest. Don't botha with the boys, Miss Daphne."

Daphne turned to face her family.

"Please forgive me, but we're all family, and going forward, my name is Daphne. Boys, you can call me Aunt Daphne if you like."

Daphne turned to Silvia and said, "Silvia and Jackson, please call me Daphne, because now I can go by the name I've longed to say out loud. My name is Daphne Smith!" she said with pride.

Silvia, Jackson, Johnny, and Billy went to embrace her. Clayton was a bit hesitant because of her injuries, but he knew how headstrong his wife was, and the sooner he got used to her independence, the better.

"Of course, I'll come to your graduation. I wouldn't miss it, boys," Daphne said eagerly. "Clayton, we will need to bring something to the graduation. Don't let me forget."

As the Smith family made their way into the mansion, another set of eyes was on them.

It makes me sick t'see that niggah touchin' Miss Daphne. I cain't believe they gonna have a baby togetha, well, we'll jest have to see 'bout that, he thought.

Tuesday

The eight summer school kids and Alvin showed up at the Scholls' house the next day for school. They had discussed the graduation with their parents. The children decided they would put on a talent show for the parents, sing songs, and have Superintendent Marcus Peters hand out a certificate to each of the eight kids.

Each child thought of what they would do for the talent show. They practiced their talents all morning.

Only three more days until their graduation. This is going to be the graduation day they will all remember, he thought.

CHAPTER 31

THE CARNIES COME TO TOWN

The Dakota County Fair happened once a year, and residents from both Grayton and Stockton came to it in droves. Everyone loved the fair. This was the time when farmers showed their horses, goats, cattle, sheep, and pigs. It was war between the livestock, farmer against farmer. Oh, what fun it was for those competing. The lawn mower races and the tractor pulls were fun for the gear heads, and every mother wanted their little princess to be voted Princess or Queen of Dakota County Fair.

The children looked forward to the fair because of the games, rides, and of course the food, but the ones who loved the fair more than any were the carnies. That's right, the carnies. They loved traveling from town to town and county to county to put on a show for a few days, and coming to Dakota County was no exception.

There were several carnies who loved to see how much money they could swindle out of the townfolk, and two of those were the Dennis brothers, Mikey and Walter.

Mikey, a.k.a. Hamerhead, and his brother, Walter, a.k.a. Squirt, were two carnies who made money at the fair. They made cash because no one ever won at their games, and people kept coming back to try and win their date or child a stuffed animal. It never happened. Hamerhead worked the game called the Strength-O-Meter. He would stand next to the a tower and goad men to show off how strong they were by using a heavy hammer to hit a pad and see if a bell could be rung at the top. He was a master at getting men who thought themselves strong to try his game. He had several big stuffed animals to give away if they did. These stuffed animals were brand-new, and they stayed that way because no one was ever successful enough to ring the bell—that is, until the fair came to Dakota County. Hamerhead met his match the night Sheriff Charles Hall showed up.

Squirt worked the game called the Shooting Star. This game men loved to play because it demonstrated their shooting skills. The rules of this game were to shoot out the entire red star, which was on a piece of paper, with the gun full of one hundred BBs, which were provided. Little did the player know there's a trick to winning this game, but as close as many would come, they would still leave a little of the star on the paper, and thus, no prize. Squirt found out he can't fool everyone when Harry Miller and Victoria Scholl laid fifty cents down to play his game.

Summer school

The eight students at summer school were so excited. They had promised to help out at the fair, and with their graduation approaching, this was an added plus.

"T'day, me an' Tati gonna hep with the animals. We gonna play with baby calves, ain't we, Tati?" "Y'all wanna hep?" Rosie asked Val and DaisyBelle.

"Ya bet we do. Momma said we can hep out, an' ya said we can put ribbons on the winners, right, Rosie?" responded Val.

"Yep, we always git t'hep with the ribbons, don't we, Tati?" asked Rosie.

"Uh-huh, I was hopin' to put a wibbon on the howses," responded Tati, shaking her head up and down.

"We never heped b'fore with the animals. I can't wait! Ya thank I could put a ribbon on a horse too, Tati?" DaisyBelle inquired.

"I let ya hep me, DaisyBelle," answered Tati with a big smile.

"Hey, Johnny an' Billy, y'all gonna hep park cars?" Monty laughed.

THE GHOST COMES OUT

"Ha ha," Johnny responded. "We only wish we could park 'em. I know we'd do a great job, right, Billy?"

"Ya know it. I thank we could park 'em betta than most of the people who drive here in Grayton," Billy said.

"Sure sure," Monty said laughing. "Hey, Deano, still wanna hep me an' Uncle Bake take pictures at the fair?"

"I asked Harry, and he said it would be okay. He's wants to go to the fair too, so I'm sure we'll see him," Dean replied.

"Hey, why don't we meet up somewhere at the fair. Maybe we could ride some rides or play some of the games togetha. What y'all thank?" Val suggested.

"I know! Why don't we meet up at the ice cream booth? Tonight they gonna 'nounce who wins the pony, so don't forgit yua tickets. I thank ya have t'be there t'win," Rosie reminded everyone.

"I thank it's 'spose t'be announced at 7:00 p.m. Y'all good with that?" Johnny wondered.

Everybody agreed to the time and place. Rosie was extremely excited. She wanted to win that pony badly. Her dad had promised her a pony when she turned eight, but now that he was gone, she knew she probably wouldn't be getting one. Even though Ree had left her family some money, neither she nor Tati knew how much, and even if their mother had told them, they would not have been able to fathom the amount; they were, after all, only eight and three.

4:00 p.m.

"Harry, is it okay if I go on over to Monty's house? I'm going to go with him and his uncle to the fair. I could take Lucy if you'd like," Dean requested.

"Lucy and I will walk you over to Monty's house. Remember Lucy must stay with you at all times. She's there to protect you. I'll be going to the fair too. So I'll probably run into the two of you. Do you need any money for food and such?" Harry asked getting his wallet out of his pocket.

"Thanks, Harry. You're the best!" Dean said as he took the money Harry handed him and put it in his pocket. He then reached around and gave Harry the biggest hug.

*****

"Come on, girls," said Victoria to her daughters. "You don't want to be late to help with the animals, do you? We'll pick up Val and DaisyBelle on the way, okay?"

"We comin', Momma. Me an' Tati was changin' owwah clothes. We thought we'd betta put on owwah playclothes. Just incase we be brangin' a pony home," Rosie said with a laugh as she and Tati ran down to meet their mother.

"We gonna bwang a pony home, Momma," echoed Tati laughing.

The three girls ran to the door to go with Midas in tow.

Tati looked down at her buddy and, giving him a hug, said, "Middy, we gots t'go to the faiuh. Yua stay heeyah. We be back lata."

*****

"Uncle Clayton, ya ready? We gots lots of cars t'park, don't we?" Johnny asked impatiently.

"Yeah, Uncle Clayton, we gots t'go!" echoed Billy at Johnny's side.

Clayton walked over to his two nephews and said, "Your dad's going to take you this time. I need to be here with Daphne."

Daphne was standing by his side, and she interrupted, "Oh, no, you don't! I'm just fine. In fact, I'd like to go to the fair too, and there's no reason why I can't go," she emphatically stated.

Johnny and Billy ran to her and hugged her.

"Yua the best aunt evah!" Billy exclaimed.

"Careful, boys, she's still healing, and she's carrying a gift from God," Clayton said with a huge smile. His love for Daphne had multiplied sevenfold since he found out she was pregnant. He knew with the loss of her sight, she would need to be careful, and he wanted her to stay at home, but she wouldn't think of it.

"I love you boys too. And as for you"—she turned and faced Clayton and said lovingly—"just because I can't see, doesn't mean I have to be put on a shelf. The sooner I get out and about, the better it will be for us. You must understand that, okay, honey?"

Daphne still had bandages on both eyes and preferred to wear dark glasses too. Despite her handicap, those who saw her thought she looked beautiful. She let her hair hang down her back, and she had a glow about her.

Silvia came into the living room where the four of them were. She had overheard most of the conversation when she spoke up, "Okay, boys, Clayton'll take ya t'the fair. Me an' my sista Daphne will ride with ya daddy. We gonna have us some fun t'day."

*****

"Deano will be here soon, Uncle Bake. Whatcha thank we need t'do first when we git to the fair? I know, can we ride some rides? Or go to the animals? Or git some cotton candy?" asked Monty excitedly.

"Hey, buddy, calm down. We'll do it all. What have I taught you?" Bake asked.

"I know, I know. First we work, an' then we play. Good stories are always there, we jest need t'uncover 'em," Monty said dejected.

Bake responded, "Okay, why don't we compromise? First, we can take pictures of the livestock winners. I don't see why we can't eat some cotton candy while we're taking pictures. How does that sound?"

"That sounds awesome, Uncle Bake!" exclaimed Monty.

The townfolk seemed to turn out for the fair. When Victoria, her girls, Val, and DaisyBelle arrived at the fair, they went immediately to the livestock. As the girls wandered around looking at the animals, Victoria went to find out what they needed to do to help. This year the judge of the fair was none other than Sheriff Charles Hall. When he saw Victoria approaching the judges' booth, his heart beat faster. He had been especially busy working Carl Shelby's murder and the fire at the Baptist Church. He had not seen Victoria since Ree's funeral.

"Well, hello, Miss Victoria," Charles said with a grin. "How is the Scholl family today?"

"Hi, Charles. We're just excited to be here and help out. The girls love the animals, and we try to help out every year with the pinning of the winning ribbons," Victoria answered with a big grin.

She tried to keep the tone of her voice steady. She didn't want him to think she was interested in him. Victoria kept reminding herself that he was being nice to her only because of the tragedies her family had gone through, nothing else. She didn't dare entertain the belief that he might have feelings for her.

"Well, we've just completed the judging. If you'd like to bring the girls up to our booth, we'll get them fixed up," explained Charles. He came down from the booth and walked with Victoria back to where the girls were.

"Hey, Mista Sheriff," shouted Rosie. "Are ya on a case or somethin'?" Rosie, Tati, Val, and DaisyBelle were standing outside the sheep's pen. Tati wanted desperately to hold one of the little lambs.

Val and DaisyBelle stayed back a little. The last time they had seen Charles was at their father's funeral, and they felt uneasy. He noticed their hesitancy.

"Hello, girls! It looks like it's my lucky day to be surrounded by all this beauty," proclaimed Charles.

Tati walked forward, looked at Charles, and said, "Mista Shewiff, ya thank I could hold a baby lamb? I pwomise I'll be good."

Charles bent down and picked her up. He could not resist how adorable she was. "I'm going to personally take you into the pen and let you hold one. If it's all right with your mother," he said looking down at Victoria. All the girls ran forward and wanted to hold one too.

Victoria smiled up at Charles. "As long as I can hold one too," she said laughing. The girls went with Charles into the sheep's pen. They were in the pen with the sheriff holding the baby lambs, totally unaware that they were being watched.

THE GHOST COMES OUT

She will be mine soon enough, he thought. *How absolutely perfect she's holding a lamb in her lap. Oh, if I could only stop time. How much longer must I wait? The moment will present itself,* he thought to himself. *I know I mustn't tarry. I don't want to stay too long for fear of being caught.* He blew a kiss in her direction before leaving.

Outside in the hot Tennessee sun stood Johnny, Billy, and Clayton. They were helping guests park their cars.

"This ain't a bit of fun, is it, Johnny?" Billy asked as sweat was rolling down all of their faces.

"Yeah, I know, but jest thank we git free tickets t'ride some rides if we hep, an' I don't have no money, an' I know ya don't eitha," answered Johnny laughing.

He motioned for an old truck to park in the space provided. Johnny held up his hand for the truck to stop, but the vehicle just kept coming. Johnny had to jump out of the way, or the truck would have hit him. Clayton rushed over to the pickup and opened the driver's door. He was ready to fight the driver.

"You almost hit my nephew. What were you thinking?" Clayton shouted at the driver as his eyes rested on the face of Mr. Joe himself, the ice cream man.

After the 5 Mile Race, there was certainly no love between the two men. In fact, even though the entire episode at the 5 Mile Race was Joe's fault, Joe blamed Clayton, and he aimed to get even with him.

Joe just looked at Clayton and said, "Niggah, ya need t'git ya little black sambos outta heeyah. They was in my wayah," screamed Joe at Clayton. "And if ya touch my truck, ya gonna git yua clock cleaned. Ya heeyah that, niggah?"

Joe had forgotten how big and strong Clayton was. Joe looked up at Clayton as he got out of his truck. Clayton had his hands clenched ready to take on Joe, but his wife, Raveleen, and daughter, Dorothy, got out of the vehicle too. Both looked like they were smelling something offensive.

"Ya lay a han on my Joe, an' I'll claim ya tried t'harm me an' he was jest comin' t'hep me. Ya don't wanna mess wid us, niggah. Got it?" Raveleen shouted.

"Ya know yua lying! Ya almost hit Johnny, an' ya know it! 'Sides, Uncle Clayton wouldn't touch a piece of ugly white trash like you!" screamed Billy at Raveleen. Clayton had to hold Billy back from attacking.

"Ya betta keep little sambo back. I'm a VIP of this heeyah fair. We givin' way a pony t'day!" Joe said gleefully.

Dorothy screamed, "Pops, that's my—"

She began to say as Joe put his hand over her mouth before she finished her sentence. All at once, Dorothy fell to the ground and threw the biggest temper tantrum. She was eight years old and going into the second grade. She had spent an additional year in first grade trying to learn the alphabet, how to read, and addition and subtraction. She had failed in all the subjects, but she couldn't be retained again. Look out, second grade, here comes Dorothy. A crowd had formed around them, not to help her but to observe her outburst in disbelief.

Looking at Clayton with beady eyes, Joe thought, *I'm not done with ya yet. The hour's comin' when I'm gonna rock ya world. Ya not only a niggah but ya stole Miss Daphne from us whites, an' worse, she's havin' ya niggah baby. Ya don't d'serve to breathe. The hour's comin' niggah, an' Joe's a comin' for ya!*

Luckily, another two cars pulled up and needed to park. Clayton and his nephews got back to work while the Puckett family left the parking lot for the fair.

Monty, Dean, and Bake were inside the livestock area eating cotton candy and taking pictures for the paper.

"Hey, look, Monty, it's Rosie, Tati, Val, and DaisyBelle!" Dean said enthusiastically.

"Hey, girls!" he yelled walking toward them. Lucy was right by his side. She greeted the girls with her tail wagging.

"Now, let me get a picture of the summer school group with one of their mascots," Bake said.

"Val, Rosie, Monty, and Dean, you guys get it in back and let DaisyBelle and Tati up front with Lucy. That way we can get everyone in the picture. I'll see if I can get this picture in the paper. Would you like that?" Bake asked.

THE GHOST COMES OUT

The kids were jumping up and down in excitement as they posed for the picture. The only two who were missing from the photo were Johnny and Billy. Bake promised the group he would take another picture when Johnny and Billy could be in the photo too.

"You are so sweet to take a group picture of the kids, Bake. Do you think I could get a copy?" Victoria wondered.

"I'm sure I can make that happen, Victoria," answered Bake. He then turned to Charles and motioned for him to come in a little closer.

"So, Sheriff, getting any closer to making an arrest on our local murder? And is the church fire an electrical fire or an arson? Do you think they're linked? Who are you looking at?" Bake asked. He had his pencil and paper ready in case there was a story.

"Bake, you know I can't divulge anything to you, but I promise when I know something, so will you," Charles responded. He turned away ready to present the prize winning livestock.

CHAPTER

32

And the Winner Is...

Time at the fair passed quickly. After the ribbons for livestock winners were given out, next came the pie-eating contest. They all entered it but were no match for Linus Hill. He ate nine whole pies in three minutes. That became a record at the Dakota County Fair. Then the group decided to walk the midway to see what to do next. They saw Billy and Johnny coming out of the house of mirrors. They ran over to see their friends. Billy was laughing as he approached the group.

"Y'all shoulda seen Johnny. He couldn't fine his way out. It was so funny!"

"Nah, I was jest seein' if yua was scared. I coulda gotten out anytime I wanted," said Johnny unconvincingly.

The other kids laughed.

"So, what y'all wanna do now?" Val questioned.

"I know, let's ride the roller coaster!" cried Dean. "I always say the faster the better!"

Monty looked up pleading to his uncle, "Yeah, can we please, Uncle Bake?"

"Is everybody in for the roller coaster?" Bake asked.

Tati looked up at Rosie and her mom. She didn't want to say she was afraid, but she was. She didn't like fast rides, and going on the roller coaster was the fastest at the fair. Victoria looked down at Tati with a knowing smile.

THE GHOST COMES OUT

"I do not like roller coasters. They really scare me. So, if anybody would like to ride the carousel with me while the others go on the roller coaster, the invitation is open," invited Victoria with a knowing smile.

"I wanna go with ya, Momma," Tati immediately responded.

"I wanna go with ya too, Miss Toria," said DaisyBelle. She and Tati joined hands ready to walk over to the merry-go-round.

"Does everyone else want to go on the roller coaster? If so, I'll go with Bake and take the others on the roller coaster. How does that sound?" Charles suggested.

The kids ran and got in line for the ride.

Victoria, Tati, and DaisyBelle headed to the carousel. The three of them had no idea another set of eyes was on them. He watched them as they boarded the merry-go-round. *You'll be mine soon*, he thought.

When the group got together again, it was fastly approaching the 7:00 p.m. hour. So, they decided to head on over to the ice cream booth. As they came up toward the booth, they saw that there were about thirty people already there. Silvia, Jackson, Clayton, and Daphne were among the crowd. Clayton was holding Daphne by her elbow. There was no mistaking the love between the two of them. It was quite apparent the way he looked and touched his beautiful wife that there was no one in the world for him but her.

He make me sic t'my stomach, Joe thought. *He stole the purest woman that evah was, an' now she's gotta niggah baby inside. I'm gonna show 'em. They all gonna heeyah fo me. I'll show 'em.*

Raveleen and Dorothy had gotten the booth ready. The pony they were to give away was just feet from them. He was tied up and not going anywhere. He was grossly overweight, and even though he was tied up, he wouldn't have had the energy to move if he had wanted to.

"Momma, ya thank that's the pony?" asked Rosie sadly. "I thank they've givin' him too much ice cream."

"Yes, honey, I think you're right. He does look a little sad, doesn't he?" Victoria answered. *Why would they do that to this animal?* she thought.

"If me an' Tati win, we gonna put him on a dite, an' we gonna exercise him," Rosie said with assurance. "He gonna love us, right, Tati?"

"Ya betcha, Wosie. We gonna excise him," Tati responded.

Rosie's job was never over. She being the teacher she was asked her friends if they had their tickets. They responded by waving their tickets in the air.

"Don't forgit Mr. Joe says we gotta have the ticket t'win," she reminded them.

At 7:00 p.m. on the dot, Mr. Joe stood up at the front of the booth. By then, fifty families had surrounded the booth with their children. Each child was clinging to the tickets in their hands hoping beyond hope their number would be drawn.

"Okay, we gonna make this short n sweet. 'Member, ya gotta have yua ticket t'win," Mr. Joe announced.

The summer school group stood together. Rosie, Tati, Val, and DaisyBelle were holding hands hoping one of them might be the winner. Johnny and Billy had already talked about where they might put the pony if they were to win, and Dean was hoping Monty would win. *I already have the greatest pet in the world*, he thought looking down at Lucy. *Monty needs a pony for him and his little brother, Alvin, to ride.*

"I would like t'have a volteer t'draw a ticket outta this heeyah barrel. Do I have any volteers?" asked Mr. Joe.

Every child waiting held up their hands, but Mr. Joe thought of a better idea.

"I thank I seen the lovely Miss Daphne in the audience. I thank she should pick the ticket. What say everbody?" shouted Mr. Joe.

The crowd broke into applause and whistles. Everyone was in favor of Miss Daphne picking the number. The only one who objected was her husband, Clayton.

"I don't trust that man, Daphne. He's up to no good," Clayton protested to his wife.

"Nothing's going to happen to me. Please, honey, I want to do it," Daphne pleaded with her husband.

"You know I can't turn you down," Clayton said with a smile. *Please, God, let this go okay. I swear if that man lays a finger on Daphne, he will live to regret it*, Clayton thought.

THE GHOST COMES OUT

And with that, Clayton led her up toward the front of the crowd. Daphne had on a pair of blue denim shorts with a pretty pink blouse and matching pink sandals. She had her hair pulled back in a light-pink scarf. Her eyes were bandaged, and she wore black sunglasses. Despite the heat, she looked cool as a cucumber. Clayton didn't trust Mr. Joe one bit, and with the episode out in the parking lot that day, it was no wonder, but he was so proud of his wife that he wanted to show her off at every opportunity. So even though he disliked Mr. Joe, the love he had for Daphne far outshadowed any ill feelings he had. Clayton was also conscious of where Mr. Joe was standing. While Mr. Joe was standing next to the pony on the left side of the barrel, Clayton and Daphne were on the right.

"Miss Daphne, ya lookin' beautiful t'day, ain't she, evrybody?" Mr. Joe cried out.

The audience erupted in great applause. Billy and Johnny were especially excited. They loved their aunt and were excited she was pregnant with their cousin. They wanted the community to know just how happy they were.

With a concerned look, Charles turned to Victoria and said, "There's just something not right about this."

"Miss Daphne, if ya do the honors of reachin' in heeyah an' gittin' a ticket out an' then give it t'me t'read, okay?" asked Mr. Joe.

With Clayton's help, she reached into the barrel and pulled out a number. She handed it to Mr. Joe, who reached in his shirt pocket for his eyeglasses.

"Ya know yua gittin' old when ya need these things," he said pointing to his glasses. The audience laughed.

Mr. Joe read the number, "0-1-1-4-5-7!"

There was silence in the audience as every child was looking through their tickets to see if they had the winning number. All of a sudden, someone screamed, "I got it! I got it! Lemme through! Lemme through! I gotta git my pony!" screamed the child.

As the child made her way up front, everyone saw that the winner was none other than Dorothy Puckett, Mr. Joe's daughter.

CHAPTER 33

FRAUD

The crowd froze as they saw who the winner of the pony was. Everyone began to stir, and as they did, one could hear them chant one word over and over again.

"Fraud! Fraud! Fraud!" the crowd yelled. They got louder and louder.

"Ladies an' gentlemen, this ain't a fraud. Ya saw fo yoself, Miss Daphne an' her niggah husband drew the winnin' ticket. If ya mad at anybody, it's them an' their sambo baby!" Mr. Joe shouted. He turned to leave the stage and passed by Daphne and Clayton on the way. He shoved Daphne hard to make her fall, but Clayton was right there and caught her before she hit the ground.

The crowd was disgusted by not only how Joe had rigged the pony draw but everyone there witnessed how he tried to push Daphne off the stage. Their ranting got louder and louder.

"Git him! Git him! Git him!" the crowd kept yelling. Sheriff Hall knew a fight was brewing, and he'd better do something quick.

Clayton carried Daphne to a nearby table. The audience parted for them to sit down.

"Honey, I'm fine, and the baby is too. I didn't fall. You caught me. I love you, Clayton, and you will always be my hero," Daphne said as she kissed him hard. The crowd started applauding and whistling. Those at the ice cream booth witnessed a beautiful romantic scene, and every woman there had tears in their eyes.

THE GHOST COMES OUT

Meanwhile...

Charles looked over at Bake Haas. "You thinking what I am, Bake?" he asked.

"You know it, Sheriff. I took pictures of it. He did the old magician's slight'o'hand trick. He held his daughter's ticket number in his left hand. Took the ticket that Daphne picked with his right hand. Reached into his pocket with his right hand for his glasses, and dropped the winning ticket there, and surprise, surprise! His daughter is the winner!" explained Bake.

Charles ran up to the front of the crowd and grabbed Joe by his collar.

"It's one thing you rig the pony draw, it's another to try to push a pregnant woman off a stage. You are despicable! Right now, Joe Puckett, we're going to handle the pony drawing. You and I both know this was rigged. I am now going to reach into your front shirt pocket and pull out the winner of this contest, or I will arrest you for assault and fraud. You won't like what punishment you will get once you're convicted. Now, are you going to give me the winning ticket, or shall I get it?" threatened the sheriff.

Mr. Joe, whose scam was uncovered, reached into his pocket and pulled out the winning ticket. Sheriff Hall grabbed it and said, "Ladies and gentlemen, there seems to be a mistake. The real winning number is 0-8-0-1-9-5."

Again, it was quiet as the children scrambled to look at their tickets. The pause seemed to go on for about a whole minute when suddenly a small little voice said, "I thank I won."

The crowd turned to see whose voice it was. It was none other than Sally Spangler. Slowly, Sally made her way up front as the crowd parted for her as she walked. When she got to the front, she handed Sheriff Hall her ticket. The crowd was silent as Sheriff Hall compared her ticket number to the winning number.

"Looks like we have a winner! Congratulations, Sally," Sheriff Hall proclaimed.

The crowd went wild, and this time they began chanting, "Sally! Sally! Sally!"

THE SISTERS SPURLOCK

Sally Spangler came from a broken home, was one of five children who lived with their mother, and small for her age. In fact, she was in the twenty-fifth percentile on the growth chart, but that didn't stop Sally. What she lacked in height she made up in intelligence. She taught herself to read and write at the age of two. She would start school at Grayton Elementary in the fall, but because of her intelligence, she would skip two grades.

Charles took Sally's hand and led her over to the pony. Dorothy was holding onto the animal for dear life. She wasn't about to let go of "her" pony.

"No! No! Ya can't take my pony! Is mine, right, Pops? Is mine! I already named him Pumkin. Ya can't touch Pumkin," Dorothy demanded.

Mr. Joe looked at his daughter and ordered, "Shut up, Dorothy! Git 'way from the pony. Is not yuas, no mo.'"

Dorothy refused to go, so he and Raveleen had to pick Dorothy up kicking and screaming. Everyone at the fair either heard or saw Dorothy throwing a fit as she left the midway.

The kids in the summer school ran up to congratulate Sally on her win. They agreed if they couldn't win, it couldn't have gone to a nicer family.

Sally's mother, Becky, came up to where they were standing. Becky bent down and looked at Sally. Her eyes filled up with tears as she talked to her.

"Sally, ya know we can't 'ford this pony. We barely have nuf t'feed owwah family. I'm so sorry, honey, but we jest can't keep 'im."

Sally didn't blink an eye when she spoke. She knew it wasn't possible for them to keep it.

"I know, Momma. Is too much. Ya thank I could hug 'im though?"

Victoria overheard the conversation between the mother and daughter and stepped forward.

"Hello, Miss Spangler, I'm Victoria Scholl. I'm Rosie and Tati's mother. I would like to talk to you about the pony you just won. I would like to purchase the pony from you for $300, but on one condition only, if at any time you are able to afford the pony, we would give it back to you free of charge, *and* your children are welcome, at any time, to come and ride at our house," she said.

Becky looked at Victoria as though she were seeing an angel. She then looked down at Sally and said, "Whatcha thank, honey? Do ya like that idea?"

Sally didn't speak a word. She didn't have to as she ran over and gave Victoria the biggest hug. Rosie and Tati joined in, and laughter and tears were witnessed by the crowd.

As Charles was watching this transaction, his heart was so full of love. He had waited long enough. He was going to start courting Victoria and was determined to win her heart. *Jeb, I pray you'd approve as I try to win Victoria's love*, he thought.

The summer school gang started celebrating, and Sally joined in too.

"This is the bestest day eva! Thank ya, Momma! Yua the bestest! Would it be okay if we call him Lucky? 'Cause we the luckiest girls in the world!" Rosie said excitedly.

"We ah so lucky, Momma!" Tati echoed.

And the eyes that had been observing them had not left. His clock was ticking, and the time was ever near.

CHAPTER 34

ALMOST HOME

The night at the fair was not quite over. Before they left, the children wanted to play some games. Now everyone knows most of the fair games are fixed, or rather there's a trick to winning them, but the kids didn't care, they just wanted to try. As they walked closer to the area the games were located in, Dean noticed Harry. He and Lucy ran toward Harry.

"Hi, Harry! Are you playing the games?" Dean inquired.

"Not yet. I've just been people watching. I thought I might give the games a try though," responded Harry as he observed the other kids and their parents approaching.

Charles and Bake were both thinking the same thing. *Who is this guy? What is the connection between him and Dean? Why does Dean call him Harry?* Charles came forward and stuck out his hand.

"I don't believe I've had the pleasure of meeting you. I'm Charles Hall," he said. Harry shook his hand with a firm grip.

"I'm Harry Miller. I believe you oversaw the Dakota County 5 Mile Race. You did a fine job, Sheriff."

Harry knew everything there was to know about Sheriff Charles Hall. He knew Charles was studying to be an attorney and had been offered a job at the prestigious law firm of Dicken, Wade, Hamm and Gouge. He knew Charles had come home from Memphis for the Christmas holiday and had never gone back due to the sudden death of Sheriff Braxton Hughes. He knew where Charles lived, the schools

THE GHOST COMES OUT

he had attended, how many women he had dated, and how much money was in his bank account. There was nothing about Sheriff Hall that Harry didn't know. He even knew Charles was interested in dating Victoria Scholl. Before Charles could respond, Harry turned to Dean and asked him, "Dean, I promised you could play some games. What would you like to play?"

Dean turned to Monty and wondered, "Would you like to play the Shooting Star with me?"

Monty readily replied, "Ya bet I would!"

Johnny and Billy joined them, and they went up to the Shooting Star booth to play. The girls merely watched. None of them were in to guns, and they agreed to cheer their friends on.

Walter "Squirt" Dennis was waiting for another group of suckers to come play his game. Each of the boys gave him fifty cents, and he in turn gave each of the boys a rifle.

"Ya know how this game works, boys? Well, Imma gonna tell ya how t'play. I've given each of ya a rifle. There are one hundred BBs in yua rifles. Ya need t'shoot the star completely off the sheet t'win. Any questions?" Squirt asked.

"Nah, this is gonna be a piece of cake!" answered Monty.

"Yeah, watchme shoot, Uncle Clayton. I'm gonna win somethin' for Aunt Daphne," Johnny exclaimed. Daphne, Clayton, Silvia, and Jackson stood right behind the boys to encourage them. Clayton had a tight grip on Daphne. It was as though if he let her go, something might happen to her again. He wasn't about to let anyone or thing hurt his wife.

"Momma, Imma gonna win ya somethin'," Billy said to Silvia.

"Sure ya are, Billy. Jest don't hut yoself!" Silvia responded with a laugh.

Before the game started, Squirt said, "I b'lieve we gonna have four winnas. Yep, I can see four winnas right heeyah. Now Imma gonna say 1-2-3, an' then ya can b'gin shootin'. One, two, three, GO!"

The boys started off shooting; *pow pow pow pow* went their rifles until the BBs in their rifles had been shot and there was nothing left. The stars on the pieces of paper were still there but hanging on.

"Ah, if I only had a couple more!" cried Johnny.

"Me too! I'd a won me a big animal," echoed Billy.

Squirt knew he had four boys who couldn't resist this game, so he led them on.

"Comeon, boys, ya not gonna give up? Ya so close t'gittin' that stuffed animal. Yua so close. I know next time, you'll git it. This was jest a warm-up," Squirt urged.

Sure enough, the four boys couldn't resist. They each laid another fifty cents down as Squirt loaded the rifles and handed one to each boy. The boys took aim at their star as Squirt said, "One, two, three, GO!"

Just like before, the boys shot all of their one hundred BBs, and then they were out. *And* just like before, the stars were still attached to the papers—no winners.

"Comeon, boys, one more time! I know, I betcha these men heeyah can show ya, an' then ya can try again, whatcha say?" Squirt insisted.

"Yeah, Daddy, ya can do it! Show us, Daddy!" cried Billy and Johnny to Jackson.

Jackson couldn't resist.

"Okay, jest one time," he replied. He laid a half dollar down on the table.

"Uncle Bake, please show me how t'do it, please?" cried Monty.

"Monty, you know your Uncle Bake is not a very good shot, but I'll give it my best," Bake said as he laid his money down on the table.

"Harry, show me how to do it! I know you can!" insisted Dean.

"Okay, Dean, this is for you," Harry responded, and he too put two quarters on the table.

"Anybody else? What about you, sir?" asked Squirt of Charles.

"No, this time I'm just going to watch, but there's someone in our company who can shoot petals off of flowers, right, Victoria?" Charles questioned. Victoria shot him a look of surprise.

"You're not gonna believe this, Charles, but Victoria can shoot the petals off of her mother's garden flowers. It's one of the things that made me love her more," Jeb had confided in Charles after he'd met her.

"Who told you that?" asked a shocked Victoria. She knew the only person who could have told him. She was just about to say

THE GHOST COMES OUT

something but was drowned out by her daughters begging her to show off her skills.

"I haven't picked up a gun in sometime, but I'll give it a try," Victoria declared while everyone cheered her on.

"Okay, lady an' gentlemen, heeyah yua rifles. Show the girls an' boys how t'win. On the count of three. One, two, three, GO!" Squirt yelled.

Jackson was a pretty good shot. He shot right at the bull's-eye of the star, but left one little bit hanging—no winner. Bake was a lousy shot. He left half of the star on the paper when he finished—no winner. Much to Squirt's dismay, both Victoria and Harry not only shot the entire star out but had ammo left in the chamber. Both were not just amazing shots but both understood there was a technique to winning the game. They knew all they had to do was shoot all the way around the star, not in the middle, and voila, the star fell off the paper. Squirt was simply dumbfounded. He couldn't hide his astonishment, and Tati and Rosie couldn't hide their delight and surprise.

"Yua amazin', Momma! How'd ya learn that?" shouted Rosie as she jumped up and down.

"Momma, yua 'mazin'!" echoed Tati as she hugged her tightly.

"Get what you'd like, girls," said a beaming Victoria.

Dean was jumping up and down and screaming, "You did it, Harry! You did it!"

Harry looked down at Dean with a smile and said, "Get what you want, Dean."

Dean got the biggest stuffed animal Squirt had. It was a brown dog almost as big as he was, and his arms didn't fit all around it. He squeezed it tightly and then gave Harry the biggest hug.

"Yua git t'git something, Tati, 'cause I got my pony, Lucky," Rosie explained as she hugged her sister.

"Could I git the little pink kitty cat?" Tati asked Squirt, softly pointing to a little animal on the top shelf.

"Cain't yua ask fo somethin' that I don't have t'git a ladder t'git, little girl?" yelled Squirt.

Charles stepped forward and stared Squirt down. Squirt retrieved the ladder and got the pink cat from the top shelf and handed it to Tati.

THE SISTERS SPURLOCK

Meanwhile, Monty, Johnny, and Billy ran over to Harry and Victoria asking them to play the game again.

Victoria turned to Harry with a smile and said, "I have officially retired, but I think Harry is a much better shooter anyway."

Harry smiled and said he would be happy to play the game again until everyone won. That night was one of the greatest nights of Harry's life. He won each of the boys a stuffed animal, and Squirt had to shut down his booth. Squirt feigned stomach problems just so everyone would leave. If anyone was going to scam someone, it was Squirt. That night he got tricked, and that didn't sit too well with him.

The group made their way past a few more booths until they came to the Strength-O-Meter. Mikey, brother of Squirt, a.k.a. Hamerhead, was there waiting for the group to approach. He noticed the boys had giant stuffed animals and the little girl had a pink cat. *Those are Squirt's animals. Well, I'll show 'em. No one can win this game. I'll win Squirt some of the money he's lost*, he thought.

"Why, hello there! Arentcha girls the cutest? Why I'll betcha wanna win these precious girls a doll," Hamerhead urged.

Tati and DaisyBelle, who were the shortest in the group, did not see the dolls Hamerhead had in his booth, but when they walked forward, they saw every Marian doll there was. There was Marian in beach wear, evening wear, play wear, and business attire. Hamerhead even had Marian's younger sister, Mippie, and brothers Hall and Hodge. He had Marian's fantasy house and magic car. He even had the newest Marian doll out, Darian, Marian's twin sister. Tati and DaisyBelle were speechless. They just stared at the dolls.

"I can see by the looks of these two, they are in heaven. So, who wants t'git these two beauties what they want?" Hamerhead invited.

Clayton stepped forward at the urging of Daphne.

"Girls, I'm going to try. I may be strong, but I've never done well at these games," he said to the girls as he laid five dimes down.

Hamerhead handed him the hammer.

"All ya have t'do is ring the bell at the top, an' one of those dolls is yuas, an' with yua muscles, it's a cinch," explained Hamerhead.

THE GHOST COMES OUT

Clayton took the mallet and stepped up to the tower. He swung the hammer down on the pad, and the puck went to the level that read 'anemic.' Clayton started laughing, which made everyone else laugh. He explained to Daphne the level he got.

"It's all right, honey. You're all the man I need," she said lovingly and kissed him.

Charles then stepped forward. He could tell how much getting one of those dolls meant to the girls.

Tati looked up at him and said, "If ya can win it fo DaisyBelle. I took huhs home."

Charles's heart tugged, and he said, "I'll do the best I can, Tati."

He took the mallet and stepped toward the tower. He knew there was a trick to winning this game and figured it out in college. He swung the hammer, and it landed in the middle of the pad. The puck went all the way up to the top and rang the bell. Hamerhead was in disbelief. No one ever won his game because no one knew the secret to winning.

Charles turned to DaisyBelle and said, "Which one would you like?"

"Can I have Marian's twin, Darian?" DaisyBelle asked Hamerhead.

"Uh, no, in order to win one of the Marian dolls, the bell must be rung five times. Sorry. You can have this one though," Hamerhead said, and he reached underneath the table and handed DaisyBelle a doll that had been handmade with the stitches coming out.

"You never said anything about having to ring the bell five times," Charles yelled at Hamerhead.

"Ya didn't hear me, sir. I said yua may have one of those dolls. I neva said which one," Hamerhead explained.

Charles turned to Victoria and said, "Would you like for me to ring it four more times for the doll?"

"I don't think that's necessary. Just look at the two of them," she answered.

DaisyBelle looked down at her doll and said, "I already love her."

Tati said, "She jest need a little mo love, that's all. She's bootiful. Whatcha gonna call huh?"

"Her name's Betsy," DaisyBelle responded with a smile.

And with that, the group dispersed. Each boy carried his stuffed animal, and with a smile on their faces, they left the midway.

"Let me help you with the pony," Charles volunteered to Victoria.

Victoria was more than grateful to have the help and happy it was from Charles. Rosie was so excited to get Pumkin, now Lucky, and take him home; and Tati had her pink cat she'd named Featha. Victoria drove her car, and Charles walked alongside the pony as the girls rode on his back all the way home.

When they got home, Midas met them and was thrilled to meet Lucky. This was going to be the beginning of a wonderful friendship between the two.

Across town in the small hidden cottage

He was just putting the finishing touches together. The last thing he did was to decorate the entire cottage with hay bales. *The time has finally arrived. Friday is the day I will act*, he thought. *I cannot wait until she's finally home.* He put the key in the door and locked it. *Until Friday*, he said to himself.

CHAPTER 35

Practice, Practice, Practice

It was Thursday, and the excitement from the day before at the fair still lingered with the summer school kids. They couldn't stop reminiscing about Wednesday's events. The boys and girls wanted to ride Lucky. The teacher in Rosie came out.

"Okay, now evrybody gits t'ride Lucky, but we must take turns. Imma thanking we each git five minutes on him. Val an' I, since we the oldest, will take Lucky's lead an' guide ya round the backyard. Sound good, everybody?" advised Rosie.

"I like yua idea," said Johnny.

"Me too," Billy reaffirmed.

"Ya always know how t'make it fair, Rosie," Monty said with admiration. He couldn't hide the fact he had a crush on her.

"Sounds good to me," said Dean.

Both DaisyBelle and Tati were busy playing with DaisyBelle's new doll, Betsy, and Tati's pink cat, Featha. They weren't paying much attention to what was going on, but when Rosie called them to attention, both said it was fine with them too.

"Wosie, can DaisyBelle an' me wide togetha?" asked Tati.

She knew she was too little to ride on the pony by herself. She would feel safe if DaisyBelle was with her. Besides, they could let DaisyBelle's new doll, Betsy, and Featha ride with them too.

"Good idea, Tati," Rosie said. "I thank me an' Val would feel betta if y'all rode togetha."

"I thank Momma would like it if DaisyBelle had someone t'ride with," agreed Val.

And so, everyone had a turn on Lucky. Then it was time for them to practice their talents for the graduation the next day.

"Me an' Val need t'see what y'all gonna do fo yua talent," teacher Rosie stated.

Tati had been practicing her talent and actually spoke up first.

"Wosie an' Val, I gonna say my ABCs," Tati said proudly. DaisyBelle nodded. She had encouraged Tati to do that.

"Good job, Tati. DaisyBelle, whatcha gonna do?" Rosie wanted to know.

"Val an' Rosie, I gonna read a letta I wrote my momma," DaisyBelle replied. When their father had died, Val had suggested to DaisyBelle she write their mother a letter telling her how much she loved her. What Val didn't know was that the letter was also about her. She wanted to surprise her at graduation.

"She gonna love it, DaisyBelle," said Val to her sister, clapping her hands in approval.

"Boys, what y'all doin'?" Rosie wondered.

"Me an' Billy thank we should do owwah timeses. We been learnin' owwah timeses. Billy gonna do zeros through fives, an' I gonna do sixes through tens. Me an' Billy are good at 'rithmetic, ain't we, Billy?" asked Johnny.

"Ya betcha, Johnny. We been practicin' owwah timeses at home too. Jest t'give ya peek, two times two equals four," added Billy.

"I thank that's great, boys. We wanna show we been studin' 'rithmetic here at owwah summa school," Rosie asserted.

"Yeah, I like that idea," agreed Val, "and if ya wanna use the little chalkboards, ya can."

"I know what I wanna do too," interrupted Monty. "Imma gonna draw a picture. I can use my chalkboard an practice tonight. What y'all thank?"

"I love it!" said Rosie. *Monty's a good drawer and if thas what he wanna do is okay by me,* she thought.

"I've been learning the Gettysburg Address. I thought I might recite it," Dean explained.

THE GHOST COMES OUT

Harry had gotten some *World Book Encyclopedias*, and Dean was fascinated with Abraham Lincoln. At night, he would read about different presidents in his new books, and Abraham Lincoln was his favorite.

"I haven't learned that yet, but is good yua have," Rosie stated.

She turned to Val and said excitedly, "Why don't we let Dean go last? He gonna steal the show, an' then we can git t'gethea an' sing 'This Land Is Your Land.' Everybody like it? One last thang, we gotta bow at the end 'cause that's jest whatcha do."

"Okay, thas good. Dean'll go last. We sing a song then bow. I thank it sounds great," said Val.

Dean couldn't wait to tell Harry. He was bubbling inside. *I can't believe I've been accepted by my friends, and they're letting me go last. Oh, how I wish my mom could be here. I know she'd be proud of me too*, he thought. He looked down at Lucy. He knew she understood because she was licking his hand.

"Okay, evrybody, I got an idea. What if we go round an' invite evrbody to graduation? We could bang our trash cans with sticks and invite Grayton. The more people come, then next year, we can have a bigga summa school. What y'all thank?" encouraged Rosie.

"I love that idea. Less take a vote," remarked Val.

The kids agreed to invite the entire community to their graduation the following day. So, the kids got trash can tops and sticks and walked through Grayton banging their metal lids and inviting everybody they saw to their graduation.

"Come one an' come all t'owwah summa school gradiation tomorrow at 6:00 p.m. at the Scholls' house on Raintree Road!" they all yelled.

Several people stopped and asked about it. Someone was watching them as they made their rounds through town. *I wouldn't miss your graduation for anything. I'll be there front and center*, he thought.

Marcus Peters was leaving the Board of Education when he ran right into the kids. They yelled at him to come.

"Yes, yes, I'll be there to hand out your diplomas," he said hurriedly. He didn't really want to be there, but Victoria has asked, and he just couldn't think of a quick enough excuse to get out of it. *I just hope they don't want to hug me. I guess I'll have to postpone my run until after the ceremony. My routine is going to be out of whack. Oh bother,* he thought as he got into his car to drive home.

"That man neva slows down, does he, Tati?" Rosie asked as they all watched him drive off.

"No, he don't, Wosie. He neva slow down," Tati echoed in the same voice Rosie used.

As they made their way back to the summer school barn building, Rosie reminded everybody to be at their house tomorrow, Friday, at 5:30 p.m.

"We don't need t'be gittin' here when the audance comes," commented Rosie.

They agreed they'd be there early, and with that, they went home to practice for their big day.

CHAPTER 36

FRIDAY MORNING

Friday came in with a hard dousing rain. The girls woke up to it coming into their bedroom from the leak in the ceiling.

"Wosie, Wosie, it's waining!" cried Tati. She burrowed under the covers with Featha as if the rain couldn't reach them there. Midas burrowed his head too.

"It okay, Tati. Rain only hurts witches, an we ain't witches, are we?" Rosie laughed.

"No, we ain't witches," echoed Tati, and she joined in the laughter. Midas looked up at the girls and started wagging his tail.

There was a knock at their door.

"Can a mother of two precious daughters who are graduating today come in?" Victoria asked.

She opened the door and noticed the rain coming in the girls' bedroom.

"Oh, bother," she said. "Well, that does it, we're getting a new roof!" exclaimed Victoria.

"Momma, can we 'ford a new roof?" Rosie asked with raised eyebrows.

Victoria brought the trash can over to catch the rain coming in. Then she sat down on their bed. The girls gathered around her just waiting for Victoria to wrap her arms around them. She did not disappoint them.

"Girls, remember when we went to BANK and met that nice Mr. Phelps?" asked Victoria.

"Momma, I 'member," answered Rosie.

"I 'memba too," repeated Tati.

Victoria hugged her daughters closely and said, "When Ree died, she left us some money, if you recall. So, we're going to fix up this house with some of the money. Rosie, when you found that letter, Ree told us to make some home improvements, and that's just what we're going to do, but today is not the day to think about that. Today is an important day for two precious girls. I wonder who I'm referring to?" teased Victoria.

"Momma, it's owwah gadiation day!" shouted Tati.

She and Rosie started jumping up and down on Rosie's bed. As they jumped on the bed, Midas would go up and down on the bed too. He seemed to enjoy himself immensely. None of them cared about the rain.

"Okay, girls, we've got a lot to do before graduation. Silvia's making cookies and punch. Daphne wants to provide flowers for the centerpiece. Harry's bringing barbecue, buns, and chips. He told me there would be enough for anyone who shows up. Isn't that nice? Bake's going to provide a fruit platter, and Rita's bringing some type of vegetable platter, and I'm picking up the cake at the store today. Doesn't that sound yummy, girls?"

"I thank it sounds great, but, Momma, ya thank the rain'll stop?" asked a concerned Rosie.

"I don't know, but you know what? If it rains, we'll just have it inside. So, no worries, okay?" said Victoria reassuring her daughter.

"No worries," said Rosie.

"No wowwies," repeated Tati.

And they got up ready to begin the day. Midas raced with the girls down the stairs and into the kitchen. He went out through the broken screen and then came back in to get his breakfast. Victoria had cereal and toaster pastries for the girls. She also had donuts she'd picked up at the grocery just the day before.

"Gee, Momma, this is the bes breakfast evah!" shouted Rosie, who was busy stuffing as many donuts as she could fit into her mouth.

"Easy does it, honey. I don't want you to choke," Victoria said with a laugh.

Tati wasn't saying anything because she was too busy eating her pastries. Midas was underneath the table, as was his place during breakfast. Tati gave him an entire donut, which he gobbled in two bites. Midas lay down content, satisfied, and ready to sleep off those calories.

"Momma?" Tati said as she looked up at her mother. "I'm weal 'cited 'bout the gadiation. I hope ya like what I do."

Victoria looked down at her youngest daughter with love in her eyes and said, "Anything you do I will love, and do you know why?"

"Because ya love me?" Tati replied with a big smile.

"Because I love you," agreed her mother, who hugged her so very tightly.

After breakfast, the Scholls started decorating the house just as the rain ceased. They put up homemade banners and signs in the yard. One read,

> Summer School Graduation at 6:00
> Evrybody Welcome!
> Free food an' pony rides for kids!

So while the Scholls were busy setting up for the graduation, Harry was busy doing other things.

"Harry, you really are a great cook, you know," Dean acknowledged as he watched Harry cook.

"Yes, sir, this here's my own special recipe, little friend. You've gotta let it cook slowly in this pot. You can't rush it, you know. And while it's busy cooking, I prepare my secret sauce," explained Harry.

"It smells so good, Harry. I can't wait to taste it," Dean declared. "I think Lucy wants a bite too."

Lucy was standing beside Harry. She never took her eyes off of the pot. She knew something good was in there, and she wanted a taste. Every now and then when he didn't think Harry was watching, Dean would give Lucy a little. Harry just smiled. He went over to the cupboard to collect some ingredients. He used various things in his sauce, but three of the items were paprika, brown sugar, and vinegar. The rest he kept secret. This was his mother's recipe, and he would take it to his grave before he disclosed what was in it.

"You know what, Harry? I think this is going to be the best day ever! I can't wait!" Dean exclaimed. When Harry had come to get Dean and Lucy from summer school the day before, Dean told him he was going to be the last one in the talent portion of the graduation. He went on to explain he would be reciting the Gettysburg Address.

Unbeknownst to Dean, Harry quickly made a phone call. After he hung up, he said, "I'm volunteering to bring barbecue and buns. There will be enough food to feed the whole town if they show up. I guarantee it, Dean," Harry explained.

While Harry and Dean were busy cooking, Rita and her girls were busy cutting vegetables for the tray they would be bringing.

"This is so much fun, Momma," said Val while she cut up the celery.

"I don't thank I eva had so much fun," DaisyBelle chimed in while cutting the broccoli.

Ever since Carl had died, the three Shelby girls had gotten even closer. Rita no longer had to worry about Carl coming in drunk and hitting either her or the girls. There was a calmness about the house now. Rita didn't know what happened to Carl after she left to take DaisyBelle to summer school. She didn't care. She was just happy he was gone, and with the insurance money they were going to get, she could move to Memphis to be closer to her family.

Rita looked at her two daughters lovingly and said, "Girls, I got somethin' I wanna discuss wid ya. Ya know we gittin' the insurance money. I thought we might move a little closer t'my family. Y'all could see yua grandmom an' be wid yua cousins. Would ya like that?"

Val and DaisyBelle hated to leave Grayton. They both loved it here. Their best friends were Rosie and Tati, and the thought of leaving them would be hard.

"Momma, I like it heeyah. We jest gittin' close wid Rosie an' Tati," explained Val.

THE GHOST COMES OUT

"Less talk 'bout it later, okay? We don't need t'talk 'bout it now," Rita explained.

The Shelbys went on cutting up the rest of the veggies and placed cherry tomatoes around the edge of the platter. No one said anything. Val and DaisyBelle couldn't stop thinking about moving away. As they were working on a special dip to go with the tray, there was a knock at the Shelbys' door.

"I go see who it is, y'all jest keep doin' whatcha doin'," Rita said as she hurried to the front door.

She opened the door slowly. Sheriff Hall was standing on her porch. Rita opened it wider when she saw who it was.

"Hi, Sheriff, this a surprise. What can I do fo ya?" asked Rita.

Rita didn't see this coming as Charles handed her a search warrant.

CHAPTER 37

CARL SPEAKS

"Whas this, Sheriff?" Rita asked as she took the paper that Charles presented to her.

"It's a search warrant, Rita," he said as he made his way into her house.

"Sheriff, ya know Ida letcha in. Ya didn't need t'go an' git this. Look around. I don't have nothin' t'hide," Rita said as she stepped aside to allow Charles access to the house.

The first thing Charles noticed was the broken chair shoved into the corner of the room. Rita hadn't bothered to throw it away. It was broken in several pieces, and on each piece, there was blood. He gathered up all the broken pieces and put them in bags. He looked around the entire house. There was a washcloth that had dried, and it appeared to have blood on it. Charles bagged that up too. Rita was not the greatest housekeeper, and when Carl had left and had been found in the pond, she just didn't have any desire to clean the house, and therefore, everything was just as it had been the day Carl left.

"Carl bled a lot. I hit 'em smack ovah the head, an' the charr broke. He was good an' knocked out. Serve him right fo hurtin' my Val. He was a mean man when he drank, Sheriff," Rita recalled as she followed Charles around the house.

Charles knew Carl had a mean streak when he was drinking. He'd heard plenty of stories. He went into the kitchen where Val and DaisyBelle were cutting up vegetables. Today was the day of their graduation. Victoria had invited him to the summer school graduation, and he was excited to be there and see her. *What a day to investigate a murder. Why couldn't this have been another day?* he thought, but one cannot pick a good day to investigate a homicide.

After finding nothing but the items mentioned, he turned to Rita and asked her if she and Val would volunteer to take a polygraph test.

"Would you be willing to bring Val and come down to my office?" Charles asked.

"Sure thang, if this'll git us from havin' any further visits from the law," answered Rita. She knew neither she nor Val had anything to do with Carl's death. *So why not?* she thought.

"I'd really like to have it done today, Rita. Kit Code is the polygraph examiner from Stockton, and he's here today. Could you come in about an hour?" Charles requested.

"Yeah, we'll come. I don't wanna take DaisyBelle. I'll see if she can stay at Victoria's house. Her an' Tati they so close," Rita said with a smile.

So, Charles took the items he'd bagged up and walked toward the door. He waved at the girls and left Rita's house. His gut feeling was that Rita and Val had nothing to do with Carl's death nor did they know who did, but he needed to eliminate them once and for all, and this was the way to do it.

An hour later

Rita and Val were at the Grayton City Hall Council Chambers, which was where the sheriff's office was located. They were met by Shelia, Charles's secretary.

"Hello, can I help ya?" Shelia asked Rita and Val. She acted as though she had no idea who they were or why they were there.

"Uh, hi, Shelia. Sheriff ask us t'come down. We gonna take that lie detector test, ya know. We ain't got nothin' t'hide, so here we are," Rita explained.

"Uh-huh, y'all can take a seat ovah there. I'll ring the sheriff," Shelia said as she motioned for them to sit on the bench across from her desk.

Shelia picked up her phone and dialed the sheriff.

"Sheriff, the Shelbys are heeyah. Ya want me t'send 'em on back?" The sheriff said yes, so she told Rita and Val to go on back.

Rita had to calm Val down because she was nervous.

"Honey, ya jest gotta tell 'em the truth of what happened. We both know we didn't do nothin'. Jest tell 'em the truth, an' ya know what? Imma gonna be right there in your heart the whole time, okay? So ya ain't got nothin' t'worry 'bout," Rita said to Val reassuring her. They hugged each other as the sheriff came out to meet them.

"Thank you for coming down, ladies. I'd like you to meet the polygraph examiner, Mr. Code," Charles said as he introduced them.

"I'd like to polygraph the young girl first, if you don't mind," Kit requested. He looked at Val and gave her a reassuring smile.

"I promise I won't bite," he added, and Val nervously smiled.

He took Val into a room and closed the door. While Val was in with Kit, Rita and Charles were in another room.

"Imma glad ya wanted us t'come down 'cause now we can put this thang t'rest. I don't thank we'd had a good night's rest since Carl died. Ya know the girls been havin' night terrors. They thank they hear thangs outside at night. I told 'em it's their 'magination. They've been sleepin' with me the past two nights. They all I got, an' I love 'em so much. Val is so protective of me and DaisyBelle, bless her heart. Sometime it seem like she's the momma," Rita rambled.

Charles asked Rita if he could get her any coffee or a soft drink. He wanted her to feel at ease. They sat in silence for about twenty-five minutes before Val and Kit came back through the door. Val immediately went over to her mother, and because it was the relief of it being over, she cried as Rita held her. Sheriff left them together and went back into the other room with Kit.

"That sweet young girl passed every single question. She has no idea what happened to her father," responded Kit.

"Okay, good. Are you ready for her mother?" asked Charles.

"Yes, send her in," replied Kit.

THE GHOST COMES OUT

Rita went into the room, and Kit closed the door behind her. Charles asked Shelia to bring Val a soft drink and some cookies from the back room. She barely looked at the cookies; she was too nervous. Rita was Val and DaisyBelle's stability, and even though Val didn't know who killed her papa or how he got into Buckley's pond, she hoped her mom had nothing to do with it either.

Charles tried to engage Val in small talk by asking her about the graduation that night at 6:00 p.m. Val only gave short answers because her focus was on what was happening in the other room with her mother.

Thirty minutes later, the door to the room opened, and Rita and Kit came through together. Rita went over to hug Val while once again Charles went back into the room with Kit.

"She's not your killer, Charles. Both of those ladies passed with flying colors," Kit asserted.

Charles was so relieved that neither Rita nor Val had anything to do with Carl's murder. Now that they'd been cleared, he now wondered, *If not Rita, then who?* Charles told them they could go home. He was just about to call it a day when his phone rang. Tyler Bush, the coroner, was on the other end.

"Hi, Charles, it's Ty. I just heard from Marshall Cross, and the results are in. Carl Shelby's blood type was O+, but we found traces of blood type A on his clothes."

"Well, maybe it's Val's. You know he hit her. She must've bled onto his clothes," responded Charles.

"Well, that can't be. Val's blood type is B, as is her mother, Rita. There's no possible way it was the Shelbys' blood. What I'm saying, Charles, if you find out who has blood type A, then you might've found Carl's killer," explained Ty.

CHAPTER 38

PAYBACK TIME

Dorothy Puckett was one unhappy eight-year-old since Pumkin had been taken away from her. *That pony was mine fair an square. Imma gonna make Rose Scholl sorry she evah met Dorthy Puckett. If she thanks Imma bully at school, jest wait t'see what Imma gonna do at yua gradiation*, she thought.

"Pops, Imma gonna go t'that gradiation t'day. Imma gonna git my pony back," she said to her father. Joe Puckett looked down at his daughter as he thought of a good plan to get back at all of that bunch of people.

"They always thank they betta than us, but they ain't. Less plan somethin' good that'll make 'em all sit up an' take notice of us Pucketts. I got an idea. Go git them eggs we threw 'way yesterdee. Ya know the ones in the garbage can," Joe explained to his daughter.

"Pops, I don't wanna put my hands in that there can. Is dirty," Dorothy complained.

She shouldn't have said anything because she knew what was coming if she ever defied her father, but she just couldn't help herself.

"What did ya jest say t'yua daddy?" Joe shouted at Dorothy as he turned and walked toward her with his hand up in the air ready to strike her.

"Nothin', Pops. I go git 'em," Dorothy yelled as she ran to the garbage can.

THE GHOST COMES OUT

She looked in the can, and it was full of trash and old food. The idea of putting her hand into the can made her sick, but then she thought of her Pumkin. She stuck her hand into the can and found the eggs at the bottom. They were rotten, and the smell was enough to make her sick. *He was my pony. He only loves me. Imma gonna show ya, Rose Scholl, ya can't take my pony!* she thought with a smile.

The Dakota County Fair had come and gone, but the Dennis boys, Hamerhead and Squirt, had not forgotten the folks in Grayton. Although these carnies didn't know who Harry Miller was, they did know they he had won every good prize Squirt had at his booth.

"Ain't right they took us, Hamerhead. Ya know I had t'buy more of them damned stuffed animals afta that man cleaned me out. Ain't right, ya know," bellowed Squirt.

"We gotta little time off 'fore our next county fair. I'm thanking we need t'take a little trip to Grayton an even the score, whatcha thank, Squirt?" Hamerhead suggested.

So the two Dennis brothers loaded up in their 1955 Chevrolet Task Force pickup truck and headed east back to Highway 69 and Grayton, Tennessee.

*****

Frances "Frannie" Boyd was getting ready to write the letter Harry had requested she pen. She could hardly wait. In fact, she had been in a tizzy since Monday when she last saw Harry. Moving to Chicago was all that was on her mind. Her husband, Pastor Allan, had even remarked on how cheery she was and how her mood had changed.

"Why, if I didn't know any better, I'd say you had another man on the side," he had said with a laugh. She had chuckled too.

She thought back to her last meeting with Harry. *Oh, if you only knew how close I had come t'bein' with another man, ya wouldn't be laughin'. What was it that Harry had said? Oh yeah, "Frannie, don't tempt a man like me. I'm only human, an' you are some woman." Boy, he had wanted me badly, an' frankly, who could blame 'em, but he knew I was a pastor's wife, and that wasn't right. Oh, I wonda what Harry* would be like in bed? Shame on you, Frannie Boyd, *she thought with a laugh.*

Allan had a full schedule that day. He had to complete his sermon, meet with the board regarding finances, counsel a young couple, look over the hymns for Sunday with the music director, and purchase the communion wafers for Sunday. So, when Allan left for the church, Frances got right to work. She had her favorite pen and monogrammed stationery to write on, and so she began.

My Dearst Allan,

I know this is going come as a surprise but Im leaving you. I have been seeing anuther man. He wants me to go a way with him. You know I wasnt happy here. I need to go to new plases. My boy frend is taking me to new plases. Dont come looking for me 'cause you aint going to fine me. Im finlly happy. Some day you will be happy to. I know its going to be hard to get over me but try ok? I think we both need to be happy and Im going to now.

Frances

P.S. I took all our money. I knew you would want me to have it.

Oh dear, is the letter too dramatic? No, Harry said the more startlin' the letta, the betta the s'prise of Allan seein' me in Chicago. I know this is gonna hurt him because it would be impossible fo him t'git ovah me, but that will make an' even bigga s'prise. Now I must figure out what t'wear tonight, an' I must pack my bags. Allan won't be back until 7:00 p.m., an' I meet Harry at 8:00 p.m. I've got so much t'do b'fore I leave, so git with it, Frannie, thought Frances.

CHAPTER 39

Friday Afternoon

Tati and Rosie had on their Sunday best dresses. They each had on matching hats too. Rosie had a red rose in her hat, and Tati had a blue one.

"Momma, how am I s'posed t'ride Lucky in a dress?" asked Rosie fidgeting with the bow in back of her dress. She looked down at Tati and fixed her bow too.

"Your sign said Free Pony Rides, right?" Victoria asked her daughter.

"Yes 'em. Me an' Tati wrote it with ya help o'course," explained Rosie.

"Well, the pony rides are for everyone else. This day, you are graduates and hostesses. Your duty is to look nice and ensure everyone else is having a good time. Don't forget, you and the others have important jobs today," Victoria explained.

"Yes 'em. Okay, me an' Tati'll look nice an' such, an' lata we can ride Lucky, right?" Rosie asked with a smile.

"Exactly." Victoria smiled. "Your friends should be arriving shortly. Let's go and look at the tables we set up. We did invite anyone who wanted to come. I just hope we've got enough food for everyone."

Victoria didn't have to worry about food. Because at that time, coming down Raintree Road was a delivery truck, and on the side of the vehicle it read, Gouge's Memphis Barbeque. It stopped right in front of Victoria's house, and a gentleman in white got out. He walked to the door and rang Victoria's doorbell.

Victoria came to the door and opened it, "May I help you?" she asked sweetly. She noticed the big truck in her driveway.

"Yes 'em. Is this the place that's having the summer school graduation?" asked the man in white.

"Yes, it is," replied Victoria with a puzzled look on her face.

The man turned back and looked at the truck. He gave them a wave, and five people dressed exactly the same way got out of the vehicle. They began unloading tables and chairs. The tables Victoria and her girls had set were for card playing. These tables were professional catering tables and chairs.

"What's this all about, sir?" Victoria asked confused. "I believe you've got the wrong address."

"This is 1362 Raintree Road, right?" asked the man.

"Yes, but I don't understand," she responded. "We didn't order this."

"The surprise is for you. Your food worries have been taken care of, ma'am. My name is Grayson, and I will take care of the food service. If you need anything, please let me know."

"Uh, Grayson, who ordered this, and how much will this cost?" Victoria asked.

"The bill's already been paid, and I'm not at liberty to tell you who ordered it," Grayson said as he started backing away off the porch. Grayson couldn't have told her even if he had wanted to. He had no idea who had paid for this order.

There was enough Memphis barbecue dropped off at the Scholls' house to feed not only the entire town but half of Stockton too. Along with the barbecue, there were chips, baked beans, coleslaw, mac and cheese, potato salad, paper plates, utensils, various desserts, and all the sauces needed for a wonderful picnic and in a buffet style. Also included in the delivery were workers to help serve the food and the tables and chairs needed. The workers were dressed in white aprons and had the name of the barbecue restaurant on their front pocket: Gouge's Memphis Barbeque.

THE GHOST COMES OUT

When Victoria and the girls saw the food, they were so excited they couldn't contain themselves.

"Momma, ain't this gonna be the best gadiation evuh?" asked Tati, whose eyes were wide with excitement.

"Yes, honey, I do believe this is going to be a wonderful day," Victoria responded. "I don't think there's anything for us to do but to enjoy ourselves, my precious girls."

"Since our work has been done, whatcha say we git t'ride Lucky?" Rosie asked with a big grin, to which the Scholl girls started laughing.

At 5:00 p.m., Rita came with Val and DaisyBelle. In her hands was the vegetable platter they had fixed for the graduation, but when they noticed the tables and the food, they were shocked.

"Where in tarnation did this all come from?" asked Rita as she handed her vegetable platter to Victoria. "I guess ya don't need this, do ya?"

"We don't know where it came from. They just showed up, but I for one will eat your vegetable platter. I promise it won't go to waste," responded Victoria.

"The barbecue looks d'licious," said Val.

"Sure does," echoed DaisyBelle.

Both of the Shelby girls were dressed similarly with floral skirts. Val had on a purple blouse and DaisyBelle a pink one. Both girls had their hair piled high on their heads. It looked a little like a woman's head on a child's body, and Rita admitted she had spent an hour on each girl to get the right look.

"Ya hayah is so pwetty, DaisyBelle," said Tati. "Can I touch it?"

"Sure. Momma put a lot of spray in it. That's how come it can stand up," admitted DaisyBelle.

"It looks like Mawian's hayah. Imma gonna git huh back. I miss huh," Tati added.

"That would be real nice of ya, Tati," replied DaisyBelle.

What did Tati tell me? Oh yeah, Mawian's home. What does she mean by that? DaisyBelle was just about to ask Tati where she had left her, but the Smith boys arrived, and the girls rushed over to them. Both Billy and Johnny were in suits. Johnny had on a light-blue suit with a navy tie, and Billy had on a light-green suit with an emerald tie. They liked the way they looked, and they kept posing like they were male models.

When Silvia and Jackson saw the tables and food, they couldn't believe it.

"I made some of my famous chocolate chip cookies fo the teacha. Thought she might like 'em, but she probly won't even see 'em fo all the food heeyah. Did ya do this, Miss Victoria?" asked Silvia.

"No, I've no idea who ordered or who's paying for this. I cannot imagine how much this is costing," explained Victoria.

"Whoeva pay fo it has more money than sense, but I spose we gonna enjoy eatin' it, huh?" Silvia smiled as she handed Victoria the cookies.

She was proud of her boys and had admitted to Jackson she was wrong about the summer school program. In fact, since Daphne and Clayton were now living as husband and wife, Silvia had changed her opinion on a lot of things. She was thrilled that Daphne was pregnant, and the two of them had bonded, especially now since Daphne's sight was gone. Silvia mothered her. She wouldn't let her do anything for fear she might fall, but Daphne had assured her she could do a lot of things without the sense of sight.

"Silvia," Daphne said softly, "I'm not as helpless as you'd think. The inside of our house hasn't changed in two generations, so I know exactly where everything's located. It's also true of what they say about losing a sense, because my other senses have really heightened. I hear birds, bees, and little animals I never heard before, and other sounds I took for granted are now sweet music. My sense of touch has really intensified. I feel every movement my baby makes, and I know she can feel my touch when I rub my stomach. My sense of smell tells me you're making chocolate chip cookies. I hope you'll save one for me and my baby."

"Daphne, if ya want the whole batch, is yuas. I make more fo the little teacha," Silvia insisted.

"No, heavens no. I'll be as big as a barn." Daphne laughed. "Just save one for me and baby Grace," she added with a smile.

THE GHOST COMES OUT

"Ya thank is a girl, Daphne?" Silvia asked with excitement. "I would love me some little princess t'pamper."

"As I said before, my senses have heightened, and I just know, but let's not tell Clayton. He's already watching over me like a mother hen. If he thought we were having a girl, he'd confine me to the bed for the next six months." Daphne laughed.

Now Silvia was a proud mother waiting for her sons to graduate from the summer school. She couldn't have been prouder. As she turned to look around at the yard full of tables, she heard a loud noise. It was a truck, and inside was Mr. Joe, the ice cream man, and his daughter, Dorothy. They got out of the truck and made their way to one of the tables.

"Wouldn't have missed this gradation fo nothin'. Me an' Dorthy had nothin' better t'do, did we, girl?" asked Mr. Joe.

"Nope, we didn't, Pops. Look at the food. We gonna need t'take home some food in a doggie bag." Dorothy laughed.

Victoria saw them and just prayed they would be on their best behavior during the ceremony. She thought she needed to greet them. Rosie and Tati came along too.

Victoria greeted them by saying, "Hello, Mr. Joe and Dorothy. I hope you will enjoy the ceremony, and please stay for the barbecue buffet."

"Of course we be stayin'. We ain't leavin' till we eat an' Dorthy rides her pony," answered Mr. Joe.

Rosie stepped forward and said, "Dorthy, ya know Lucky ain't yua horse. I let ya ride 'im if ya want, but he's our pony. He didn't like it at yua house, an' he didn't like his name. He's lucky he's outta there, an' now he's finally happy."

Before Dorothy could answer, the Scholls had already dismissed them and turned to see their next-door neighbors approaching. Monty Hutchins and his Uncle Bake brought over their fruit platter they had prepared. Monty looked like a mini-Bake. His suit was a light gray with a red tie, and it matched his uncle's, down to the handkerchief in the breast pocket.

Bake turned to Victoria and said with a laugh, "Who is the one responsible for this spread? There's enough food here to feed three counties."

"I don't know. Gouge's Memphis Barbeque came out of the blue, and the man in charge, Grayson, won't tell me who ordered or paid for it," she answered.

"Interesting," said Bake aloud. His mind was already thinking who could afford it. The only one he could think of was Daphne Montague. *I'm going to ask Daphne Montague. It has to be her*, thought Bake. *Why would she do this? I know her nephews are in the graduation, but would she have ordered this? I will find out.* He didn't have to wait long because Daphne and Clayton came riding up. No one could miss Daphne's sports car, and as Clayton parked the vehicle, Bake was already on his way over to talk to them.

"Hello, Miss Daphne and Clayton. It's going to be a great day to have this graduation, don't you agree?" Bake asked.

"It's going to be lovely. Daphne couldn't wait to get here," explained Clayton. "I'll help get the flower arrangements, honey. You stay with Mr. Bake." The Grayton Florist Shop was just pulling up to the Scholls' house. Mr. Wooldridge, the florist, got out, and he and his helper brought out the most beautiful centerpiece for the buffet table. There were asters, dahlias, gladiolus, daisies, and peonies in an array of colors.

"Miss Daphne, that arrangement is the most beautiful centerpiece I believe I've ever seen. I realize you can't see it, but trust me, it's beautiful," Bake said.

"Oh, but I can see it, Mr. Bake. I see it in my mind's eye. I can also smell it, and just by breathing in the aroma, I know how lovely it must be," answered Daphne.

"Can you also smell the barbecue? Were you the nice person who bought enough barbecue for the entire town?" Bake demanded.

"I don't know of what you speak, Mr. Bake," Daphne said softly.

Clayton came and stood by his beautiful wife and said, "Honey, there's enough barbecue here for everybody in town and plenty to take home for leftovers."

THE GHOST COMES OUT

Victoria saw Daphne and rushed over to greet her. She whisked her away to give her a special table so that she could hear what was going on. It was just as well because Bake got the feeling she had no idea what he was talking about, but he was determined to find out who had sent the barbecue.

The last two people to arrive were Harry and Dean, with Lucy by Dean's side. Dean looked sharp. He too was in a suit, but his was more conservative. He wore a brown pin-striped suit with a brown skinny tie. There was no doubt it was expensive. He had a tall crown Victorian top hat on his head. He had made it out of black construction paper. Dean looked the part of Abraham Lincoln. All he needed was a beard. When Bake saw them arrive, he walked over to them.

"It's Harry, right? Did you see the grand buffet we're having tonight?" demanded Bake.

"No, I didn't," Harry remarked as he came closer to have a look. He was carrying the barbecue he'd made.

"You brought barbecue too? Odd that someone else thought of bringing the same entrée, only on a much larger scale. You wouldn't know who is responsible for this order, would you?" Bake asked.

"How would I know? I made my own barbecue with my special sauce," Harry shouted. He was a little frustrated, but then he thought of who might be behind the buffet, and he smiled.

"I'm going to eat yours, Harry. I know how long you've worked making it," Dean noted.

Rosie came forward and ushered the summer school group into the house. She wanted them to be ready at 6:00 p.m. The seats were filling up as more and more people came. There were so many people there that Rosie was worried they couldn't be heard in the back. Victoria called Marcus Peters and asked if he could bring the public address system to the ceremony. Marcus had just gotten back from his run.

"Yes, I'll bring it, Victoria. I really wish you'd asked me earlier. I need to shower and then run by the office. I hope you know this is a bit of an imposition, but I'll bring it nonetheless," he said in exasperation.

Victoria was a little taken aback by her boss's attitude. *Oh well, I mustn't let that ruin today. He's probably got a lot on his mind. I shouldn't let that get to me*, she thought.

The audience seemed to grow by the minutes. It wasn't quite clear if those attending were there to see these children graduate or if the barbecue had enticed them, but whatever the reason, they seemed excited. There was one person who wasn't from Grayton. The figure fit in well with dark trousers and a work shirt. A baseball cap was pulled down along with dark glasses to cover the face. The figure was there for one reason and only one reason, and it wasn't the barbecue.

Another person was there to observe and be seen. What was his agenda? He was waiting until nightfall when the ghost would come out.

CHAPTER 40

THE GRADUATION

The last one to be seated at the graduation was Sheriff Charles Hall. Victoria had told him a seat would be saved for him at the front table, but he chose to sit in back. He wanted to get to Victoria's house earlier, but Arnold Deal had kept him on the phone for some time. Charles had returned Arnold's call several times, but they seemed to just miss one another. When they finally were able to converse, Arnold kept talking, and it was hard for him to stop, but Charles had to hear what the Stockton fire investigator had to say regarding the church blaze.

"I was telling your secretary, Shelia, the other day that I needed to talk to you. I've investigated 367 fires in my career, Charles, did ya know that?" Arnold bragged.

Everyone knew how many fires he'd investigated because he told anyone who looked at him twice.

"The fire at your colored church in Grayton makes 368 fires. Yep, I've investigated more fires than anyone in this here volunteer state, ya know that?" Arnold proclaimed.

Everyone also knew he'd investigated more than anyone else in Tennessee. He was proud of himself and his job, but he was good at what he did, and he knew it.

Arnold went on talking, "Sheriff, your fire wasn't an electrical fire nor was it caused by the lightning that night. What you've got, Sheriff, is arson. Someone deliberately set that church on fire. I found traces of accelerants in the basement of the church. Gasoline was poured on every piece of furniture in the basement. That's what started your fire, Sheriff." Arnold went on talking, but Charles tuned him out when he mentioned arson. *Who would want that church burned down, and why? Could it have anything to do with Carl's murder? Are they connected in any way? It just doesn't make sense,* he thought.

As Charles took a seat in the back, he couldn't help but look around at the people there and wonder if the arsonist or murderer was in the audience. *I see Mr. Joe and his daughter, Dorothy, are here. Wonder why they'd want to come to this graduation. There seemed to be trouble wherever Joe went. They better not try to take the pony back. I need to keep my eyes on them. I know most everyone here, but some are strangers. They're probably here for the food. Those two guys in the back by the cars look familiar. Where have I seen them?* Charles thought. *Something's strange. I feel like something's going to happen. I need to be on my toes.*

The time was exactly 6:00 p.m. when Rosie and Val came out of the house and called everyone to attention. Rosie stepped up to the microphone.

"Hello, y'all. We wanna welcome y'all t'owwah gradiation. We worked hard this summa, an' we wanna show ya a little of what we been learnin'," greeted Rosie.

Val then stepped up and said, "This has been the best summa school. We all learned a lot, but I wanna thank Rosie Scholl fo havin' this here school." She stepped over to Rosie and gave her something.

"We all went in t'getha t'git ya somethin', Rosie. We hope ya like it." Val presented Rosie with a wrist corsage to wear, and she hugged her as the audience applauded. Rosie slipped it on her wrist.

"I hate that Rose Scholl," Dorothy said to her father in a voice many could hear. "Stole Lucky—I mean Pumkin, an' Imma gonna git her for that."

"Shhhhh!" said an elderly woman sitting behind Dorothy.

Dorothy turned around to face the woman and was just about to say something to her when her father punched her and told her to

THE GHOST COMES OUT

sit still. "Jest wait," he said. "Ya need t'shut yua mouth. Her time's a comin'."

Rosie went back up to the microphone.

"Me an' Val were the teachas of the summa school. We worked hard, but the others worked even harda, an' they wanna show ya some thangs they learned," she said.

"Tati wants t'show ya what she learned," Rosie introduced Tati and then sat down.

Tati went over to the microphone carrying her pink cat, Featha, for courage to get her through her performance and began saying her ABCs. She was so little and cute that the audience immediately went crazy with applause when she finished. She bowed and took a seat next to DaisyBelle. Then Val got up and introduced her sister, DaisyBelle, who walked to the microphone carrying a piece of paper and her doll, Betsy.

"My name's DaisyBelle Shelby. I'm repeatin' first grade, but I learned a lot this summa. I wrote my momma a letta when Papa died. Imma gonna read it fo ya."

> Dear Momma an' Val,
>
> Yall have alwayz ben theeyah for me. When Papa died I was sad an scard. Why can't he come back like Jesus? Yall told me Im gonna see hem agin one day. I blieve ya 'cause when I cry yall both hold me an yall tel me its gonna git bettr. I know it is 'cause I dont cry all the time now. God gave me a gif when I got yall for a momma an sista.
>
> I love yall so much.
>
> Yua frend,
> DaisyBelle

When DaisyBelle finished reading her letter, both Rita and Val rushed over to hug her. The only ones in the audience with dry eyes were Mr. Joe and Dorothy.

THE SISTERS SPURLOCK

Why's everyone cryin'? That letta was stupid. I could've done betta if I wanted, I jest don't happen t'want to, Dorothy thought.

Rosie went back up to the microphone and introduced Monty. He ambled up to the mic and said, "Name's Monty Hutchins. I live next door. My uncle's Bake Haas, an' he's the best uncle in the world. Imma gonna draw a picture of my uncle," explained Monty.

He preceded to draw a picture of his uncle on the little chalkboard. He also drew a picture of Midas and Lucy. For a second grader, he was quite good, and the audience showed their pleasure with a healthy applause. He bowed and took a seat next to Dean.

Val went up to the microphone next to introduce the Smith brothers. They wanted to do their talent together. While they made their way up to the podium, Joe and Dorothy made their way to their truck. Silvia and Jackson were sitting up front. They didn't want to miss a thing, so they had borrowed Daphne's Kodak Brownie camera to take pictures of the children. Jackson was a pretty good photographer and had managed to capture the boys and girls in the summer school and had taken a lot of random photos of the crowd.

Billy Smith spoke up first in the microphone, "Name's Billy Smith. Me an' Johnny, we like t'do our timeses. Imma gonna do my timeses from zero t'fives. I like my timeses," he said as the audience chuckled.

The boys were nervous. Neither Smith brother had ever been on stage before. Billy didn't realize how nervous he would be, so it didn't take him long to recount his multiplication facts up to the fives. When he stepped aside, it was Johnny's turn, and he was speeding through the times tables as fast as he could so that he could sit down too.

While the boys were on stage, Joe and Dorothy were rummaging around in their truck. They located the newspaper they had put the rotten eggs in and quickly got out of the truck. Before they could get back to their table, the Smith boys had bowed and were leaving the stage as the audience applauded and cheered. No one was prouder than Silvia or Jackson.

The two men Charles had seen were not part of the audience. They were actively going through the parked cars looking for any-

THE GHOST COMES OUT

thing that wasn't nailed down to take. They had stolen money, cigarettes, and one of the men carried a radio he had seized from the unlocked cars. As they were making their way back to their truck, Joe and Dorothy made their way through the crowd loaded with the rotten eggs. Charles saw Joe and Dorothy approaching the front, and he intervened. Then he started running in their direction, but they doublebacked, and Dorothy ran right smack into the two men. The eggs broke all over the two men, Hamerhead and Squirt. While Joe hurled unbroken eggs toward the stage. He got four eggs off before Charles tackled him. The eggs hit Dean's tall crown Victorian hat. They slowly dripped down from his hat onto his suit.

The two men who ran into Dorothy dropped their stolen loot. They were dripping in rotten eggs too, and that's when Charles remembered who they were.

"Okay, Dennis brothers, you're under arrest for burglary, but you're not getting into my squad car until you've washed yourselves off. Go get the hose," Sheriff Hall admonished.

"Joe and Dorothy, you're under arrest for disorderly conduct and disturbing the peace," Charles added.

"Nah, I ain't rided Lucky...er Pumkin! I wanna ride my pony, an' we ain't got our babeque yet, Pops! I want my food!" screamed Dorothy.

"Get in, Dorothy! You're not getting to ride the pony or eat the food! You're going to jail! Now get in!" Sheriff Charles shouted.

The four who were arrested crammed into the squad car as Charles sped off to the jail, with the windows down, of course.

The smell of the eggs had disrupted the graduation as some of the audience was gagging from the aroma, but then Dean stood up. He didn't move as the eggs dripped down on his suit. He didn't even get upset. Instead, he turned and faced the audience, and without the aid of a microphone, he recited the Gettysburg Address. When he completed his recitation, he bagan singing "This Land Is Your Land," and the other boys and girls joined in, as did the audience. Those who attended the graduation said they'd never seen anything like it. The children went on with their graduation as if nothing had happened. Before giving out diplomas, Dean washed off and changed into shorts and a shirt, and Superintendent Marcus Peters didn't recoil too much when Dean accepted his diploma.

The caterers got rid of most of the rotten eggs smell with detergent and peroxide, and not one single person left. One spectator never took their eyes off of the children, especially Dean, and one of them was just waiting until nightfall when the ghost would finally come out.

CHAPTER 41

THE GHOST COMES OUT

The barbecue was enjoyed by the entire town and a few visitors who just happened to stop by. The boys and girls couldn't wait to eat, but first had to make sure all of their guests went through the line first.

"Why can't we go first?" Monty began. "It's our gradiation."

"Momma always says the hosts an' hostesses go last, an' that's jest how it is," explained Rosie.

"Ya don't need t'worry, Monty. Food ain't goin' nowhere. There's nuff food fo us all," Val said reassuringly. So, the graduating group of boys and girls were at the very back of the line waiting their turn to eat.

Jackson Smith took pictures of the boys and girls as well as the crowd attending the ceremony. He wanted them to remember the day and who attended. There was one individual at the back with a baseball cap, shades, and dark trousers who would turn away every time Jackson got near to take a photo, but Jackson was able to capture the person in the distance in one of his pictures. *Wonder why he don't wanna have his picture made? He jest camera shy*, Jackson thought. Little did Jackson know.

Daphne and Clayton were seated with Victoria and Rita at a table close to the front.

"This is delicious barbecue, Victoria, and you say you've no idea who ordered it?" Daphne asked between bites of the the sandwich she was eating.

"No, I've no idea, and the head caterer, Grayson, would not tell me. It's such a mystery," Victoria explained.

"Ya know, I don't care," Rita replied. "I'm jest so grateful owwah kids did such a wonderful job, an' whoever paid fo the barbecue is A-OK in my book!"

"I agree, Rita," Daphne acknowledged. "I think your kids did remarkably well, and I'm so glad Dean stood up and recited the Gettysburg Address. I know that couldn't be easy with rotten eggs dripping down the front of his suit. He did such an amazing job."

"How did you know the eggs were dripping down his suit, honey? Oh my gosh, you can see, can't you?" shouted Clayton.

"Remember what the doctor told me? He said I may get vision back in my left eye. Well, it's not perfect, but because I was up front and close to the children, I could see. I still have no sight in my right eye. I didn't want to say anything for fear it was a fluke, but I think it's just going to keep getting better, honey, but could we keep this quiet? Until it's certain, I don't want to let it out just yet," Daphne explained. Before Daphne had finished talking, Clayton was out of his seat and was kneeling by Daphne's side. He had her in such a tight embrace.

Clayton looked at her and said, "God is so good to us, Daphne. He's bringing back your sight, and he's blessing us with a baby. How can two people be as lucky as the two of us?"

Victoria and Rita were wiping away tears as they witnessed this sweet scene between the two lovebirds.

"If y'all don't stop it, Imma gonna have t'redo my makeup, an' if y'all only knew how long it took me t'look this way, y'all would stop," Rita explained as the group started laughing.

"I'll second that." Victoria laughed.

Unbeknownst to them, the stranger at the back could not stop staring at Daphne and Clayton. The figure watched the two of them and how they acted together and was aware Daphne had lost her sight. *What was it I heard? Oh yes, she had lost her sight due to that fire. How tragic. She seems to have adjusted well,* the stranger thought.

*****

THE GHOST COMES OUT

The crowd of people who came to the ceremony were dwindling. They came to see the kids and eat, and as they had accomplished both, they were leaving, but not before they came to say something to the children. The one figure in the baseball cap with dark pants and a plaid work shirt who had stood at the back and watched the ceremony did not come close to the kids. The figure seemed to be watching them but never approached and was one of the last to leave. No one seemed to notice other than Jackson, who had taken pictures of everyone in attendance. *Odd fella, didn't even git any barbecue. Weird. Wonda why he came in the first place? Oh well, we all gots owwah reasons*, he thought.

After the kids had eaten, Rosie ran up to her mother and asked if they could have a slumber party at their house.

"Ya know, Momma, we done a lot of good thangs t'day, an' we was all wondrin' if we could have a sleepovah at the house. I know what ya thankin' the boys'll have t'stay downstairs, but that it be okay, wouldn't it, Momma?" Rosie asked so earnestly, and of course, Tati had to echo her sentiments.

"It be okay, wight, Momma?" echoed Tati.

"Well, I think we would need to ask parents if it's all okay with them," said Victoria smiling. "If they say it's okay, then it's fine with me. Everyone have a sleeping bag?"

"Yay, Momma. Me an' Tati'll go ask," answered Rosie.

So each child went to their parents and asked. When Dean went to Harry to ask, Harry responded without hesitation.

"Yes, Dean, you can go, but make sure Lucy goes with you," he added. *This works out great. Now I won't have to worry about Dean while I keep my appointment with Frances Boyd. I can't be late for my 8:00 p.m. date*, he thought with a smile.

The other kids got permission from their parents to attend. They went to their homes to change clothes and get their sleeping bags. They were going to have a night they would all remember.

By the time the children got back over to the Scholls' house, the sun was going down. They rode Lucky once more before it was time to put him up for the night.

"Ya know, this been the best day evah!" exclaimed Johnny.

"Ya got that right, Johnny. I don't know when I had so much fun," echoed Billy.

"I gotta idea!" shouted Monty. "Y'all know the story 'bout Polly Tartar?"

"Nope, nevah heard of her," Billy answered.

"Well, y'all know the old Summers house? Ya know the one with the painted window upstairs?" Monty explained.

"Oh yeah, I always wondered why it's painted," noted Val.

"That's 'cause old Polly Tartar was this girl, an' she got invited t'this outdoor dance. Her momma got her the prettiest dress in all of Grayton. Well, story was that there was a storm comin', an' the dance had to be cancelled. Ya know what Polly did then?" testified Monty.

"Nuh-uh!" responded Val.

"Well, she cursed God fo sendin' the storm," yelled Monty.

"Uh-oh, what happened then?" DaisyBelle asked transfixed to Monty.

"From outta nowheres came a lightnin' bolt, an' it went right through that window an' struck her down an' killed her," Monty insisted.

"Aww, ya kiddin'. That didn't happen." Johnny laughed.

"Then why is that window painted white?" stressed Monty.

"Ya know, he's right. It is painted white. I go by that house all the time, an it's painted white!" asserted Val.

"That's not all, ya know. They say the reason it painted white is 'cause if it wasn't, then yua could see Polly Tartar's impression on the window. If Imma lyin', Imma dyin'!" shouted Monty.

"I b'lieve ya, Monty!" yelled DaisyBelle.

"Me too!" echoed Tati. "I don't wanna go by that house 'cause Momma say it ain't nice to cuss God. Wosie, we don't cuss God, do we?"

"No, Tati, we don't. It ain't right!" Rosie added, "But the only thang I gotta say is Polly must've wanted t'go to that dance pretty bad, huh?"

"Okay, now that everybody agrees it's not right to curse God, why did you tell us about this story, Monty?" Dean questioned.

THE GHOST COMES OUT

"Well, I learnt this new game called the Ghost Comes Out, an' it has t'do with Polly Tartar. She's the ghost," answered Monty.

"How d'ya play it?" Billy asked.

"Okay, y'all, this is how ya play the game. There is one Ghost Polly, an' evrybody else is here at home base. While Ghost Polly goes an' hides, we all say, 'One o'clock, two o'clock, three o'clock, four o'clock, five o'clock, six o'clock, seven o'clock, eight o'clock, nine o'clock, ten o'clock, eleven o'clock, twelve o'clock, the ghost comes out.' After we say that, we go an' look fo the Ghost Polly. If Polly catches us, then we become ghosts. If ya make it back t'the front porch an' touch this here chair, which is home base, then Polly can't touch ya. The first one t'git caught becomes Ghost Polly the next round. Any questions?" Monty asked.

"If I get touched and become a ghost, can I touch somebody else?" Dean asked.

"Yep, ya sure can. An' the last one t'git caught is the winna. I might tell y'all I've been the winna a lot," Monty said confidently.

"What if the Ghost Polly don't touch nobody?" Johnny asked.

"Then that person is the ghost agin. Make sense?" explained Monty.

"Yeah, Imma gonna tell y'all right now, when I b'come the ghost, all y'all are gonna be touched 'cause I am f-a-s-t!" Billy proclaimed.

"Yeah, whatever, Billy, I ain't scared of yua at all!" replied Johnny as he nudged him off the porch. The other boys and girls laughed.

"Okay, y'all ready t'play? Who's gonna be the ghost?" Rosie wanted to know.

"I can be it t'show ya how t'play," replied Monty. Everyone agreed that Monty should be the first ghost.

So, the other children stayed on the porch and began the game by saying, "One o'clock, two o'clock, three o'clock," and went all the way to twelve when they said together, "twelve o'clock, the ghost comes out!"

Dean looked down at Lucy and said, "Okay, girl. You stay here."

The boys and girls began looking for Monty. Billy and Johnny were the first to venture out beyond the front porch followed closely by Rosie and Dean. Val, Tati, and DaisyBelle were more reluctant to venture out too far. All at once the ghost, Monty, came out from nowhere and touched Val first then DaisyBelle and Tati.

"Where'd ya come from?" inquired Johnny. "Ya scared us to deaf!"

"That's the whole purpose of the game," Monty said as he raced to get Dean.

Val, Tati, and DaisyBelle ran around trying to help Monty touch the others. Rosie and Billy got past them and managed to touch home base. Johnny saw an opening and took it to run past all the ghosts to touch home base, but Dean was caught trying to run around a bush. Everyone came back to the porch exhausted and excited.

"This game is crazy!" said Billy. "Ya neva know where the ghost is."

"I know," responded Rosie. "Great game, Monty!"

"Okay, whoja touch first?" asked Johnny

"I think I got Val first, right?" Monty replied.

"Yep, I guess Imma Ghost Polly," Val admitted. "Y'all watch out 'cause Imma gonna be a ghost who don't come out."

The boys and girls started the count of, "One o'clock, two o'clock," until they reached twelve and said, "Twelve o'clock, the ghost comes out!" While they were counting, Val snuck around the back of the house and went in through Midas's doggie door through the house. She waited while everyone ventured beyond home base.

While the others embarked on their quest to seek out Ghost Polly Val, Tati wouldn't venture off the porch.

"Tati, ya can't base stick. Them's the rules," Billy reminded.

"I ain't a base sticka, am I, Wosie?" Tati wondered as she bit back the tears in her eyes.

"Okay, everybody, listen up. Tati is three, an' if she wanna sit on top of the base, she can!" proclaimed Rosie, taking up for her little sister.

"But everybody else gots t'git off the porch, right, Rosie?" insisted Billy.

"Yep, them's the rules!" sanctioned Rosie.

All at once, the door of the house opened, an' Val came out screaming, "Imma the ghost, and y'all about t'git a taste of Ghost Polly Val!"

THE GHOST COMES OUT

The other boys and girls raced around screaming. They were trying to make it back to the base safely. Tati, because she hadn't ventured too far, touched the chair as Val made her way down the steps, but DaisyBelle wasn't so lucky. Val reached out and touched her as she tried to follow Tati to the chair. Together both Val and DaisyBelle went out and managed to touch everyone with the last one caught being Dean. He was thrilled he had won that round.

"Did ya see me? Did ya see how I dodged all of you? I think I'm a natural at this game. Whatcha think, Monty?" Dean cried out.

"Yep, I'da say yua meant t'play this game," Monty admitted while nodding his head.

"Okay, I guess DaisyBelle, you're it!" Val said.

"DaisyBelle, ya wanna take Betsy wid ya?" Tati asked as she handed her the doll.

"Good idea, Tati. Betsy likes t'hide," replied DaisyBelle.

The rest of the kids started their counting while DaisyBelle hid. She raced around in back of the house and took cover behind a big tree. She heard the boys and girls counting and was startled when someone walked up to her.

"Did I scare you, DaisyBelle? I didn't mean to. What are you playing?" he asked softly.

"Ghost Comes Out, an' Imma the ghost," DaisyBelle whispered.

He bent down and quietly asked her, "Would you like to find a hiding place where no one could find you? You'd be the best ghost that ever was. I can guarantee it."

"Really? Ida like that. Oh, they on eleven. Let's go!" DaisyBelle said hurriedly.

He bent down to pick her up as she eagerly went into his arms, but dropped Betsy in the process. *Nobody gonna fin' me. Imma gonna be the greatest ghost eva*, she thought as they raced away. Ghost Polly would've been proud, she had escaped into the night.

CHAPTER 42

THE MEETING

I'm so glad Dean had some place to go tonight. Now, I need to get myself ready to meet Frances Boyd. She's such a strange woman, and she has no idea who's coming to our meeting tonight, Harry thought with a slight smile.

Harry left his house at 7:30 p.m. and drove to the city limits. He saw an old truck by the side of the road and pulled over. The passenger side of his car opened, and his boss jumped in.

"What a day. It's such a perfect night, and the sky is so clear. I think we might change our plans, but let's see how it goes first," explained his boss.

"You wanna meet her first?" Harry asked looking at his passenger.

"No, I'm thinking I can go behind the shack and wait while the two of you talk. I'll listen to what's going on and will make my appearance known when the time's right. I'd like to hear how much she knows or thinks she knows," Harry's boss stated.

Harry pulled out again and headed for the shack. They wanted to arrive early so his boss could be hidden, but when they approached, they saw Frances Boyd waiting. Harry shut his lights off, and his boss climbed in the back seat of the car and hid under Harry's coat. Harry and his boss always had a plan B ready just in case. As Harry drove next to the shack, Frances walked over to the car carrying her purse and a piece of luggage. She was just about to open the door to the back seat when Harry jumped out of the car and took her luggage from her. He helped her into the front seat and placed the bag in the trunk.

"I like ya car, Harry. It's nice. I can always tell a man with money by his car, ya know? Men who drive nice cars have money t'spend, an' I like t'spend money," Frances said as she laughed.

Harry looked over at her and asked, "Did you just have that one suitcase, Frances?"

"Member yua t'call me Frannie," she said flirting. Frances eased over in the front seat where she was sitting close to Harry. "Do ya like my perfume, Harry? It's called I Don't Know, 'cause I don't know if ya want me or not. I wore it fo you."

Harry said, "Yes, it's lovely, Frannie. I just want to make sure you brought all of your clothes and left nothing behind because we want Allan to think you've really left him."

"I gotta notha two pieces of luggage in my car. Ya wanna git 'em now?" Frances asked as she handed Harry her keys and edged closer.

"I will in just a second, Frannie," Harry said with a smile. He put his arm over the back of the seat, and it lightly touched Frances's back.

"Did you leave the letter for Allan like we planned?" asked Harry. His breath was so close to her face, and Frances felt it and leaned back so that his arm draped over her shoulder.

"Ya know I did," she said as she leaned in for a kiss. He lightly touched his lips on her cheek and then found her mouth. She moaned as her right arm found its way around his neck. The embrace lasted what seemed like an eternity for Harry and just a few seconds for Frances until he pushed away.

"I can't do this, Frannie. You're a married woman, and your husband's a minister. It's just not right."

"What Allan don't know—," she started, but Harry wouldn't have any more of it. He wanted to get this job done.

"Frannie, I wanted to ask how you came about calling the number in Chicago. I was really surprised when my boss told me," asked Harry.

"Oh, that was easy. 'Member I kinda fainted at ya house an' y'all carried me in? Well, I memorized one of the numbas on ya pad.

Imma good actress, don't ya thank? I didn't really faint, jest wanted t'see what yua was hidin'. Pretty good, huh?" explained Frances.

"Yes, it was. You're pretty crafty, Frannie. So, do you know who I work for?" asked Harry.

"Nah, but I've a feelin' he's an elder or a gansta," Frances said with a laugh while planting a kiss on Harry's lips.

Harry pushed her away and looked at her and was just about to come clean when Frances asked, "Hey, ya hear what happened t'day? Some kids here in town had a graduation, an' one kid got rotten eggs all ovah him! Can ya b'lieve it? I would've loved t'have seen that! I'll bet the place stunk t'high heavens. The kid probly d'served it." Frannie couldn't stop laughing at the thought and didn't notice as Harry's face grew darker. Nor did she notice someone pop up from the back seat.

"What kind of a monster are you?" said the voice from the back seat. Frances was so startled her head nearly hit the roof of the car.

"Who...who...are you?" Frances demanded as she recovered from the shock.

"My name's Rocky Frederella, I'm from Chicago. Ever heard of me?" Rocky asked while opening the back car door.

"Oh. My. God. You're...head of the... Frederella Gang. Oh. My. God! You *are*...a gangsta! But you're a—," Frances started, but Rocky interrupted her. Rocky got out of the back seat and opened the passenger front door and climbed in front, sliding over to Frances.

"So, Frances, you're really smooth, you know that? It's bad enough you torched the Church of the Southern Baptist of Grayton, but then you laugh at the expense of a child. Tsk tsk, Frannie," Rocky said calmly. Rocky gestured using the right-hand pointer finger moving it back and forth in front of Frannie's face.

"H-h-h-how...did ya...know that?" Frances cowered and moved closer to Harry. She was frightened by the look on Rocky's face.

"Now, Frannie, we know everything. You didn't like the attention Reverend Andrew Anglin Greer was getting at his church, did ya?" Rocky demanded.

"Yes... I mean...no. I...mean...well, it jest ain't fair. Y'all... understand...he's a color'd. He...was takin'...'tention...away...

THE GHOST COMES OUT

from me… I mean Allan. Don'tcha thank? Y'all know it ain't right," Frances appealed to Rocky and Harry.

"What we do know, Mrs. Boyd, is you're not only a pathetic racist, you could've been a murderer. The Reverend Greer been at the church that night as was his usual schedule. God works in myserious ways, Mrs. Boyd, and that night he came down with the stomach flu. Lucky for him and sad for you, huh? Harry and I have been watching you for sometime. Harry, why don't you give Mrs. Boyd a rundown on what we know about her," insisted Rocky.

"With pleasure, Boss," Harry began. "So, uh… Frannie, we know you've not spent too many nights alone, have you? Your latest affairs have resulted in two unwanted pregnancies with two miscarriages where you almost died…twice. Coat hangers are not a way to terminate pregnancies. As a result, you're no longer able to have children. Why, I guess that makes you happy, huh? Recently, you've been dipping into the collection plate to the tune of $123.67. Why, Frannie, at that rate, you'll be able to buy that Daimler SP250 you want in no time at all. Oh, and I almost forgot, when you were fifteen, you 'accidentally' pushed your baby stepbrother into the lake. How unfortunate for him that he couldn't swim. Why, I can't believe a two-year-old child can't tread water, can you, Boss? And all because you didn't want him taking any of your inheritance. Funny how life is though, your grandparents left you with nothing. Wow, living can be a bitch sometimes, can't it, Frannie, don'tcha thank?"

"But you won't need to worry about that anymore. Oh, and by the way, the child you made fun of who was slimed with the rotten eggs is my son, Dean," Rocky whispered.

Looking at Harry and in a very cool even voice, Rocky said, "I think we're done here, Harry. I'll get rid of her car. You get rid of the load."

Harry handed Rocky Frances's keys.

Rocky got out of the automobile and hopped into Frances's car and sped off just as Frances let out a bloodcurdling scream.

CHAPTER 43

DaisyBelle's Missing

"DaisyBelle must be hiding in a great place," Dean expressed as he slowly walked around the yard.

"Hey, Rosie, ya thank she went in the house like Val?" asked an exasperated Billy.

"I go look, Wosie. She come out fo me," Tati said as she opened the front door to her house.

Val shouted, "Okay, DaisyBelle, ya win! We can't fin' ya. Come on out! Now's a good time t'touch us 'cause we ain't by home base."

They waited, but no movement from anywhere. Then suddenly someone yelled, "Boo!" And they jumped. It was Monty trying to be funny.

"Stop it, Monty! DaisyBelle, ya can come out now. We ain't gonna fin' ya, an this is gittin' old," Johnny cried out.

Tati came outside with her mother. Victoria had a flashlight in her hands.

"I thought this might help you locate the ghost," she noted smiling and handing the flashlight to Val. She then made her way back into the house.

"Thanks, Miss Victoria. DaisyBelle, we gonna fin' ya, now. We have a flashlight. Heeyah we come!" proclaimed Val.

The six other children got behind Val as they walked around the front yard. They looked behind every tree, bush, or shrub. Then they scoured the backyard, and behind a tree, they found something as Val reached down to pick it up.

"Look, it's DaisyBelle's doll!" Dean exclaimed.

"Is Betsy. DaisyBelle wouldn't go without huh," Tati remarked sadly.

"DaisyBelle, yua the best ghost! Come out now. We wanna play somethin' else," Rosie shouted. No one made a sound. The only noises were the sounds of crickets, and the only light was from the flashlight and intermittent lightning bugs.

"DaisyBelle, this ain't funny. Come on out! We taared of this game!" Billy yelled.

"If ya don't come out, DaisyBelle, Imma gonna have t'tell Momma," Val shouted in desperation.

They waited for five more minutes, and then Rosie marched into the house to get her mother. In less than a minute, both Rosie and Victoria were running out the front door.

"DaisyBelle? DaisyBelle? You've played this game so well that we're getting a little worried. Come on out, now. Tell us where you've been hiding because it's a great hiding place!" Victoria cried out.

The desperation began to sink in when Val showed Victoria the doll they had discovered behind a tree in the backyard.

"So, you found this behind a tree in the backyard?" Victoria asked, and the girls and boys nodded.

"Okay, well, that's where we'll start. We know she was in the backyard. I want three of you to go look in the barn. Maybe she's hiding with Lucky. Three of you look behind every tree, bush, and shrub, and Tati and I will look inside the house and the front yard, again. If…uh…when you find her, yell to everyone and let's meet back on the front porch," directed Victoria.

Monty, Dean, and Val searched the inside and outside of the barn. No luck. Billy, Johnny, and Rosie searched every tree, bush, and shrub—still no luck. Victoria and Tati searched the house from top to bottom and the front yard too. There were no signs of DaisyBelle.

As they all met on the front porch, the concern on their faces was visible.

"What…we…gonna…do, Miss Victoria?" asked Val as she began to cry. Rosie reached over and put her arm around Val.

"Okay, no need to get upset. I'm going to call Rita. Maybe DaisyBelle went to your house, Val. Let's call and see," Victoria said. *Oh, please let her be at her house. How could she have just disappeared?*

The boys and girls followed Victoria into the house. Rosie held Val's hand for reassurance. Victoria went straight into the living room to their telephone. The boys and girls crowded around while Victoria dialed Rita's number.

"Hello, Rita? It's Victoria. I know this may sound silly, but is DaisyBelle down there with you by any chance?"

"No? The boys and girls were playing a game outside, and DaisyBelle was the one hiding, and well…she's just such a good hider. No, Rita, I'm sure she'll get tired of hiding and give up."

"No, there's no reason to get upset. I'll call you when she shows up," Victoria said and hung up the phone. She looked at the children.

"I'm sure she'll be back in no time. Why don't I make some popcorn and lemonade, and you go outside on the front porch and wait for DaisyBelle. How does that sound?" asked Victoria trying to reassure the children.

"Yeah, less go outside. When DaisyBelle stops hidin' an' comes t'fin' us, we can say we all win an' touch home base," Rosie explained.

"Yeah, good idea," replied Dean. Everybody else followed and went outside to wait.

While Victoria was in the kitchen making the children some snacks, there was a commotion at the front door. Victoria raced from the kitchen to find Rita running toward her, and the boys and girls followed.

"Where…is…she? Where is she? She…my…baby, Victoria. She…my…baby," Rita said in between sobs.

Victoria held out her arms to comfort Rita.

"Shhh, shhhh, it's okay. She'll be back in no time. There's no need to cry and get upset. If you like, I can call the sheriff. Would that make you feel better?" Victoria wondered. She seemed to feel better when Charles was around.

THE GHOST COMES OUT

Rita simply nodded her head. She couldn't speak, and now the children were crying too.

Victoria called for Rosie and Tati to come help her in the kitchen.

"Girls, I want you to help me calm everyone down. Bring the other children in here to eat, and I'll take care of Rita, okay?" Victoria pleaded.

"Ya got it, Momma. We'll take care of 'em. Ya don't need t'worry 'bout us," Rosie stated while Tati just nodded. She too was upset. Besides Rosie, DaisyBelle was her best friend.

So, while Rosie and Tati served lemonade and popcorn to their friends, Victoria comforted Rita and called the sheriff.

She picked up the phone and dialed his number.

"Charles, this is Victoria."

"Hi there, what can I do for the woman who put on quite a spread today? You just name it!" Charles said excitedly. *I can't believe I was just thinking about her, and then she calls*, he thought.

"Uh, well, the summer school kids thought it would be fun to have a sleepover, and they were outside playing a game. DaisyBelle Shelby was it, and she hid from the others. They were supposed to find her, and, well…we can't find her," explained Victoria.

"So, she hasn't been found? Would she have gone to her house?" asked Charles.

"No, I've got Rita Shelby here with me now," Victoria answered. When Rita heard what Victoria said, she just cried louder, so Victoria rubbed her back to soothe her.

"Okay, then I'll be there in three minutes," Charles said as he hung up. He was concerned DaisyBelle was missing but was thrilled to have an excuse to see Victoria.

When he arrived at Victoria's house, the tables, chairs, buffet had been cleared. It was as though nothing special had occurred there that day. The front door was open when he arrived, and so he just went inside.

"Victoria? Victoria?" shouted Charles.

"We're back in the den, Charles," Victoria yelled in response.

When he found them, Rita was sobbing uncontrollably, and Victoria was rubbing her back trying to get her to breathe and calm down.

"Rita?" Charles asked. Rita turned and looked at Charles. She could hardly talk, but she got out a few words.

"Karme...is karme," she said and began to sob again.

"What, Rita? What did you say?" Charles couldn't understand her through the crying.

"Is karme. Is my fault...is my fault," Rita kept repeating over and over.

"What's karma got to do with this, and why could this be your fault?" Victoria demanded softly.

"Is...my...fault. I... I...have...secret, Victoria," Rita started to tell her. "I...was...there...when... Jeb...died. I...caused...him...t'run...off...the...road...an...wreck. Is...karme...comin'...back...to....me." She sobbed.

CHAPTER 44

EVEN BULLIES SLEEP

Mikey, a.k.a. Hamerhead, and his brother, Walter, a.k.a. Squirt, had been humiliated by the people of Grayton. First, two of Grayton's citizens had cost them money they had earned from manipulating their fair events so there would be no winners. How dare anyone win at these games? It had cost them *their* own money to replenish the stuffed toys that had been won by the folks of Grayton. *How dare anybody takes advantage of us carnies? It's our job t'exploit them. That's jest part of us an' the carnie life. An' now, we been 'rested fo takin' some treasures that was owwahs fo the takin', an' t'make thangs worse, some white trash fatha an his ugly fat daughta soaked me n' Squirt in rotten eggs. I'll git 'em fo what they did*, Hamerhead thought as he looked at Joe and Dorothy.

Ya don't know who ya recknin' with. Ya ain't seen the last of us! thought Squirt as he stared a hole through Dorothy in the back seat of the squad car. Hamerhead didn't like children, but Squirt liked them even less. Joe and Dorothy Puckett felt uncomfortable in the three-minute ride to the sheriff's office and jail. They felt the Dennis brothers' eyes locked on them.

Dorothy turned to Squirt and said, "Take a picture, mista. It'll last longa. Ya jest bein' rude."

"Shut up, Dorothy! These ain't nice people," Joe yelled at this daughter as though he and his daughter were the epitome of goodness. Joe was worried they'd made enemies of Hamerhead and Squirt, and he didn't need any more.

When they got down to the sheriff's office, Charles placed them under arrest, but because Dorothy was a minor, he couldn't lock her up. She had been read her rights, and the judge would decide what to do. The others were put in cells next to one another. There were three holding cells, and Joe was placed in the middle one with one of the Dennis brothers on either side of him. *That ought to make Joe feel good and cozy*, Charles thought.

Charles then made a call to Raveleen to come and get her daughter.

"Raveleen, it's Sheriff Hall. I've got your husband and daughter down here. They were arrested for disorderly conduct and disturbing the peace. You'll need to come and pick up Dorothy," Charles informed her.

"Ya tellin' me ya gots my baby? Why?" demanded Raveleen.

"She interrupted a children's ceremony with rotten eggs. She attempted to throw them at the kids," Charles retorted.

"Did she hit 'em?" Raveleen shouted over the phone.

"No, she hit two men," Charles replied.

Raveleen was laughing. "I'll bet that was funny, huh?"

"The two men she doused are not amused. Are you going to pick up Dorothy?" Charles barked.

"I ain't gotta car. Guess she gonna have t'stay put. 'Sides, my stories are on," Raveleen answered and hung up.

"When's Momma pickin' me up? Imma gittin' hongry," demanded Dorothy.

"She's not. She thinks it might do you some good to stay here in the lockup," Charles answered her as he stared her down.

Dorothy wasn't used to not getting her way and didn't know just how far she could push the sheriff. So she did what she always did when she got in trouble. She cried. She cried and cried and cried. Then she would stop and cry some more. Charles didn't have to listen to her because the small room he was in was soundproof. Her father and the Dennis brothers weren't so lucky.

THE GHOST COMES OUT

Charles left her in the room until he knew the graduation ceremony and barbecue lunch would be over. Then, he went into the room and found Dorothy crawled up in the fetal position sucking her thumb. She had cried herself to sleep. *Even bullies rest*, Sheriff Hall thought.

CHAPTER 45

You're Home

As they ran deeper and deeper into the thicket of weeds, crabgrass, and vines away from the others, DaisyBelle was beginning to think this wasn't a good idea.

"I really 'preciate ya helpin' me, but I thank the othas are gonna wonda where I'm at," said DaisyBelle.

"Nah, they're going to think you're the best Ghost Polly that has ever played the game the Ghost Comes Out," he said. "We're almost there anyway."

They came upon something that DaisyBelle couldn't make out in the dark. As they got closer, she realized it was a small cottage house colored in camoflouge. He seemed to know where everything was located because he put the key in a lock that DaisyBelle had not seen. *Wow, not only it's dark but the color of the little house matches the grass. Wonda why it's same color? It'd be prettier if it were blue or pink. He must like the color green*, she thought.

"Here we are!" he said as he carried DaisyBelle across the doorway. He turned on the lights, and just like that, DaisyBelle forgot about the game. She was staring at the most beautiful sight she'd ever seen. An entire room with all the Marian dolls and accessories that were available. There were shelves of dolls, and each one was different. There was a shelf full of Mippie dolls. Mippie was Marian's little sister, and two shelves of Marian's brothers, Hall and Hodge. All the dolls had multiple accessories. There was even a shelf with Darian

THE GHOST COMES OUT

dolls, Marian's twin sister. DaisyBelle had never seen such a sight in her life. She raced over to see Marian's magic car.

"Is okay if I play with 'em?" DaisyBelle asked, reluctant to touch them.

"Of course, DaisyBelle, I got them for you," he responded smiling.

DaisyBelle raced over to play with Marian's magic car, and then she noticed the Fantasy House. She couldn't resist but run her fingers over the strong cardboard with divisions placed in the middle to separate the rooms in the Fantasy House. *Is more beautiful than on TV!* she thought.

"This place is splendiferous!" she said excitedly as she took some of the dolls off the shelves to place them in the magic car and the Fantasy House. She lost track of time while she played. *Momma an' Val gonna love this place. Tati gonna thank this is a magical place*, she thought.

"This entire room is all for you," he insisted as he interrupted her thoughts.

"Me? Why ya doin' it fo me?" DaisyBelle inquired as she played.

He came closer to DaisyBelle as he talked and bent down so he was at her eye level. He cupped her hands in his when he said, "You deserve the world, and I'm going to give it to you, DaisyBelle. You are the only one who has ever seen this room, and you are the only one who will ever see it," he explained.

"Am I in heaven?" DaisyBelle asked.

"No, DaisyBelle. You're home!" he replied.

CHAPTER 46

Pastors Cry Too

Pastor Allan Boyd was one of the finest men ever to grace Grayton. He was gentle and kind and the sort of person some might want to comfort them in an hour of need. Pastor Allan, as his parishoners called him, was too good for his wife. The congregation could not understand what he saw in her. The Women's Bible Club, which met every Thursday at 7:00 p.m., had all but disbanded because of Frances. She had insisted on being not only its president but the treasurer too. When she nominated herself for both positions, she said, "Since my Allan is the minister of this fine church, I should be the president. Don't ya thank? And y'all jest know Imma gonna do a great job. I thank I should be treasurer 'cause the president an' treasurer have t'git along, an' who gits 'long betta with me than me?"

And that was that. No one said a word. They were afraid to. They loved Pastor Allan and didn't want to insult him by dissing his wife. So, she became the president and treasurer of the Women's Bible Club and stole them blind.

When Allan came home that night to discover the letter Frances had left for him, he was distraught. He couldn't believe she would leave him. He had loved her from the minute he had laid eyes on her and thought himself the luckiest man in the world to have a woman like Frances as his wife. What had Frances told him recently?

THE GHOST COMES OUT

"Ya neva pay me the 'tention I d'serve, Allan. Why ya not much of a man in the bedroom? Ya need t'look at some girlie magazines or somethin'. I need a real man, not a boy!"

Had I not provided Frances with sufficient love? Should I have tried to find another church in a bigger town? Would that have kept her? I need to find her, but where do I look? Who had she run off with? Was it someone I know? These were the thoughts that kept running through Allan's mind. The only thing he could do was to go to the one source that never let him down. He picked up his favorite Bible, and as the tears rolled down his, face he opened the book to 1 Peter 1:6–7.

> *So be truly glad. There is wonderful joy ahead, even though you have to endure many trials for a little while. These trials will show that your faith is genuine. It is being tested as fire tests and purifies gold—though your faith is far more precious than mere gold. So when your faith remains strong through many trials, it will bring you much praise and glory and honor on the day when Jesus Christ is revealed to the whole world.*

And the pastor wept.

CHAPTER 47

THE SECRET'S OUT

"What…did you…just say?" Victoria requested of Rita. She reached over and put her hands on Rita's shoulders and shook her.

"Me…and… Carl was…havin' a fight. He…got…drunk as… usal, an's we was on our way to… Stockton. The…snow…was beginnin'…to add…up. I was…drivin' 'cause Carl…was…impaired, but he kept…grabbin' fo the stirrin'…wheel, an' we came…up ovah the top…of the hill, the…car kept sliddin'…on the ice. All a sudden… Carl fell…on the floor…and he jest…liked laid…on the gas… I… couldn't git him…off, an', well, I…reached down…t'move 'em, an' I…lost control…of the car. Ya husband, Jeb, tried t'avoid…us. I didn't…know he…had wrecked… I swear it… I didn't…know… until lata… I swear it, Victoria." Rita sobbed into her hands.

Victoria couldn't hide her anger.

"And you just left him there?" she demanded. *How could anyone not know they had caused a wreck? I now know what had caused Jeb to wreck—and to think it's my neighbor. My Jeb…my precious Jeb…*, Victoria thought.

Rita was so upset she was shaking all over. She knew she had kept a secret from Victoria and thought she would be upset, but now her child was missing, and she attributed it to karma coming back to her.

"I'm…sooo…sorry. I'm…sooo…sorry," Rita kept repeating over and over as she cried. It was then that Victoria realized she

THE GHOST COMES OUT

couldn't think about what Rita was telling her. There would be time for that later, but for now they must work together to find DaisyBelle. So, she reached over to Rita and pulled her into her arms and let her cry. In fact, Victoria joined in too.

As Charles watched the scene in front of him, he discovered how deep his love for Victoria had grown. He reached over and embraced both women as they cried. When the sobbing slowed down, he gently released the two women and, looking down at them, said, "I know there's a lot of questions that need answering, but for now let's get the kids together and go and search for DaisyBelle."

Both women nodded and tried to compose themselves as Charles called to the children in the kitchen.

"Hey, kids, could you please come in here?" he asked urgently.

The boys and girls ran into the den and asked, "Did ya fin' huh?" Tati asked. "Where huh at?"

Victoria looked down at her daughter as Tati ran to be held.

"Not yet, honey. That's why we need all of you," Victoria said.

"Okay, let me get some facts first. When was the last time you saw DaisyBelle?" Charles questioned them while getting his notepad and pen out of his front coat pocket.

"We was playin' the Ghost Comes Out, an' she was it," Monty explained.

"DaisyBelle had to go hide, Sheriff, and we were to find her," added Dean. Lucy was right by his side and seemed to confirm what he said. She was at attention just ready for a command, and Midas was by her side lying flat on the floor.

"So, she was it and went to hide. Then what?" Charles asked as he wrote in his pad.

"We went t'look fo her, Mista Sheriff. We counted all the way up t'twelve o'clock, an' then we started lookin' fo her," Rosie explained.

"How long was it before you went looking for her?" Charles wanted to know.

"I say 'bout four or five minutes. We was jest learnin' the game, but was havin' fun. If I only had gone with her. Momma, I'm sorry. So sorry," Val cried. Rita got up from the sofa and came over and hugged her daughter.

"Is not yua fault, honey. Is nobody's fault," Rita replied and hugged Val tightly.

"Okay, so five minutes. What could've happened in five minutes? Surely she's gone somewhere to hide and will be back shortly," explained Charles.

"Sheriff, that ain't like DaisyBelle. She don't go runnin' off. She always does the right thang, an we found Betsy, on the ground." Val interjected.

"She...wouldn't have lef... Betsy," Tati added softly as she cried. Victoria rocked Tati as she sat in her arms.

Charles looked at Victoria with eyebrows raised as though asking, "Who's Betsy?"

Victoria read his mind and mouthed, "Her doll," to Charles.

"So, we've got DaisyBelle playing a game, and she's it. It's kind of like a reversed game of hide-and-go-seek, right?" asked Charles.

"Zactly. So, what'll we do now, Mista Sheriff? Do ya thank we should round up a posse?" asked an inquisitive Rosie.

Charles had to suppress a laugh. "Rosie, that's a very good idea, but I think you all could be my posse, and we can find DaisyBelle." *I'm sure she's just found a great place to hide, and she may have fallen asleep*, he thought.

"Did you hear that, Lucy? We're going to be in a posse to find DaisyBelle," exclaimed Dean. Midas's ears perked up then too.

"I thank Midas wants t'join," Rosie added.

"I'm thinking we'll need flashlights to aid us. Monty, why don't you go next door and get as many flashlights as you can find. Victoria, how many do you have? Rita, do you have any flashlights? We also need people. See if your uncle is at your house, Monty. Dean, what about you? Could you call your...uh... Harry? Johnny and Billy, you think your dad and Clayton could help out?" Charles asked.

Johnny made a call to his father. Jackson told Johnny that he and Clayton would drive down and bring four flashlights and walkie-talkies too.

Dean tried calling Harry, but got no answer. *Funny, I thought Harry was going to have a quiet evening at home*, Dean thought.

THE GHOST COMES OUT

Monty went next door, and his mother sent over three flashlights. *Uncle Bake must be downtown at the newspaper or back at his house,* Monty thought. *Bummer, I was hopin' he could hep us. This could be a big story fo him.*

"Mom, ya need t'call Uncle Bake an' tell 'em what's goin' on. This might be a big story, an' he don't wanna miss it," Monty told his mother.

"Great idea, Monty! I'll call him," Mrs. Hutchins said.

When Jackson and Clayton had gathered at the Scholls' residence, Charles explained the details of DaisyBelle missing and when she was last seen. He divided the group into teams. Each team had an adult and a walkie-talkie with them. Everyone except Rita went on the search. She stayed back in case DaisyBelle returned.

They set out in different directions to find DaisyBelle. Charles and his team went back toward the barn and woods. Victoria and her group went toward the Shelby house and the creek. Clayton's team went toward the square in town, and Jackson's group went toward the churches on Christian row.

Before they started out, Charles looked at this watch. It was 8:43 p.m.

"Let's meet back at Victoria's house in one hour. Call DaisyBelle's name as you go. She may have crawled up and gone to sleep, so hearing her name will help," he instructed.

It started out being more of a game to locate DaisyBelle, but the longer they walked with no result, the more afraid they became. In one hour, they came back to Victoria's house and found a hysterical Rita, and Bake Haas, who was there comforting her.

"Did ya fine my baby?" demanded Rita. When no one answered, she fell to the floor. Bake bent down and gently picked her up. He cradled her in his arms while trying to reassure her DaisyBelle would be found.

Charles motioned for Victoria to follow him into the kitchen.

"I need to call Stockton and keep reinforcements to assist us. Do you think you could get everybody settled while I make a phone call? This was going to be a slumber party, right? So, let the kids get their sleeping bags and put them together in your den. They need to have each other to lean on right now," explained Charles.

"I think that's a great idea, Charles. I'm really concerned. No, I'm scared," Victoria replied.

Charles couldn't help himself as he reached over to her and pulled her toward him. He embraced her as though he would never let her go. They stayed like that until there was a noise at the the door.

"Momma, I scawed. DaisyBelle is my fwend," Tati said running toward her mother. Victoria picked her up and carried her into the den. She sat down, and the other boys and girls curled up around her. She told them to get their sleeping bags and find a place to rest.

"We're going to sleep in here together and make sure you save a place for DaisyBelle. So when she comes in, she can go right to her spot. How does that sound?" she asked.

Val unrolled hers and DaisyBelle's sleeping bags. She placed them beside each other, and Tati put hers on the other side of DaisyBelle's. Rosie was right beside her sister, and the four boys put their sleeping bags in a circle around the girls as though they were their protectors.

"Daddy, ya gonna stay too, right?" Johnny asked Jackson.

"Ya bet I am, son. I ain't goin' nowhere," he replied.

"What if the ghost took DaisyBelle?" Billy asked.

"Ya thank the ghost's gonna git us too?" Monty added.

"No ghost is going to get you. Why, I'm a ghost hunter, didn't I tell you guys? Huh, I was sure I had...oh, well...when I was in my teens, I hunted ghosts with Jackson. So, you are in good hands with us. Now, you boys and girls get some sleep," answered Clayton.

Charles came into the room, and the five other adults followed him into the kitchen. They left the door open for the kids.

"So, Sheriff, what's going on?" asked Bake. "What's the plan?"

Charles was just about to answer when there was an emergency call for him.

"Sheriff? It's Shelia."

"We gotta little trouble down here. Joe Puckett's escaped," explained Shelia.

"How in the hell did that happen?" Charles demanded.

THE GHOST COMES OUT

"I dunno. I went t'take my dinna break. I'd already brung dinna back fo the prisoners, an' when I came back, he was gone!" she countered.

"Are Mikey and Walter still in their cells?" asked Charles.

"Uh, yeah," Shelia replied sheepishly.

"Uh, yeah? What else aren't you telling me, Shelia?" shouted Charles.

"They both in their cells, an' they dead," she answered.

CHAPTER 48

APB

Immediately there was an all-points bulletin out for Joe Puckett, who had escaped from the Grayton Jail. The APB read:

> White male, 45 years old, brownish hair with a bald spot in the back, 5'10" tall with a beer gut, scraggly beard missing one front tooth. Be on the lookout he may be armed and considered dangerous. Do not approach him. Call authorities immediately!

"Hey, Joe, there's an APB out fo ya. Whatcha thank of that?" And they both laughed.

Joe was barely conscious. He was bruised from his head down. They had done a number on him. When they came through the jail doors, he thought they were there to hassle him.

He wasn't upset he had to stay in jail. It was the first hot meal he would have in some time. *Raveleen may be good-lookin', but she can't cook a lickin'. Truth is her looks are a fadin', an' she gottin' fat. Fact is she ugly. I might trade her on a younga model,* he thought with a smile.

His thoughts had been interrupted by these two who had come for him. Joe wasn't ready or prepared for what the two of them had in store. If he had only known, he wouldn't have gone willingly with the pair. Poor Joe, he never was good at choosing friends.

CHAPTER 49

HOW MANY GHOSTS ARE THERE?

What started as a mundane summer in Grayton suddenly turned into a place everyone talked about over coffee and a smoke. What exactly was going on in this small community had people from out of town guessing, but most of all the citizens of Grayton. Reporters from both the *Commercial Appeal* and the *Tennesseean* had mobbed this quiet town. Folks from the area weren't sure if they could trust their neighbors, and homeowners no longer left their doors unlocked and opened. Who was next? That was the question they were asking.

"I don't know what t'thank, sista," Barbara said to Elizabeth. After Barbara had read aloud the news in the *Grayton Gazette*. "What should we do, sista? Why, I'm 'fraid t'go out."

"Now who in their right mind would want a couple of old ladies like us? I say let the ghost come on out. I'll show Polly a thang or two. I used t'be a sight t'be reckoned with in my youth. 'Member I was good at kickin'," proclaimed Elizabeth.

"Ya say ya like t'kick?" asked Barbara. "I 'member playin' that kickball when I was young. 'Member?"

"No, I said I was good at kickin'. Ya really need t'git them ears checked," Elizabeth commented.

"Is not my eyes that need a check, is my ears. You the one with the bad eyes, sista," Barbara remarked.

*****

Others in town were just as scared after the news was broadcasted. Where was precious DaisyBelle? What had happened to her? Did someone abduct her? Was it a local person or a stranger? These were the questions everyone was asking, and how many ghosts were out there?

"Momma, whatta we gonna do? Me an' Tati are scared b'cause DaisyBelle's missin'," cried Rosie.

"I scawed, Momma," said Tati. "Is Polly gonna git me too?"

Victoria held her daughters in her arms. Each child sat on one of Victoria's knees.

"Nobody or no ghost is going to get my babies. You know why?" she asked. The girls just shook their heads.

"It's because they would have to get through me, and that's not going to happen. You understand?" Victoria explained.

"Momma, DaisyBelle wouldn't fogit huh doll. She love Betsy. Huh went t'see Mawian," Tati commented.

"Whatcha mean, Tati? She must've dropped Betsy. Right, Momma?" Rosie suggested.

"I think DaisyBelle found the bestest place to hide and left Betsy on the ground to give us all a hint of where she is," Victoria insisted.

That seemed to placate the two girls. Actually Victoria was beyond scared. *What if someone had taken DaisyBelle? Could someone take my daughters too? Is someone watching us? I must stay calm for my girls. Midas may not be the best guard dog in the world, but he loves the girls, and he would make a lot of noise if someone tries to take them*, she thought.

Victoria looked down at Midas and said, "You're a good dog, Mr. Midas! We're so glad you're a part of this family."

The two girls jumped off of their mother's lap and got down on the floor and gave their pet some love and much needed attention. The three of them stayed in the den for a few more minutes.

THE GHOST COMES OUT

"I'm going to check on Rita and Val. I'd like you to come with me, okay, girls?" Victoria pled. The girls got up and went upstairs to dress. Midas went with them of course.

When they came down the stairs, Victoria did something she hadn't done in years. She locked the door. When they went out of their house, they noticed the street was lined with different cars. There were three Hemi-wagons, a green Impala, and four different black-and-white Plymouth squad cars from surrounding counties. They couldn't have driven to the Shelbys' house if they had wanted to.

Before they got to Rita's door, it flew open, and Rita and Val came bursting out. Rita fell into Victoria's arms, and Val reached for Rosie and Tati to hug. Both of them looked exhausted.

"Thank God, Victoria. I was hopin' you'd come. We a mess, ain't we, Val? We a mess!" Rita exclaimed.

They went inside the house, and there were two plainclothes men standing in the living room. Each one had on a black suit with a skinny tie, and both had a cigarette hanging out of their mouths. On each of their coat pockets, one could see a police shield. They were detectives.

"This here's my bess friend, Victoria Scholl. She the nicest person in the world, an' she gonna hep us fin' my baby," Rita insisted.

"Ma'am, we were just coming up the street to talk to you. May we talk to your daughters too? I believe they were there when DaisyBelle disappeared, right?" the tall detective inquired.

"Of course. I know they want to help as much as possible," she said.

Turning to her daughters, she stated, "Rosie and Tati, these gentlemen are going to ask you some questions. So try to remember exactly what happened, okay?"

"Yes, Momma," said Rosie.

"Yes, Momma," echoed Tati.

The tall detective bent down to talk to the girls. He introduced himself as Joseph McClanahan, and his partner was Nobel Douglas.

"Rosie, how old are you?" Joseph asked.

"Imma eight years old, an' Imma goin' into the third grade," remarked Rosie.

"Rosie, I need for you to think real hard. Did DaisyBelle say anything about running away?" Joseph asserted.

"No, she nevah said anythang 'bout runnin' away. She was the ghost, ya know?" Rosie reminded him. "We was playin' a game."

"Rosie, was DaisyBelle unhappy? I know her father recently… uh…died, was she distraught?" asked Joseph.

"DaisyBelle was the ghost. She was excited. Don't know what *distraught* is, but she was happy. She an' Tati is best friends. Ask her," added Rosie pointing to Tati.

Joseph wasn't getting anywhere with the eight-year-old. *What could the little one add?* he thought.

Joseph turned his attention to Tati, but his partner, Nobel, butted in and said, "Let me take the little one."

"Your name is Tati?" asked Nobel.

"Uh-huh," Tati replied shyly.

"Can I ask you a couple of questions?" Nobel wondered. Tati nodded.

"I understand DaisyBelle's your best friend. Is that correct?" he asked. Tati nodded again.

"What do you and DaisyBelle like to do?" asked Nobel.

"Me an' huh play wid dolls. Huh has Betsy," Tati answered.

"I understand Betsy was found in your backyard by the big tree," stated Nobel. Tati nodded.

"Why do you think she didn't take Betsy?" Nobel wanted to know.

"Huh pwobly went t'see Mawian," Tati explained.

"She probably went to see Marian? Now, who's Marian?" Nobel queried.

"She huh doll, an' huh lives in a house," Tati replied.

CHAPTER 50

SADIE HARGIS

When word spread that seven-year-old DaisyBelle Shelby was missing, the entire town came out to assist. The *Commercial Appeal* and the *Tennesseean* sent journalists to the sleepy town of Grayton. Anybody who walked down the street would get a reporter hounding them with how long they had lived in Grayton and how well did they know DaisyBelle Shelby.

Television stations from Memphis and Nashville sent reporters to interview any and everybody in the quiet town of Grayton. One reporter, Palo (pronounced Pay-lo) Lankford, was a good-looking single male who loved the ladies. He had no plans on changing his bachelor status. Palo knew women, and he especially knew how to play them. He had done his homework and discovered DaisyBelle Shelby's first-grade teacher was Sadie Hargis. So, he paid Miss Hargis a visit.

Sadie Hargis was a single female who was married to her job. Teaching was her life, and she had known at a young age she would be a teacher. She had made sure every runner had a flower with his/her name on it written in chalk on the route for those who ran in the 5 Mile Race. Sadie loved all of her students, but she had no idea what was heading her way until that fateful day when her doorbell rang and on the other side was Palo Lankford.

"Uh, Miss Hargis?" Palo began. "My name is Palo Lankford, and I'm with the NBC affiliate from Nashville. I am so sorry to bother you, but if I could ask you a few questions regarding DaisyBelle Shelby." Sadie Hargis shut the door on Palo's face.

Palo turned to his cameraman and said, "Take two," with a laugh.

Palo did not give up. He was going to knock all day until she opened it and let him in.

"Mr...uh... Lankford, as you can see, we are torn up in this town over the murder, fire, and the disappearance of DaisyBelle. Please leave me alone," she insisted.

"How absolutely distasteful and inappropriate on my part, Miss Hargis," Palo said sincerely, inserting his foot in the door.

"I just so badly want to help out and thought maybe you could shed some light on your knowledge of DaisyBelle, but I understand if you'd rather not share any information," he said and turned to go.

"No...uh... Mr. Lankford, I'm sorry. I've...not slept...since she went missing," Sadie said apologetically.

"Miss Hargis, you have nothing to apologize for. I understand completely," he maintained.

"Please come in," Sadie said with a half smile.

Palo knew how to work a source without that person being aware of it, and he had just worked his magic into Sadie's home.

Both Palo and his cameraman took a seat on her couch. Sadie sat opposite them in an off-white wingback chair. She loved her chair because it had belonged to her grandmother, and it was the single piece of furniture she had inherited from her. Only she sat in that chair.

"Now, Miss Hargis, if I might ask you some questions for the news, it might prove to be the one lead detectives and the sheriff need in finding DaisyBelle. Would that be all right with you?" he asked.

"Yes, that would be fine. Maybe I should put on some makeup. I'm afraid I've been crying and—" She didn't finish as he held up his hand.

"You look lovely, Miss Hargis, and I do believe the camera and the viewers are going to love you," he said earnestly.

"Well, if you're sure...," she began.

THE GHOST COMES OUT

"I am," he said as he turned on the bright light for the camera. The photographer stood up and aimed the camera toward Sadie. He knew only to get Palo's left side for the story as that was his best side.

"Shall we begin?" Palo asked, and Sadie nodded.

Palo faced the camera and began his intro, "Hello, viewers, this is Palo Lankford, and I'm reporting from Grayton, Tennessee. As you know, Grayton has had its share of tragedy and drama recently with the murder of Carl Shelby, a fire at the colored Baptist Church, and the disappearance of DaisyBelle Shelby. I am here with DaisyBelle's first-grade teacher, Sadie Hargis."

Turning to Sadie, he said, "Tell me, Miss Hargis, how long have you known DaisyBelle?"

"Uh, I've known the Shelby family for several years. We all go to the same church," Sadie said with a smile.

"You were DaisyBelle's first-grade teacher, right?" he asked.

"Yes, DaisyBelle was in my class," she answered nodding her head.

"Was she a good student?" Palo inquired.

"She was the sweetest child. In fact, I don't know of anyone as sweet as DaisyBelle. She was my special student," she maintained.

"What do you mean by your special student? Did you give her special treatment? Did you show favoritism to her over the other children?" he demanded.

"No, no…of…course…not. I… I…mean she…was just…so sweet. I loved DaisyBelle." She blushed.

"Do you know something we don't know? You just said you *loved* DaisyBelle and she *was* so sweet—in the past tense. Do you have something you want to tell the viewers? Do you know where she is?" he insisted.

"No, I… I…didn't…mean…*loved*. I… I…mean *love* and…*is*, not…*was*," she stammered choking back tears.

Palo turned toward the camera. "You heard it here, folks. Sadie Hargis *loved* DaisyBelle Shelby. I don't know about you, but I think those in law enforcement might need to check up on our teacher Sadie Hargis. For now, we're signing off in Grayton, Tennessee," Palo said with a smile.

He turned back to Sadie to thank her for the interview, but she had run to the bathroom. Palo and his cameraman heard her regurgitate. Palo pulled a card from his jacket pocket and wrote something on it: "If you have anything further to add, please give me a call. Your new friend, Palo." And he left.

The next day, Sadie turned in her resignation, effective immediately.

CHAPTER 51

CAN THIS BE BAKE'S BREAK?

Bake could not believe his good luck. *We've got two unsolved deaths, a dead body in Buckley's pond, an escaped prisoner, an arsonist who burnt down the only black church in town, and a missing child—all in our wonderful town of Grayton! This is my chance to prove to the bigger marketable papers what a small-town journalist can do*, he thought.

Bake headed for the sheriff's office to talk one-on-one with Charles. He arrived at the City Hall to find several news crews and newspaper journalists already there. They had been told Sheriff Charles would make a statement shortly, and they were to wait until he did. Bake didn't need to wait. He lived in the town and had already reported on Carl's murder and the burning of the black church. Bake had also been out looking for DaisyBelle, so he had an advantage, and he planned on using it. He walked through the front door to find Shelia at her desk. He noticed she looked awful. There were tear stains on her cheeks, her lipstick was smeared, and her mascara had run down her face.

"Shelia, are you okay?" Bake asked delicately.

She looked up at Bake and said, "It's so nice to see a familiar face, Mista Bake. I don't know what happened. I only know when I got back from my dinna break, the Dennis brothers were dead an' Joe Puckett had escaped. They was all locked in when I lef 'cause I made sure by tryin' t'open 'em. They was all locked," Shelia said sadly. Bake was busy taking down every word Shelia uttered.

"Shelia, you think someone came in here and killed the brothers? Or you think Joe somehow killed them and then got loose? Just between us, how did they die?" Bake asked as he wrote in his notebook.

Before Shelia could answer, Charles and two other men came into the waiting area.

"Hello, Bake. You're going to have to wait along with everyone else when I make my statement. Please stop harassing Shelia. She's had enough on her plate," Charles explained.

"I understand, Sheriff, but remember I've been helping search with you for DaisyBelle. Do you have any leads on her?" Bake wondered.

"Off the record?" Charles asked.

"You bet, Sheriff, off the record," Bake replied as he grabbed his notebook.

"We have no leads. It's as though she just disappeared, but I'll tell you this: I will not rest until that sweet child is back with her mom," Charles insisted.

Bake looked at Charles and knew he meant business.

"Thanks, Sheriff, for your candor," Bake noted.

Bake turned to the two men who were on either side of the sheriff. They both had *TBI* on the sleeves of their jackets.

"So, you guys work for the Tennessee Bureau of Investigation?" Bake asked the question, but it was more of a statement.

"Do you guys have any news about the Dennis brothers? What happened to them? How did they die?" questioned Bake.

"As Sheriff Hall just remarked, you're going to have to wait until he gives his statement, end of story!" exclaimed the shorter of the two men.

Sheriff Hall excused himself from the other two men and went back into his office to make a phone call. He picked up the phone and dialed a local number. A voice answered on the other end.

"This is Charles. Watch the news tonight." And he hung up.

CHAPTER 52

THE SEARCH

Everyone in Grayton, Stockton, Clifton, and even Savannah came to help in the search for DaisyBelle Shelby. No stone was left unturned in the small town of Grayton. It was quite the circus. Grayton Burger and Shake set up stands around the town. Anyone who searched for DaisyBelle could stop by one of the stands and get a hamburger, shake, and fries for free. There were signs around town that read,

> Help us locate our DaisyBelle
> And send who took her straight to jail.
> If you've searched both high and low
> Take a burger, shake, and fries to go!

People came from Nashville and Memphis to help hunt. Two college students from Memphis came into town to assist. Their names were Bubba and Scott. They were sophmores at Memphis Tech and had skipped classes to locate DaisyBelle.

"I think someone in that town took her, Scott," proclaimed Bubba while driving into Grayton.

"I dunno, Bubba. I'm of the opinion a stranger took her. And what kind of game is the Ghost Comes Out? It's like a real ghost took her," Scott shared as he shivered.

THE SISTERS SPURLOCK

When Bubba and Scott arrived into Grayton, they rolled all the windows in their car down and yelled, "DaisyBelle Shelby, you need to go home. Your momma wants ya!"

They drove from one end of the town to the next yelling the same thing over and over out their windows. Then they went to the closest burger stand and collected their food and headed out of the city limits.

"I think we did a good thing today, Bubba," Scott contended.

"I couldn't agree with you more, Scott. I think because of us and our dedication in trying to locate DaisyBelle Shelby that she will return home soon," Bubba stated as they ate and drove back to Memphis. They both had night classes that evening, which they skipped in favor of a keg party at their fraternity house.

What they didn't realize was at that moment, DaisyBelle was yelling for someone…anyone to come and get her. "Hep! Please hep me! I want my momma!" She sobbed.

DaisyBelle was in a room that was soundproofed. There were stacks of bales of hay in the cottage, and because of its absorbency and composition, it allowed high-pitch sound waves to travel through untouched, and therefore, it was soundproofed. She had made herself hoarse by yelling, but it was to no avail. No one could hear her.

When she was taken to this little cottage, she was thrilled to see the Marian dolls and the accessories too, but when she asked to go home, he said, "Why, DaisyBelle, you are home!" and had left locking her in.

DaisyBelle began looking around the room, and her eyes found something she hadn't noticed before. There in between several Marian dolls was one that stood out. It had spots on it in red Doh. This was her doll, the one she had taken to Tati when she had the chicken pox. *Oh my goodness*, she thought. *This the place Tati tole me 'bout. Tati's been heeyah. What did her say? She tole me Mawian's home. She gonna come git me. Tati's gonna git me! Oh, please come git me, Tati! Why he let her go? Maybe he let me go too.* And then she began to cry. She cried until it was dark outside. She put the Marian doll back on the shelf amongst the others. She didn't want him to know she had found it.

THE GHOST COMES OUT

She had began yelling again when suddenly the door opened. She ran to see who it was and then stopped in her tracks. He was back.

"DaisyBelle, you shouldn't waste your voice on yelling. No one can hear you. You're safe now. You're with me," he said in a comforting tone.

"I wanna go home. I wanna see my momma an' Val. Please take me home," DaisyBelle pleaded.

"Sweetie, I've saved you from your bad family. You don't have to worry anymore about those awful people. You're with me now," he explained.

"But I want my momma. She not bad. She loves me," DaisyBelle insisted.

"You come from a family of abuse. Your dad hit your momma and your sister. He was a bad man, and what did your mother do? Nothing. She allowed it to happen. But now, you are safe. No need to worry," he stressed.

"How you know he hit Val?" DaisyBelle asked.

"Oh, I was there. I saw it all through the window. I've been watching you all for some time. I came to rescue you from your horrible family," he replied.

"Ya…ya saw…wh-what…happened? Did…ya…see…my…papa?" DaisyBelle asked through tears.

"Carl? Oh yes! I saw Carl, and I saw him smack your mother around, and then he laid into your sister. It was only a matter of time before he would've hit you too. He was an evil man, DaisyBelle, very evil," he noted.

"Do…ya know…what hap…pened…to Papa?" wondered DaisyBelle in between sobs.

"I do, my little princess," he said with a smile.

He continued, "After your mother took you up to the Scholls for summer school and your sister was resting on her bed, I came in and had a little talk with Carl. I took him on a joyride out to Buckley Flohr's farm. I beat him to death with the back of my gun, but not before your papa bloodied my nose. Then I silenced him for good," he said with a laugh, remembering the look on Carl's face. "Anyway,

I pushed his car into Buckley's pond, and, well, as they say, the rest is history," he said matter-of-factly.

"Now, who wants dinner? How about a burger, shake, and fries? They're just giving them away," he stated.

Chapter 53

The Statement

Charles and the two TBI officers, Joseph McClanahan and Nobel Douglas, prepared a statement that Charles read, but wasn't comfortable with it and changed it when the cameras were on. Reporters and journalists from all over the state were present in that room. Bake had a front-row seat, and sitting next to him was Palo Lankford. As Charles made his way into the room, the audience silenced immediately, and the cameras starting rolling. Charles made his way up to the podium with Joseph and Nobel.

"Good evening, ladies and gentlemen. My name is Charles Hall, and I'm the sheriff here in Grayton. Recently, we have had our share of crime here in our fair town, and my friends from the TBI will go into more depth in a moment, but right now I would like to talk to the person who knows where our own DaisyBelle Shelby is. I know you are watching because that's how you get your kicks, but I promise when I find you, and I will, you're going to wish you'd never come into our fair town.

"Our criminal profilers from the Tennessee Bureau of Investigation have analyzed information needed to come up with a possible suspect. We know you're a white male between the ages of thirty and forty-five. You have a need for power. You feel inadequate around women your own age, so you must look for those who are younger. You may have been abused yourself, or you've witnessed abuse. Your father was most likely not in your life, and your mother most likely submissive. And lastly, we think you're a local man who's been watching DaisyBelle for a while. We're coming for you!" Charles was not supposed to let the audience know they thought the person who had DaisyBelle was a local person, but the sheriff wanted him to know.

And with that, Charles walked out of the room. He left Joseph and Nobel to answer the reporters' questions. Sheriff Hall went back into his office and made a local phone call.

"This is Charles. Did you see it?"

"Yes, I did. Nice job. Do you think he was watching?" said the voice on the other end of the line.

"I know he was," Charles said and hung up.

CHAPTER 54

THE REVEREND ANDREW ANGLIN GREER

Andrew Anglin Greer was the minister of the Church of the Southern Baptist of Grayton. When it burned down, the fire took with it his sermons, marriage, baptism, and christening books. It was a devasting blow to him, but he took refuge in the Lord's word and knew what was gone could be replaced and built stronger than ever. The reverend also had a secret weapon in his wife, Queenie Mae. She was the epitome of optimism, and the glass was never anything but half full with her.

"Brother Andrew," she would say to her husband, "it's not for us t'question the Lord. It's up to us t'follow the plans *He* wants us t'do, an' I say let's git on with the rebuildin' of owwah church."

"Queenie Mae, ya know the fire investigator has ruled it an arson. I don't know if he gonna need any additional pictures or if he's through lookin' through the debris."

"Well, Brother Andrew, you ain't gonna git any answers by jest sittin' there. Why don't ya pick up the phone an give 'em a call? The mountain ain't gonna move if ya don't try pushin' it. Let's see what he got t'say. Oh, Brother Andrew, I feel the Lord is callin' ya," Queenie declared as she threw up her hands and looked upward as though God was calling them.

THE SISTERS SPURLOCK

Before Brother Andrew could make the call, their phone rang, and it was Clayton Smith on the other end.

"Hello, Brother Andrew, it's Clayton and Daphne Smith calling."

"Yes, Brother Clayton, what can I do fo the two of ya, an please tell me Sista Daphne's doin' well? You know, I pray fo her eyesight t'come back an, of course, fo yua unborn chile."

"My wife is doing so well, Brother Andrew. I feel your prayers are working because my Daphne is glowing. Doctor says our baby is developing and healthy. We are indeed blessed."

"Great news, Brother Clayton. Great news, indeed. Now, what can I do fo ya t'day?"

"Daphne and I would like to help rebuild our church. We have a check made out to the Church of the Southern Baptist of Grayton and wanted to drop it off some time today. Would either you or Sister Queenie be available around 3:00 p.m.?"

"Brother Clayton, we'll both be here, an' we 'preciate yua generosity. The church insurance hasn't paid up yet, an' this would really hep us git a start on rebuildin'."

"The sooner we can lay the foundation, the sooner our chuch can be rebuilt," proclaimed Clayton.

"Amen, Brother Clayton! We will see you at three!" stated Andrew, and he hung up.

Clayton hung up the phone and looked at Daphne with a smile.

"You've nothing to worry about, honey, the church will be rebuilt soon. I told you I would take care of it," Clayton said as he kissed his wife on the forehead.

CHAPTER 55

MARCUS PETERS MAKES A MISTAKE

With the town in a frenzy over the recent deaths and DaisyBelle's disappearance, Superintendent Peters had to show support for what was going on in his town. He attempted to go to work, but he was the only one. His loyal secretary, Victoria Scholl, was absent. She was too busy searching for DaisyBelle. *I know the child is missing, but I have lots of work to do to get ready for the school year. You'd think somebody could help me. I'm sure DaisyBelle will turn up. She's like a little lost sheep. "Leave her alone, and she'll come home"…isn't that the way that nursery rhyme goes? Lord, I pray she finds her way back soon because this might mess up the start of the school year, and I do not want to delay that!* he thought.

At around 12:00 noon, he left for lunch. The only place he could go was to Grayton Burger and Shake. *If I tell them I've gone out looking for DaisyBelle, then I'll get a free burger, shake, and fries. Do I dare? Why not? Everyone else is milking this for everything it's worth. Why shouldn't I?* he thought.

He went into the restaurant, and the owner, Parralee Barmore, came up to him.

"Hello, Superintendent Peters, ya out lookin' for DaisyBelle? Of course ya are! Yua the superintendent. It's a shame, Mista Peters. I don't know what to thank. It's jest a shame," Parralee rambled. Before

Marcus could respond, Parralee continued, "I'll betcha have yua own team lookin' fo her. It breaks my heart, ya know? Jest breaks my heart. We gotta fin' her! We gonna fin' her," she insisted.

"Uh, yeah," he said a little sheepishly.

"I tell ya what, sir. Imma gonna give ya three burgers an' fries. How bout some milkshakes fo ya team?" Parralee asked. Without waiting for an answer, she yelled back, "I need four cows through the garden, four frog sticks, an' four black cows."

Turning back to Marcus, she said, "I ordered four of everythang, will that be enough, sir?"

"Uh, yes, thanks!" Marcus mumbled.

They bagged everything up for Marcus, and Parralee handed it to him saying, "No charge! Ya jest go an' fin' that precious girl an' brang her home."

"Uh, yeah," Marcus said and left with the food.

There was no way he could eat all that food, so he dropped by Victoria's house and left three burgers, fries, and shakes on her doorstep. He rang the bell, and when Rosie answered the door, he waved as he drove away.

Marcus realized work was a bust, so he drove home. He turned off to go to his house when he noticed someone walking quickly on the nature path.

How odd, he thought. *No one ever uses that path. It's a shame, but I'm so glad they don't. The last thing I want around my sanctuary of my house are people!*

After Marcus ate his lunch, he thought he would watch the television and lie down for a few minutes. After watching TV for about twenty minutes, his eyes closed, and he fell fast asleep.

He woke up, and it was just getting dark. He put on his running shorts and checked his hair in the mirror. *Oh, you look good*, he thought. Too bad his mirror didn't show him the bad comb-over or the huge balding spot at the back of his head. No, his mirror always lied to him. Anyway, he quickly headed out for his five-mile run. *Gotta run off the burger, fries, and shake*, he thought.

As he was just finishing up his run, he thought he saw a light coming from behind his house. He was just about to enter the home when he saw it again. He went to retrieve his flashlight and walked in back of the house and along the nature trail. The sky was now dark, and it was hard to see, but his flashlight shone on the way. He was getting into the thick brush when he saw the light again, and then it went dark. He kept walking for several minutes and was just about to turn around when he saw something in the brush. *What is that?* he thought. *It looks like a shed or a little house like a cottage. Why, I never would've noticed it because it's painted in colors to camouflage it.*

CHAPTER 56

FORENSIC AUTOPSY REPORT IS IN

The reason Charles did not field any questions regarding the deaths of the two Dennis brothers was because the report had not been conclusive. He did not know the origin of their deaths. When he came back to City Hall to the jail, he immediately went into the cells of both brothers. Each brother looked like he had a skin rash, and both had vomited several times on the floor of their cells. Charles didn't know what to think.

Marshall Cross, the pathologist from Stockton, was called in to determine how the brothers died. He along with Ty Bush did an extensive autopsy. Both men went to see Charles at City Hall.

"Ty and Marshall, do you have the results from the Dennis brothers?" Charles asked as he shook both of their hands. They took seats opposite the sheriff.

"We do. This is a very rare occurrence, but both brothers died from an allergic reaction to the eggs they were covered in," Marshall explained.

"What? An allergic reaction? So they died of a freak accident?" demanded Charles.

"Well, yes. It seems as though both brothers were highly allergic to eggs. This means they couldn't eat them or touch the egg yolk or egg white. In most cases, when a child has an egg allergy, they outgrow the allergy by their midteens. These two were rare cases. I think if you do some digging that you will determine the brothers never ate eggs. Perhaps their parents never told them, or maybe they didn't know themselves, but these two brothers were very allergic," asserted Marshall.

"So, why did it take so long for the reaction to occur?" Charles asked.

"Sometimes the reaction can occur in the first few minutes, and sometimes it takes a few hours. In their case, they probably started feeling strange, and hives began to break out followed by vomiting, and lastly their breathing became obstructed, and they died from asphyxia, and that is what is indicated on their death certificates," Ty noted as he handed Charles the papers.

"Well, I'm a little relieved, but I'm also baffled. If they died from an allergic reaction? Was Joe still in his cell when that occurred? Did he hear anything? Where is he, and how did he get out of the cell? Was he helped?" questioned Charles.

"Sorry, Charles, those are questions you're going to have to find out. We did our job," Ty said as he and Marshall laughed.

After Ty and Marshall left his office, Charles got in his car and drove to Joe's house. *I believe Raveleen and Dorothy haven't told me everything. They must know where Joe is, and I'm determined to find out*, he thought.

On his way to their house, Shelia radioed him.

"Sheriff, this is Shelia."

"Go ahead, Shelia," Charles radioed back.

"TBI here. There's a break in DaisyBelle's disappearance," Shelia said.

Charles turned the car around and drove back to City Hall.

CHAPTER 57

ROSIE LISTENS

It had been seventy-two hours since DaisyBelle was missing. The townfolk were questioning everyone they saw, and if they happened to view an out-of-town license plate, then Sheriff Charles would get a call. No one was as upset as the children who were there when she disappeared. They were dealing with her missing differently.

The Smiths' house

Johnny and Billy had been very restless since DaisyBelle's disappearance. They didn't feel like doing anything. They wanted to go and see their friends, but their parents wanted to keep an eye on them. Jackson had been out searching for DaisyBelle.

"Any luck, Daddy?" asked Billy and Johnny.

"No, sons, yua dad struck out. I been everywhere lookin' fo huh. I thought she might have gotten stuck somewhere. I jest don't know, boys," an exasperated Jackson said.

"Y'all thank she was kidnapped, don't ya?" Johnny inquired.

"Son, I don't know what t'b'lieve. She jest disappeared," Jackson answered.

"Daddy, can me an' Johnny go lookin' fo huh? She know us. We huh friends," noted Billy.

"Yeah, she come if we call huh," Johnny expressed.

THE GHOST COMES OUT

"I tell ya what, if she still missin' in the mornin', Imma gonna take ya boys with me t'look fo huh, deal?" asked Jackson.

"Deal!" responded both Billy and Johnny.

Harry and Dean's house

Dean was so worried about his friend DaisyBelle. He hadn't seen his other friends since the night the girl went missing. Harry was afraid to let Dean out of his sight.

"Could I just go and see Monty? I promise I'll take Lucy," Dean pleaded to Harry.

"Dean, you know I would if I could, but with DaisyBelle missing, I do not feel comfortable in your being anywhere that I can't see you," Harry explained.

"You know, Harry, it makes no sense as to how she just disappeared. I've tried to figure out where she could go. I love my new friends, and I would do anything for them," remarked Dean.

"I know you would, Deano. You've got such a wonderful heart, and that's why everyone is drawn to you," stated Harry.

There was a knock at the door, and Dean and Lucy went to answer it. It was their pastor, Pastor Allan Boyd.

Harry went to the door.

"Won't you come in, Pastor Boyd?" Harry greeted the pastor.

Harry could see how gaunt and pale the pastor looked. *Poor man,* Harry thought. *He really loved that woman. You don't know it now, Pastor, but you're better off without her.*

"What can we do for you, Pastor? I know, you're here to give us some encouragement about DaisyBelle, right?" Harry wondered.

"Yes, uh…yes, of course. I know we're all so worried about that precious child. Dean, I know you were last with her, right? How are you doing?" Pastor Allan questioned.

"I'm okay, sir. I miss her and my other friends. We get along so well," explained Dean as he rubbed his dog, Lucy.

"Of course, my son. Of course. Would you like for me to say a prayer?" Pastor Allan suggested.

"We would welcome one, Pastor," Harry insisted. And they got in a little circle and held hands and bowed their heads.

"Dear Jesus, we come to You today asking You for guidance as we search for the precious child DaisyBelle Shelby. May You help us locate her so that we may bring her back to her family. And, Father? Would You look out for Frances too?"

Harry's eyes opened when he mentioned Frances. He looked at the pastor as he was praying. Pastor Allan continued, "I pray she will be happy wherever she is. In Christ's name, we pray." And together they all said, "Amen!"

The Hutchinses' house

"I wish Uncle Bake could take me on a reportin' job!" Monty stressed to his mother as she was feeding his little brother, Alvin.

"Honey, ya know yua Uncle Bake is busy. This might be the story that takes him t'great places like Nashville or Memphis. This jest could be his big break," explained his mom.

"Me an' Uncle Bake could fin' DaisyBelle togetha. I jest know it!" Monty exclaimed.

"I wanna fine DaisyBelle as much as anybody, but I don't want anythang happenin' t'you, ya know?" advised his mom.

The door to the kitchen opened, and Bake Haas walked in.

"Uncle Bake! Uncle Bake! I missed ya!" cried Monty.

"You know, Monty, this is my biggest story to date. I'm working around the clock. I was just curious what you guys may have heard. You know, word on the street and all that?" Bake questioned.

"We know nothin', Uncle Bake. No parent'll let their child come out an' play fo fear of gettin' taken," Monty added.

"Can you blame them, Monty? They're just being cautious, and that's a good thing, right?" Bake asked.

"Yeah, I guess so. Hey, can I go t'work with ya, Uncle Bake? I promise I'll be quiet," Monty pleaded.

"You know I'd take you if I could, but my boss'll have my hide." Bake laughed. "Tell you what, sport, when all this dies down, I'll take you fishing. Would you like that?"

THE GHOST COMES OUT

"You bet I would, Uncle Bake!" shouted Monty.

"In the meantime, if y'all hear anything, let this starving reporter know, okay?" Bake laughed again.

As Bake and his sister were talking, Monty snuck out of the house and got into his uncle's car and ducked down in the back seat. There was an old raincoat in back that he used it to cover himself up.

Imma gonna be a real reporter, he thought. *Imma gonna hep my Uncle Bake!*

The Shelbys' house

"Momma, Imma not givin' up on DaisyBelle. She gonna come back, Momma. I jest know it!" Val expressed to her mother.

"We gotta have faith. Ya know owwah pastor says that, an' he know," said a subdued Rita. She was holding DaisyBelle's Betsy doll for dear life. This was the last thing DaisyBelle touched before she disappeared, and it gave her strength.

"Val, would ya thank I was bad if we went t'see a fortune-teller? I jest have t'know if my baby is safe," Rita commented.

"Where is they one, Momma?" Val inquired.

"They's one on the otha side of town. I heard 'bout her," Rita replied.

"Momma, if it git DaisyBelle back, I don't see no reason not t'try," Val responded.

They drove to the other side of town and found the home of the fortune-teller. Rita and Val approached the front steps holding hands. Both were a little leery. Rita clutched the Betsy doll in her left hand. Before they could knock, the door opened, and there was a small woman with white hair.

"Come in. I've been waitin' fo ya," she said.

Rita and Val came in together holding hands.

"Y'all ain't got nothin' t'be 'fraid of. Y'all jest want some answers, huh?" questioned the woman.

Both Rita and Val nodded.

"Please take a seat. Tell me y'all's names," she insisted.

"Imma Rita, an' this here's my eldest daughter, Val," Rita explained.

"Y'all wanna know where DaisyBelle is, don't ya?" the old woman asked.

Rita and Val nodded again as the old woman looked deep into her crystal ball.

"Did ya brang somethin' of DaisyBelle's?" the old woman queried.

Rita handed her DaisyBelle's Betsy doll. The old woman rubbed it and began to say a lot of mumble jumble. Rita and Val looked at one another not knowing what was going on.

"I see someone starting with an *M*," said the old woman while still gazing into the crystal ball.

"Uh, I dunno. Do ya know anyone with the letter *M*, Val?" Rita asked.

"Ya know Monty, Momma? His name starts with an *M*," stated Val.

The old woman kept gazing at the crystal ball. Then she looked up at Rita and Val and asked, "Who's Marian?" the old woman wanted to know.

"Uh, she's DaisyBelle's otha doll. She lost somewhere," Rita stated.

The old woman pushed Betsy back into Rita's hands and shouted, "Go! When ya find Marian, ya find DaisyBelle!"

The Scholls' house

"Momma, me an' Tati don't thank DaisyBelle's gone. Me an' Tati thank she round here somewhere, an' we gonna fin' her," Rosie asserted.

"I want to believe she's close by too, but you girls don't need to be going anywhere without me or another adult. Is that clear?" warned Victoria.

"Me an' Wosie won't go wifout ya, Momma. I pwomise. Midas won't let us," Tati asserted as she looked down at her dog.

Rosie and Tati went out on the front porch to talk. Midas followed obediently. Rosie was sure they had missed something, and she was resolute in discovering what that was.

THE GHOST COMES OUT

Rosie looked at Tati and questioned, "What do y'all talk 'bout with DaisyBelle when y'all are t'getha?"

"Um, we talk 'bout Betsy," Tati said as she held her pink cat Featha and rubbed Midas.

"Yeah? What y'all say?" Rosie asked.

"Um, we talk 'bout huh cwose," Tati answered.

"So, ya talk about her clothes. What else?" wondered Rosie.

"Mawian. We talk 'bout Mawian," Tati explained.

"Yeah? What about Marian? Tati, why do ya always say Marian's home. She ain't in owwah house, an' she ain't in DaisyBelle's house," Rosie stated.

"Nuh-uh," agreed Tati.

"So, whatcha mean?" queried Rosie as she looked down at Tati.

"Huh in da house in da woods," replied Tati.

CHAPTER 58

TBI TAKES OVER

Charles got back to City Hall in five minutes, and there waiting for him was Joseph McClanahan, Nobel Douglas, and two more of their TBI colleagues. They were just about to leave when Charles got there.

"Good thing you got here when you did, Sheriff. We've got a great lead. A man approximately forty years old has been spotted in Memphis with a young girl around seven or eight who looks like DaisyBelle. They were acting suspiciously when a waitress asked them who they were. The man even said, 'No busness of yours. She my niece if ya gotta know.'

"And then they got up and left and didn't even stay to eat. Then they were spotted in a shopping center. He was getting her some clothes when an attendant asked if she could help him. She asked him how old the girl was, and he didn't know.

"He looked at the girl and said, 'How old are ya?' The girl didn't reply. The attendant said she was very scared. The attendant asked the girl what size she wore, and the girl just stared at her scared to say anything. I think we got our man. They're tailing him. He checked into the Soft Pillow Hotel in Memphis. We got our eyes on him now. This might be over tonight, Sheriff. We're going to take over the case from here, Sheriff. You just hang loose," Joseph said.

Charles hoped the girl was DaisyBelle and that they were going to get her, but something just kept gnawing at him. He couldn't shake the belief that DaisyBelle had never left Grayton. He believed all along the perpetrator was here in the town right under his nose, but if he was wrong and they were bringing the child home, he was thrilled. *I shouldn't call Rita yet,* he thought. *I need to make sure the child is DaisyBelle. I wouldn't want to get her hopes up again. She's gone through too much.*

Charles watched the TBI pull away. He headed back into his office when his phone rang.

"Sheriff's Office. This is Shelia speaking."

"He's right here, Victoria. I'll put ya through." Shelia turned to Charles, who was already picking up the other phone.

"Hi, Victoria. Are you okay?" Charles asked.

"Charles, I think you need to get to our house as soon as possible! I think we might know where DaisyBelle is," she stated.

"What? You think you know? Where? How? Nevermind, I'm on my way!" Charles exclaimed, and he ran out of the office and jumped into his squad car.

CHAPTER 59

WHERE'S MONTY?

The phone rang, and Harry went to pick it up.

"Hello?" Harry answered. Harry listened to the voice on the other end of the phone.

"Yes, I will. I'll see you in ten minutes," Harry responded as he hung up the phone.

Dean was in his room reading one of the *World Book Encyclopedias* Harry had purchased for him. Harry came to the door of his room.

"Dean, would you and Lucy like to spend some time at Monty's house?" Harry asked.

"You bet I would!" Dean said excitedly. He jumped up, and Lucy was at his side ready to go.

Harry, Dean, and Lucy got into Harry's Studebaker Gran Turismo Hawk. They drove the short distance from their house to the Hutchinses' house. When they arrived Harry went to the door and knocked. Mrs. Hutchins came to the door carrying Alvin on her hip.

"Hello, Mr. Miller, how are ya t'day?" Mrs. Hutchins asked.

"I'm doing very well, Mrs. Hutchins. I have a meeting I must get to and was hoping if Dean and Lucy could play with Monty. I realize this is short notice, and I apologize for any imposition," Harry acknowledged.

THE GHOST COMES OUT

"Nonsense, Mr. Miller. Why, I know Monty'd love t'have Dean an' Lucy. Take as long as ya want, an' I'll watch 'em for ya," she replied.

Dean and Lucy got out of the car and ran into the Hutchinses' house as Harry drove away.

"Monty? Monty? Ya got compny!" Mrs. Hutchins yelled in the direction of Monty's room. Monty didn't come.

"I'll betcha he's listenin' t'that radio. He likes it loud. Ya young folk like it loud, don't ya?" Mrs. Hutchins laughed.

"Jest go in t'his room an' surprise him, Dean. He'll be so excited."

So Dean and Lucy went down the hall and into Monty's room, but he wasn't there. Dean called for him. *Maybe he's in the bathrooom*, he thought, but no one was there. Dean and Lucy walked into the kitchen.

"Mrs. Hutchins, Monty's not here," Dean asserted.

CHAPTER 60

MARCUS'S MISTAKE

He knocked on the door of the cottage house. *I wonder who lives here. I cannot believe this house is so close to my residence, and I had no idea it was here, but how would I? It's camouflaged*, Marcus thought to himself. There was no response with that knock, so Marcus tried again with a harder and louder knock, and then the door opened.

"Hey! I didn't know you lived here. I thought you lived in town," Marcus said with a shocked surprise.

Before anyone could respond, there was a small little voice that yelled, "Hep!"

Marcus Peters pushed his way into the house and saw DaisyBelle Shelby tied up in a chair surrounded by a roomful of dolls. They all seemed to be looking at them.

Marcus looked at him and said, "You? You're the one who took her? Why? Who the hell are you? What kind of freak are you? What's with the dolls?"

Before he got an answer, Marcus did the most courageous thing he had ever done in his life. Without thinking of himself, his hair, or his safety, he rushed to DaisyBelle's assistance. The moment he got to her, he heard a loud noise and felt a sharp pain in his right shoulder. As he tried to untie her with his left hand, he saw blood dripping down and heard another loud *bam* and felt a bullet enter his back. He tried to protect and save DaisyBelle, but as he fell to the ground, his foot got tangled in a leg of the chair, which sent DaisyBelle down with him. Her head hit the hard concrete floor, and she was knocked unconscious. Marcus Peters was dead before his body hit the floor.

Because the door was left open, the loud gunshots were heard outside and awoke Monty, who was sleeping in the back of his uncle's car. He quickly opened the car door and ran into the camoflouged cottage house and found his uncle, DaisyBelle, and Superintendent Marcus Peters.

He ran up to his uncle and yelled with excitement, "Ya found her, Uncle Bake! Ya found DaisyBelle! Oh my gosh, Uncle Bake, this is gonna be the best story ever! Ya gonna be famous! I can't wait t'hep ya write it." He was thrilled with emotion but then turned his attention toward the two on the floor.

"Hey, what's wrong with Mr. Peters an' DaisyBelle? Why ain't they movin'?" Monty demanded. He then quickly looked around the room and took in the dolls. He was trying to grasp what was going on. He looked at his uncle and shouted, "Uncle Bake, Mr. Peters is bleedin', an' DaisyBelle is…is she dead? We gotta git hep, Uncle Bake! Ya want me t'run an' git hep? Can ya call the sheriff?"

Bradley Bacon Haas never said a word. He simply shut and locked the door and turned back to his nephew. He had a look on his face Monty had never seen before. Bake's eyes were jet-black and piercing as they stared at his nephew. It was only in that moment that Monty realized he was in the presence of the devil, and that evil just happened to be the one he most admired…most loved…his dear Uncle Bake.

CHAPTER 61

Don't Mess with Rocky

Harry drove quickly to meet Rocky, his boss. He arrived at the burned-down building where his boss told him to meet. When Harry arrived, Rocky was already there.

"Quick, Harry, we don't have much time. Are you packing?" Rocky queried.

Harry nodded as Rocky jumped into Harry's car and told him where to go. Harry pulled out and onto Highway 69. They drove about four minutes when Rocky told Harry to pull over.

"We're going to need to walk the rest of the way from here, but first, open your trunk," Rocky commanded.

Harry opened the back of his trunk, and Rocky looked in and found the jacket and a tan polypropylene rope and gave them to Harry. He looked down at the jacket with a question, but didn't dare inquire what he was to do with them. Rocky slammed the trunk door shut and started walking. They came upon a path that was overgrown with weeds. Harry was surprised to see the path. He thought he knew every inch of this town, but he had never seen or been on this trail. They were walking fast when Rocky started to run. Harry did his best to keep up, but his boss was much faster. They ran for about five minutes until they came to a building that was colored in khaki.

I never would've found this building. It's disguised so no one would find it. I wonder what's inside. It must be something extremely important, or Rocky wouldn't be this determined, Harry thought.

THE GHOST COMES OUT

Rocky turned to Harry and whispered, "That's where he's holding DaisyBelle!" Rocky pointed at the house.

Harry had had his eyes on Bake for sometime and knew he, like his father, was a peeping tom, but he didn't know it had escalated to kidnapping. Rocky had figured that out, and both of them were waiting to catch him and find out where he'd taken DaisyBelle.

"Okay, I know the door is locked. Use your talent for lockpicking. Deano's buddy is in there too. So, you don't need to be visible, Harry. Give me three minutes. I'll get Monty and DaisyBelle out, and then you come in and complete the job," Rocky instructed.

"Right, Boss!" Harry said.

Harry immediately went to work using the skill he had accomplished so many years ago—lockpicking. He pulled out a screwdriver, Allen wrench, and a paper clip out of his breast pocket. In less than a minute, he gave his boss the go-ahead sign, and Rocky stormed through the door.

CHAPTER 62

EVERYONE LISTENS TO TATI

Sheriff Hall pulled up to Victoria's house and almost hit Rita and Val as they were running up the yard to the front door. Charles jumped out without shutting his car door. Rita grabbed Charles and yelled, "We gotta fine Marian! We gotta fine Marian, an' then we fine my baby!"

"Rita, settle down. I don't know what you're talking about," he claimed as he held her shoulders with his hands. He noticed she had DaisyBelle's doll, Betsy, in her hands.

Victoria ran out of the house followed by Rosie, Tati, and Midas.

"The fortune-teller. She tole us t'fine Marian!" Rita pleaded and looked down at Tati.

Victoria intervened and said, "Charles, I think we can help you. Tati thinks she might know where DaisyBelle is, and Rosie figured it out."

Charles dropped down on two knees so he was just a little taller than Tati. He knew he needed to be very gentle when talking to a three-year-old.

"Tati," he said softly, "can you tell me where you think DaisyBelle might be?"

"Huh in da woods wid Mawian," Tati answered while rubbing her pink cat, Featha.

Charles had absolutely no idea what she was talking about, so Rosie stepped up to interpret.

THE GHOST COMES OUT

"Mista Sheriff, I thank I can hep ya. When Tati got the pox, DaisyBelle gave Tati her Marian doll, an' she put some red Doh on it t'make it look like she had the pox too. It looked really real. Anyway, Ree sent Tati away, an' she went in the woods an found a house with some dolls in it. She lef DaisyBelle's doll there. Imma thankin' DaisyBelle's in that house," explained Rosie.

Charles turned to Tati and pleaded, "Can you take us there?"

"Um, I thank so. Midas an' Lucy know da way," Tati responded softly.

And just like it was on cue, running across the front lawn were Mrs. Hutchins, Dean, and Lucy.

"Monty's missin'! Ya thank one of those ghosts got him too?" Mrs. Hutchins cried as she came closer to the group. She went to Victoria, who draped her arms around her for comfort.

"He was with me one minute, an' then he gone. I thank he snuck out an' went with Bake, or one of them ghost got 'em," she added with a sob. With Mrs. Hutchins crying, that only made Rita wail louder.

Charles stood up. He looked over at Victoria, who seemed to know what he was thinking.

"Why don't I stay here with Rita, Mrs. Hutchins, Dean, and Val? There's no sense in all of you going into the woods. I'll make lemonade and coffee and heat up some pastries. We'll wait here until you come back. Rosie, can you go with Sheriff Hall and Tati?" Victoria asked her daughter.

"You betcha, Momma. Tati, we goin' t'gether. Dean, can we take Lucy?" Rosie wondered.

"Of course," Dean immediately answered and took Betsy out of Rita's hands. He brought it up to Lucy's nose and, as he looked into her eyes, said, "Go find DaisyBelle and Monty!" And just like that, Charles, Tati, Rosie, and the two dogs left to search the woods.

CHAPTER 63

THE SMITHS COME A CALLIN'

It was precisely 3:00 p.m. when Daphne and Clayton Smith rang Brother Andrew and Sister Queenie Mae's front door. Daphne always prided herself on punctuality.

"Nobody likes to be kept waiting. Just remember, Daphne, your time is just as important as the person you're making wait on you," Franklin Montague informed his daughter. Daphne had never forgotten that.

As she and Clayton stood at the door waiting for it to be answered, Daphne thought back to a few nights ago when she and Silvia had entered City Hall to visit with one of the prisoners there. It was not their intent to kidnap Joe Puckett, but the opportunity seemed to present itself, and, well, who were they not to take advantage of the situation? They had waited until Shelia, Sheriff Charles Hall's secretary, had gone out for dinner. She had already brought food back for the inmates, and now she had one hour to eat, and then she would return to do night duty and keep an eye on the prisoners.

Ya know, Imma not paid nuff to watch these bad people, she thought. *Why, I do b'lieve Imma gonna ask Charles fo a raise. He always says Imma the best secretary. Yeah, that's what Imma gonna do. Imma gonna ask him tomorrow*, Shelia thought happily.

Both Daphne and Silvia knew they had an hour to visit, and when they walked into City Hall, Daphne's heart began to beat faster. She knew she was getting close to the man who not only had burned down the Church of the Southern Baptist of Grayton, but had blinded her in the process and tried to knock her off the stage in order to harm her baby. Joe Puckett was one of the lowest forms of human beings. He was a no-good sadistic racist. *What kind of a man hates another simply for the color of the skin? Why do people like that exist?* she thought.

As Daphne and Silvia turned down the hall to go toward the cells, they heard shouting going on.

Silvia turned to Daphne and said, "Them prisners show make a lot of noise, don't they, Daphne?"

"Yes, they do, Silvia," Daphne affirmed nodding her head.

When they got into the room with the three cells, they noticed one of the Dennis brothers was up against the bars of his cell. His face was red and blotchy. He saw Daphne and Silvia even though Daphne had her hair pulled back in a scarf and was wearing dark glasses. She was still so beautiful, and anyone could tell that.

"Hey, hey, beautiful!" Mikey, a.k.a. Hamerhead, yelled at Daphne. "Come ovah heeyah. Someum's wrong with me. Imma itchy. I feel funny. Ya gotta hep me!"

"Hey, Hamerhead! Imma itchy too. Whas goin' on? Somethin' ain't right. Imma feelin' funny," Walter, a.k.a. Squirt, yelled to his brother.

Neither Daphne nor Silvia paid any attention to them as they got louder and louder because the two women had their eyes on the prize, and that was Joe Puckett.

They approached his cell and saw him eating his dinner. *What a slob*, Daphne thought. *He eats like a pig would at a trough. No, that's not true. He's worse. At least pigs were made to grunt and gorge. He's a man with no manners, no backbone, and no usefulness on this earth.*

As Daphne and Silvia came into the view of Joe, he looked up.

"Well, well, if it ain't the princess of Grayton and huh niggah friend," Joe said while chewing his food. Some of it spit out of the corner of his mouth.

"So what y'all doin' here, huh?" Joe demanded.

THE SISTERS SPURLOCK

Neither Silvia nor Daphne spoke. Silvia simply retrieved a small tension wrench from her pocket and a paper clip and went to work on the keyhole on Joe's cell.

"Whatcha doin', niggah? Ya thank ya can break me free?" Joe said with a laugh.

"What if I don't wanna git outta heeyah? This best meal I had in long time. I kinda like it heeyah cept fo those brothas. Would ya shut the fuck up? Imma tryin' t'eat," Joe yelled at the Dennis brothers.

Hamerhead's and Squirt's moans got louder and louder. It sounded like their breathing was becoming labored, but Silvia and Daphne paid no attention. They were there for one reason, and nothing was going to distract them from their business. At last Silvia heard the click of the lock, and she nodded to Daphne, who opened Joe's cell door. Daphne walked in and put a gun up to Joe's head.

"You're coming with us, Mr. Puckett. Don't make a move, or I promise I'll shoot your brains out," Daphne said in a low calm voice.

Joe looked at Daphne as though he couldn't believe what was going on. He actually had a frightened look on his face. *She can't see me!* he thought. *When that colored church was burned down, she went blind. I can make a run fo it. She won't see where Imma goin'.*

Daphne stared at Joe through her dark glasses.

"If you think I can't see you, then you're wrong, Mr. Puckett. I regained my sight, and if you're thinking about making a run for it, I'd think again if I were you," she said coldly.

Silvia came in and put a knife up to Joe's throat.

"Gimme a reason t'slice yua throat, Joe. I really wanna reason," Silvia demanded as the knife she was holding cut ever so lightly into his dirty white skin. Daphne reached into her purse and pulled out some handcuffs. She quickly slid them on Joe before he knew what was happening.

"Hey! Ya don't have t'do that. I'll be good. I promise," he said as he smiled with a cavity-filled mouth and one front tooth missing.

"Ya disgust me, white boy!" Silvia shouted. "When's the last time yua teeth came into contact with a substance called toothpaste?"

"Whatcha sayin', niggah girl, my teeth not pwetty?" he said and then shut his mouth. *How dare this niggah girl say anythang 'bout my*

THE GHOST COMES OUT

teeth. Momma always says I's gots the pwettiest teeth in the Puckett family. This niggah girl know nothin', he thought.

Hamerhead began to shout, "I'm...n...trouble! Somebody... hep...me...!" And then he began gasping for breath.

Squirt echoed his brother's rant, "Me...too! Hep...somebody!" And then his breathing became labored.

But their shouts went unnoticed. Silvia and Daphne put a pillowcase over Joe's head and marched him out of the building and into a truck, which was parked outside. They drove to the place where the Church of the Southern Baptist once stood and took the pillowcase off of his head. Joe looked around and noticed the lot had been scraped, and except for a lot of ash that remained, everything about the church had been demolished. There was a dump truck and a backhoe, which were going to be used to make the footers. The concrete foundation was to be laid the very next day.

"What we doin' heeyah?" Joe demanded.

"This is the place where we all came togetha. Because of you, owwah church ain't here. Because of yua, Sista Daphne lost huh sight!" Silvia explained.

"I ain't got nothin' t'do wid huh sight goin' way or burnin' ya niggah church," Joe insisted.

Silvia turned toward Joe and, with a swift move, stabbed him in the leg.

"Ооn!" Joe yelled as he fell to the ground. "I swear, nig—I mean...lady, I didn't do it!" he begged.

"Yeah ya did!" Silvia persisted. "Ya burnt my church, an' ya blinded my sista. Ya don't d'serve t'breathe owwah air!"

"Mr. Joe, you know why we're here. I could've forgiven the realization of your blinding me. What I can't forgive, forget, or overlook is that you attempted to injure my husband at the 5 Mile Race, you set fire to his church, you intended to swindle innocent children out of their chance to win a pony, and you and your pathetic daughter sought to ruin the graduation of the summer school students. And lastly, the proverbial straw that broke the camel's back is your wanting to hurt my unborn child," Daphne explained as she rubbed her stomach, and then she added, "My daddy always told me that the only way t'take care of scum is to erase it…and well…you're scum, Mr. Joe."

Joe looked up at Daphne pleading with her. "Please, Miss Montague, don't 'rase me. I… I…b'betta, an' I swear I ain't the one who burned da church. I ain't! I swear it! I sorry ya went blind, but I ain't the one who blind ya, I swear! My daughta, Dorthy, know who did it. She was there. Ask her! Ask her!" He put up his two fingers like he was giving the Boy Scout pledge.

"You know, Mr. Joe, there's only one thing I hate more than a racist," Daphne said as she took off her glasses, took a knife out of her handbag, and stared down at him. She didn't have to tell him. Joe knew she could see, and the look she showed gave him the shudders. If he was worried about Silvia, then he was doubly concerned about Daphne.

Scared to ask, but he just couldn't help himself. "Uh…whas… that?" he asked slowly, afraid of her answer.

"A stupid one!" she shouted as she plunged her knife into his chest.

CHAPTER 64

LOIS COMES TO THE RESCUE

"Uncle Bake...please. I... I... I'm...your...buddy...please," cried Monty as Bake came toward him. Monty's heart was beating so loud and fast he thought his uncle could hear it. *Why would Uncle Bake do this? What's wrong wid him? What's he gonna do to us? Would he kill us like he had Mr. Peters?* These were the questions that were going around in Monty's brain.

Monty looked down at DaisyBelle, who was beginning to stir on the floor. When she had fallen, the ropes around the chair had come undone. *I can't let anything happen to her.*

"Aaah," she cried as she moved about and opened her eyes.

Monty stepped closer to DaisyBelle and sat next to her. He wrapped his arms around her as she looked up at him.

"Monty? Ya...found...me?" DaisyBelle asked quietly as she looked up at him. She viewed the room and saw Bake coming toward them. "Oh no!" she cried softly as she clung to Monty.

Suddenly the door swung open, and Rocky charged in. Rocky ran toward Bake and surprisingly him knocked him out with the butt of Lois. Lois was Rocky's .38 revolver, and Rocky never left home with her. Bake's injury made a puddle of blood next to him on the floor.

Rocky looked around and quickly assessed the situation. *Who's that on the floor? Oh wow, that's the superintendent of Grayton County shools. Why would he shoot him?* Rocky thought. *Must've surprised him.*

Superintendent Marcus Peters looked dead from the gunshot wound. Rocky quickly went over to him and felt for a pulse. *Nothing. Just as I thought. He's dead.*

Monty and DaisyBelle were huddled together on the floor. They looked at Rocky with wide eyes, and they used the chair to shield them from this intruder. Rocky came closer to them, and they started shaking.

"Who...who...who...are...you?" Monty questioned as he held DaisyBelle closer to him. He wasn't about to let anything happen to her now that he'd found her.

"It's okay, Monty. I'm a friend," Rocky explained inching closer to the two children.

"Ya...ya...know...my...name?" wondered Monty as he hugged DaisyBelle closer still.

"Yes, buddy. I know your name, and I know DaisyBelle's name too. Now, we don't have much time before he comes around," Rocky said pointing to Bake.

"Can you walk, DaisyBelle?" Rocky asked DaisyBelle.

"Uh, I... I...thank...so," DaisyBelle replied meekly.

Rocky reached down and lifted DaisyBelle up and held her close for a moment. Rocky gave her a big hug and said, "Everything's going to be okay, honey. I promise. Monty's going to take you home to your mom, okay?" And DaisyBelle looked at Rocky and nodded.

Monty stood up, and he put his arm around DaisyBelle, who leaned into him. They slowly walked toward the door when DaisyBelle shouted, "Wait!"

She moved quickly to one of the shelves in the cottage and grabbed her Marian doll, the one with red Doh dots still on its face.

"Okay, now Imma good," she said to Monty, and they hurriedly left the cottage, putting as much distance between them and Bake Haas.

CHAPTER 65

HARRY'S TURN

Harry rushed into the cottage when he saw DaisyBelle and Monty leave.

"Good, you're here. We don't have long, so help him into his jacket and don't forget to keep his T-shirt on him. We don't want to show marks under his armpits," Rocky instructed Harry.

"Right, Boss," Harry replied and quickly put the jacket on Bake. He had done it many times before, so it was an easy task. It took him about five minutes to get it on him just right, and he sat him up in the chair. Then, he threw a glass of water on Bake to wake him up.

"Wake up, Reporter Bake! You're missing the story of your life!" shouted Harry at Bake.

Bake began to come to and found himself sitting up in a chair. He looked around the room and saw someone he'd never seen before, and then his eyes found Harry looming over him. *What's he doing here? Where's my love, DaisyBelle? Where's Monty? Oh, when I get my hands on those kids, their punishment will be slow and long*, he thought with a smile, but then Bake tried to move around, but his arms were in a tangle. He then noticed he was in a straitjacket. *How did I get in this?* he thought.

"Who…who…are you?" Bake demanded.

"My name is Rocky Frederella. Have you ever heard of the Frederella Family from Chicago?" Rocky quizzed.

"The Frederella Family? You...you're Rocky? But you're a—?" Bake started, but Rocky interrupted him.

"You've been a very bad boy, Mr. Bake. I don't like bad boys, do I, Harry?" Rocky calmly asked.

"No, you don't, Boss," answered Harry.

"Oh...my god! Y...y...you...work for Rocky?" Bake asked Harry.

"You know if I were you, Mr. Bake, I would be saying a prayer or getting my head right before I meet my maker, but yes, to answer your question, he works for me," concluded Rocky.

"W...w...why are you here? Uh, I was...protecting DaisyBelle... from her family," explained Bake.

"Is that what you call it? I would call it kidnapping, molestation, and pedophilia to start with," Rocky responded.

"Yeah, Bake, we don't like creeps like you who go out of their way to harm children," Harry interjected.

"What...what if... I turned myself in?" begged Bake.

Both Rocky and Harry started laughing.

"Too late," Rocky answered after much laughter.

Rocky came toward Bake holding the polypropylene rope. Harry took it from Rocky and threw the end over the lighting fixture on the ceiling. He swung on it to see how sturdy it was. It was strong because Bake had nailed it to a beam that supported the structure of the cabin. His eyes were alert, but Bake still hadn't figured out what was going on when Rocky said, "So, Mr. Bake, I sincerely hope you've watched the greatest magician in the world, Benny DaPortia, get out of these contraptions. If you have, then you're home free or at least until Sheriff Hall finds you. If not, then I would suggest you saying a few prayers before you meet your end. Either way, it's a win-win for Grayton."

"What do you mean? What are you going to do?" Bake nervously asked. His brain was working overtime, and he was scared. He now knew exactly what was going on but thought he might buy some time while his hands were working nonstop to get him out of this constraint.

THE GHOST COMES OUT

Harry gave Rocky the rope after he'd put a hangman's knot in it. Rocky placed the rope behind Bake's left ear. Harry lifted Bake and stood him up in the chair.

Rocky turned to Harry to give him directions.

"What's my motto, Harry?" Rocky insisted.

"No messes, Boss, no messes. Messes mean questions, and we don't like questions," Harry responded with a smile.

"Righto!" Rocky replied and then added, "Give him four minutes to free himself before you kick the chair away," Rocky said with a smile and grabbed Lois, the .38 revolver, and turned to leave.

"Right, Boss!" Harry replied.

Harry turned to Bake and said with a grin, "If it makes you feel any better, Mr. Bake, you'll pass out in thirty seconds, and then, well, it's just a wait-and-see game until you stop kicking."

The last thing Rocky heard before the door closed was Bake screaming, "Nooooooooooooo!"

Meanwhile...

DaisyBelle and Monty were walking at a very fast pace. Monty stopped when he noticed DaisyBelle was having a hard time keeping up.

"Git on my back, DaisyBelle. Imma gonna carry ya," Monty insisted. So Monty stooped down on the ground, and DaisyBelle got on his back. Because she was so little, it wasn't much of an effort for Monty to carry her even though he was only a year older.

"Thank ya, Monty. Ya saved me," DaisyBelle whispered into Monty's right ear as he carried her. She held on tight and never wanted to let go.

They really didn't know where they were going but knew they needed to get as far away from the cottage as possible. They must've been walking for fifteen minutes when they heard a noise in front of them. Monty stopped walking. Something was in the thick brush coming toward them. They were afraid to move. *Could it be Bake? Could he have gotten away? What would he do to us?* they both thought. All at once they saw something move. Their hearts were beating out of their chests, and both of them froze. They saw an animal staring at them. In fact, there were two of them.

"DaisyBelle, it's Lucy and Midas!" Monty shouted.

Following right on their heels were Sheriff Charles, Rosie, and Tati.

CHAPTER 66

THE CHECK

The door opened, and Reverend Andrew Greer and Queenie Mae both were there to greet Daphne and Clayton. Queenie Mae had on one of her fanciest dresses. It wasn't every day that Daphne Montague-Smith made social calls. Although since both she and Clayton had announced to the town they were married and having a baby, she had been seen around town a lot and had recently joined the Church of the Southern Baptist of Grayton. After the fire, services were conducted at the Grayton Grocery Mart until the grocer had noticed candy and pop had gone missing. Many parishoners suspected the Smith boys, and they would've been correct. Now the services took place at the white Baptist Church, with each minister taking turns delivering the sermons. Some commented the sermons were better with both ministers assisting and hoped they could continue getting together after their church was rebuilt.

Before they arrived, Queenie had been making a fuss over what to wear.

"Ya don't needs t'dress up so fancy, Queenie. Jesus knows why ya dressin' up so, an' he know it ain't fo him. Ya do know she blind, right?" Reverend Greer was teasing his wife.

"I ain't dressin' up fo nobody. I jest happen t'wanna look nice t'day. Is that okay by you, Reverend? Maybe I wanna look good fo you! And yes, I know she blind. I was there when she went blind. Ya know what the Lord say? He say ya always do yua best when ya look yua best!" Queenie said looking in the mirror and fixing her hair.

"Uh-huh, ya git that outta the good book of Queenie Mae?" asked Andrew laughing. "He know the truth, Queenie Mae," as Andrew looked up to the heavens.

Queenie Mae invited Daphne and Clayton into their home.

"Y'all come on in. I take ya hand Daphne an' lead ya to a seat. Ya look so purdy t'day. That color yellow look so nice with yua hair," Queenie Mae commented.

Daphne was wearing a yellow sundress. Her hair, with a yellow band, was hanging down. She looked stunning and was just barely showing that she was pregnant. Clayton couldn't hide his delight. He was dressed in light-colored pants and a blue navy jacket.

My, they make a beautiful couple. And t'thank they havin' a baby. That baby gonna be gorgeous or handsome 'pending on what she be havin', Queenie thought.

Daphne was a little nervous, but having Clayton by her side made her feel safe. She knew her husband was watching out for her.

"Well, like I told you on the telephone, we would like to give a check to you, Reverend Greer, for the new church. Daphne and I think waiting for the insurance money will take time, and we need to build our new church. So, we were hoping that with this check, Baker Brothers Construction can begin laying the foundation, tomorrow," Clayton explained with a smile while handing Reverend Greer the check.

"This is mighty nice of y'all. I talked to the fire inspectors, and they say we can begin rebuilding, so this is gonna hep, I'm sure," he said, and then he looked at the check. It was a $10,000 check made out to the Church of the Southern Baptist of Grayton. Reverend Greer had never seen a check for that amount. He stared at it and then looked at both of the Smiths.

"I cannot b'lieve ya generosity. I don't know what t'say otha than 'praise the Lord!'" Andrew said with excitement as he laid it down on the side table.

Queenie Mae was itching to see how much it was. When Andrew asked Clayton to help him get some cold drinks in the

THE GHOST COMES OUT

kitchen, Queenie Mae couldn't contain herself. She walked over to the table and picked it up. She gasped.

"Are you okay, Mrs. Greer?" Daphne asked Queenie Mae. Daphne saw what was going on but knew Queenie Mae thought she was blind.

"Oh yes, Miss Daphne, I'm jest fine. I dropped somethin' on the flow. Imma gonna pick it up," she said and acted like she was picking something up.

Yeah, you dropped your mouth on the floor, thought Daphne with a smile.

The two men came back into the room with cold lemonade and homemade chocolate cookies. Clayton handed Daphne her drink and brought her some cookies. He laid two cookies on a napkin and placed it on her lap. Then he sat down beside her on the couch.

"Um, so do you think the Baker brothers could lay the foundation tomorrow?" Daphne asked nervously.

"Oh, Imma gonna call 'em t'day. They gonna start t'morrow, guaranteed!" Andrew said enthusticastically, and with that, Daphne got up forgetting the chocolate cookies were in her lap.

"Oh my," she said. "I've made a mess of your pretty blue rug."

"Don't ya even thank 'bout it. It'll vacuum right up," Queenie Mae explained. "Imma glad the chocolate didn't git on ya purdy yellow dress."

It would be many days later when Queenie Mae was thinking back over the conversation that took place in their house that she remembered what Daphne had said about the color of the rug. *How did she know the rug was blue?*

Daphne wanted to get out of the house as fast as she could. The guilt of what she had done was now getting to her, and she just wanted it to be over.

Andrew and Queenie Mae walked the Smiths to the door.

"Clayton an' Daphne, could we say a prayer b'fo y'all go?" asked Andrew.

"Of course," Clayton replied. Everyone clasped hands and bowed their heads as Andrew began, "Heavenly Fatha, we so grateful. We know Ya sent us the Smiths so we could rebuild owwah church.

Lowd, we are Yua clay, so mold us as we reconstruct Ya house. Lowd, bless the Smiths fo what they done fo owwah church an' bless they unborn chile that he or she may grow up t'be as fine a Christian as his or her momma an' daddy are. Amen."

And Daphne began to cry.

CHAPTER 67

HOME AT LAST

Charles ran toward DaisyBelle and Monty and hugged them both tightly. Rosie and Tati came in behind them and put their arms around them too. It was one big group hug, and it felt good to all of them.

"Are you okay? Are you hurt?" he asked anxiously pulling himself away to look at both of the children.

"DaisyBelle fell and h-h-hit her head. She's got-ta real g-g-goose egg on it, Sheriff, but y'all betta run afore Uncle Bake g-g-gits us all!" Monty stuttered while pushing DaisyBelle forward.

He was still scared, and he and DaisyBelle tried to run again. Charles intercepted the children and held them close. He knew they were frightened, but he needed answers to his questions.

"Monty, settle down, son. You've got to tell me what happened. What's this got to do with your Uncle Bake?" Charles demanded to know.

"We can't stop, Sheriff. He gonna git us!" DaisyBelle yelled as she and Monty tried to run again.

"Who's going to get you?" Charles wanted to know. "I promise you I will not let anything else hurt you, but I need to know what happened."

"Uncle Bake is gonna git us! He-he-he da one who t-t-taked DaisyBelle!" stammered Monty.

Charles was trying to comprehend what Monty was telling him. He couldn't put all the pieces together—that would happen later when he had these children home safely and when he had Bake under arrest. His mission now was to take them home to their mothers.

"Okay, kids, we're going home!" explained Charles.

Before they started for home, DaisyBelle went over to Tati and hugged her tightly. DaisyBelle looked down at Tati and said, "I knew ya was gonna come fo me, Tati. I jest knew it!" DaisyBelle said with tears in her eyes and handed Tati the Marian doll she had left.

"I b'lieve ya forgot somethin', Tati," she said.

Tati hugged her back and said, "I lef huh fo ya, DaisyBelle," and kissed her on her cheek.

Charles then reached down and lifted DaisyBelle into his arms. She held out both of her hands for her two best friends. Monty took hold of her right hand, and Tati grabbed her left. She gladly relaxed in Charles's arms as they hurried home and even rested her head on his shoulders. DaisyBelle was going home to her momma and Val, at last.

Meanwhile...

"How long's it been? I jest know the ghost of Polly Tartar has got 'em," cried Mrs. Hutchins as she fell into Rita Shelby's arms.

"Ya thank she got my DaisyBelle too?" sobbed Rita while cluthing DaisyBelle's Betsy doll. Both of the ladies wailed while hugging each other. Victoria, Val, and Dean tried their best to comfort and give them hope, but they were completely ignored.

"Ladies, it's only been a couple of hours, and I know for a fact that Sheriff Hall will not give up until he's brought all of our children home," Victoria said reassuringly while waiting and watching to see if she saw any movement coming in the direction they had gone.

The ladies quieted down for a moment when Dean spoke up, "Hey, I hear something! I hear Lucy!" he shouted as he ran off the porch. He was closely followed by Rita, Val, Victoria, and Mrs. Hutchins. They ran in the direction of the noise and couldn't believe the sight they saw. Coming up over the ridge was Rosie, Midas, and

THE GHOST COMES OUT

Lucy followed by Sheriff Charles with a sleeping DaisyBelle and Monty and Tati on either side.

"My baby! My baby!" Rita cried as she reached for DaisyBelle. "Ya brought my baby home t'me." Rita and Val surrounded DaisyBelle in a huge bear hug.

"Ya miss me, Momma?" DaisyBelle asked with tears rolling down her cheeks. She didn't need a response as she was hugged tighter by her mother and sister. Rita handed her Betsy, and DaisyBelle hugged her tightly.

Mrs. Hutchins was just as anxious to have Monty back and enveloped him with kiss after kiss.

Victoria looked at Charles with tears flowing down her cheeks.

"You did it! You found our children and brought them home safely." Victoria couldn't resist and gave him the kiss he had longed for. It only lasted a few seconds, but it was enough for both of them to know there would be plenty more where that came from. Charles regained his composure quickly and moved Victoria over to the side so that he could speak with her out of the earshot of the mothers.

"We've got a huge problem, Victoria. When the truth gets out, all hell is going to break loose. Starting with Rita," he said as they both looked over at Rita.

"Where did you find her? And where was Monty?" Victoria wanted to know.

"Let me use your phone. You just keep the two families away from one another before the truth comes out," he stated firmly.

Charles went in to use the phone and called his office.

"Shelia?" Charles asked.

"Yeah, Sheriff. Go ahead," Shelia responded.

"Call off the 10-41! DaisyBelle has been found! She is safe!" Charles yelled into the phone.

"Repeat! DaisyBelle has been found—safe!"

"Sheriff! What wonderful news!" Shelia cried.

"Shelia?" stressed Charles.

"Yes, Sheriff?"

"Call TBI, tell them to meet me in ten at the office! And tell Dr. Walker to meet us there too," Charles instructed.

"Ten-four, Sheriff! Out!" squealed Shelia. After she notified the TBI and Dr. Walker, she called Wanda, owner of the Grayton Nails and Salon, and gave her the good news. From there it wasn't long until every citizen of Grayton was out in the streets hollering.

"She's home! She's home! DaisyBelle came home!"

Charles went back outside and asked Rita and Mrs. Hutchins if he could speak with their children.

"Sheriff, ya gonna go git Uncle Bake?" Monty questioned.

"Whatcha talkin' bout Monty? Oh, ya wanna know if Bake'll come up to interview ya, right?" Mrs. Hutchins asked and then added, "I thank that's a great idea."

"No, Momma, that ain't what I mean. Sheriff, ya gonna git Uncle Bake fo takin' DaisyBelle an' hurtin' her an' Mr. Peters?" asked Monty.

Oh no! This is not how I wanted this to come out. What did Monty mean about Mr. Peters? What does he have to do with this, and how was he hurt? thought Charles.

Before Rita had time to react Charles stated, "We need to get DaisyBelle to Dr. Walker. Victoria, would you take the Shelbys down to my office? I know DaisyBelle would want Tati to go with her. Then I'll take the Hutchins in the squad car. I'm sure Dr. Walker will meet us there."

As fast as he could usher everyone to the cars, Charles got into the squad car with the Hutchins family. On the way to Grayton City Hall, people were lining the street to get a glimpse of DaisyBelle. Mothers, fathers, and children were jumping up and shouting as the squad car passed by. It was assumed DaisyBelle was in the squad car. Instead, she was in Victoria's car, which was following right behind.

Oh great! This is not how I wanted the community to find out. Shelia just can't keep her mouth shut, Charles thought.

When both cars pulled up in front of City Hall, there were newspaper journalists and television reporters from Nashville and Memphis. Cameras were rolling as they tried to catch a glimpse of DaisyBelle.

"Okay, this is what we're going to do. Mrs. Hutchins, you and Monty need to walk slowly into the office. Everyone thinks

DaisyBelle is in my squad car. While the journalists are surrounding you, I'll get DaisyBelle and her family into the office, okay?" Sheriff Charles asserted.

"Okay, Sheriff. I only got one question. Was Bake involved?" asked Mrs. Hutchins in a low whisper that only he could hear.

"We've got many things to work out, Mrs. Hutchins," Charles pointed out. "Ready? On the count of three. One, two, three." And Charles threw open his door followed by Mrs. Hutchins opening the passenger seat door and Monty opening the back door. They both got slowly out of the car.

Charles ran to Victoria's car and opened the back door and picked up DaisyBelle, who was holding Betsy, and ran with her into City Hall. Rita, Val, Victoria, Rosie, and Tati shadowed behind him.

Inside City Hall waiting for them were the TBI detectives, Joseph McClanahan and Nobel Douglas; Cane Summers, the mayor; and Dr. Elsworth Walker.

Charles completely ignored them and carried DaisyBelle into the back room. The TBI detectives trailed behind them and closed the door. Rita and Val tried to follow, but Victoria prevented them from going back.

"Let the doctor take a look at DaisyBelle. I know you want to make sure she's okay. You and I can plan a welcome-home party for DaisyBelle. How does that sound?" urged Victoria.

The idea of a party for DaisyBelle helped Rita to focus on something positive. Victoria had a talent for making others feel better. This was one of the qualities everyone loved about her, including Sheriff Charles Hall.

Charles rang for Shelia and said in a commanding voice, "Bring Dr. Elsworth Walker and Monty Hutchins back to my office ASAP!"

Tati walked over to Dr. Walker and gave him the Marian doll.

"DaisyBelle need huh too," she said and handed him the doll.

Shelia showed Dr. Walker and Monty Hutchins back to Charles's office. She knocked on the door and ushered them in. The door closed suddenly behind them.

Shelia would love to have been invited back too. She wanted to see DaisyBelle and hear about what happened, but she could tell by

Charles's tone, she would not be welcome. *Oh well, maybe I'll hear Rita Shelby talkin' an' learn some information from her*, she thought.

Charles's office

The two TBI detectives and Sheriff Hall were standing around watching. It had been decided that Dr. Walker would do his examination and ask some probing questions before the detectives took over. They agreed that DaisyBelle's care came before anything else, but the detectives had put out an APB on Bradley Bacon Haas as soon as Charles told them who the perpetrator was.

"Would one of you take Monty Hutchins into my side office? You can question him there," directed Sheriff Hall.

So the smaller TBI detective, Nobel Douglas, took Monty into the side office to ask him questions about Bake's whereabouts and exactly what happened.

Dr. Walker gave DaisyBelle her doll, Marian, and had her sit in the sheriff's chair as he did a rudimentary job of looking DaisyBelle over to make sure she was okay. He took her temperature, took her pulse rate, and felt all over her head for bumps, scrapes, brusies, etc. He discovered the bump on her head.

Dr. Walker asked softly, "DaisyBelle, do you recall how you got the bump on your head?"

"Uh-huh," DaisyBelle answered shyly while all the time rubbing Marian's and Betsy's hair.

"Can you tell us what happened?" Dr. Walker urged in a voice just barely over a whisper.

"Uh-huh. I was in…da…chair… Mista Peters…came…ovah. He don't know Imma there, but he…gonna git…me…outta there. Mista… Bake…he…shoots him. I don't…member…what happens…but…then… Monty…came…t'git…me…"

Dr. Walker asked, "Do you think you passed out when you hit the floor?"

"What that mean?" DaisyBelle asked him.

"You said you don't remember what happened, then Monty was there. So was there a lapse of time? Meaning was Monty there the entire time, or was he there when you woke up?" Dr. Walker questioned her.

"Uh, um... Monty...hep...me...git up. He...wasn't there afore," DaisyBelle replied.

Dr. Walker instructed, "I'm going to get you an ice pack for your head. I can give you some children's aspirin. I think you're going to be just fine, but I'm going to have your mom sleep with you tonight and wake you up every hour just in case. Okay, DaisyBelle?"

Dr. Walker handled the next phase of examining very carefully.

"DaisyBelle, did the man who took you ever do anything to you?"

"Uh, he...wouldn't...let...me go t'Momma an' Val. He...tole...me I was home," DaisyBelle slowly responded.

"Did he ever touch you?" Dr. Walker asked gently.

"Uh-huh...he...combed...mah hair. Uh...one time, he...braided it. Momma nevah braided my hair 'cause...she didn't...know how. Ya wanna watch...me braid...mah doll's hair? Mista...Bake...he...taught...me," DaisyBelle said.

"Did Mr. Bake ever touch you in a private place?" Dr. Walker inquired.

"Yeah, he...touch...mah...feet. He said he...was gonna...clean 'em...'cause...they was...dirty," explained DaisyBelle.

"Did Mr. Bake touch you anywhere else other than your feet and hair?" asked Dr. Walker.

"You mean...afore...or afta...we got...married?" wondered DaisyBelle.

CHAPTER 68

MONTY TELLS ALL

When Nobel Douglas took Monty into the side room, he had no idea what was in store. Nobel deliberately sat Monty in a chair across from him so they could look at each other eye to eye. Nobel had two children of his own and wanted this to be as casual and friendly as possible. He had his notebook on the table in front of him and was ready to take notes on what happened. He also had a bottle of pop for Monty.

"Hi, Monty, I'm TBI Officer Nobel Douglas, but why don't you just call me Nobel?"

"Yessir," Monty said nervously.

"Now, Monty, there is nothing to be scared about. I just want to get to the bottom of what happened. Can you start from the beginning and tell me, son?" Nobel asked in a fatherly tone.

The only father Monty had ever known was Bake. So trusting another fatherly figure was going to be hard, and Nobel knew it.

"Um… I don't know what ya want me t'say," Monty began. "Where ya want me t'start at?"

Nobel leaned in. "Can you tell me where you went when you left your house?"

"Uh-huh. I wanted t'go with Uncle Bake. He's or… *was* my… bess friend," Monty said weeping.

Nobel gave Monty a tissue and gently tapped him on the shoulder. Monty responded to the kindness, and he looked up at Nobel and half smiled. Nobel offered Monty the bottle of grape pop, which Monty readily took.

"I snuck out the house an' got in Uncle Bake's back seat. He didn't know I was there. I jest wanted t'be near him, ya know?"

Nobel nodded.

"Well, I guessin' I was kinda sleepy an' fell asleep in the car. I didn't wake up til I heard a gunshot. Then I heard 'nother one. I got outta the car. I was scared, ya know?"

Nobel nodded while writing furiously in his notepad. Monty stopped talking. He was remembering what happened next, and Nobel was not going to push him. *Don't rush him, Nobel. He's a child. Go slow and easy and let him tell you what happened*, Nobel thought to himself.

"Anyways, I saw this cabin, er…cottage, ya know? It was like painted funny. Ya know like those lizards that change colors?" Monty asked looking at Nobel.

"Chameleons?" Nobel offered.

"Yeah, like those thangs. Anyway, ya wouldn't know it was there if ya weren't b'side it. I don't know. Does that make sense?" Monty queried.

"Yes, it does, son. Did you go in?" questioned Nobel.

"Uh-huh. I thought Uncle Bake might need me. I guess that was stupid, huh?" whispered Monty. Without much of a pause, Monty began again, "The door wasn't locked. It was a little opened, that's why I went in, an' ya not gonna b'lieve what I seen." Monty paused. "I seen a room full of them dolls, ya know?"

Nobel looked at Monty and asked, "Dolls? What dolls?"

"Ya know them Marian dolls. They was everywhere," answered Monty.

Nobel stopped writing to ask, "There were dolls over the entire room?"

"Yeah, that an' hay bales everywhere. They was dolls on every shelf, an' they wasn't jest the girl dolls. They was the boy dolls too," explained Monty.

"Okay, let me get this straight, there was hay bales and Marian dolls in the room, right?"

"Yep, they was everywhere. They was starin' at ya, ya know?" Monty insisted as he drank a sip from the pop.

"Then I saw DaisyBelle on the floor next to Mr. Peters. They was blood everywhere, an' I saw Uncle Bake… I thought…he…had…found… DaisyBelle. I aksed…him…if…we should…call Sheriff. I went…ovah…t'DaisyBelle… I didn't…know what…was wrong… with her… I…looked at… Uncle Bake. He…close…the door… an' he…had the meanest…look on…his face," Monty answered in between sobs.

Nobel sat very close to Monty and just held him as he cried. *I wish I had a dad like this guy. I don't have nobody, an' now I don't even have my Uncle Bake*, thought Monty as he teared up.

When at last Monty's cries began to slow down, Nobel sat up in his chair and waited for Monty to continue.

"Are you okay, son?" Nobel asked softly.

"Uh-huh. I'm okay," he said as he took another sip of the pop.

"Was Mr. Peters okay?" Nobel questioned.

"Uh-uh. He weren't movin' at all. He was really bloody. After that, DaisyBelle began t'make a noise like she was wakin' up or someum. All of a sudden from outta nowhere came in this man," Monty recalled.

"Wait! A man came in the cottage?" asked a surprised Nobel.

"Uh-huh. He surprised us all, even Uncle Bake. He took a gun an' hit Uncle Bake until he was on the floor. Then he came ovah t'me an' DaisyBelle. We was scared. I held on to DaisyBelle 'cause she's only a first grader, ya know?" Monty said as he was remembering the details.

Nobel nodded.

"Then ya know what happened?" Monty didn't wait for Nobel to answer, he just talked on.

"This man knew my name. He knew DaisyBelle's too, an' he said he was a friend. He tole us we was gonna be okay an' we needed t'git outta there. He picked DaisyBelle up an' held her for a minute then put her down an' tole me t'hep her git home safely. I swear if Imma lyin', Imma dyin'. I nevah saw him afore, I swear," Monty said as he raised his hand.

THE GHOST COMES OUT

"So this man came in and knocked your uncle out and then came over to you two and told you to leave and go home, is that right?" Nobel repeated.

"Yep. Then we started walkin', an' we saw the dogs, Lucy and Midas, an' then we saw the sheriff an' Rosie an' Tati. We all walked home afta that. The end," stated Monty.

"Monty?" Nobel asked as he looked at him. "I'm going to let you and your mother into the kitchen area of City Hall. The two of you can eat snacks and drink another pop, how would you like that?"

Monty jumped out of his chair.

"Can DaisyBelle come too? She could use a pop," Monty asked excidedly.

"When she gets through, we'll send her in there with you. Why don't you pick out a soft drink and snack for her, and then when she comes in, you can give it to her. Sound good?" Nobel asked with a big smile. Monty readily agreed.

While Monty and his mother were in the kitchen, Nobel went into the other room with his partner, the doctor, the sheriff, and DaisyBelle. Nobel noticed the look on everyone's faces. *What in the world had DaisyBelle been telling these men? The looks on their faces tell an unbelievable story. Bless those kids*, he thought.

"I'm so sorry to interrupt, but I need to ask DaisyBelle one question, please," Nobel asked gently.

He sat down across from DaisyBelle. She was playing with her dolls.

"DaisyBelle, my name is Nobel Douglas. Mr. McClanahan is my partner," he said pointing to Joseph, who was standing.

"I've just been talking to Monty, and he tells me there was a man who came into the cottage and rescued you and Monty, is that what happened?" he inquired.

DaisyBelle looked up from playing with her dolls.

"Uh-uh, it weren't a boy," she said shaking her head from side to side and then paused, "it was a girl."

CHAPTER 69

BAKE HAAS IS FOUND

The TBI and law enforcement from Stockton were out trying to locate Bake Haas. They had been given additional information of the cottage Bake had taken DaisyBelle to. When at last they found it, the instructions were to surround it and wait until everyone was in place before they stormed in.

Police Chief Spencer Dicken from Stockton was the man in charge of the situation. His men had already established a perimeter around the cabin, but since there were no windows in the cabin, throwing tear gas cannisters through windows was not an option. Police Chief Dicken signaled on the count of three, they would break the door down and go in.

He raised his hand and put up one finger, then two, then three. Four men broke the door down and rushed inside of the cabin with guns drawn. They looked around and lowered their weapons. One of them came to the door of the cabin and motioned for Chief Dicken to come inside. There were two dead bodies in that room. One on the floor and one hanging from the ceiling.

The first thing the chief saw was Bradley Bacon Haas swinging by his neck from the light. Chief Dicken had seen enough suicides by hanging to know what he was looking for. He went over to examine the body and noticed the capillaries in his eyes had burst; thus, Chief Dicken determined Bake had not died immediately. Bake had the death erection, which meant his genitals were engorged. *Bake, you*

THE GHOST COMES OUT

suffered a little before you died, didn't you? Good. And, it looks like you hanged yourself when you knew we were coming to get you, you son of a bitch. What a coward you were, he thought.

After he had inspected the body, he asked his men to take pictures, dust for fingerprints, and collect anything not nailed down. Next, he went to examine the body on the floor.

"Have we any idea who this guy is?" asked Chief Dicken pointing to the body on the floor.

"Yeah, Chief, he's the county's school superintendent. Name's Marcus Peters," Detective Luther Montgomery replied. Luther had grown up in Grayton but moved to Stockton after graduating from college.

"He was a pretty good fellow, Chief," Luther added.

Chief Dicken noticed Marcus Peters had two gunshot wounds, and both appeared to have come from behind. The first one went through his right shoulder. The second one was that one that took him down. It went straight through his back into his heart. *Huh, I wonder if the two of them worked together? Could both of these men have kidnapped the little girl? What was the connection between them? I will find the answers to these questions*, he thought.

Finally, he turned his attention to the rest of the room, and then did he notice the dolls and all the hay bales.

"Holy cow! What kind of a freak was this guy?" Chief Dicken asked examining the dolls. Then he turned his focus to the hay bales. *This guy thought of everything. He used the hay bales to muff the sound so no one could possibly hear the child when she screamed. He made this cottage into a soundproofed area, and then he brought in all these dolls. What a weirdo!* Chief Dicken thought.

"Hey, Smitty, come here!" Chief Dicken yelled to a small man who was taking evidence outside of the cabin.

Smitty came in and was shocked by dolls in the room. He asked, "What the fudge, Chief? How many dolls did this perp have?"

"That's what I want you to find out. Count them, categorize them, and check for fingerprints on all of them. Right now, I'm going to meet up with Sheriff Hall. There's a lot going on in this room," Chief Dicken replied.

CHAPTER 70

THE MARRIAGE

"So, you say it was a girl who rescued you and Monty?" asked a surprised Nobel.

"Uh-huh, it was a girl," DaisyBelle repeated.

"What did this person look like, DaisyBelle?" Nobel prompted.

"Um, her had on a pair of men's pants an' a ole shirt," DaisyBelle stated and then added, "Her look like a boy, an' her hair was short."

"If she looked like a boy, how do you know she was a girl?" Nobel questioned.

"Her pick me up an' held me. Her smell jest like Momma," DaisyBelle answered.

Never underestimate the wisdom of a child, Nobel thought to himself.

"Did she say anything to you?" asked Nobel.

"Uh-huh. Her say t'git outta there. Her tole Monty t'take me home. Her smile at me an' knew my name an' knew Monty's too," DaisyBelle commented with a smile as though she was remembering what had taken place.

With that, Nobel had no more questions for DaisyBelle, but the others were just getting started.

Charles just got down to business and asked the question they all wanted to know.

"DaisyBelle, you said Mr. Bake touched you before and after the wedding. Tell me about the wedding," Charles insisted softly.

THE GHOST COMES OUT

"Um, well... Mista Bake...tole me...we was...gittin' married. He...say...the dolls...was the...witnesses. He...say...we git...married...infront...of 'em. He...git...me...a dress...with lace. It was... purdy...too. He...say... Imma beautiful," answered DaisyBelle.

Charles knew DaisyBelle could possibly use a break, so he asked to send Rosie and Tati in with some soft drinks and snacks. He thought the girls and DaisyBelle have a strong friendship, and if anyone could make DaisyBelle feel comfortable, it would be Rosie and Tati, and how right he was. When they entered the room, DaisyBelle got up and brought her two dolls to share. She gave Rosie a hug and Tati a bear hug and handed Marian to Tati.

"I want ya t'have her, Tati. I gave her t'you. When I saw her on the shelf, I knew ya gonna git me, Tati," DaisyBelle explained as she handed her Marian doll to Tati.

The dots on the doll's face were missing a few, but it was still obvious she had the pox. The girls played together for a few minutes while eating cookies and drinking sodas. The men stood around not wanting to appear they were watching and listening, but they were.

"Ya okay, DaisyBelle?" Rosie asked.

"Uh-huh, Imma good, Rosie," DaisyBelle answered while eating another cookie from the bunch.

"Did Monty hep ya git away?" questioned Rosie.

"Uh-huh. He heped me git outta there," DaisyBelle recalled. "I was scared until he came." And she smiled remembering how he had rescued her.

"Did Bake hurt ya, DaisyBelle?" quizzed Rosie. Charles and the TBI detectives were listening closely to what they were saying.

"Um...when I...didn't wanna git married...he spank me. I... I...didn't...know why he...spank me. I cried...and then...he cried. I jest...knew you'd come...alookin' fo me... I jest...knew it," DaisyBelle stated as she patted Tati with a smile.

"Did ya see all them dolls?" Tati asked suddenly while brushing Marian's hair.

"They...was my friends...an' Mista Bake says they...was witnesses too," DaisyBelle declared.

"Whatcha mean they was witnesses?" Rosie asked.

"Uh, well, they was watchin' when...we got married. Mista Bake say...they was my friends. He kissed me...on my head, an' then we jump ovah a broom. He say...he was savin' me for...t'night. I don't know...what he mean... Imma...glad to be...home," DaisyBelle announced.

Charles, Dr. Walker, and the two TBI detectives breathed a sigh of relief. *At least he didn't get to make it official. What a disturbed man Bradley Bacon Haas was. How could I not have noticed what was going on? Bake Haas was a pervert all right. Just wait until that makes the paper!* Charles thought.

"DaisyBelle, Imma so glad you ah home. I missed ya so much," Tati said sweetly.

"Um... I missed...ya too... Tati," DaisyBelle replied, and then she broke down. She started sobbing.

Tati rushed over and hugged her. "Whas wrong, DaisyBelle? Ya safe now," Tati stressed while rubbing her back.

"I... I...jest...'memebered somethin'... Mista... Bake...tole... me...he killed...my papa." DaisyBelle sobbed.

Charles and the other law enforcement came over toward the girls.

"Tati and Rosie, I'm going to take you back to your mom, okay?" Charles asked gently. Rosie said goodbye to DaisyBelle as Tati got up and hugged DaisyBelle tightly.

"Ain't ya glad Ghost Polly Tata didn' fin' ya?" Tati whispered in DaisyBelle's ear.

"That's jest it, Tati, I thank she did," DaisyBelle whispered back, "but I had...this...p'tectin' me." And she opened her hand and showed Tati the buckeye she always kept with her.

CHAPTER 71

GHOST BAKE CAME OUT

The headline for the *Grayton Gazette* read, REPORTER BRADLEY BACON "BAKE" HAAS WAS THE GHOST WHO CAME OUT! Sadly, Bake didn't live long enough to see his name in print in the *Tennesseean* or the *Commercial Appeal*. He felt he would be famous one day, and how right he was. The name *Bake Haas* was on every Grayton citizen's tongue and those in Nashville and Memphis. He was renowned from Gatlinburg to the banks of the Mississippi. Fame had found Bake, but not in the way he had dreamed.

The entire town came out to see and welcome DaisyBelle home. The mayor and every public official joined in the celebration, but there were still many questions everyone had as the truth began to unfold. Who was Bake Haas? Had he been watching DaisyBelle, and how long? Had he killed both Carl Shelby and Marcus Peters, and why? Why had he kidnapped little DaisyBelle? What had he been planning? Did he hang himself because now the jig was up? These were the questions that the *Grayton Gazette* did their best to answer. The paper was so popular that five hundred more copies had been printed, and that still wasn't enough.

At noon there was a great celebration with the entire town to recognize DaisyBelle's safe return. Sheriff Hall was especially eager to observe the women. He was hoping to locate the woman who had saved DaisyBelle and Monty. *Who is she? She would've have to been a local to know both Monty's and DaisyBelle's names. What did she do after* the kids left the cabin? Did she have anything to do with Bake's death? Was it truly a suicide, or was it murder? These were Charles's thoughts.

Before the big event began
The elderly sisters' house

The elderly sisters, Elizabeth and Barbara, had several questions on their minds about the entire kidnapping.

"I don't know, sista. I always kinda liked that Bake. He seemed nice t'talk to, ya know? Not that I could see him. He probly looked like a bad guy. Whatcha thanking, sista?" asked Elizabeth.

"Bake Haas yousta d'liver me my newspaper, 'member, sista? He was our paperboy. Should've know he was bad. He nevah got the paper on the porch. I thank he went outta his way t'make me git up an' retrieve it from the bushes," Barbara responded angrily.

"Yeah, I do, sista. I forgot that. Now Imma thankin 'bout it, he was a bad little boy. Ya know his father left 'em when they was little. He liked t'peep in on his neighbors. He was a peeping tom, ya know?" Elizabeth asked.

"I didn't know his name was John. I thought it was Bake, but if ya say so, sista," Barbara replied shaking her head.

"No, I didn't say his name was John, I say his daddy was a peeping tom," shouted Elizabeth.

"Oh, so ya saw him creeping? I knew I didn't like that Bake," muttered Barbara, and by now, Elizabeth had lost interest in the subject altogether.

The Shelbys' house

"Imma gonna run them Hutchins family outta town. They is very bad people. To thank Bake Haas was the one who took my DaisyBelle an' killed my Carl! I will not let this go, Sheriff!" Rita screamed into the receiver of the phone as she slammed the phone down.

"Somebody's gotta pay fo this, an it's gonna be those Hutchins. They was watchin' us and plannin' this the whole time. They gonna pay!" Rita said to herself.

"Momma, do I have t'wear this?" Val asked as she put on a floral dress with big poofy sleeves.

"Val, ya look so purdy. Let's see if we can't do someum t'tame that hair, hmmn?" Rita suggested as she led Val over to the ironing board.

"I know ya don't like this, Val, but let's see if we can iron yua hair straight. Girls, these days jest love the straight hair, right?" Rita asked absentmindedly. Val was blessed with naturally curly hair, but that was not the style in the '60s, and she hated her frizzy locks. She put her head down on the board and turned to the left and then the right as her mother ironed. It was straight now but very stiff, so Rita put it back in a ponytail, and both she and Val looked in the mirror and smiled.

"DaisyBelle honey, ya gotta git ready, okay? Yua the toast of the town, ya know that? Jest thank a Shelby is goin' t'git the key t'the town. Why, DaisyBelle, yua can do anythang in this here town. Evrybody loves you," Rita exclaimed.

But DaisyBelle just played with her doll, Betsy, on the living room floor. She was oblivious to what was going on. She was lost in her own little world.

The Hutchinses' house

"Momma, aint we goin' to the celebration?" Monty asked his mother, who was still in her pajamas.

The only way Mrs. Hutchins got any sleep after Monty returned was from her good friend, Jack Daniels. Mrs. Hutchins wasn't shy about her drinking, but during stressful times, she upped the ante from a pint to a fifth. The telephone had not stopped ringing with obscene callers until she finally took the receiver off the cradle, which rang busy to those calling in. She was struggling with the reality that it was her brother who had kidnapped DaisyBelle Shelby and murdered her father. If that weren't bad enough, Bake had killed himself and left her and her family to answer questions and sweep up his mess.

How could he have done this? He was a good brother, or at least I thought he was. Why, Bake, why? Mrs. Hutchins thought.

"Momma? Momma?" Alvin pled.

"Momma, Alvin has a stinky diaper. Where the clean ones? I hep ya, Momma," Monty said cheerfully.

Mrs. Hutchins looked at her sons. How could they be so sweet and loving when their uncle was a despicably vile murderer and pedophile? She had wanted them to grow up to be like their Uncle Bake, but now she couldn't face anyone. The entire town and state knew what a horrible person her brother was, and she and her innocent boys were left, and the town was going to make her pay.

What will I do? How can we live in a town where everyone knows who we are and who we were related to? Sadly, I miss my brother, or the person I thought he was, Mrs. Hutchins thought as she began to sob again.

The Scholls' house

Tati, Rosie, and Midas had gone outside to feed Lucky. Victoria was inside the house making breakfast. Because of the events that had occurred, she had put her own thoughts on the back burner, but now as she was trying to make sense of DaisyBelle's kidnapping, Bake's suicide, and the murder of her own boss, Marcus Peters. Her mind returned to the conversation she had had with Rita concerning Jeb. *What was it she said? Oh yeah, "Is my fault. I… I…have…secret, Victoria. I…was…there…when… Jeb…died. I…caused…him…to…run…off…the…road…an…wreck. Is karme…comin'…back…to…me."* Victoria couldn't believe Rita had been the cause of her Jeb's death. *How can I ever forgive her? Why had she not stopped? The medical examiner had said Jeb had died on impact, but the least she could've done was to stop.*

Those thoughts kept playing over and over again in her mind. When at last she decided she must acknowledge them. She went over to the telephone and called the sheriff.

THE GHOST COMES OUT

"Hello, Shelia? This is Victoria Scholl. Could I speak with Charles… I mean Sheriff Hall, please?"

"Hi, Victoria. He jest came through the door," Shelia said happily.

"Sheriff, it's Victoria. I'll transfer the call t'your office," stated Shelia.

Charles went into his office. Any excuse to hear from Victoria was a good one as far as Charles was concerned. With all the happenings in Grayton, he had barely slept, much less spending time with Victoria.

"Hi, Victoria. I was going to call you today. How are you doing?" Charles asked.

"Hi, Charles. I'm well. I…uh…well…do you think you could come to the house?" Victoria blurted out.

"Of course, I can. Do you want me to come now, or can it wait until after the big celebration at twelve o'clock?" Charles asked.

"I think this needs to be addressed before the celebration, Charles," Victoria demanded.

This sound ominous, Charles thought.

"I'm on my way," said Charles as he hung up the phone.

Then Victoria called her neighbor down the street.

"Rita," Victoria said in the receiver of the phone, "it's Victoria."

"Hi… Victoria," said Rita.

"I was hoping you could come up to the house. Please bring your girls too. I know Rosie and Tati would love to see them, and then we could go to the celebration together," suggested Victoria.

"Um…well…we were jest gittin' ready, but…okay, I thank… we can be there…in about ten minutes. That okay, Victoria?" Rita answered. *What she have in mind? I got too much to do, but… I betta go*, Rita thought.

Ten minutes later, both Charles and Rita arrived at Victoria's house. Charles was surprised to see Rita and her girls getting out of the car.

DaisyBelle and Val had on pretty floral dresses. DaisyBelle's hair was pulled back in a headband with a flower on top. Her light-brown hair was shining in the sun. She looked like a little princess. Val's hair was pulled back in a ponytail, and she too looked happy and quite lovely. In fact, it was the first time he had seen Val smile since before Carl's death.

As they made their way to the front door, it was opened suddenly by Rosie and Tati. They came running to give the Shelby girls a hug. Tati was holding Marian, and Featha and Midas came bouncing behind them.

"Don't y'all look bootiful," Tati said to both Val and DaisyBelle. The girls smiled at Tati and Rosie.

"Ya excited, DaisyBelle?" Rosie asked.

"I jest wish it was ovah," DaisyBelle said shyly.

"Why, DaisyBelle?" asked Rosie.

"'Cause Imma...widow, and... I don't...wanna be," sobbed DaisyBelle as she sat down on the front step.

Rita and Val sat down next to DaisyBelle and put their arms around her as she cried. Victoria heard the commotion and came outside to find the three Shelby girls in a big embrace. She looked at Charles.

"Rita, what's wrong?" asked a concerned Victoria.

"DaisyBelle thanks she's a widow," Rita responded.

Victoria stood in front of the three Shelby girls, and then she squatted down so that she was at eye level with DaisyBelle.

"Honey, when you and Bake got married, it was just for pretend. You didn't really marry him," Victoria gently explained.

"Nuh-uh, Miss Victoria. Mista Bake tole me we was married. He even tole me them dolls was our witnesses. He tole me. I didn't wanna marry him. He hurt me," DaisyBelle contended.

"How he hurt ya, DaisyBelle?" asked Rosie.

"When I tole him I...gonna grow up...and marry Monty, he...s-s-slap me. It...hurt. He tole me...neva talk bout... Monty 'cause Imma...marrying him...not Monty. Monty...save...me. He...my...boyfriend," cried DaisyBelle.

Rita interjected, "Honey, is that why you've been so quiet? Ya b'lieved yua was married t'Bake Haas, an because he dead, yua b'lieved you was a widow?"

THE GHOST COMES OUT

DaisyBelle nodded her head while big teardrops fell to the ground.

"You ain't evah gonna have anythang t'do with the Hutchins family. They are bad, an' Imma gonna run 'em outta our town. They need t'go!" shouted Rita indignantly.

DaisyBelle stood up and begged her mom, "No, Momma… ya…can't do…that. Monty…save…me. He…my…boyfriend. Please… Momma," cried DaisyBelle.

Victoria asked Rita and Charles to join her in the house for a moment. She led the way into the foyer and turned around to face them both.

"You know, Rita, we all make mistakes, but we can't punish the young for what the elders do, can we?" Victoria softly spoke. She went on, "I asked you to come here so that I could tell you in front of Charles that what happened earlier in the year in the snow with Jeb was an accident. It wasn't anyone's fault. It just happened." She continued, "I have no right to hold you accountable. Sometimes things happen, and we don't know why, but I do know you've got two beautiful loving girls, and you've done a wonderful job teaching them how to love and forgive."

Rita hugged Victoria like she would never let her go.

"So, let me get this straight, Victoria, you do not want to press charges?" Charles appealed.

"No, I do not," Victoria answered.

"Thank ya, thank ya, thank ya, Victoria. Yua the bess friend anyone could have. I sorry fo what happened, but I thank ya from the bottom of my heart fo ya goodness. I guess I need t'forgive too. It ain't right I punish Monty fo what his uncle did," Rita cried.

"Now that we've got that behind us, let's celebrate DaisyBelle!" said Victoria smiling. In that moment, Charles knew he would do anything in his power to win Victoria over and make her his wife. Their eyes connected, and for what seemed like minutes, they were lost in each other's gaze.

"Mista Sheriff? Mista Sheriff?" Rosie demanded as she came through the door with Val, Tati, and DaisyBelle following.

Charles broke the gaze with Victoria and looked down at Rosie with a grin.

"Yes ma'am, what can I do for you?" he inquired.

"Can us kids all ride in yua car down t'the square?" Rosie questioned.

"And can ya turn on them sirens?" Val added.

"Can we ride down in yua car?" echoed Tati.

Rosie looked at Tati and shouted, "What did you say?"

"I say 'can we ride down in yua car?'" Tati repeated.

Rosie looked at Tati and said, "What's my name, Tati?"

"Rosie!" Tati replied laughing.

"Momma, did you hear that? Tati's saying her *Rs*. She called me Rosie! Ya know what that means?" Rosie yelled.

"You fixed me, Rosie. I now talk jest like you!" Tati shouted with excitement.

"And you know what that means, girls? You are all going to ride in the squad car with the sirens blaring!" interjected Charles.

"Yay!" Rosie screamed.

"Yay!" echoed Tati.

"Less go see Lucky a'fore we go downtown," said DaisyBelle smiling, and off the girls went.

Rita excused herself to go freshen her face, and Victoria and Charles were left alone on the porch.

Charles immediately took Victoria into his arms and said, "When this is over, I would like to court you exclusively. Would you be opposed to that?"

"Only if you court my daughters too!" Victoria eagerly agreed.

"I wouldn't think of doing anything else." Charles smiled as he reached in to kiss her.

The Smiths' house

Since Daphne and Silvia had taken care of Joe Puckett the old-fashioned way, Daphne had worried about what effect it might have on her unborn child.

THE GHOST COMES OUT

"Now, Daphne, ya know God'll take care of ya. He probly glad Joe finally met his demise. 'Sides, they ain't eva gonna fin' 'im. He's where he should be, ya know?" Silvia explained.

"Do you really believe that, Silvia? I don't want my transgressions to fall to my child. My baby shouldn't have a negative spirit around her. She should have only beautiful thoughts flowing through and around her," said Daphne.

Clayton stepped in, "Honey, listen to Silvia. It's all taken care of. We will never have to look at that creep again. He will spend an eternity in the one place he tried to abolish and destroy." He put his arm around his wife and gave her a reassuring hug.

Billy and Johnny came running into the room.

"Momma, we can't be late. We gotta go see DaisyBelle. She gonna be lookin' fo us," Billy shouted.

"Yeah, Momma, we ah part of the summer school club, an' she's one of our bess friends," bellowed Johnny.

"Okay, everybody, if we gonna git down t'the square by 12:00 p.m., we betta git goin'," Jackson interjected as he grabbed an umbrella just in case.

The Pucketts' house

"Momma, it ain't fair we gotta go an celebrate that girl DaisyBelle comin' home. Ya know Rose'll be there too, an' I jest hate her. She stole my horse, Lucky—I mean, Pumkin, an' she don't d'serve him," Dorothy complained.

"Ya gonna go downtown an' be nice fo once. Since yua pops broke outta jail an' lef town, yua momma's gotta git herself anotha suga daddy. Ya understand? My looks ah ventually gonna fade, an' I gotta have somebody t'take care of us. So, ya gotta be nice, an' could ya comb yua hair? Ya lookin' like a street urchin, Dorthy," Raveleen responded to Dorothy as she put on another coat of lipstick.

"Momma, why didn't… Pops come…an' git us…when he broke outta jail? I hep that woman set the colord church…on faar fo Pops, ya know? Didn't even say goodbye…he jest took off." Dorothy sobbed.

"I don't know what ya talkin' 'bout, an' I don't care. Quit ya cryin', Dorthy. Least he didn't hit ya. Now go an' comb ya hair an' put on a shirt that don't have traces of yua supper from last night on the front," clarified Raveleen.

I know there'll be lots of men at this celebration fo that DaisyBelle girl. Don't really care if the men ah married. That's what a de...vorce is fo, she thought with a laugh. *Oh, I wish this skirt were a few inches shorta. Oh well, gotta make do wid what I got*, Raveleen thought as she looked at her reflection in the mirror.

If Raveleen and Dorothy had only known that Joe had never left town. In fact, he would forever be a part of Stockton. Oh well, on with those who were still breathing.

Harry Miller's house

Dean was so excited about DaisyBelle's homecoming, he could hardly stand it, but Harry had insisted he go and rest before the big excitement. Harry also knew he would be getting a visitor soon, and he wanted to get ready. Dean was asleep in his room when a soft knock came at the door. Harry rose to get it just as the visitor came through the door.

"Hi, Boss," Harry said as he greeted his guest.

"Hello, Harry. I want to make sure all loose ends have been tied. What did you do with that meddling piece of garbage Frances Boyd?"

Harry laughed. "She always wanted to be a part of a new church. She got her wish."

"Good. I hope she'll be happy," Rocky said sarcastically. "Do you think anyone suspects the death of Bake Haas?"

Harry clarified by answering, "Don't know how they could, Boss. The straitjacket did the trick. When I left him, he was hanging as though it was a suicide."

"Good. I want to thank you for all you've done to keep my Deano safe. You know I chose you to watch over him, and you've done a brilliant job of it," Harry's boss said.

THE GHOST COMES OUT

Harry actually blushed. He wasn't used to his boss bestowing such compliments on him, and it really meant a lot.

"Ya know I'd do anything for Dean. If I ever were to have a kid, I'd want him to be just like Dean," Harry stressed.

While Harry was talking, his boss was busy cleaning up. Harry watched as the makeup applied came off so easily. The wig his boss wore was pulled off, and long red hair came flowing down. Contact lenses were removed, and now beautiful green eyes appeared. The padding used under clothes was taken out, and now a small curvaceous body emerged. Now no one would mistake her for a male. She was a ravishing woman who would cause anyone to take a second look. Harry's boss was Rochelle "Rocky" Frederella and the only woman in the Frederella mafia clan. The Chicago Mafia assumed Rocky was a man, and she used that advantage when she needed to.

Rocky's goal in life was to be a wife, mother, and cosmetologist. She had gone to school and had received her certification; and her husband, Gregory, had bought her a shop of her very own. The day before her grand opening, she had come home to share good news with Gregory. They were going to have a baby, but Gregory never made it home. He had been out running errands and was caught in the cross fire between two rival Mafia families and had been gunned down.

Rocky vowed she would get even, and she had. She became the most feared Mafia head of them all. She aimed to right the wrongs and clean up Chicago, but her son Dean was not going to be a part of the violent life, and so she gave Harry Miller her most prized possession, her son. She wanted him to have a normal childhood and had chosen the small town of Grayton, Tennessee, for her son to be raised. Harry was her eyes, and if he saw anything amiss, he called his boss. Rocky wanted Dean to grow up in a town without crime, and she was going to ensure it stayed that way.

"I want to see my baby before I leave, Harry," Rocky said gently.

"He's sleeping, Boss. I thought with the excitement, he needed to rest before the ceremony," Harry explained.

Rocky smiled at her friend and said, "I knew I chose the right person to raise my boy. Thank you so much for loving him as your own. You know, when I see him, it's all I can do not to rush and put my arms around him. One day, I will come back for him, but there's still work to do in Chicago. You just keep me informed on what's going on here, okay?"

Rocky walked over to the bedroom door. She quietly turned the doorknob, and the sunlight shone into the room. There were two beds in the room, and on the smaller bed lay a young boy with light-brown hair. He seemed to be asleep as Rocky crept into the room. She stood over the small figure and looked down as tears filled her eyes. She reached down to touch his hair. *He's so beautiful. I cannot believe Gregory and I made such a perfect little boy. Oh, how I want to hold you and shield you from the world. Jesus, would You please watch over my boy and protect him?* she thought as two tears came falling from her eyes and onto his pillow. She left the room and never saw Dean's eyes open as he watched her walk away. He kissed the pillow where his mother's tears had landed. That was the last time he would ever see his mother again.

Across town, at the site of the new Southern Baptist Church

No one would've guessed that the ground on the site of the colored Baptist Church had been disturbed not once but twice. Harry Miller and Daphne Montague-Smith and Silvia Smith had all made a deposit in the dirt.

The next day, the concrete company came and poured the foundation of the church. Now Frances "Frannie" Boyd had at last found a new church because both she and Joe Puckett were forever interred in the cement slab of the "new" Church of the Southern Baptist of Grayton.

Epilogue

The celebration that summer day went off without a hitch. The towns of both Grayton and Stockton were in attendance to welcome DaisyBelle Shelby back home. Sheriff Hall brought the girls down to the square as promised, in his squad car with the siren blaring. The crowd went crazy when the girls stepped out of the vehicle. DaisyBelle was last and was clinging to her doll, Betsy. Tati held DaisyBelle's free hand and was clutching her Marian doll with the other.

The four boys who made up the rest of the summer school were there to greet the girls. Johnny and Billy Smith looked dapper in their light blue and gray suits. Dean was the epitome of fashion in his gray slacks with a blue jacket and light-brown vest. Even at seven years old, DaisyBelle had eyes only for Monty, who had a light-brown suit with matching tie. Each boy had a white rose to give to DaisyBelle. When Monty gave his rose to DaisyBelle, he hugged her. There was not a dry eye on any woman's face and several of the men's faces as well.

It was determined that the blood found on Carl Shelby's body matched Bake Haas with a blood type of A. He was responsible for the two murders in Grayton: Carl Shelby and Superintendent Marcus Peters.

The Hutchins family stayed in Grayton. Monty graduated high school and went on to the local community college. He graduated with an associate's degree in technology. He became the financial officer at the car dealership in Stockton. The day after DaisyBelle graduated from high school, they got married, and the entire town came out for it. The bond they formed the summer of '64 was so tight neither one ever sought out another. They became the parents of twin boys and lived down the street from their mothers.

Rita Shelby used the insurance money to fix up her house. She actually had a knack for interior design and used her skills to decorate many of the homes in Grayton, including a makeover at Daphne Montague-Smith's mansion. Val went into business with her mother, and they opened a store called the Fashion Designers of Grayton. Val married a law enforcement officer who swept her off her feet when she remodeled his home, which was coincidentally next door to DaisyBelle's.

Raveleen Puckett went on to marry five more times and eventually moved into a double-wide trailer. She felt like she'd won the lottery.

And Dorothy? Well, she dropped out of school at the eighth grade, but hit it big by selling cosmetics. She became the leading saleswoman in the south. While her sales tactics may not have been conventional, they were just the words needed to sell in small towns.

"If ya dab a little of this here cream all ovah ya face, ya gonna wake up an' look like Cinderellie," she would say. She became a hit, but the art of the swindle was in her blood and before long found herself on the other end of the law. Dorothy kept the money given to her by her customers. Unfortunately, she forgot to give them what they had purchased. Dorothy received one to two years in prison. Rumor has it she's running a gang behind bars.

Pastor Allan Boyd eventually got over losing his Frances to another man. Having seen what Palo Lankford had done to DaisyBelle's teacher, Sadie Hargis, he came to her aid. They began courting, and these two lonely souls found one another. After dating for a year, she became the second Mrs. Allan Boyd and, unlike her predecessor, was the perfect pastor's wife and never wanted to leave her town, Grayton.

Daphne and Clayton Smith welcomed a baby girl the following winter. They named her Grace, and she was as beautiful inside as she was out. Even the women in the Garden Club had nothing but compliments to bestow on Baby Grace. Daphne and Clayton raised her to be a pillar of the community. She fought hard for the rights of everyone no matter their sex, race, or religion. Years later she became the first African American mayor of Grayton and then the governor of Tennessee.

Billy and Johnny Smith became entrepreneurs in Grayton. They opened the first pizza delivery place and were most successful. Their good fortune led them to open two more stores in Stockton. Their slogan was,

> If ya have a hunger need
> And don't want to overfeed
> Call the Brothers Smith for speed!

While it was a silly slogan, it worked. It stuck in consumers' heads, and they did extremely well. Rumor was they never left home without their buckeye nuts.

Harry Miller became involved in the community. He opened his own barbecue stand, and Dean would help him run it after school. Harry ran for mayor twice and was elected on his second try. He realized politics were not for him and resigned suddenly. One night Harry dropped Lucy off at Victoria Scholl's house. There was a note attached to her neck, which read, "Please take care of me." He and Dean left town that night in Dean's sophomore year of high school and weren't heard of again.

The Grayton community wanted to change the elementary school's name to Marcus Peters Elementary School. It passed the council unanimously. The board also voted to put Victoria Scholl in as interim superintendent until she could finish her certification. After all, she was the brains behind the office anyway, and the entire town knew it. With Victoria's financial windfall, she remodeled Ree's house, and it became the showplace on Raintree Road.

Sheriff Charles Hall and Victoria married one year later, and all of Grayton turned out for the wedding. Rosie and Tati were her bridesmaids, and Clayton and Jackson were Charles's groomsmen. Charles and Victoria welcomed a baby boy the following year and named him William. Rosie and Tati helped raise William, and Rosie helped educate William as only she could do.

Sheriff Hall never stopped looking for the woman who rescued DaisyBelle and Monty, but to no avail. Jackson Smith gave him the pictures he had taken at the summer school graduation, and both DaisyBelle and Monty had ID'd the photo of a person who was dressed like a man in the back of the crowd, but Charles was never able to positively ID the figure. The TBI have labeled Joe Puckett's file as a cold case.

Rosie Scholl graduated high school and went on to Peabody College in Nashville. She graduated summa cum laude and went on to receive her master's in education at Vanderbilt and then her PhD. She married one of her professors, and they had two children, Katie and John. She taught for twenty years before becoming principal of Elkhorn Elementary School.

Tati Scholl graduated high school in Grayton and attended Auburn University majoring in zoology. She graduated and was accepted into its prestigious veterinary school of medicine. She got her DVM and stayed in Auburn, where she married a financial advisor and opened a veterinary clinic in town. She had a set of twins whom she named Christian and Lucy and stayed in Alabama for twelve years until…

Boston, Massachusetts, 2015

A beautiful young woman carrying a newspaper knocked on her boss's door.

"Come in," he said from behind his desk.

"I thought you might like to see the news from the *Grayton Gazette* today, Boss," she said as she handed the paper over to him.

He read the caption of the paper: THE SCHOLL GIRLS RETURN HOME. The article talked of how Rosie Scholl was to follow her mother and become the superintendent of Dakota County Schools and her sister, Tatiana, was opening a veterinary clinic in Grayton. The sisters were coming home to raise their families after the sudden death of their stepfather, Sheriff Charles Hall.

He quickly put the paper down.

THE GHOST COMES OUT

"Get me a plane to Memphis, please, Alice, and I'm going to need a car."

"How long, sir?" Alice asked as she took out her phone to dial.

"Make it one-way, Alice. I'm not coming back," he answered.

Grayton 2015

The pace in Grayton wasn't like a big city. Even though Grayton had been hit by the technology bug and Wi-Fi was present, it was slow, but life was good. Those who were there in '64 still talked about what happened that summer although their memories were getting a little jumbled. Families moved in to Grayton because of the high achieving schools and low student-to-teacher ratio, but mainly because it was a step back in time and the feeling of being safe was in the air. The freedom of unlocked doors and allowing children to play outside even after dark was apparent. The laughter of children and catching lightning bugs at night was an activity seen on most summer nights.

Everything seemed good. Everything seemed safe and normal, and it was. That is…until the ghost comes out again.

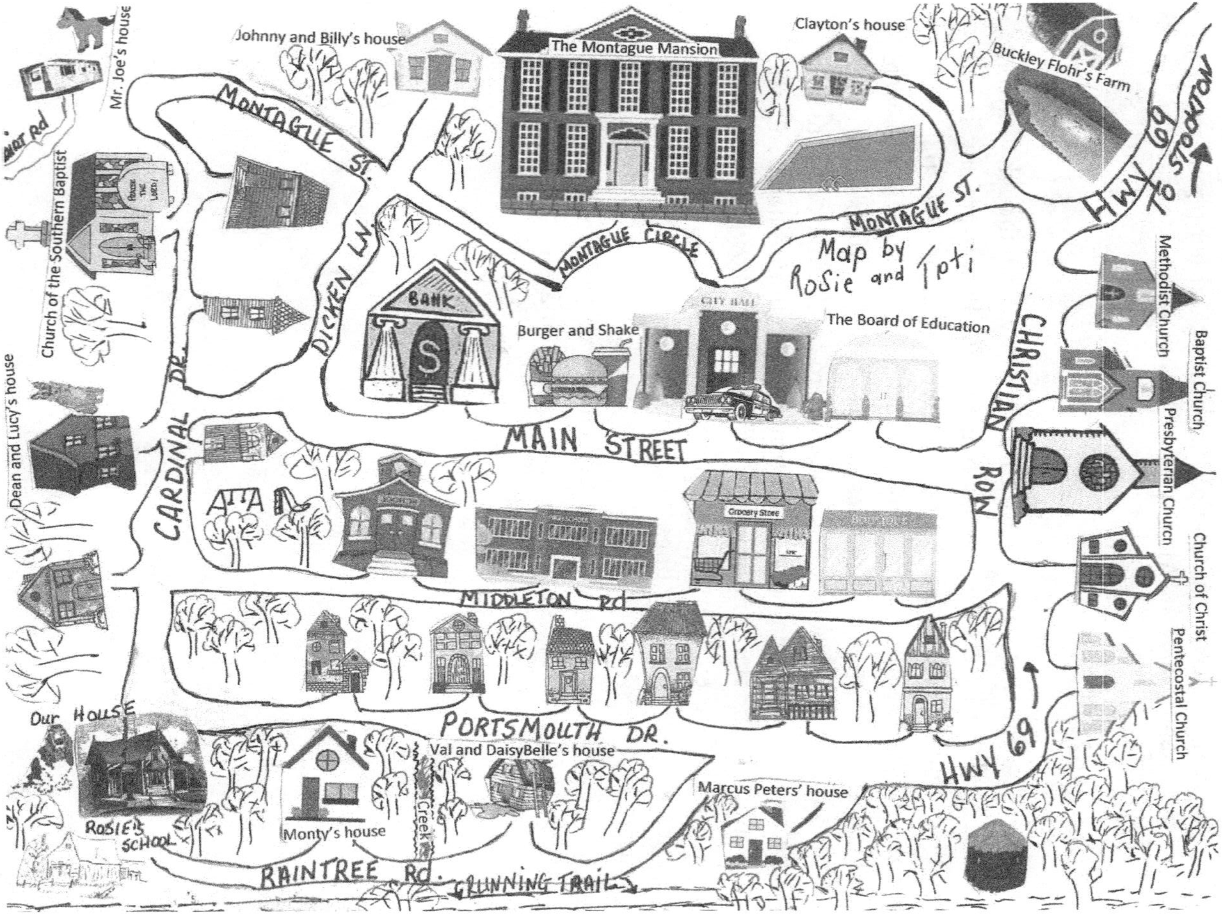
Map by Rosie and Toti
HWY 69
TO STOCKTON
Buckley Flohr's Farm
Clayton's house
The Montague Mansion
Johnny and Billy's house
Mr. Joe's house
MONTAGUE ST.
MONTAGUE ST.
MONTAGUE CIRCLE
DICKEN LN.
Church of the Southern Baptist
PRAISE THE LORD!
Dean and Lucy's house
CARDINAL DR.
BANK
Burger and Shake
CITY HALL
The Board of Education
Methodist Church
Baptist Church
Presbyterian Church
Church of Christ
Pentecostal Church
CHRISTIAN ROW
MAIN STREET
Grocery Store
MIDDLETON Rd
PORTSMOUTH DR.
HWY 69
Our HOUSE
ROSIE'S SCHOOL
Monty's house
Creek
Val and DaisyBelle's house
Marcus Peters' house
RAINTREE Rd.
GRUNNING TRAIL

About the Author

The Ghost Comes Out is the Sisters Spurlock fourth published book but their first attempt at a fictional novel. Their other works include *Navikate and the Sound of the Sea, I Give You the Olive Tree,* and the award-winning *No Mask, No Home!*

CPSIA information can be obtained
at www.ICGtesting.com
Printed in the USA
LVHW042059280420
654635LV00002B/117

9 781098 025823